Trapped

JILL PETERS

Trapped

HODDER

First published in Great Britain in 2009 by Hodder & Stoughton
An Hachette UK company

First published in paperback in 2009

1

Copyright © Freda Lightfoot 2008

A CIP catalogue record for this title is available from the British Library

ISBN 978 0 340 97771 2

Typeset in Plantin Light by
Palimpsest Book Production Limited,
Grangemouth, Stirlingshire

Printed and bound in the UK by CPI Mackays, Chatham ME5 8TD

Hodder & Stoughton policy is to use papers that are natural, renewable and
recyclable products and made from wood grown in sustainable forests. The
logging and manufacturing processes are expected to conform to the
environmental regulations of the country of origin.

Hodder & Stoughton Ltd
338 Euston Road
London NW1 3BH

www.hodder.co.uk

Author's Note

This book came about as a result of a casual conversation with my editor, when I happened to mention that I had once suffered a short and violent marriage. My own story took place in the early sixties, but the problem of violent men still exists to this day and many of the incidents which Carly has to deal with, and the control Oliver imposes upon her, are written from personal experience. Writing this book was rather like opening Pandora's box. I've been happily married now for almost thirty-nine years, certain that I'd successfully blocked the bad memories of that painful period from my mind. But as I began to write I soon realised that I still carried a sense of shame for having 'allowed' it to happen to me, for having stayed in the marriage for almost three years in a futile effort to make things come right. No woman should feel such guilt, or have to tolerate abuse. Fortunately, although some attitudes still need to change, help for the abused woman suffering domestic violence is more readily available today. If you are in need of such help, don't hesitate to contact the organisations listed on this page.

Women's Aid or Refuge, run in partnership on the 24-hour National Domestic Violence Helpline: Call 0808 2000 247
http://www.refuge.org.uk
http://www.womensaid.org.uk

I

I'm lying sobbing on the floor, head reeling, unable to believe that my husband of just four weeks has knocked me flying. The force of the blow took me completely by surprise and I'm huddled in a tiny ball, shaking with shock.

He's saying that it's all my fault, that I drove him to lose his temper because I provoked him, and as I sob I'm thinking that maybe he's right in a way.

I'd told him about the anonymous letter, the one my parents received only days before our wedding, warning me that he'd been seen kissing another girl, Sandra or Shirley, I can't quite remember. He fiercely denied it, of course, and I can see now that it was stupid of me to even joke about Oliver cheating on me.

We'd got back home this evening after a meal out, just the two of us to our favourite Italian restaurant. I'd slipped out of my dress and was hanging it in the wardrobe when, quite out of the blue, he asked me why I'd flirted with the waiter.

I couldn't help but laugh at the very idea of my looking at another man, let alone flirting with one so soon after our honeymoon. 'Don't be ridiculous, Oliver. Why would I?' I went to rub myself against him, clad only in my skimpy black bra and panties, wanting to tease him into a better mood. We'd enjoyed a bottle of Muscadet with the meal, and I was in the mood for loving, not a silly quarrel.

'Because you're a stunning girl and it was obvious the guy couldn't take his eyes off you,' Oliver said, his usually handsome face cold and unsmiling.

The compliment touched me deeply. I'd never thought of

myself as stunning. Reasonably attractive perhaps, some might even say pretty with my long fair hair framing a heart-shaped face in a tapered cut and a thick fringe above big amber eyes. But I'm not thin enough, or tall enough ever to be classed as beautiful. It took weeks to trim off half a stone for my wedding and hone my curvy figure, more kindly termed voluptuous by my lovely new husband, till I felt slender enough to show off the satin sheath dress I'd set my heart on. Even then my bottom stuck out too much and I had to keep hoisting up the strapless bra in an effort to control my ample cleavage. No, indeed, I'm not at all the sort of girl to cause men's heads to turn. Not stunning at all. More the girl-next-door type.

Which was one reason I couldn't believe my good luck when I hooked up with Oliver Sheldon. I met him on a girl's night out at a club in Manchester. I'm not usually into clubbing, being too shy to be comfortable in crowds, and some guy was giving me a hard time, harassing me to dance with him when I really had no wish to. Oliver stepped in to rescue me like the gentleman he is. I spent the rest of the evening in his arms, which turned my friends green with envy.

He was good company, great fun, and charming. He's an accountant working for a large reputable firm in Lancaster, although now that we're married he's been transferred to the Kendal branch. He's the dynamic sort and promotion is on the cards. He's also utterly gorgeous with dark good looks and captivating grey-blue eyes. I guessed he could have his pick of any girl but for some reason he chose me, claiming I was the sweetest of the bunch. I've been pinching myself ever since. So for him now to be jealous of me, instead of the other way round, seems incredible, and surely proof of his deep feelings for me.

'Oh, don't I just love it when you're jealous,' I teased, kissing his perfect, aquiline nose.

His face seemed to darken and his jaw tightened, forming a thin white line of tension above his upper lip. 'Is that why you encouraged him, in order to wind me up?'

'For goodness' sake, I didn't encourage him. Like I say, why would I? I never even noticed the flipping waiter.' It was then that I foolishly mentioned the letter.

I saw anger flare instantly in his pale eyes. 'Who sent it?' he shouted, furious there should be gossip about him behind his back.

I seemed to find this question funny, and foolishly giggled. 'It was anonymous, darling, so I wouldn't know, would I? Maybe it was from one of your jealous ex-girlfriends?' I teased.

My joke fell on stony ground as he didn't even listen when I tried to say how my parents hadn't mentioned it at the time, had thrown the letter straight on the fire. His face was contorted with rage, then, quite out of the blue, he gave me a shove, digging me painfully in the shoulder and sending me sprawling. I must have caught my heel in the rug, he surely couldn't have *meant* to knock me down?

I like to think I'm reasonably intelligent, ambitious in a modest sort of way, even if I am a bit of a wallflower at social occasions. I certainly don't believe that allowing a man to knock me about is the right way to behave. I was filled with a sudden spurt of anger, and, being the sort of girl who's always been ready to stand up for myself, I quickly got to my feet and pushed him right back.

'Hey, what the hell are you doing? You made me trip!'

But this wasn't a silly squabble with my sister Jo-Jo in junior school, this was a grown man, and with barely a pause he strikes me full across the face with the flat of his hand. This time the blow sends me crashing to the ground where I crack my head on the polished, cedar-wood floorboards. The room seems to tilt around me and I fear I'm going to lose consciousness.

Which is how I come to be lying here, sobbing my heart out.

Seconds later he's by my side, cradling me in his arms. 'Carly, darling, I'm so sorry. I can't think what came over me.' There are tears in his eyes as he strokes strands of damp hair from my face, kissing me as I continue to sob. 'I never meant to hurt you, but you know I can't bear the thought of you with another man.'

'Y-you h-hit me,' I cry, unable to believe what's happened. 'How could you *do* that? What on earth were you thinking of? You knocked me down!'

'It was meant to be just a tap, a little reprimand. I really don't appreciate my own strength. I'm so sorry, darling. It's all your own silly fault though,' he gently scolds, 'for making me love you so much.' He kisses my trembling mouth, thumbs the tears from my cheeks. 'Let me help you up, sweetie. Are you OK?' He's running a hand over my bare stomach and thighs, checking for bruises, and my traitorous flesh is responding. I love him so much, and we've been married barely a month, after all, so how can I resist him?

'You really shouldn't provoke me, you silly goose. You know how much I care about you, and the last few months have been so stressful with the wedding and everything.'

My heart softens as I see the depth of his remorse, feel the power of his love as his skilled fingers slip off my bra and slide down my panties. He knows just where and how to apply the right degree of seductive pressure to have me gasping with need in seconds. Then he's inside me, right there on the hard wooden floor, filling me, holding me tightly in his arms and to my shame I am responding.

Later, as I lie curled beside him in our huge new king-sized bed, I think that maybe he's right about the wedding. It was indeed stressful. Could it be anything else when two families who are little more than strangers are brought together for the first time? And no one could call my own family easy to get along with.

Mum smiling tightly as she politely touches cheeks with Mrs Sheldon, plainly revealing, to me at least, how she was mentally comparing her own store-bought dress and jacket with that of the chic designer outfit worn by Oliver's more affluent mother.

My sister preening herself in her ice-blue bridesmaid's dress, looking harassed as she desperately sought to avoid the sticky fingers of fifteen-month-old Ryan, her youngest.

And my father constantly whispering in my ear, 'Are you sure you want to do this? It's not too late to back out.' Dad wasn't quite so enamoured with my choice of husband as Mum, even though he liked Oliver and was grateful for his willingness to help with trimming the hedge, or fixing the car. Poor Dad found it hard to let me go. 'You hardly know him,' he kept saying over and over again in the weeks leading up to the wedding. 'You're only young, where's the rush?'

I would sigh and remind him we'd been going out together for nearly a year, that I was twenty-five and old enough to make up my own mind.

Mum, however, whole-heartedly approved. 'Such a lovely man,' she said when first she met Oliver, and hasn't stopped singing his praises since. She thinks he's the bee's knees and is completely bowled over by his charm. For once in her life she didn't complain that she had enough to do looking after Gran and Grandpa without helping to organise a big wedding. Nor did she moan about how fussy Oliver was for insisting on the most expensive hotel in which to hold the reception, a full three-course meal rather than a finger buffet, what a big family he had compared to ours, or who was paying for it all? Even when he generously offered to contribute a large sum towards the cost she declined gracefully, saying it was their privilege to pay, as parents of the bride. I could hardly believe my ears. My parents aren't well off and it was a stretch for them.

But then she could see how happy we were together.

From the moment I first met him, Oliver has made no attempt to disguise his utter devotion to me. He has this happy knack of making me feel special.

'You're the girl for me,' he would say. 'You are my life!'

No one was allowed to criticise anything I wore, anything I said, or even to swear in front of me, particularly not my tempestuous sister or he'd severely rebuke her, much to Jo-Jo's annoyance.

'He's such a prude,' she'd bitterly complain. 'I don't understand what you see in the guy.'

'Oliver has high standards, that's all, and he loves me.'

'He needs to get real,' she'd scoff.

It was true that he did put me on some sort of pedestal which felt wonderful, almost unbelievable that a gorgeous man should care for me so much. I was always the shy mouse at school, the plain, dumpy one with braces on my teeth and more than a smattering of freckles. The one who never got the guy.

'You're a rogue,' I'd say to him, loving him for the way he was always so adoring and protective towards me.

Throughout all the months we went out together Oliver showed himself as forever loving, tender, and most considerate.

He sent me roses every single week, took me out for romantic meals and on regular trips to the movies or the theatre by the lake, where he'd whisper in my ear how much he was aching to make love to me while I was trying to concentrate on the film or the play. He did this once when we were supposed to be taking tea with my grandparents, which was so embarrassing.

'I can't help myself. I just love you so much,' he'd say, whenever I gently scolded him for being so naughty.

How could I blame him? We couldn't seem to get enough of each other. He took me on a weekend trip to Paris and spoiled me rotten, which was so romantic. The best hotel, finest cuisine, the most expensive shows. Nothing was too much trouble. But my favourite times were when we were alone in his flat, or the times he would drive us out to a quiet spot by Coniston Water where we'd enjoy a champagne picnic, then make love beneath the canopy of green.

He made it clear from the start that I'm the only girl for him, so why do I sometimes find it hard to believe in his love and allow myself to be truly happy? Why do I still have doubts?

I was so crazy about him I'd quite happily have moved in with him once it became obvious we both felt the same way about each other. Oliver, however, wasn't satisfied with that. He was determined to make me his wife, wanting to provide me with the very best of everything. He'd talk for hours about the dream home he planned for us with a designer kitchen and two bathrooms, tastefully furnished in pale neutral shades, wired for internet access and with high-tech sound systems. He had his eye on a four-bedroom detached being built on a new estate on the edge of a pretty village not too far from my parents in Kendal. How could I protest that a small traditional cottage would do just as well so long as we were together? Nothing was more important to him than the wonderful future he planned for us.

I was surprised and excited by his proposal of marriage, carried away by his enthusiasm and his dreams, so if I suffered any niggling doubts that it was all a bit of a rush, that maybe we should perhaps live together in his rented flat for a while first, I pushed those worries to one side.

We're in love, I thought. What can possibly go wrong?

It was Jo-Jo, naturally, who told me about the letter. Never one to miss an opportunity to put one over on me, she seemed to take great pleasure in the process. She's been jealous of me, as the baby sister, for as long as I can remember, and for no good reason that I can think of. My marrying a good-looking man with a comfortable lifestyle hasn't helped in this respect. Even though she is herself happily married to the ever-patient Ed who absolutely adores her, has three lovely kids, a garden, a large car, even a mutt of a dog, all the accoutrements for a happy life. Yet, despite what for some women would be everything they could wish for, my good fortune still seems to increase her own sense of inadequacy.

'Has Mum told you about the anonymous letter?' She tossed this little firecracker into my lap as I was checking out the seating plan for the reception just days before the wedding.

My beloved sister was supposed to be helping by setting the gifts out on display, together with their appropriate card, although she kept breaking off to pluck her eyebrows, or buff her nails, making it clear she was bored by the whole performance. My thoughts had been up in the clouds, mentally flying to Italy on my honeymoon with my wonderful new husband, but her words brought me down to earth with a bump.

'What letter?' This was the first I'd heard of any letter. Mum had made no mention of it, so I'd no idea what she was talking about. 'When did she get it?'

'Oh, a week or two ago, I believe.' Jo-Jo gave one of her artless little shrugs, pouting her pretty lips as she coated them with plum-coloured lipstick. 'It was utterly malicious so she burnt it. Probably didn't mention it because she didn't want to upset you.'

So why did you, you nasty little bitch? I thought, loathing myself for feeling so distrustful of my own sister, yet hating her for putting me in this invidious position. If someone really had sent Mum and Dad a malicious, anonymous letter, was this the right time to reveal it, just days before our wedding?

'So what did it say then, this letter?'

Jo-Jo took great pains to search her normally empty mind and dredge up every nasty phrase she could recall, all about how Oliver had been seen kissing another girl, that in fact he had a reputation as a womaniser. I listened, horrified.

'That's a complete lie, Oliver's not like that at all. He would never cheat on me. He loves me. It was obviously written by one of his old flames, someone with a grievance, perhaps because he jilted her for me.'

'Why don't you ask him?' Jo-Jo airily remarked, turning to smile at me, dark eyes gleaming with triumph at my discomfiture.

I pushed back my chair. 'Some people simply can't bear to see me happy,' and I was no longer referring to the unknown writer of that letter. I walked away, head high, slamming the front door behind me. I'd no idea where I was going, feeling only a desperate need to escape. I certainly had no intention of asking Oliver any such thing. That was my first mistake.

My home at that time was my parents' bungalow, and it wasn't easy to escape prying eyes when seeking a bit of privacy.

There always seemed to be someone watching from behind twitching curtains.

The hills surrounding the auld grey town, as Kendal is fondly known, are my favourite place to go when I'm troubled, as you can walk for miles in absolute silence without seeing a soul, save for a lone buzzard or a few lapwing. But I didn't go walking on the fells that evening as it was already growing dark. Instead, I wandered the streets in utter despair and disappointment. I don't really remember where as my mind was taken up completely with wondering how I could possibly marry Oliver if this anonymous letter were found to be true. How could I even still love him? He'd betrayed me, so he couldn't possibly love me, not as he should.

It still seemed astonishing that he'd even looked my way. My puppy-fat might have fined down, the braces had done their work and were long gone, but I still felt lucky to have him. Oliver could have any girl, and there are plenty better looking than me.

Stomach churning, I worried over losing him, and of practical things like having to resell the new house we'd bought, let alone the embarrassment of calling off the wedding and returning all those lovely gifts. Nor was it a happy prospect, at twenty-five, to settle for staying on with my parents, not when I'd dreamed of happy-ever-after in a home of my own.

Perhaps I was worrying unnecessarily. I told myself that Mum was probably right to burn the letter. It was no doubt nothing more than jealous mischief from some ex-girlfriend.

When I got back to my parents' bungalow, Jo-Jo had gone home to Ed and her children. Mum offered to make me a mug of hot chocolate, then started discussing our choice of hymns, the flowers in church and a myriad other details. I never plucked up the courage to ask her about the letter. I shut it right out of my mind, which was perhaps my second mistake.

The wedding took place on a perfect, if rather breezy, summer's day at the parish church where we threw pennies to the local children from the lychgate, according to custom. Oliver thought

I looked utterly beautiful in my satin gown. The wedding photos seemed to go on forever as he kept making the young photographer take a few extra shots, just in case he hadn't quite captured the perfect picture of me. My face ached with all the smiling by the time he finally called a halt, but I was so happy, so proud to make my vows and start on our new life together.

The reception followed with champagne flowing, a band playing, and everyone having a great time throwing themselves about like demented idiots, while Oliver and I enjoyed the sexy, smoochy dancing. My dizzy, tactless, interfering sister acted as if she hadn't a care in the world, as if she hadn't done her utmost to scupper my precious happiness.

We enjoyed a wonderful honeymoon in Florence, visiting the Uffizi and the Ponte Vecchio, marvelling at the pavement artists, exploring the narrow historic streets, the famous designer shops and the many museums and galleries of this beautiful, romantic city. And now here we are, newly married and settled in our beautiful dream home.

But as I curve myself against the warmth of my husband's body, I wonder why I don't feel happier. I try to block the awful incident from my mind, tell myself the slap was nothing more than the result of stress, of my clumsy response to a perfectly reasonable question. And it's true, I did smile at that damn waiter, so isn't Oliver's jealousy only proof of how very much he cares for me?

Deep in the pit of my stomach there's a knot of dull pain, and a solitary tear rolls down my cheek on to the pretty, lace-edged pillow. Stressed out by the wedding or not, he really shouldn't have hit me.

2

At breakfast the next morning Oliver is his normal self, behaving as if the assault of the night before never took place. I come swiftly to the conclusion that this is probably the right way to deal with the matter. The least said about that dreadful incident, the better. I'm quite sure he must be smarting with shame, and it won't help one bit for me to add to his guilt by reminding him of it.

He eats the breakfast I've cooked for him, gives me a long, lingering kiss, then grabs his briefcase and strides out of the door, throwing the usual instructions over his shoulder as to when I might expect him home.

'I could be late too,' I say, as I rush after him with his mobile phone which he's left on the kitchen table, and lean in through the open window of his Ford Mondeo to steal one last kiss. 'I have to wait to hand over the key of Jasmine Cottage to the Williams family, and they warned me they might arrive a bit late.'

Oliver pulls a face. 'Leave it under the mat, for goodness' sake. You've got the damn place ready for them, surely you don't have to wait on them hand, foot and finger?'

I smile at his impatience, understanding why he wants me home early. Even after almost a year of going out together, and a whole four weeks married we can still barely keep our hands off each other. Sex is very much an important part of each day, and dinner often comes second to this need in us both. I kiss him again. 'I'll be ready and waiting for you if it's at all possible, I promise.'

'I do hope so, Carly. I expect to come first in my wife's life, not second to some tinpot holiday business.'

I'm annoyed by Oliver's description. 'It's all part of the job, sweetie.'

'No, it's you allowing yourself to be put upon, as always.'

This was too much. 'Hardly, I'm my own boss, after all. Both Emma and I work very hard. Perfect Cottages are known for taking proper care of owners' property, and we certainly wouldn't dream of leaving keys lying about under mats where some sneak thief can easily find them. I'll leave something in the fridge for you, in case I get held up.'

'Just don't expect me to cook it,' Oliver growls, as he drives off frowning.

I shake my head in fond despair. Nobody could accuse Oliver of being a 'new man'.

Shortly before we got together I'd started my new business, Perfect Cottages, a holiday letting agency. I'm not exactly the academic type and I'd been working in Mum and Dad's shop, a Spar convenience store, up to a couple of years ago when I decided I wanted to do something more interesting and worthwhile with my life, something that suited me better.

My best friend was equally frustrated with her job, so we happily teamed up as partners to start a new business. She's great is Emma, a funky feminist with hazel eyes and pink-tinted, auburn hair that looks as if it's been cut with a knife and fork. She has a particular fancy for eating jam doughnuts, which she claims are not responsible for the way her backside fills out the dungarees she's so fond of wearing. We sat next to each other all through school, shared homework, and endured heart-rending agonies over unrequited love during our teenage years.

Emma was a bridesmaid at my wedding, and I would do the same for her only she's opted for a more modern arrangement with Glen, her partner. She's fiercely independent and absolutely refuses to marry him, on the grounds that a piece of paper will make not a scrap of difference to their happiness. My feminist friend sees no reason to 'sign over her freedom', as she puts it, and didn't entirely approve of my doing so. Unconventional she may be, but she's also loyal and great fun; warm, friendly and really quite shrewd. I'd trust her with my life.

Setting up the business together was exciting. We devised a brochure outlining the services we had to offer, set up a website and advertised for property owners looking for rental income. We had to take out a small loan from the bank as it took a few months to really get going but gradually the bookings started coming in, and we're building steadily, improving and growing all the time.

Nothing ever fazes Emma. She's calm and unruffled, the more organised of the two of us. I'm much more the ideas person, but Em is the practical one, the one who knows instinctively if something is possible. We make a good team, happily working side by side cleaning and making up beds, tidying gardens, and generally caring for the self-catering holiday cottages and apartments. The work is demanding and time consuming, with long, unsocial hours. We prepare the properties for occupation, and often answer calls at odd times if clients have a problem, such as the plumbing going wrong, or they can't work out how to switch on the central heating, an essential here in the Lake District.

Admittedly this did create a degree of tension between Oliver and me at the start of our relationship, still does occasionally if I'm honest. He wasn't at all happy when our evenings together were interrupted by frequent calls on my mobile.

'Can't they find the damn thermostat?' he'd complain, or curtly suggest they should call my partner, not me.

'They do call Emma when she's on duty, but I'm on call tonight, so it's my responsibility to keep our clients happy. Sorry!' I'd feel embarrassed and apologise profusely, but I'd no intention of giving up my job, which I love.

Once, a poor woman needed to call an ambulance when her husband suffered a heart attack, and I went with her to the hospital. Oliver didn't seem to think this should be part of my remit. Probably not, but I didn't mind. It was really no trouble and as the couple were on holiday, she had no family or friends nearby to support her.

I'd often find him waiting for me at the end of a shift. He'd unexpectedly turn up, quite out of the blue, just as Emma and I were off out for a drink. I'd apologise to Em, yet be secretly flattered that he couldn't wait to see me. He hated every moment we were apart.

It's vitally important to Emma and me that we make everything as perfect as possible for our guests, including a welcome pack of groceries for their first day, which means a quick trip to Mum and Dad's shop for fresh bread, cheese and wine. Clients are expected to vacate the apartments by ten-thirty, when we move in and blitz the place. We never know what we might find. Some guests leave a property immaculate, as if they've hardly slept there, while others somehow manage to leave evidence of every meal they've eaten.

On days when there is no changeover to deal with, we work in a small rented room above a hairdressing salon in Bowness on Windermere which we use as an office to do paperwork, keep the website updated, and take bookings. We dream of employing someone to man the phone, and cleaners to help deal with the cottages, but can't quite afford to yet. Maybe next year, when we hope to really break into profit. I enjoy my job enormously, and being able to share each day with the lively, ebullient Emma makes it so much more fun.

I give her a quick ring now on my mobile. 'Meet you on the roundabout at the top of Windermere Road on the dot of ten, then we'll have time for a quick coffee at the Gateway before we start.'

'Right you are, unless the lovely Oliver is still busy ravishing you, of course, then I'll go on to the flats and start without you, shall I?'

Jokes about newly wedded bliss somehow fall a bit flat this morning, but I attempt to laugh at her humour, promise to pick up a new pack of washing powder fro. on the way, and ring off.

I hurry to stack the dishwasher, quickly wipe do marble worktops, in which I take great pride, and gl. at the kitchen clock hung high on the pristine white-til decide I've time to bake a quiche before I meet Emma, i I hurry. Then when I do get home, I need only quickly heat it up while I toss a green salad.

Once the quiche is baking in the oven, I dash about running a duster over the polished surface of our new bookshelves and display unit, plumping up cushions on the two white leather sofas. I'd thought these a touch impractical but Oliver fell in love with them at sight, so how could I refuse? He was lavishly generous when it came to choosing furniture for our new detached house, and I too have poured my small savings into it. He's not a man to tolerate second best in anything. Again I think how lucky I am to have him, resolutely blocking last night's petty display of jealousy from my mind.

I carefully flick a feather duster over the backgammon set laid out on the smoked-glass coffee table. He's teaching me to play and I've discovered an amazing ability to throw doubles, which seems to give me an advantage. The very first time we played I won three games in a row. Oliver is hugely competitive and hates to be beaten, so he sulked for a while, putting it down to beginner's luck. When it became clear I was about to win a fourth game, he suddenly leapt to his feet, for no reason I could see, and sent the board flying.

'Oh, no, and I was doing so well,' I cried.

'For goodness' sake,' he laughed. 'I didn't knock it over on purpose. In any case, you were absolute rubbish. You have no skill at all. I was letting you win, you silly goose. Come on, time we went to bed and played more interesting games.'

I frown now as I flick the duster over the pieces and wonder if it was really true about him not knocking the board over on purpose, or whether Oliver's need to win had compelled him

...et so childishly. I was beginning to see that my new husband was far more complicated, and a good deal more sensitive, than I'd given him credit for. I shake my head in fond despair. Men, they have such egos. Then I put away my dusters, set the quiche to cool in the fridge and head off to work.

It's just after nine as I call in at my parents' shop, meaning to purchase one or two essential items before meeting up with Emma. Perfect Cottages has an account with them for the welcome packs, which makes it easier for us and keeps the trade in the family, as it were. My parents have always been business people and I know that they will have been working in the shop since seven o'clock this morning or even earlier, sorting newspapers, taking delivery of the milk and fresh bread. I put some of each in a basket, together with wine and cheese, not forgetting the washing powder for the never-ending laundry. I hope one day to be able to afford to pay Lakeland Laundry to do it for us; meanwhile I do the lion's share myself since Emma has nowhere to dry sheets in her one-bedroom apartment.

As I approach the counter with my loaded basket, Mum finishes serving a customer and turns to me with a distracted smile. 'Hello, love, off to work?'

I agree that I am and refuse her offer of coffee, but then as she checks the items on to the till, she looks at me keenly and makes some joke about married life making me look tired and how I should try to get more sleep. I laugh, explaining we were out late last night, and suddenly my eyes fill with a rush of tears.

She's immediately all concern. 'What is it, love? Has something happened?'

I shake my head and smile. 'We had our first matrimonial tiff, that's all. Nothing important. Oliver was a bit miffed because he thought I was flirting with the waiter.'

Mum frowns her disapproval, an expression I'm very familiar with. 'What a thing to do, and with a lovely new husband like Oliver. You don't know when you're well off, girl.'

'It was only a smile,' I say in my own defence. My mind is racing, wondering how much I should tell her, and what her reaction would be if I said that Oliver hit me, but her next words stop me in my tracks.

'Actually, we've heard all about it. Oliver popped in earlier on his way to the office, explaining how you'd had a few words over an incident at the restaurant, and how concerned he was about your state of mind.'

A few words! I stare at her in complete shock. Grabbing her arm, I draw her into the stockroom at the back, away from the queue of customers Dad is busily dealing with, all earwigging in on our conversation. 'There was *no* incident at the restaurant,' I hiss. 'It was just a damn smile I gave that waiter, nothing more. I never even noticed it bothered Oliver until we got home.' Again I hesitate to reveal exactly what did happen, not wanting to put my husband in a bad light, or admit to what felt like failure on my part.

'Well, that just shows how very insensitive you can be at times, Carly. You always were very careless with those winning smiles of yours, imagining everyone will love and flatter you because you're the baby of the family. Well it's time you grew up a little, madam, and learned to be more circumspect and caring of a husband, like your big sister.'

'What?' I gasp in astonishment. 'Jo-Jo is like a big kid, always spoiling for a fight. It's a miracle Ed puts up with her.'

'He absolutely worships her, and you know it. Jo-Jo may not be as fortunate as you are materially, but she's blessed in her marriage. She's a loyal, affectionate wife and mother. Untidy, a bit scatterbrained, and lacking in confidence I will admit, but without a selfish, cruel bone in her body.'

'Oh, pleeease!' My sister may be an over-anxious worrier at times, very like our mother, particularly where her children are concerned, but I'd never thought of her as lacking in confidence. Quite the opposite, in fact. A bit defensive because she married so young at just nineteen, but rather full of herself and certainly over-critical of me. 'What about that anonymous letter you received, the one saying Oliver had been seen with another girl, which you failed to mention and Jo-Jo told me about just days before our wedding, bless her sweet heart?'

Mum looks deeply uncomfortable for a moment, then turns away to glance anxiously through the open door, ostensibly to check that Dad is coping all right on his own, before folding her arms across her chest in that bossy way she has. A small, pretty woman with dark hair the colour of burnished chestnuts, and not a sign of grey, I notice for the first time that she's looking tired herself. Her long face droops with unhappiness and the bags beneath her brown eyes have surely never been quite this bad before. I remember how burdened and inhibited she must feel, hemmed in by caring for elderly in-laws, and I'm filled with guilt for seeming to add to her difficulties.

'This isn't the place to discuss private family matters,' she's sharply informing me, wagging a scolding finger as she used to do when I'd arrived home late as a teenager, or not done my homework on time. 'I can see that Oliver was right to be concerned about you. You're making a big fuss over nothing. Your dad and I thought that letter was pure mischief-making. Oliver is a nice-looking lad. It's only natural other women should fancy him. Anyway, if you want to know, without even mentioning the letter we did casually speak to him about a rumour we'd heard that he'd been seen with another girl. Apparently, it was nothing more than a misunderstanding which he explained to our complete satisfaction, and reiterated how much he loved you, which was very plain to us both.'

My jaw falls open and my cheeks grow warm with embarrassment and annoyance. 'You *questioned* him, without even mentioning the matter to me?'

She doesn't answer my question but embarks on a lecture about trust in marriage, how she and Dad may have had their ups and downs over the years but always trusted each other. I begin to feel distinctly uncomfortable for seeming to doubt my own lovely husband. It doesn't occur to me to wonder exactly what Oliver told them about Shirley or Sandra or whatever her name was, that he might have lied to my parents, giving his version of events rather than the truth. Not for a moment do I imagine that he might not have admitted to actually kissing the girl. Snogging, as we call it. My mother, who has never looked at another man since she started going out with Dad in her teens, can be very naïve. But then so can I, I suppose. The fact is, I *want* to believe Oliver is innocent.

I make one last effort to sort out my troubled thoughts. 'So you and Dad were always love's young dream, were you? Viv and Ken, Mr and Mrs Perfect. Never a cross word and neither of you ever doubting you'd done the right thing by getting together. No problems at all, eh?'

Mum doesn't look at me as she pins my receipt into the account book, so that she'll have a record for the monthly bill she'll send. 'Oh, there were quarrels all right, and plenty of problems, but only for the first twenty-five years. It gets easier after that.' She looks up at me and smiles, her brown eyes warm with affection.

I smile too at her dry humour, knowing she and Dad adore each other, and hoping that Oliver and I will be half as happy.

'Don't worry, love. You've got a good man there, and you'll be fine once you get the hang of sharing your life with someone.' She puts her arms about me and gives me a hug. 'Just remember to tell him how much you love him, every single day. I still tell your dad, and he tells me.'

'I do, I do. But I never realised what hard work marriage is. All that emotional stuff, and jealousy can be very draining. And I never seem to stop working from morning till night, what with getting the house organised and coping with a load of new tasks, as well as keeping on top of things at the agency. So yes, I suppose I am a bit overtired.'

'Marriage is certainly not all red roses and champagne,' she drily remarks, and I chuckle, feeling foolishly naïve and adolescent.

'I'm not quite such a hopeless romantic, Mum, but with summer almost upon us, we're coming up to our busiest time, and today is no exception.' I'm fervently wishing I'd never started on this conversation; I should have kept my lips firmly buttoned. But I can see she's no longer listening, her mind having moved on to other things as she bustles back to the counter, me trailing disconsolately behind.

'Speaking of being busy,' she's saying, as she packs my goods into a cardboard box, 'could you find time to take Gran to the doctor for her check-up this afternoon? I'll be helping your dad in the shop all day today as Friday is one of our busiest days.'

My heart sinks. This could well be the straw that breaks this particular camel's back. The day ahead seems horrendous enough as it is, and I've made it worse by lingering here and making myself late. Yet I'm instantly washed with guilt at these selfish thoughts. There's me dreaming of a time when Perfect Cottages will be making sufficient profit for me to employ someone to help while Mum copes marvellously with twice my workload. Most days she does a ten- or twelve-hour shift in the shop, including dashing home to make a meal and care for two frail old people at midday.

Gran hasn't been well for some time, and Grandpa can be very difficult at times as he's becoming increasingly senile. He has been known to wander off in his dressing gown and slippers and get lost. Last time the police found him down at the timber yard, where he'd worked for forty-odd years, at five in the morning.

I try to politely point out that I'm pretty busy myself. 'It's changeover day for three apartments and two cottages. Can't you get Pat to stand in for you for an hour or two?' Pat is a friend who comes to help in the shop occasionally, but Mum is shaking her head.

'She's on holiday. I've tried everyone and I'm really stuck.' Again she turns all huffy. 'I thought you might be prepared to help, but if it's too much trouble . . .'

'That's not what I mean,' I interrupt, feeling somehow weary at the way she always manages to twist my most innocent remarks. 'I've got a long day myself, that's all, with clients arriving at all hours, some quite late.'

She huffs a bit more, puffing out her chest in that martyred way she has. 'There are times when I don't know whether I'm on my head or my heels. I run myself ragged round those two old dears on top of a full-time job. How your father expects me to manage, I really can't imagine. He seems to think I'm Superwoman while he never lifts a finger to help. And they are his parents, after all.'

I can't help but smile, having heard a version of this complaint a thousand and one times. 'What about Jo-Jo, can't she drop Gran off at the doctor's on her way to picking up the kids?'

My mother stiffens and starts to stack cans of soup, slapping one on top of the other with a clang. 'Jo-Jo may only have a part-time job, and you may not consider her work to be half as important as yours, but she does have three lively children which makes her far busier than you, dear. Nor does her husband earn what Oliver does, so no, I didn't even ask her. I wouldn't ask *you*, only Gran's blood pressure has been up quite a bit lately.'

I sigh. I could remind Mum that I'm wrestling with a new business, a new husband and a new life myself but I know when I'm beaten. Besides, I love my gran so I buckle under the emotional pressure, nod and agree to take the old lady to the doctor, even though it will throw the day's routine into chaos. 'I'm always happy to help, you know that.'

I do some rapid rearranging in my head. Fortunately, the people for two of the properties aren't due to arrive until seven this evening, so, with luck, I can get everything done and still be home by eight at the latest. I'm sure Oliver won't mind, for once.

I drive to the Gateway Inn and Emma and I down our coffee at rapid speed while quickly running through the chores lined up for the day. No two are ever the same, which is what I love about the job, cleaning aside that is.

Sometimes I worry that I might have bitten off more than I can chew. Starting a business of my own seemed like a great idea a couple of years ago when I was still single and without any commitments. Now, on top of a full day's work for Perfect Cottages, for the first time in my life I'm entirely responsible for the running of a home, for dealing with the laundry, cooking delicious meals, and keeping everything just so, as Oliver likes it. In addition, I feel it's important that somehow I manage to get home in time to make myself look beautiful for my new husband, no matter how tired I am.

There are days when I feel overwhelmed by it all, and long to slip back to the carefree freedom of my youth. I love my family and miss coming home at the end of a tiring day to find my tea ready, my clothes all washed and ironed, a home-baked cake in the tin. Now I'm responsible for providing these things for myself, which is proving quite a shock to the system.

I miss lazy Sunday mornings reading in bed, which seem to be very much a thing of the past. Oliver insists upon a cooked breakfast every single morning, including weekends. And he doesn't at all approve of my reading in bed. It even irritates him if I curl up in a chair with a good book, claiming there are far more exciting ways of spending our time together. But then, we are just married.

I'm thankful that Mum and Dad don't live far away and are very supportive, despite occasional differences and disagreements. But I'm a married woman not a teenager, so I can't keep running to them every five minutes to ask advice. I do enjoy being able to pop into the shop for a chat now and then, although the one this morning didn't exactly solve anything. I welcome the fact that Mum can pop round to my house whenever she feels like it, even if it is only to sound off about Gran and Grandpa. I'm very fortunate in my family, so tell myself not to worry too much about a bit of tiredness and overwork. If Mum can cope, so can I.

My sister has always been something of a favourite of hers, but she makes a valid point nonetheless. Jo-Jo has enough on her plate. She always seems harassed these days, and I make a mental note not to start a family too soon. Not that Oliver would welcome one. He's made it very clear that we should enjoy a few years on our own before taking on such a responsibility, and I agree with him.

I mention to Emma about having to take Gran to the doctor's surgery later for a check-up. She smiles sympathetically despite the fact that my absence, even for an hour, will add to her own workload considerably. She's such a warm, easy-going sort of person. Immensely loyal, and very understanding.

'She's lovely, your gran, take as long as you need. But we'd best get on our way right this minute if we're going to get five properties ready in time.' She pays the bill and we each climb into our separate cars and I follow her to the first cottage, which should be vacated by now, since it's already ten forty-five. We find it generally quicker for us to work together, and within an hour we're done and moving on to cottage number two. But by four o'clock it's a different story.

Despite having made an appointment, Gran has a long wait at the surgery before finally being seen. She's in a bit of a state so I stay with her, holding her hand till the doctor has reassured her all is well. I drive her safely home again, and pop on the kettle for us to enjoy a quick cup of tea together. I'm relieved to see Grandpa is happily watching the racing on TV, and hasn't wandered off again.

While we're chatting, Emma sends me a text to say the Williams family rang to explain they are running late as traffic is dreadful on the M6. I kiss my grandparents bye-bye and dash off to finish getting Jasmine cottage ready for them.

On the way I remind myself of the quiche in the fridge, which I had the foresight to make this morning. Admittedly in something of a rush, and I suspect it will have sunk as it seemed a bit soggy in the middle. Mum's always rise and look all fluffy and appetising and I wonder if I can ever hope to make as good a wife as she has been to Dad. Oh, I do hope so. More than anything I want to make Oliver happy. I again make a mental note to get home this evening just as soon as I can. But if I am held up for any reason, all Oliver has to do is pop a slice of the quiche into the microwave.

It's ten past nine when I slot my key in the door. The kitchen is in darkness and it's quite clear Oliver hasn't given a thought to supper. I sigh and wonder why I'm not surprised. But I haven't seen him since first thing this morning so I call out his name as I pull off my coat, drop it on a chair and rush into the lounge, eager for my usual kiss and a cuddle.

3

The fridge door is open and Oliver has my arm pinned halfway up my back. The pain is horrendous and I'm quite certain my shoulder is going to slip out of its socket at any moment.

'What the hell do you call *that*?' he roars at me. 'What sort of meal is this for a man to come home to after a long day's work?'

I can hardly see the quiche for the tears of agony welling up in my eyes, nor can I think of anything to say in its defence. It does indeed look thin and pathetic, sunk in the middle with a rim of hard crust, a pale imitation of Mum's deliciously plump offerings. I try to whimper an apology but his grip on my arm tightens still further and I don't know how much more I can take. My heart is racing and a pink haze seems to be blocking my vision.

'More importantly, where the hell were *you*?' He has his mouth against my ear and he hisses these furious words into it.

My teeth are starting to chatter, which must be because of the cold from the fridge chilling me through. It surely can't be fear. This is my husband, for God's sake! Oliver, who adores me. I ache to be held in his warm embrace and loved. *What is happening here?*

'Oliver, please, darling, stop this! You're hurting me.' I can't think why he's so angry. What is causing him to behave like some sort of lunatic? 'Please let go of my arm, Oliver.'

Instead, he gives me a furious shake which bangs my head against the top shelf, bringing a sting of tears to my eyes. Then, to my intense relief, his hold on me eases and my arm drops to my side. A pain grips my shoulder and I wince in agony.

Worried it might be broken or dislocated, I gently flex my fingers to check. I wonder what on earth can have upset him. This whole silly tantrum can't really be about something as stupid as a failed quiche, can it? I turn to face him, all concern. 'What is it? What's wrong, darling? Has something happened?'

'Yes! My incompetent wife expects me to eat cold quiche.'

I manage a shaky laugh. 'OK, it may not be up to Nigella's standard, or even Mum's, but you didn't marry me for my cooking, right?' I give him one of my sexy smiles, which usually melt away his black moods. Sadly, it doesn't have the effect I hope for.

He glares at me coldly through the eyes of a stranger. 'I married you because I love you, which means I expect to come first in your life. Not too much to ask of a wife, is it? I certainly deserve more consideration than this. In future you'll make sure you're home in good time to cook me a decent meal.'

There's a short pause while I absorb the implications of what he has just said, too startled for a moment to speak. I may not be quite so aggressively feminist as Emma, but I'm no doormat. I can't believe what I'm hearing, that we're standing here in our beautiful kitchen engaged in yet another terrible row. 'I did warn you that I might be late home tonight.' I try to sound calm and reasonable although even to my own ears there's a tremor in my voice. 'I do my best but I work too, darling, and I don't always have time to cook a big meal. I'm sorry I'm late, but heavens, what a fuss about nothing. Why didn't you set the oven to warm, or at least put the lamps on?'

I'd found him sitting in complete darkness when I'd entered the lounge, presumably waiting for me. No lights on, and the room felt cold and damp as the log-effect gas fire hadn't been lit. He wasn't even watching TV, simply sitting on the sofa in his camel coat and business suit, his briefcase on the floor where he'd presumably dropped it when he came in. It's as if he was incapable, or unwilling, to lift a finger to do anything, simply because I wasn't there to welcome him home. Making the point I was neglecting him, presumably.

His next words confirm this. 'Being married means that you do things for each other. What do you ever do for me? You're always far too busy to find the time to make your husband happy.'

I'm appalled that he should think such a thing. 'That's absolutely untrue. I cook your breakfast every single morning and . . .'

'Is that too much trouble as well?'

I answer him with measured patience. 'No, I'm only saying we need a bit of old-fashioned give and take here.'

'Don't push me too far, Carly.'

'What? You're the one doing the pushing. I wasn't aware when I said those immortal words – *I do* – that I was agreeing to be your slave. Women have shaken off the shackles in today's modern world, remember. They're even allowed to vote.' I laugh, hoping to tease him into a better humour. It's a bad mistake.

This time he grasps me by the hair and thrusts me back so hard against the open fridge that the bottles and jars inside rattle and fall about every which way. I can feel cold milk running down the back of my leg as he spits his fury in my face. 'Don't you dare to lecture me. Am I supposed to do everything? I've had a shit of a day and I come home to an empty house. No wife, no lights on, no fire going, not even any fucking dinner. Nothing!'

I start to cry, quite unable to control my emotions any longer, which seems to annoy him even more.

'Don't think weeping and wailing will get you off the hook. I've been waiting hours for you to come home. It's half-past nine, for God's sake!'

I struggle to swallow my tears, try to speak on a half-choked sob. 'I've said I'm sorry, but I've had one hell of a day too. Gran isn't well and . . .'

'I don't want to know. This is where you should be, in our home, being a good wife to *me*. Not running round after your stupid family, or playing housemaid for holidaymakers. *I'm what matters in your life now. You and me. This house, and our life together!*'

I stare at him in shocked dismay. 'What's got into you? Why are you shouting?'

He instantly drops his voice and becomes strangely calm and controlled. 'I wouldn't have to shout if you started listening for once.' Yet there's a wildness in his eyes still. It feels as if he's turned into a complete stranger, as if he's possessed. I can't think what could possibly have this effect upon him. What would make him so angry? Certainly not a simple quiche, no matter how badly cooked it might be, or even my being late. I've been late before, although that was before we were married, admittedly. Even so, his reaction seems completely over the top. 'You haven't lost your job have you, because if so . . .'

'Don't be bloody stupid. I've told you what's wrong. *You*!'

Angry suddenly, I push him away to grab a tea towel and start to mop the milk from my leg. 'If that's really all this is, then you're behaving like an idiot,' I tell him. 'Where is it written that only the little woman can switch on the oven or toss a green salad? You knew how important my work was to me when you married me. Surely we can share the chores a bit more?'

He looks at me with something like pity, speaking slowly as if to a child. 'Your trouble, Carly, is that you've been spoiled, and the result, basically, is that you simply can't cope with real life. You're incompetent, think only of what *you* want. You still haven't taken into account the fact that you're married now. Things have changed, and it's long past time you put your priorities in order.'

I stare at him, stunned. His words are so dangerously close to my own secret concerns that he's put a doubt in my mind. It's true that I'm not coping very well, either with running this house or the business. Emma shouldered the lion's share of the work today, which isn't fair on her. Is it true that I think too much of what *I* want, instead of what's good for *us*, for Oliver and me? Are my aspirations too high? Maybe I have been spoiled, and now expect to have everything: a profitable business and a happy, fulfilled life with my husband. But if my unrealistic ambitions succeed only in damaging my marriage, where is the value in that?

I chew on my lip, saying nothing, worrying that perhaps he might have a point.

Oliver reaches into the fridge, pulls out the offending quiche and drops it into the pedal bin. 'Now make me a proper dinner, good and hot. I'm off to the pub for half an hour. I'll expect it to be ready and waiting by the time I get back.'

Only when the front door slams shut behind him, do I put my face in my hands and start to cry.

'Carly has it so easy. She wants to try swapping places with me for a day.'

It had taken over an hour for Jo-Jo to prise her three children away from their various toy cars, and bricks and Barbie dolls, go through World War III in the bathroom, read an episode of Bob the Builder and finally tuck them all up and escape for a bit of peace with her husband. She and Ed took it in turns to put the children to bed, so tonight he had cooked their evening meal: a delicious lasagne which Jo-Jo was eating with very little appetite.

'She swans off every day driving round in that natty little Peugeot, looking all smart and prosperous, earning her own money as well as raking it in from her rich new husband. She even gets to talk to grown-ups while I'm stuck in this house most of the time watching Teletubbies and trying to stop our Ryan from scribbling all over Samantha's books.'

Ed chuckled. 'This wouldn't be a display of petty jealousy, would it?'

Jo-Jo scowled at her husband as she sulkily pushed her food about the plate. 'Don't you start. Carly accuses me of that all the damn time. She even did it today when she rang to ask if I could take Gran to the doctor's because she was having a 'frantic' day. I told her she didn't know the meaning of the word.'

'You two are speaking again then? This must be a first since the wedding. But then Carly was hardly likely to welcome being told her fiancé is suspected of playing away, right before her big day, was she?'

Avoiding her husband's accusatory gaze, Jo-Jo carefully loaded her fork with meat and pasta and put it into her mouth. 'It has been a bit awkward between us recently, but I was only concerned for her, that's all. If she doesn't choose to believe me, that's her choice.'

'And you *were* sure of your facts, were you?' Ed's voice was soft with concern. 'Is it worth risking your relationship over a rumour?'

Jo-Jo gave a harsh little laugh. 'What relationship? Don't you know sisters always quarrel?'

'But you still love her,' Ed gently reminded his wife.

'Of course I still bloody love her. That's why I told her about the letter.'

'Right, not because you wanted to spike her guns,' Ed teased, 'or because you were in a bad mood about something?'

Jo-Jo slammed down her fork. 'Who knows whether it's true or not. I just thought she should be warned, that's all.'

'Your parents did the right thing by throwing the letter on the fire. You should never have mentioned it, Jo-Jo. It was very naughty of you.'

Jo-Jo pushed her plate away, cheeks bright with guilt. 'For goodness' sake, don't make me out to be the wicked sister. There was no need for her to get so uppity, but that's our Carly. Always knows best, and thinks the sun shines out of that man's ass. Maybe it does. Maybe I'm wrong. No doubt the beautiful newly weds are even now enjoying the best wine at some smart restaurant or other. I bet they eat out every night. I can't remember the last time I didn't spend all evening running up and down those stairs putting our Ryan back to bed. I'll tie him to the bedpost, I swear it.'

'That's a good idea,' Ed chuckled. 'Come on, eat up. At least it's good that you two are talking again, so don't get too upset about it.'

'I'm not upset,' Jo-Jo snapped.

'Just jealous.'

'No. Bored. I'm bored, bored, bored! I hate Bob the bloody Builder.'

Ed laughed, not taking her too seriously as he tucked into his own supper. 'Well, if you want to make life more exciting you should win the lottery, or you could always consider taking a lover. Just remember to check the guy's bank balance first.'

'Don't tempt me!' This was an old joke between them but for once Jo-Jo wasn't laughing.

Ed glanced at his wife's barely touched plate and embarked upon a gentle lecture. 'You're not on another diet, are you? I've told you a million times I love you exactly as you are, sweetie. I like cuddly women.'

Jo-Jo promptly burst into tears. And with that instinct which comes from having lived with a woman for almost ten years, and seen her in this emotional state on at least three previous occasions, Ed knew instinctively that her tears were not caused by her having taken offence at his ham-fisted compliment, but because there was a reason for the extra inches. 'Oh, my God, you're pregnant!'

Ed Dickson had been in love with Jo-Jo Holt ever since the fourth form at Kirbie Kendal School together. And with his teasing, gentle manner and cheerful smile, his good looks, dark hair cut close to his head, and soft brown eyes, she had been instantly smitten by him. He made her laugh, was a perfect foil to her highly strung, over-emotional personality.

Now he abandoned his own meal and quietly led his wife to the sofa to cuddle her close as the crying notched a pitch higher.

'I never meant this to happen, I swear it. Three is more than enough for anyone. And I'd just got back to work, even if it was only part-time for Mum and Dad. Oh, Ed, we can't afford another child, what are we going to do?' she wailed.

Ed was stroking her hair, kissing the tears from her cheeks, while looking as if he'd been hit head on by an express train. 'Well,' he said in that quiet way he had. 'We can't send it back and ask for a refund, can we?'

Despite her misery, Jo-Jo gave a spurt of laughter.

He smoothed back her ruffled curls, fair, like her sister's, only with a wildness to it, rather like her personality. But then Jo-Jo hadn't been near a hairdresser in years, resorting to chopping bits off it herself, whereas Carly had the income to spoil herself a bit more, and was far more businesslike and efficient in every way. Carly was the quiet one, the steadying influence and nose-to-the-grindstone sort, whereas Jo-Jo relied more on impulse, rushing through life by the seat of her pants. He rather loved that in his wife. He preferred the untamed look, the unpredictability of her personality, always thought she looked prettier when she forgot to apply lipstick and nail varnish, although she would sometimes use both when she was trying to impress.

He cupped her face between his hands and considered it with serious concern. There was usually a cheeky light to her brown eyes, a quirky smile to the wide mouth, but not today. 'You aren't going to go all hysterical on me, or do anything stupid, are you?'

Their gazes locked in perfect understanding and accord. 'As if. You don't mind too much then?'

'Well, another boy might be a good idea. Even things up nicely, that would. I reckon our Ryan will need all the support he can get to stand up to our Stacey and Samantha, once he grows up a bit and stops being such a novelty.'

Jo-Jo smiled at her husband through her tears. 'He's only just started walking. He'll be little more than two when this one is born.'

'They'll be chums for each other then. Just make sure it's a boy. Although I do love little girls. Happen we'll have another one of them too.'

'On your bike, mister! You can have that one yourself.'

Ed began to unbutton her blouse. He didn't notice the stains of baby food and tomato ketchup down the front. He was more interested in the lacy, peach-coloured bra his wife was wearing underneath. Instinctively she started to fend him off, and then remembering the damage was already done, laughingly started to kiss him instead. 'Oh, I do love you, you daft article.'

'I'm quite fond of you too. A quick shag isn't entirely out of the question then?' he asked, pushing her back on to the sofa. 'Doesn't seem anything to lose, does there? I'll make it quick in case our Ryan does his usual trick of going walkabout.'

'Pity he didn't do that the night you got me into this mess,' Jo-Jo complained as she helped him tug off her jeans, then busied herself with Ed's zip. 'I'm going to have to go on the pill you know. Other women do. Or you could have the snip.'

'So you've gone off the idea of making it a round dozen then?'

Giggling, she hit him with the cushion, then bit her lip to stop herself from making too much noise as he entered her. Upstairs came the creak of a floorboard and the sound of small feet.

Life settles down into some sort of normality over the next few days with no repetition of that tantrum. Oliver returns to his usual good humour, even profusely apologising for behaving like a prat. While he was at the pub I'd quickly defrosted and grilled a couple of pork chops, tossed a salad and microwaved a jacket potato each. It wasn't exactly cordon bleu but seemed to pass muster. Afterwards, he slept untroubled while I lay awake, worrying about what on earth had got into him, what he was trying to prove.

I still can't understand what triggered such a ferocious attack. He seems to think he can shout at me as much as he likes, but if I dare to complain, I'm in trouble. Presumably I'm supposed to merely listen and obey. If I don't, then I'm being inconsiderate of his feelings. My task, apparently, is to look after him. The thought makes me feel very slightly sick. This wasn't at all how I imagined married life would be.

But I block the memory of that awful night from my mind. He said himself he'd had a shit of a day. It was an aberration. It won't happen again, I tell myself.

We go for Sunday lunch to my parents' house and he's all sweet and charming, as usual. Quite his old self again. He compliments my mother on her cooking and makes some joke that she should perhaps give me a few lessons. I laugh, and confess to the failed quiche.

'Perhaps you used too much milk and not enough eggs,'

she suggests, preening herself at Oliver's compliments on the tenderness of her beef and the lightness of her Yorkshire puddings.

'I did my best in the time I had available, Mum.' I risk a further comment, casting my husband a smiling glance as I do so. 'Like all men, Oliver approves in theory of my running my own business, but I believe he'd much prefer it if I devoted myself exclusively to him.'

'Not at all,' Oliver demurs. 'I believe a woman has every right to be independent and do her own thing. Anyway, I don't mind chipping in and doing my bit to help.'

'Of course you don't,' Mum says, smiling into his clear blue eyes.

'And I'm so proud of her,' he says.

'Indeed, and why would you object to Carly's efforts when you've made such a good start in life yourself? Besides, you're a nice person,' Mum agrees, putting another slice of beef on to his plate.

He shakes his head sadly. 'Sometimes she thinks she's Superwoman, asks far too much of herself, so I have to give her a little lecture about priorities.'

They continue in this vein for some minutes while I listen in astonishment to the unexpected spin my husband is putting on the very same subject about which we rowed. I'm confused, hardly able to believe what I'm hearing. Is he deliberately telling lies or did I misread his attitude completely?

'She does her best but her cooking is pathetic, bless her,' Oliver says, patting my cheek fondly. 'But she's so sweet, and she is getting better.'

'Our Carly makes great scones,' Dad says, and I smile at him gratefully. At least someone is on my side.

'Whatever have you done to yourself? That's some bruise on your arm,' Emma said, examining her friend with concern.

Carly had taken off her overall in the heat of a warm spring day in order to scrub the bath properly, and Emma had unexpectedly come in and caught her. She gave a self-deprecating laugh. 'Whacked it with the cupboard door.'

'Not one of those brand-new cupboard doors in your beautiful new designer kitchen?' Emma teased.

'The very same.'

'Then get the corners chopped off, sanded down or whatever. You could do yourself a mischief.' She glanced at her watch. 'Have you nearly finished in here? I'm just about done with my bit.'

'Yep,' Carly agreed, head down in the bath as she dried it with paper towels, mentally kicking herself for her carelessness. 'I'm done.'

The two girls returned to the office together but Emma couldn't help noticing that despite the lack of air conditioning and unexpected warmth of the day, Carly rolled down the sleeves of her shirt. Is that the only bruise she's carrying? Emma worried. Should she say something further, or was it best not to interfere?

It had irritated Emma recently that Oliver had taken to calling Carly on her mobile around five each day, to check that she'd finished work and would soon be on her way home. She'd hear Carly assuring him that she was about to leave, 'Yes, darling, I'll be on my way any minute.'

'Make sure that you are,' Oliver would retort, in a voice loud enough to carry halfway across the office, and Carly would roll her eyes in amused despair. Of course, it often took another half hour or so to finish off, but she was always frantic to leave, which was a pity. The end of the day was generally the only time the two girls got the chance to really talk.

This evening Emma insisted they finish early and grab a quick drink at the John Peel pub. She was keen to discuss a few pressing issues, not least the question of working hours. The moment they were both settled with a couple of lagers in front of them, she made her suggestion.

'How about if I take over the evening work for a while? It seems fair, since you're still newly weds, and Oliver is obviously desperate to keep you wrapped in romance and red roses.'

Emma was careful not to mention to Carly that her husband rang the previous evening, insisting upon this change. Oliver had made it very clear that he was sick of his lovely new wife being tied up of an evening, that he expected her to be home on time every night from now on. Emma had resisted, naturally. She'd tried to explain how they divided the task between them, how evening work couldn't be entirely avoided during the summer months. Unfortunately, he'd then threatened to stop Carly working altogether, and she'd been forced to back down. The last thing Emma wanted was to lose her partner. 'It's occurred to me that you might need a bit more space in these early months together,' she finished, rather lamely in her estimation.

Carly was surprised by this generous offer, but suitably grateful, as well she might be. 'Oh, Emma, you're so kind. Are you sure?'

'Wouldn't have offered otherwise.'

'It would indeed help marital relations, at least for this first summer. Then we'll get back to normal, OK?'

'No problem.'

The words were barely out of her mouth when Oliver himself walked in, quite out of the blue. 'So this is where you are? Not working at all. I did wonder when I got no response to my text.'

Carly stared at him in horror, then glanced in panic at her mobile, which showed no evidence of a signal. Her cheeks reddened with embarrassment and Emma lifted her eyebrows slightly, longing to comment but not quite having the nerve to do so. She simply met Oliver's iron-hard glare with one of her own, while Carly gulped down her half of lager and leaped to her feet. 'I must go. I didn't realise it was so late.'

'Still love's young dream then?' Emma said, with a wry smile.

'My wife has other responsibilities now,' Oliver informed her, rather coldly, and hustled Carly out of the door. Emma watched them go with a troubled frown.

4

As summer progresses Oliver and I settle more comfortably together. We seem to be perfectly happy and content, so that I forget things ever went wrong between us. I start to believe that I've been worrying unnecessarily, that it's all going to work out fine and he's got over whatever was bothering him in those early days.

Even so, I find myself being far more attentive towards my husband, trying hard to please him and make him happy. I carefully follow recipes in my new cookery book, make certain that I don't forget to buy mushrooms if he wants a full English breakfast, to fry his egg without breaking the yolk. The last thing I want to do is to put him in a bad mood. And thanks to Emma's generosity, I get home early each day, which helps enormously.

Oliver is incredibly punctual himself and I discover that routine is strangely important to him. He likes me to run his bath for him, to have it ready and waiting as he walks through the door. Everything has to be perfect, not only the bath but also the right kind of shampoo and soap, or he complains and makes me change it. He expects a hot meal beautifully cooked the moment he's finished bathing; the house all neat and tidy with no sign of any books or papers or account sheets littered about. I can be a bit untidy in this respect when I bring work home, and he makes it very plain he doesn't care for that either.

He has incredibly high standards, and, I feel, somewhat unrealistic expectations. He expects to live in this perfect world which I am obliged to provide and maintain for him. If he's not satisfied, then it must be me who has failed in some way.

One evening I see him run a finger over the windowsill.

'It's the building work that's going on next door,' I say, jumping to my own defence, nervous he might get angry again. 'There's dust everywhere.'

'Don't blame other people for your own failings, Carly,' he says, scolding me gently. 'Look, I can write my name in it.'

Not strictly true but I don't argue. I run and fetch a damp cloth and wipe over every surface. I'm aware this is a weak and feeble thing to do, not something I could imagine Emma doing for instance, but I'm tired and really can't face another row. Besides, if I object, or say there's only so many hours in a day, that I've been busy cleaning the cottages and thought my own house could wait till my day off, he simply tells me it isn't good enough, that I must try harder. He's clearly used to being waited on.

'My own mother seems to manage,' he sternly reminds me, as if reading my thoughts.

Oliver's mother has never worked outside the home so doesn't have my problems. This doesn't seem the moment to remind him of that fact.

In any case, I can never succeed as the rules change, the goalposts are constantly moved. Sometimes it's good that I put flowers on the table, as his own mother does. At other times he insists I remove them as they only encourage insects and create mess. I generally go shopping on a Friday, but if I change my mind and go on a Thursday instead, he objects to this change in routine. Yet if I find I've run out of rice, as I did the other day, he tells me off for not having realised and gone shopping earlier. He would not then have been obliged to eat potatoes with his chilli, which he so hates to do.

Sometimes, there seems to be no way of pleasing him.

'So how's married life, old chap? Is the back holding up to the extra workload? Not to mention the libido?' Tony Clarke asked with a wry grin.

Oliver gave a small self-satisfied smile. 'I spend every waking hour shagging the life out of my lovely new wife, if you're interested. But there's more to marriage than that,' he added, somewhat sanctimoniously. 'Carly and I are a good team. We're friends as well as lovers.'

Tony smirked. 'Course you are, especially in the sack. Speaking as an old married man myself, marriage is great.' Both men watch as a new young assistant gets up from her desk, sashays over to the filing cabinet and, pushing back her long blonde hair with one careless hand, busies herself with the files. Tony lets out a heavy sigh. 'Puts a curb on the wandering eye a bit, though, doesn't it?'

The blonde was now leaning over her own desk, and the low neck of her top fell open to reveal a delectable view of her breasts. 'Not necessarily. What's her name?' Oliver casually enquired.

Both men swing back in their chairs to get a better view of the girl's legs as she moves over to the photocopier.

'Poppy.'

'Hmm! Nice. I don't see marriage as some sort of strait-jacket. No reason why a wife should deprive a chap of his little pleasures, is there?'

'Very true. You can look, even if you can't touch, eh?' Tony agreed, giving a nostalgic little sigh.

'Women are good for two things, and we both know what those are.'

'Yeah, right,' Tony laughed. 'Try telling that to *my* wife.'

'Ah, but you've got to train them right from the start. Women need to be kept in line otherwise they turn into useless, emotional wrecks, or nagging harpies. Give them too much rope and they'll hang you, ever ready to take advantage of a man's good nature. I fully expect to benefit from a few extra comforts in my life, now that I have Carly to care for me. I'll give her plenty of loving attention in return, as it were, but that doesn't mean she *owns* me. Women are only really happy when they're organising you, telling you what to do, what to wear, and constantly insisting you're tidy. Nurturing and caring they call it, which we call nagging.'

Tony snorted with suppressed laughter. 'Tell me about it.'

'Women's rights are all very well, but in their place, which is right behind the man's. I've certainly no intention of allowing a ring on my finger to greatly curtail *my* freedom.'

Tony was rolling about with laughter by the end of this little speech. He'd known Oliver Sheldon for only a short time in comparison to the long years he'd been friendly with Carly, and couldn't help wondering how she would view such a comment. 'Spoken like a true newby. You'll soon change your tune after a year or two. Look at me, it took Jane only six months to bring me to heel and have me washing up and everything. I've even been known to drive the vacuum cleaner. Although admittedly I do still leave my socks on the floor, which drives her mad.' He grinned, looking pleased with this small rebellion.

Oliver made a dismissive sound in his throat. 'OK, you have to jolly women along a bit, play the good-husband card, exercise the charm offensive to keep them happy and nicely on the boil, as it were. The ladies love that sort of crap. They lap it up. Make no mistake, I love Carly. Absolutely adore her, and I'm proud of what she's achieved. She's my wife, after all! But it's all about respect, isn't it? You can't have them turn you into a mummy's boy.'

'Too right,' Tony agreed. The telephone rang at that moment and Tony snatched it up. 'Harrison Accounts – Oh, hi, love.' A pause while he listened. 'Yeah right, a tub of sour cream or what – right, plain yoghurt. Yep, got that. Fresh bread . . . wholemeal, yeah, and . . . wait, I'll make a list.'

The new assistant cast Oliver a sly glance from across the room, then slowly crossed her legs, deliberately rubbing her Italian glossy tights one against the other so that the sound brought Oliver's head swivelling round, and his languid gaze to settle on her. Poppy felt goose bumps run up and down her spine. Oliver Sheldon was gorgeous, and mega-powerful. She didn't see little wifey as any sort of encumbrance, since he was quite obviously the kind of man who made up his own rules.

And Poppy would be quite happy to play by them, given half a chance.

She rather hoped he might be regretting rushing into matrimony quite so quickly. Men often did. Probably it had sounded wonderful, in theory, having a woman to take care of you, regular sex on tap, as it were, but as everyone knew, putting a ring on a girl's finger was far more complicated than that. Some women could turn frigid, start nagging, or be demanding attention all the time. From what she'd overheard Oliver saying just now, it sounded very much as if Carly was like that. Serve the silly little housefrau right if her man looked elsewhere.

Really, Poppy thought, some women were their own worst enemies.

Oliver shook his head sadly at his friend as Tony put down the phone, still scribbling madly. 'See what I mean? They'll have you running all over the damn show. What women find to do all day, I really can't think. Their nails, presumably. Look, keep an eye out for old Harrison, will you? I'm going to take a quick coffee break.'

'OK,' Tony agreed, looking faintly sheepish as he tried to hide the long shopping list his wife had given him, then watched in astonishment as his friend moved over to the new girl. Oliver whispered something in her ear which made her giggle, and then left the office. Barely two seconds later, she followed him. Now what was that all about?

I stand in the shower and see that my legs and arms are a mass of bruises. The sight shocks me. It's true that there have been one or two more incidents recently, but I hadn't realised that Oliver's black moods, as I call them, were leaving such brutal evidence. Fortunately they aren't obvious, so long as I keep them covered up. Some are already fading and turning yellow but I find the sight of them quite disturbing. They look as if I've been beaten up by some thug. I touch the marks gently with my fingers, feeling the soreness. Tears gather at the back of my throat. I hadn't realised how strong and powerful he is, or that I looked such a mess. But why hadn't I?

Because of a sense of disbelief, I realise, that this is happening to me. I feel so guilty for allowing it to happen at all. I'm not sleeping well, and I feel this creeping sense of depression deep in the pit of my stomach. I can't seem to think straight, or concentrate on anything. I have a terrible fear that our marriage is already falling apart.

Too often I find myself flinching in anticipation of an impatient hand reaching out to slap me, which he always insists is for my own good. Or he'll grab me by my arms and shake me like some recalcitrant child while he instructs me in a cold, calm voice as to the extent of my supposed transgression. I remember my sister telling me about the letter, insisting that Oliver was already cheating me. What satisfaction it would give her if my marriage were to fail. But he isn't cheating on me, I tell myself firmly. He just loses it occasionally. I examine the imprint of his fingers on the soft upper flesh of my arms and quietly weep.

I hear a car draw up and my heart starts to race before I recognise the engine as being not Oliver's, but Jo-Jo's.

'Heavens,' I murmur, as I quickly rub myself dry and pull on jeans and a long-sleeved shirt. 'Have I come to this? Does my heart skip with fear every time I think my husband has arrived home early?'

I rush down the stairs to open the door and Jo-Jo breezes in, Ryan clutched tightly in her arms. 'God, I'd kill for a coffee. Put the kettle on, sis. Our Stacey is turning into a right little madam, threw a real tantrum just now outside the school gates when she discovered I'd forgotten her PE kit. For goodness' sake, I told her, I'm only human, I can't remember everything.'

Plonking Ryan down on the kitchen floor she gives him a rusk to eat as he starts to grizzle, then collapses into a chair. She rakes her fingers through her tousled hair, looking more like the wild witch of the north than the drama queen she usually is. 'Truth is, I'm a useless mother. Utter crap.'

I smile as I hand her a coffee, with hot milk and loads of sugar, just as she likes it. 'You're a wonderful mum and your kids adore you. Instead of feeling sorry for yourself, why don't you pop back home, pick up Stacey's PE bag and take it into school for her. Much more productive than self-flagellation, don't you think?'

She gives me one of her dark looks. 'Why is it you always have the answer to everything? What makes you so bloody perfect? Perfect home, perfect husband. Even your business is called Perfect Cottages.' There's the usual sharp edge to her tone but I don't rise to the bait, determined not to take offence.

I sit opposite her, cradling a black coffee as I avoid her gaze. 'Maybe the cottages are perfect, or at least we try to make them appear so, but I certainly am not, nor is Oliver.'

She casts me a quizzical look of disbelief. 'Good heavens, don't tell me the gloss has worn off *Mr Wonderful* already?'

I frown, embarrassed now, and instinctively go on the defensive, smoothing down the sleeves of my shirt. 'I'm not saying that. I'm simply pointing out that nobody is perfect, there's always a flaw somewhere.'

'So what is dear Oliver's flaw? Have you discovered it yet?'

I meet her amused gaze and hold it for a second longer than normal, wondering how she would react if I told her the truth, that my beloved new husband was a wife-beater. Shame washes over me, and I know I simply can't do it. Admitting the truth to myself is difficult enough, even in the privacy of my own head.

There are five years between the two of us so perhaps that's why we've never been exactly close. As girls we had different friends, were always at different stages in our education, different schools for much of the time, and different hobbies. Jo-Jo was into Guiding and outdoor sports, whereas I was the quiet, stay-at-home, head-in-a-book sort. Then she took up boys and clubbing and I became what she termed a bit of a swot. Not true, but a bookworm certainly. She was always gorgeous and out-going, and I was plump and rather shy. Our relationship is getting easier as we grow older but Jo-Jo does tend to use words rather like a blunt instrument, as she is doing today. Before I can decide how best to answer she jumps up to catch Ryan who has vanished into the lounge. She carries the toddler, squirming and squealing in her arms, back into the kitchen and closes the door, barring his escape. 'Better not let him loose in your perfect house.'

'Stop it, Jo-Jo. It isn't funny.'

She sips her coffee in silence for a while, then launches into a familiar complaint that she hasn't been out of the house for weeks, that her life consists entirely of Huggies and Bob the Builder, PE kits and chauffeuring children about to school, nursery, Brownies, Rainbows, ballet, you name it. 'They have a better social life than me. I've ceased to be a person in my own right, and it's going to get worse. You're so lucky, our kid. Look at me, knocked up yet again. Can you believe it?'

'Oh, no!'

'Yeah, great huh?'

I look at her round, cosy figure, never having quite lost the weight she put on after Ryan, her tired face with the dark rings under her eyes. 'How far gone are you?'

'Three and a half months.'

'Why didn't you tell me?'

'I was waiting for the scan, just to be certain, but it's true enough. I've been sick and everything.' Tears form in her lovely brown eyes and I'm filled with remorse for thinking so badly of her. No wonder she's been in a foul mood lately, snapping at me the whole time.

Jo-Jo and Ed had been happily living together for a couple of years or so when she'd found herself pregnant with Stacey. That was almost seven years ago. Samantha had followed two years later, then Ryan who is almost eighteen months now, I suppose. She swore he was a mistake and would be the last. Now there was to be a fourth child, and I know money is tight. Ed earns only a modest wage at the garage where he works as a mechanic.

'I'd just got both girls into school, Ryan into a playgroup for a few hours each week, and I was loving my part-time job, even if it is only working for Mum and Dad in the shop. In any case, we desperately need the money. You're so lucky, Carly, that everything is working out for you. I'm at my wits' end.' Whereupon my strong, feisty sister bursts into tears.

I hold her close while she has a good cry, my own troubles paling into insignificance against this disaster. Ryan sits on the floor looking up at his mummy with a small frown of concern. I smile to reassure him.

'It's just as well you like babies then, isn't it? Ed too,' I joke, handing her a box of tissues.

She takes a handful and blows her nose. 'Oh, he's been great about it. Ed loves kids. He'd have a nursery full but I hate being pregnant, getting fat, seeping milk, feeling moody, all that stuff. Oh, I wish I was you.'

'No, you don't,' I tell her, my voice barely above a whisper as I help her to mop up the tears. 'You'll cope, you and Ed. You always do. Look, what you need is a break. Why don't I come over and babysit for the terrible trio tonight, while Ed takes you out somewhere intimate and romantic?'

She looks at me all red eyed, hope bright behind the tears. 'You'd do that for me?'

'You're my sister.'

'But I was a real pig to you before the wedding, about that letter.'

I shrug. 'All forgotten. Shall we say seven o'clock?'

'Can lover-boy spare you for the evening?' she asks, with a touch of her old sarcasm. 'Maybe you should ring and check.'

I give a little laugh. 'I don't need his permission. We're not joined at the hip. It'll be fine. I've been home every evening on time for weeks. Now go get Stacey's PE kit or you'll have her teacher on your tail, then you'll really have problems.'

She gives me a quick hug, swoops Ryan up in her arms and dashes off, grinning from ear to ear. She practically bounces down the drive, already reaching for her mobile phone to tell

Ed the good news, no doubt mentally planning what she's going to wear that evening. I smile and wave, pleased that things are back on an even keel between the pair of us, but I don't envy her the task of coping with four small children.

I know I should ring Oliver with this change of plan yet I'm reluctant in case he tries to talk me out of it. I send a quick text instead, briefly stating there's an emergency and I'm baby-sitting for Jo-Jo this evening. I'll explain when I see him. He doesn't reply but I don't have time to worry about that as I get caught up in traffic and then face the usual raft of problems which crowd my own day. Perfect life indeed. Where does Jo-Jo get these ideas from?

Later that night as I slip beneath the covers and snuggle up beside my husband, he turns to me with a sigh of resignation and asks me what the crisis was this time. He's well used to Jo-Jo's histrionics, as he calls them, so I tell him about the unexpected pregnancy.

'God, can't those two use safe sex or something? They breed like rabbits.'

I giggle as he starts to kiss me, delighted there isn't going to be any confrontation this evening. He's relaxed and sleepy, the way I love him to be, his hands moving over my breasts and thighs, clearly in the mood for something other than a row. 'Ed says he only needs to throw his trousers on the bed and she's off.'

'Then why doesn't she go on the pill, for heaven's sake?'

'Some health issue or other. The pill isn't a solution for every woman.'

'Thank God you're on it,' he says, pushing up my night-dress as he moves on top of me, nudging my legs apart with his knee. We move together in a familiar rhythm, so entirely suited I think happily to myself, so why can't this natural harmony spill over into other sections of our life? 'Don't let this babysitting lark become a habit,' he murmurs, kissing my flat stomach, doing things to me that make me gasp and cry out.

'And for God's sake, don't start getting broody. The last thing we need is for you to get pregnant.' Once I can catch my breath, I promise that I won't.

Our sex life is undoubtedly good, getting better, if anything. Oliver is a generous and imaginative lover, and I have absolutely no complaints in that direction. We can still hardly keep our hands off each other and he only has to look at me for my limbs to turn to liquid fire and my heart to race. I find making love in the early morning particularly sweet and fulfilling when we're both warm and relaxed. he has a lovely habit of waking me before the alarm goes off, so that we have time before the day begins.

Apart from the sex, married life seems far less interesting and exciting than I'd expected. Little has changed for Oliver except that he's moved house and has someone other than his mother to cook his meals and do his washing for him, while I'm feeling run down and deprived of fun. Bored, I suppose, like Jo-Jo. I'm equally tired of the domestic goddess routine and desperate for more fun.

'Even married women still need romancing,' I gently remind him one evening, slipping into a peach negligee to entice him. He laughs and takes me up to bed, but doesn't seem to think we need do any of that social stuff now that we're married. Much more fun at home, he insists, where the bed's handy.

5

We haven't seen much of our old friends since the wedding and I begin to wonder why. One couple, Tony and Jane, with whom we used to be really friendly, still live close to Mum and Dad. I've known them both most of my life, but Tony and Oliver soon became firm friends too. Oliver even helped Tony get a job as a clerk in the same office, once he was transferred to Kendal. Yet we seem to have lost touch lately. Maybe the fault is mine and I should make more of an effort.

One Saturday afternoon in early September, with no urgent calls or cottages to clean, and Oliver happily ensconced on the golf course, I decide to call in and say hello to Jane. She was one of my bridesmaids after all, and Tony was best man.

Jane looks surprised to find me on her doorstep but invites me in for coffee. I chat about inconsequential gossip, and about mutual friends as she boils the kettle and fills the cafetière but I notice that her manner is odd, rather stiff and awkward. She's certainly at pains to explain how busy she and Tony have been these last few months. 'Anyway, I expect you've got new friends now you've moved into a big detached house on a smart estate,' she says, as she carries the tray through into the lounge.

I follow her with a frown, puzzled by her attitude as much as by the remark. Does she imagine that we've gone all posh and toffee-nosed? 'We're slowly getting to know people, although it isn't easy. The place feels a bit like Stepford at times,' I laugh. 'Or as if everyone has died, it's so quiet. People seem to work late, and they all drive cars. You never see anyone walk anywhere so there's precious little opportunity to chat over the garden wall. I've missed you, and all the old gang in town. I do hope we're still friends.'

She plunges the coffee and pours it into two earthenware mugs. 'Course we are, only I'm just saying . . . well, actually I think Oliver sees Tony as a bit dull and boring these days, now he's moving onward and upward. I don't think they're as friendly as they used to be.'

'Don't be daft. I'm sure they're still good mates. They work in the same office, after all.'

Jane seems about to say something more but then evidently reconsiders, thinks better of it and sips her coffee instead. I wonder if the two have fallen out over something, and Oliver has forgotten to mention it to me. 'I thought you might pop over to see us,' I say. 'View the new house.'

'I'm sure it's very grand,' she comments, her voice flat and uninterested, and I'm even more puzzled, wondering what I've done to deserve this cool treatment. 'I'm sorry if I've neglected you a bit recently, only Em and I have been run off our feet all summer, as you can imagine. It's been hectic. And of course Oliver makes huge demands upon my time these days.'

'You surprise me,' she says tartly. 'Tony says he's a real gadabout. Never at home in that beautiful house of yours.'

I feel a burst of resentment over this comment. It's true that Oliver is out quite a lot, but it's not like Jane to be so bitchy. I've obviously upset her badly through my neglect. 'Look, you're welcome to pop in any time for a coffee, or come over for a meal some time. Work isn't so all consuming now the season is largely over. I'll give you a ring.'

'I think you'd best ask your darling husband first. The last time Tony suggested we got together, Oliver seemed to be saying that we no longer had anything common.'

I'm shocked to the core by this remark, and say as much. 'I don't believe you. Oliver would never say such a thing.'

'Not in so many words perhaps, but it's clear that's what he thinks. You don't need to feel obliged to keep in touch, Carly, now that you're married and living on that posh estate.'

'Why do you say that? You and I, and Tone, have been friends all our lives. My marriage doesn't change that, does it?'

Her cheeks grow quite pink. 'Of course not. I'm just saying . . .'

'What are you saying, Jane?'

She looks at me, takes a breath, and then launches into what sounds very like a well-practised speech. 'Well, to be honest, we've been a bit worried about you, Tone and I. I mean, it was a surprise when you married Oliver Sheldon. It was a bit sudden, wasn't it? I never thought you'd actually go through with it, hoped you'd eventually see sense. You'd only known him for a few months after all, and hadn't lived with him or anything.'

I can't quite believe what I'm hearing, that one of my oldest friends is saying these things to me. One of my *bridesmaids*, for heaven's sake! 'What does that matter whether we lived together or not? You've seen us together. You know how much in love we are. What on earth has got into you?'

'Nothing.'

'Well then, where is all this nonsense coming from?'

'We're just concerned, that's all.'

'Why?'

'No reason. Like you say, we're friends, right? I just hope your coming round here doesn't mean things have gone pear-shaped already, although it wouldn't surprise me in the slightest. If I'm honest, I never thought Oliver was good enough for you, Carly. I wouldn't trust him as far as I can throw him and I'm surprised you do.' Her face is flame red by this time and I can't quite believe what I'm hearing.

I set down the coffee mug very carefully and stand up. 'I think I'd best be getting back. Since my choice of husband doesn't seem to meet with your approval, I'll say goodbye. No need to show me out, I can find my own way.'

As I stalk to the door, Jane leaps to her feet and rushes after me. 'Don't take offence. I didn't mean anything by it, not really. Look, Carly, it's not me saying this, it's Tony. He can't stand

Oliver, that's all it is. They've had a bit of scrap over something, but it needn't affect you and me.'

'Obviously it has affected us. It's affected *you* by the sound of it.'

'We can still be friends though, can't we?'

I look at her, eyebrows raised. 'I don't think so, do you?'

There's a small silence, then she pulls open the door and says with a false brightness, 'I'll pop in some time . . . for coffee . . . as you suggest.'

We both know that she won't.

'Have you and Tony had a falling out?' I ask Oliver that evening as I flit about the kitchen cooking pasta, chopping onions, mixing a cheese sauce, trying to appear cool, calm and collected, while frantically attempting to catch up after my couple of hours out by making something quick and easy. I feel even more depressed after an afternoon with my old friend, not less. Oliver pours us a glass of red wine each while I relate to him my strange conversation with Jane. He shrugs and says he has no recollection of any row between himself and Tony.

'Her attitude was most puzzling,' I explain, taking a welcome slurp of the wine. The encounter has upset me more than I'm prepared to say, but Oliver can't understand what's wrong either.

'Don't go round to see her again.'

'What?'

'They're just jealous of my success, suffering from some sort of inverted snobbery. Forget them.'

I'm appalled by the idea, reluctant to let them go completely. 'I can't do that. Jane has been one of my best friends for most of my life, since junior school. I can't just cut her off.'

'You can if that's her attitude. She's made it very clear what she thinks of me.'

'She said she was only repeating Tony's opinions. Are you sure you and Tone haven't had a scrap, a few ill-chosen remarks, or a falling-out of some sort?'

'Are you doubting me? Are you blaming me for this?'

'No, of course not. I just wonder what's wrong.'

'I'll tell you what's wrong. She's jealous. She's a stupid, interfering woman. It's a bloody cheek to suggest our marriage has gone "pear-shaped", as if you'd gone round there looking for a shoulder to cry on. Forget her. Ignore them both.'

But I don't feel that I can. 'Maybe I should get to the bottom of this, apologise or something for whatever it is I'm supposed to have done. I need to know what it is that's really bothering her.'

'Leave it! Do you hear me? I don't want you to see her again.'

'But . . .'

Oliver lets out a heavy sigh, one I'm growing familiar with, which usually indicates he's running out of patience. I stop arguing and dash over to check on the pasta, wishing I'd never started on this conversation.

Later, as we sit opposite each other at the dining table, he swirls the wine in his glass, blood red and glinting in the candlelight. 'If it's a choice between me, your loving husband, and some old friend you happen to have known for a while, who would you choose?'

There really is no answer to that, but somehow, losing a good friend in this way makes me feel more isolated than ever.

As autumn approaches, I'm finding that I'm spending quite a few evenings at home alone. Oliver often goes out after dinner, playing golf, cricket or football with friends, or he'll stay late at the office dealing with a client. On Tuesdays he's in a quiz league, and, of course, Friday night with his mates is sacred.

Privately I feel a little jealous of his bachelor-style social life. When I mention this to Oliver, say how lonely I get on the nights he's out, he brings me home a pizza, as a treat, he says. It's not exactly what I had in mind. I was hoping he'd take me to a movie, or a meal out occasionally at that little Italian restaurant we used to go to before we were married.

I consider getting involved with some hobby or other myself, and mention an aerobics class available locally that I might attend, but Oliver isn't in favour.

'I thought you said your job leaves you exhausted every night, and you've still got all the washing and housework to do. How would you manage to fit it all in?'

I sigh. Maybe I have got enough on my plate right now. After a busy summer with the holiday letting business perhaps this isn't a good time to start an aerobics class. 'I'll see how I feel in a month or two,' I agree. 'Maybe in the new year.'

This creeping sense of loneliness is doing me no good at all, though if I complain too much he accuses me of whingeing.

'We have a beautiful home, what more do you want?'

'Nothing, I'm fine, really I am.'

'I should hope so. I'm just about broke after paying for this house.'

I'm filled with guilt at this comment and, of course, he's right, I am very fortunate. It's just that it's beginning to grate that while he's fiercely protective of his own freedom, determined that, married or not, he has the right to come and go as he pleases, my own free time is another matter entirely. Oliver likes to think of me sitting at home, waiting for him. If I pop over to see my sister and my nieces and nephew, he wants to know exactly where I'm going and what time I'll be back. I caught him once checking the mileometer on my car and I had to laugh.

'You know how far it is to Jo-Jo's, a little under two miles. I haven't done any detours, or wasted too much petrol. You can be a real skinflint at times, do you know that?' I teased him, kissing his nose.

'You might be meeting your lover for all I know,' he drily remarked, and I laughed all the more.

One evening I can't find my car keys. I've promised to pop over to Emma's to talk over how we can develop a better strategy for following up enquiries, and cope more efficiently with bookings as they come in. The keys aren't in my bag where I usually keep them, and I spend ages hunting high and low. I look everywhere, turn the house upside down. In the end I'm forced to ring Emma and postpone our meeting. An hour later, when I search in my bag for something else, there they are, tucked in the side pocket.

'I must be losing my mind,' I say, flopping back on the sofa beside my husband. 'The keys were in my bag all the time.'

'You're too stressed,' he calmly informs me, a small smile on his handsome face, and with such a tenderness in his tone that it melts my heart. 'Lucky for me though, I'd much rather have you here,' he says, starting to kiss me.

After we've made love he goes off for a shower, says he might pop out for a quick drink at the pub.

'I'll come with you,' I say.

'Looking like that?' he teases. 'As if you've just fallen out of bed.'

I giggle. 'I never got as far as the bed.'

He leans over and gives me a long lingering kiss. 'Well, go to it now, darling. Don't wait up, you need your sleep.'

I sigh and cuddle the cushion as I wave him off. He's so considerate, fussing over me like an old mother hen that I forgive him the fact that he's the one going out again, and not me. Why can't things always be this way between us? Why am I always whingeing? And why am I turning into such a scatterbrain and always losing things? Maybe he's right, and I am doing far too much.

It's a week or two later and again I'm at home alone watching a video of *Pride and Prejudice* while working on a new brochure for Perfect Cottages. I've printed out the basic design from my laptop, now I'm sticking on photos, and adding little sketches. Once the whole thing is finished to my satisfaction, I'll scan it back in, adjust the formatting a little, then get it printed up professionally.

I hear his key in the lock and look up with a smile. 'Hello, darling. Had a good evening?'

He doesn't answer immediately but looks pointedly at the

laptop on the floor, the stack of books on tourism I've been browsing through, and at the papers I'm working on. 'I thought I told you never to bring work home?'

I smile and shrug. 'Needs must when the devil drives. It's too hectic at the office to deal with this sort of thing. I didn't think it mattered, since you were out. Anyway, darling, you bring work home all the time and hide yourself away in your den, so why shouldn't I occasionally do the same?'

I can see by the way his jaw tightens that I've said the wrong thing and I feel a small flutter of concern. 'You surely aren't comparing your work with mine?' he asks, giving a sarcastic little smile.

'N-no, of course not,' I stammer, feeling a curl of unease.

'Don't tell me that partner of yours has got you doing the books? You know nothing about accounts. You're a first-class idiot over money.'

'I'm not doing accounts. This is a brochure I'm designing,' I say, feeling my cheeks start to burn, for it's true, I'm not good with figures. I generally leave all of that to Em. I am, however, very careful with money though judge it wise not to argue that point.

'You've no flair for design either. I made all the decisions about this house. You were hopeless.'

I want to say that I was never given the chance to offer an opinion, that everything was settled between himself and the builder without reference to me, but it seems petty, so I try to smile and say something about doing my best.

He gives a heavy sigh of exasperation. 'If you must make a fool of yourself, Carly, at least do so where I can't witness your folly. I won't have your pathetic work cluttering up our beautiful home and intruding on our time together.' Mouth tight, he snatches up the papers off my lap, opens the door of the wood-burning stove, and throws them on the fire.

I gasp in dismay as the flames lick and blacken the photos, quickly consuming my detailed design. '*What have you done?* I've been working on that all night.'

'I'm sure you have a copy on your laptop,' he says, his sneering tone tight with disapproval.

'Not the drawings and photos, I don't. They still needed to be scanned in. Oh, Oliver, that's a whole night's work wasted.' I can feel a great wodge of tears forming at the back of my throat, misery and frustration almost overwhelming me.

'Oh, for God's sake don't start getting hysterical.'

'I'm not hysterical, but I am cross. I don't understand what devil gets into you at times.'

'*Oh, Oliver, I am cross,*' he says, sarcastically mimicking my voice. 'Are you daring to question me? I won't have it,' he coldly informs me. 'How was I to know you foolishly hadn't scanned those stupid photos onto your computer? Now I'd like a cup of tea, *if* it's not too much trouble.' Instantly dismissing the dispute he switches off the video and reverts to a football match on TV, settles himself comfortably on the sofa, unperturbed by my distress.

Upset as I am, I march to the kitchen and switch on the kettle, quietly seething. I'm nearly bursting with frustration but realise it's useless to protest. Besides, it's true what he says, I should have scanned the damned photos into the computer first. I feel so stupid and inadequate. Why can't I do anything properly?

I feel I'm walking a tightrope, striving to remember all his little rules of what I may and may not do, the things I'm allowed to do and the things I'm not. I'm nervous of upsetting him, constantly afraid of making a mistake. Yet I'm beginning to recognise a pattern. It's as if he likes to pick fault with me in order to assert his authority, to prove he's the one with the power, the one in control. Does putting me down in some way make him feel better about himself? I wonder.

He's been calm and content in recent weeks, quite his normal self and in a good mood, yet I'm only too aware that he's watching my every movement like a hawk. The more he picks on me, the more I feel the tension mount and I daren't risk upsetting him. He could easily go into a sulk which can last for days as he gradually gets more and more edgy and the anger simmers to boiling point.

There are even no-no's with regard to suitable topics of conversation, certain subjects I mustn't mention, such as my job, or a book I've read which he knows nothing about. He doesn't care to hear me talking about my friends either, and certainly not Em, whom he sees as some sort of threat.

I realise with a chilling certainty that my husband enjoys belittling me, actually takes pleasure in putting me down; and the more he does that, the harder I strive to please him. Otherwise he might hit me again.

Perversely, he can also be kind and loving, good fun when he puts his mind to it, and a wonderfully generous lover. I always feel so grateful for the times when he shows me some love and affection. I feel this great surge of relief and gratitude whenever he shows any kindness towards me. Is that because I feel I don't have anyone else to turn to? Because I'm not brave enough to confess the bleak truth to my family, that I might have made a bad mistake in my choice of husband?

I still love Oliver, still hope and pray that one day he'll grow up a little and change, that it'll all work out. Love isn't something you can turn off like a tap.

Or am I just in denial that this is even happening to me?

I can't seem to think clearly, can't get my head round even the most mundane task, let alone make long-term decisions about the future. I'm simply concerned with getting through each day with the least possible problems.

At least our social life is improving and we're starting to go out a little more. We have a lot of fun over the coming weeks going on car rallies with friends, and once we take a boat out on Lake Windermere. Sometimes we'll just drive up into the Central Lakes for drinks or a meal at a pub. It's such a relief to get out and about again and I'm beginning to feel less isolated, far more relaxed.

And every week, without fail, he brings me flowers, telling

me that he loves me, that he finds my new wifely skills endearing. Thankfully, these do seem to be improving despite my apparent incompetence at ironing his trousers, which I never manage to get right.

Everything is going to be fine, I tell myself. Every marriage has its teething problems, which we seem to be resolving at last. It's early days yet but we do love each other, very much, which is surely all that matters. I must continue to have faith.

I admit though that there are still irritations, like when he sits down to dinner and expects to be served as if he's a client and I'm the waitress in some restaurant. He'll send me scurrying for horseradish sauce, ketchup or whatever, as if he doesn't possess the capabilities to fetch it himself. I never object. Where's the point? He's a hopeless man, after all.

Sadly, his image of our respective roles is not mine, and I'm having one devil of a job to change his attitude.

He also insists that I keep proper household accounts and note down everything I spend. I realise that being an accountant makes Oliver a bit fussy in this respect, so do my best to make sure the details are accurate.

My own new business isn't bringing in much of a profit yet, and I do worry about money a great deal. Everything seems to be far more expensive than I'd bargained for. Oliver does too, I realise, and he hasn't yet got the partnership he's been promised. He's generous enough with my housekeeping allowance yet time and time again when I go to my purse expecting to find a twenty-pound note still in there, I find it empty, or in fact I only have a fiver. I try to be more frugal and better organised, visit thrift shops and look out for bargains at the supermarkets but money doesn't go nearly as far as it should.

Oliver constantly reminds me how expensive this house is to run, demands to know where my money goes because he insists every penny be accounted for. It never occurs to me that he might be taking money out of my purse for himself, and then one day I happen to walk into the kitchen and catch him rummaging in my bag.

'Were you looking for something?' I quietly ask, and see him start, looking almost guilty for a second although he quickly recovers.

'I was checking that you weren't overspending again. You really are rather careless with money, darling. Very wasteful with food too.' He opens the fridge door and points to some leftover chicken. 'Look at that,' he says. 'What are you going to do with it?'

'It's for my lunch tomorrow,' I tell him, beginning to feel edgy, as if I'm the one who has done something wrong.

Next he goes to the pedal bin, opens it and shows me the leftover remains of some spaghetti bolognaise we had yesterday. 'Look at that, pure waste.'

'It's not always easy to judge how much to make,' I bleakly respond.

'Try harder to get it right next time. I can't afford to see the good money I earn being thrown away. Surely that too could warm up for a snack for your lunch,' he snaps.

'A sandwich on the hoof is usually all I have time for, but you might be right,' I hastily agree, as I see his expression darken.

When he goes off to his den I check my purse. One ten-pound note, a fiver and a few pound coins. I'll swear there were also a couple of twenty-pound notes in it the last time I looked. What is going on? Surely Oliver isn't taking my money? I look at his closed study door then put the purse back in my bag. I can't be certain. I could be mistaken. I make the decision to check more carefully in future, and to keep proper accounts.

But then I always do as he asks. Life is easier that way.

'I've had an idea how to cut down on our expenses,' he tells me the next morning at breakfast as I place a plate of bacon and eggs before him.

'Oh, what's that?'

'We could sell your car.'

'What?' I'm paralysed with shock. 'You are joking? You can't live in the Lakes without a car, and I certainly couldn't do my job without one. These holiday cottages are often in remote, inaccessible places, and it's not as if we have a reliable bus service.'

'I've thought about that, but I don't see why you shouldn't use Emma's car during the day. You usually work together, don't you?'

'Yes, but not always. Sometimes one of us does the cleaning and the other stays in the office, or we're forced to prepare a property individually because we've got so many that need doing. And I don't exactly work nine to five, my hours vary so much. Sorry, darling, but it wouldn't work. I need my little car.'

'I could pick you up every day after work,' he insists, stubbornly sticking to his argument, and I feel a strange claustrophobia creeping over me at the thought of being entirely dependent upon my husband for transport.

'Would you want to drive me to the supermarket, or into Kendal every time I need a hairdresser or dentist, or to see Gran and Grandpa? I doubt it. Sorry, but you'll have to think of some other way to economise.' I get up and start clearing the table and a new thought occurs to me. In any case, the cost of my car is charged against *my* business expenses, not yours.'

I smile, pleased with this realisation, this small victory. He isn't smiling back but looks annoyed, as if I've caught him out in some way. Surely he wasn't simply trying to curb my independence, I think, as he strides away, back rigid with disapproval. That would be too silly for words.

6

Oliver seems to think that if I don't do exactly as he asks, it must be because I don't think *he's* important, because I don't respect him or love him enough. Usually I've learned to hold my tongue, to tread the thin blue line my husband has drawn for me in the sand of our marriage and do my best to keep to his rules. The trouble is, he has so many requirements it's hard to remember them all, and the tension does get to me at times.

He sees himself as a person who's not fully appreciated, and I'm expected to constantly reassure him that this is not the case. But when I agreed to 'love, honour and obey', I never expected those words to be taken quite so literally.

Quiche has been very much off the menu since that first dreadful incident. I've bought myself half a dozen new cookery books and I'm learning to prepare more tasty meals, using only the kind of food he likes, of course. But it isn't easy. I buy only his favourite soap and shampoo, watch the TV programmes he chooses, and the remote is very much his toy. I only read when he's out, and don't touch his newspaper until after he's read it. I make certain the house is immaculate with not a speck of dust anywhere, and always remember to put on lipstick and make myself look attractive before he comes home.

I still spend my days watching the clock and worrying about being late home, of dinner not being ready on time, which is sure to cause him to fly into a rage.

'Can't you get one thing right, for God's sake?' He'll rail at me. 'Don't I deserve a little attention after a long hard day at work?' He certainly isn't interested in hearing about mine.

I devise little strategies like quickly plonking a few pans on top of the cooker if I hear his car in the drive before I've had time to prepare anything, hopping against hope he won't lift a lid. When he asks if I've remembered to pay in a cheque or call to collect his dry cleaning, I lie and pretend that I have. It's only a little white lie, I tell myself, but safer that way. So long as he never discovers the truth.

I'm learning to practise deceit, which seems dreadful so early in my marriage.

He's in a bad mood for days following my refusal to sell my car, which always happens when he doesn't get his own way in something. Then one evening he comes home all sunshine and smiles, insists on taking me out for a huge steak, and afterwards we make love like teenagers. He can be so loving when he wants to be, once again the charming man I married. If only he could always be this way.

I find it hard to admit that I'm being bullied, probably because I love him so much and still nurture hopes that his temper will eventually calm down and he'll stop being quite so volatile. How can I admit to anyone that Oliver is abusing me when he can be so charming, so loving and sexy towards me? I'm supposed to be this capable, strong, reasonably intelligent woman, not some pathetic victim.

I don't feel able to discuss this problem with anyone because everyone else thinks he's a great guy, so who would believe me if I told them what he does to me? If we go over to Mum and Dad's he's soon chatting and laughing with them, offering to mow the lawn or put up curtains to save Mum from stretching.

'He's so thoughtful,' she'll say.

And it's true. He can be very loving, tender and caring, considerate and good fun, but I've noticed this is mainly when we're in the company of other people. He makes less effort when we're on our own, unless he can see that I'm becoming very unhappy, or 'difficult' as he calls it, then he will make a special effort to fuss over me, as he has been doing lately. It's as if consciously, or perhaps subconsciously, he sets out to bewitch and charm me in order to bring me back into line, back under his control. A weird concept I can't quite come to terms with, yet it must be true because his behaviour deceives everyone, even me at times.

Emma and I talk about marriage in general terms. She cannot see the necessity for it at all, believing women get a raw deal, and that it pays to keep a man on his toes. I've often teased her about these radical views of hers, although I'm always careful not to divulge too much about my own situation. She can be very dismissive and judgemental. She's suffered from relationships going wrong in the past, been round the block a bit before she settled down with Glen and has rather a jaundiced view where men are concerned. I take great care what I say to her about Oliver, as she doesn't seem too well disposed towards him for some reason.

One lunchtime we're having a girly chat over a snatched sandwich and a mug of tea at our desks, and I casually mention that Oliver isn't the easiest person in the world to live with.

'I haven't quite got used to having another person by my side day and night,' I explain with a smile. 'It takes some getting used to.'

'Hell, don't I know it. You should hear Glen snore, he'd lift the roof if it weren't nailed on,' she laughs.

'Oliver thinks my cooking is dire. I never realised how difficult it can be to produce a simple meal. My rice is always soggy, and yes, I do always rinse it through with boiling water, but it's never quite right. I love jacket potatoes but Oliver hates them, and he won't touch fish, won't have butter or any sort of spread on his bread, doesn't care much for salads. Oh, and he's not too good on vegetables either.'

She looks at me askance. Emma's partner Glen is that rare creature – a builder who cooks, and food is something they very much enjoy preparing together. 'Heavens, what a nightmare. Anyway, why should you only cook the food *he* likes? Give him what's good for him, and have what *you* fancy for a change.'

'Well, I do occasionally, of course I do,' I hastily agree. 'He's just a bit fussy, that's all.'

'Huh, never pander to a man, it only makes him more demanding.'

'I suppose you're right.'

She frowns at me, looking unusually stern. 'I hope you don't allow this fussing over your new husband, or this newly wedded bliss, to block your ambitions for the business.'

'I wouldn't dream of it.' But the slight criticism snaps me to attention as we get back to work, and I privately concede that I may well be overly distracted at the moment, and really must try to sharpen up and pull my weight more.

Communication, they say, is vital in a relationship, and this evening, as we prepare for bed, we're talking for once. I'm desperately trying to put things right, attempting to convince Oliver that even if I do like to do my own thing from time to time, if I fall short of the standards he sets, or make mistakes occasionally, I don't do these things out of malice, or disrespect.

'I do love you, and desperately want to make our marriage work. I hate it when we row and you get angry.'

He looks at me with strained patience. 'These things wouldn't happen if you didn't provoke me. I wouldn't need to get angry, Carly, if you did things properly in the first place.' He's calmly attempting to explain his behaviour, or perhaps justify it to himself.

'You must try to stay calm,' I gently remind him.

'I only lose it because I have such powerful feelings for you. I love you too much.'

I try to work this out, but it doesn't make sense. 'But . . . you love your mother. Would you hit her?'

'Don't be ridiculous.'

'I'm not being ridiculous, Oliver. It's a perfectly reasonable question. You love your mother but you'd never hit her, would you? You love me, so why do you hit me?'

He gives an exasperated sigh. 'Because you drive me to it.

You're like all women, Carly, you nag, nag, nag, believing you can change the world to suit your own little plans and schemes.'

'I do not!'

'What is it they say, behind every successful man is a woman pulling his strings? Giving the poor chap hell more like, in order to get her own way. Women want men to pander to them, and fall in with their little schemes and plans. And there are plenty of men-haters out there, believe me.'

'Well I'm not one of them, and I don't try to pull your strings.'

'Yes, you do, darling. You don't think to ask if I mind your coming home late, you assume I'll be happy to buckle to after a long day's work and start cooking dinner, for God's sake! You don't check that it's OK to swan off and babysit for your sister at a moment's notice. Yet I allow you to work, and to see your friends occasionally. Those who are worthy of you, that is. But you're still not satisfied. Want, want, want. All women are the same. Utterly selfish.'

There's that word again – 'allow'. It's ringing alarm bells in my brain but I smile, anxious to placate him.

'What is it you think I'm up to, visiting some secret lover?' Too late I remember the row we had when he accused me of flirting with the waiter. I hasten to reassure him that I'm only making a joke. 'You have absolutely no reason to be jealous, or to get angry. But these black moods of yours have got to stop, Oliver. It's cruel and heartless of you to bully me in this awful way. I'm covered in bruises.'

He looks at me in cold fury for several long terrifying seconds while I hold my breath, worrying I may have gone too far. Then his face dissolves into hopeless despair as he sinks down on the bed and puts his head in his hands. 'Oh, God, I don't know what comes over me, I really don't. I accept that sometimes I do go a bit over the top, but can you blame me, after what I've been through? My boss, my parents, friends and neighbours, even my own wife seem to be against me these days. Everything seems to be going wrong, and I'm not always responsible for my actions.'

I can't follow what he's saying but I'm so concerned to see actual tears in his eyes that I sit beside him and put my arms about him. 'Tell me what's wrong, Oliver. Why do you imagine everyone is against you? Which I'm sure isn't true.'

'It's because I've been through all of this before,' he says, his voice raw with pain. 'Julie was exactly the same, even though she claimed to love me. You remember we were an item for a while.'

I nod, since we'd readily swapped stories of previous relationships at the start of our own.

'There was nothing she loved more than to boss me about, issue orders, nag me to death the whole damned time to get her own way. She never showed me the slightest bit of respect or consideration. She was always so full of herself.' The contempt in his voice tells me he feels no regret over their failed relationship, which is a comfort in a way, and yet disturbing too that he feels such venom towards her. I kiss his cheek.

'You don't have to talk about it, if you don't want to.'

He pulls me close. 'No, I want to. I want you to understand, darling. I never fought back or even tried to defend myself, but I can't take it a second time, that's the honest truth.'

I smile at his little boy sulks, yet can't help feeling sorry for him. Men are so pathetic. 'Well, I'm hardly nagging you to death, am I?' I know this is true because I weigh every word before I say it. I'm becoming adept at biting my tongue. 'Anyway, you're hardly the victim type. There are usually faults on both sides, so what did *you* do to make her behave in that way?'

He blinks in surprise, startled by the very idea. 'Nothing. I did nothing to her at all. She blamed me for everything, quite unreasonably, when the fault was quite clearly hers. She accused me of having affairs, of not treating her right.'

'And were you?'

'What?'

'Having an affair?'

'Only after our relationship had completely broken down. She was involved with someone too by that time, I'm sure of it. We went our separate ways in the end, as I told you, but she hurt me badly. There was no pleasing her. And I'm sorry to say that you're starting to nag and boss me in exactly the same way. Yet if I object and stand up for myself, or give you a taste of what you're giving me, I'm labelled cruel and heartless. Women can do whatever they like but a man becomes a pariah, a bully. Women think they own the fucking world.'

I'm appalled that he should think this way, that he sees me as some sort of harridan, and can think of nothing to say in my own defence. Here's me trying to persuade him to stop hurting me and the whole problem has been turned on its head, and now I'm apparently the one abusing him.

He gives me a pitying glance. 'The fact is, Carly, just because we're married doesn't mean that you can mentally abuse me, selfishly force me to fit into *your* way of doing things, *your* plans.'

'I – I don't! Really, I don't mean to.' I can feel my fragile confidence starting to shatter. It doesn't take much these days for me to start to doubt myself. I'm so concentrated on appeasing him I can't seem to think clearly any more.

'Yes, you do. You show me no respect at all. You're perverse and rebellious, determined to make my life as difficult as possible.'

I look at him, perplexed and confused. He's the one making all the rules, the one with the power doing all the bullying, not me, yet for some reason my courage is rapidly evaporating and I can't bring myself to say this to him. But then everything I say is wrong and open to criticism. I'm worn out by this mind game he's playing, these mental gymnastics. All I want is for the conversation to end, to give in, kiss and make up, find a little peace.

'I'll try not to nag you in future,' I promise him. 'Or ever get angry with you, and maybe you can promise me the same thing? We'll make a pact, shall we, to try harder to be nice to each other?'

'Married life is all about being *nice* to your husband and telling him you love him every day,' he calmly reminds me, quoting my own mother to me. 'If you remember to do that, Carly, I'd never need to get angry with you ever again, now would I?'

'How are things in wonderland?' Jo-Jo asks me over the phone. I respond with a heavy sigh at the tired joke. 'Sorry, just teasing,' she says, not sorry at all.

I ask her how she's feeling, which is far more to the point as her pregnancy progresses. She tells me all about her latest checks and scans and then gets to the real reason for her call. 'I saw Oliver in town the other evening. Did he mention it? Or perhaps he didn't see me. I was in the car on my way back from visiting a friend when I spotted him. He appeared to be coming out of the Brewery Arts Centre. I didn't see you, but I assume you were there too. Did you go to see a movie or something?'

I pause a second before answering, momentarily startled, wondering what indeed my husband was doing there when he was supposed to be at the quiz league. I'm determined not to allow Jo-Jo to sense my doubts. 'What if he was coming out of the Arts Centre? I believe his firm is responsible for their accounts so why wouldn't he be there one evening? And no, we hadn't been to see a movie.'

'Oh, so you weren't with him?'

'I've just said that I wasn't. Oliver is a busy man with clients all over Kendal and the Lakes. So what point are you making exactly, Jo-Jo?' She surely isn't harping back to that damn anonymous letter, I think, irritated. I refuse to give her the satisfaction of seeing my supposedly perfect life reduced to tatters. My sister is a gossip and a troublemaker of the first order.

A small silence in which I hear Ed's voice in the background, no doubt some crisis with the children. 'Nothing,' she says. 'I wasn't trying to make any point, merely commenting that I saw him, that's all.' She rushes on to relate some anecdote about the children and the dentist, the position of the baby in her womb which is creating problems for her going to the loo, and I listen sympathetically, trying to take an interest.

I hear the front door open and Oliver walks in. I smile a welcome but his face instantly darkens as he sees me on the phone, no doubt half expecting me to jump up and give him a kiss the moment he walks through to door, as they do in those old Hollywood movies.

Jo-Jo is deep in some convoluted story about how she got a place for Ryan at a local playgroup and I signal to him that I won't be a moment. He flaps an irritated hand back at me, mouthing that I should put the phone down now. I pull a teasing face and shake my head.

Without waiting for me to finish, he reaches down and pulls the plug out of the wall socket. I hear the phone go dead, my sister cut off in her prime.

I look at him in horror. 'Why did you do that?'

Mouth tightening into a thin line, he icily enquires, 'Dinner?'

I want to object to this draconian behaviour, to protest that I've every right to talk to my sister, or my friends, but I see that white line of tension etched above his top lip, forming into a familiar snarl, and all fight drains out of me.

'Just coming,' I agree with a sigh, and slip quickly into the kitchen, hoping the joint of pork hasn't burned to a crisp while Jo-Jo and I were talking.

Sometimes I recklessly break Oliver's rules and slip out for a quick drink with Emma without telling him, particularly on a Friday when I know he's going to be late home. Sadly, there are curfews. Unless I'm home by ten he rings me on my mobile to check where I am, and to remind me of the time. He talks about 'allowing' me to call on my friends, but if they say or do something he doesn't like, he stops me from seeing them altogether, as he did with Jane. It feels at times as if I'm a child again, as if he's 'allowing' me privileges which he can withdraw at a moment's notice if I overstep the line.

'You should be grateful I give you as much freedom as I do. Most husbands wouldn't.'

'I'm not saying you aren't good to me, most of the time,' I hedge, 'but Emma is my friend and business partner. Surely you've no objection to my having a drink with her occasionally, perhaps after a pretty rough day. We often have things to discuss and thrash out that can't be done in the office, or while we're cleaning bathrooms. You don't mind?'

'Of course I don't mind,' he tells me, kissing my nose and being all sweet and agreeable. 'So long as you don't overdo things, darling.'

The following week as Em and I are enjoying a half shandy in the John Peel pub, Oliver breezes in.

'I thought I'd find you here.' He kisses me on the cheek, giving Emma a perfunctory nod.

'Oliver!' I'm too embarrassed by his sudden appearance to think of anything sensible to say.

Emma is giving him one of her hard stares. 'My goodness, you must be keen to come this far out of your way on your way home.'

'I was passing anyway, so thought I'd pop in.' He's clearly lying, I can tell from his face. Besides, his office is in Kendal and Emma is quite right, he would actually need to drive past our house to reach Windermere, and further still to drive down into Bowness.

Emma smiles. 'Why don't you get yourself a beer and join us? We're having a great time.'

'Evidently,' he coolly remarks. 'But I don't think so. You've had her all day. Surely it's not unreasonable for me to want to spend some time alone with my wife?' And before either of us has time to answer that one, he turns to me and says, 'Finish your drink, darling, we're going.'

Emma and I exchange a glance but I've no wish to cause a scene in front of my best friend so I do as he asks.

Later, I gently scold him for intruding upon our time together. 'It was only a quick drink. I would have been leaving any minute. There was really no need for you to drive all those miles out of your way. Anyway, I thought we were supposed to be economising with petrol?'

'It was perfectly reasonable for me to be concerned that you weren't home. It was past six o'clock.'

'So?'

But I can see by the closed expression on his face that if I push it any further, there'll be trouble, so I quickly change the subject and ask him what he would like to do for the evening. We watch football on TV, as per normal.

'Can you believe it, she put the phone down on me?' Jo-Jo was telling her mother the story of the latest conversation with her sister in a tone of total disbelief. 'Who the hell does she think she is? I just rang for a friendly chat and she was so prickly, so couldn't give a toss. It was her I-really-don't-have-time-for-this attitude. Then bang, gone! No doubt His Majesty had arrived home so I was no longer of any importance. She only ever rings me in an evening when she's feeling lonely and short of someone to talk to. I'm a *convenience*, nothing more.'

'Isn't that what sisters are for, to pick up and put down at will?' Viv said, not taking her elder daughter too seriously.

'Hell, no! Why can't we have a proper relationship? Why can't she pop over and see me occasionally, help with the kids, *talk* to me? If I suggest it, all I get is excuses. Mainly she ignores me. She'll do anything to avoid coming over, presumably because I'm not good enough for her any more.'

Viv frowned. 'She doesn't pop in here as often as she used to either, but then they haven't been married all that long. I'm sure she has much more interesting things to do with her time than visit old folk and boring relatives.'

'Huh!' Jo-Jo grabbed Ryan who was about to de-head a dahlia flower in her mother's precious garden, and tried to stuff him back into his buggy. The small boy vigorously protested by stiffening his body and refusing to bend his knees, squealing loudly in outrage. 'The trouble is, that little madam doesn't know how lucky she is. Wait till she's got four kids, see how her perfect life stands up to that sort of disruption. Not that it'll ever happen. If she even has one baby it'll no doubt be by immaculate conception and delivered by Caesarean. Too posh to push, that one.'

'How are you feeling?' her mother asked, judiciously changing the subject as she persuaded her grandson to buckle up in his baby buggy.

'Lousy. Exhausted. Like a wrung-out dish mop. Fat! This is absolutely the last. I shall get them to sterilise me or send Ed for the snip. Never again!'

Viv laughed. 'You're probably wise, considering how easily you conceive, but we wouldn't be without one of them, would we, little one?' she said, tickling Ryan under his chin and making him giggle. 'Quickly, get the strap fastened now. There's a good boy.'

'Thank heaven. Now I've got to dash and collect the girls. At least Gran and Gramps seem full of beans at the moment. Has Carly been over to see them lately?'

'Not for a week or two, but I know she's been busy at the agency. Maybe I'll invite her and Oliver over for lunch one Sunday. You should too. Make an effort to be friends.' Straightening up, Viv helped her daughter ease the buggy on to the path, then for no apparent reason, asked, 'You don't think there's a problem, do you?'

'Problem? What sort of problem?' Ryan had kicked off his shoe by way of protest and Jo-Jo was struggling to put it back on.

'With Carly and Oliver.'

'How could there be with Mr Wonderful?'

'I'm not sure, but what you said about her only ringing you of an evening when she's alone. Does that happen often? I mean, surely Oliver doesn't go out much, does he?'

'Of course it doesn't happen often,' Jo-Jo snapped, too wrapped up in her own problems to even remember the reason she rang in the first place, that she'd seen Oliver coming out of the Brewery Arts Centre, but then Ed had told her off for gossiping again, so perhaps it was a selective memory loss. 'That's what I'm saying. I might as well not have a sister for all I see of her, and if she puts the phone down on me one more time, that's it. We're finished.'

Smiling, Viv gave her daughter and grandson a goodbye kiss, then went back into the house to make tea for her parents-in-law and didn't give the matter another thought.

7

Oliver seems to be in complete denial over the way he tries to control and manipulate me, over his behaviour in general. If I complain that he's hurt or abused me, or keeps me on too tight a rein, he absolutely rejects the idea. He retaliates by reminding me how good he is to me, how kind and attentive, reciting a litany of the times he's taken me out, or bought me flowers. It's as if he has it all on file.

'How much do you want from me, woman? I can surely defend my rights,' he'll yell, furious I should dare to criticise him. Then his temper will flare, the danger signals flash and I'll feel the ice beneath my feet beginning to crack.

On these occasions it takes all my skills to calm him down, and I'm rarely successful. It's far easier to agree with his every whim, accept his opinion and keep my own to myself. It feels like collusion but really it's self-preservation. It's the way I'm trying to resolve this issue, the way I survive. Better to concede defeat over less important matters than later be accused of deliberately starting an argument which he then takes it upon himself to win. I only get hurt more that way. I'm rapidly learning not to challenge anything unless it's absolutely necessary.

It's also important that I keep well out of his way when I see the tension mounting. It builds inside him like a volcano gathering pressure, then for no apparent reason he'll erupt and become this totally different person. He's always sorry afterwards, devastated by where his temper has led him. He'll nurse me better, swear that it won't happen again, but sadly it always does. Some silly thing will annoy him and like a spark to a fuse the path of his anger will run its course to its inevitable, violent conclusion.

'Look, it's not important,' I'll say, but for some reason it is, to him at least.

I do my utmost to tease him out of these black moods, but if I could just understand what it is I do that upsets him so much, then perhaps I could stop things from degenerating quite so badly.

And if sometimes I feel I'm losing my identity, I remind myself that marriage is about learning to co-exist with another person, which isn't always easy. I believe that if I love him enough, if I get things right, he'll eventually stop being so uptight and aggressive, resolve whatever problems are screwing up his head, and relations between us will gradually become easier. That old girlfriend of his, Julie, obviously has a lot to answer for. But surely with a bit of give and take on both sides, a little time and patience, we can work things out.

The trouble is Oliver seems short on both, and I warn myself not to expect too much. I shouldn't simply assume that this will be the kind of idyllic marriage my parents have enjoyed, although I certainly intend to do my utmost to be a better wife to him. This is what I wanted after all, isn't it?

I can't even remember what started the row today. Oh, yes, I do. I opened his bank statement, by mistake, and he caught me reading it. He reads mine every month and I don't object. He reads my letters, my emails, even listens in to my phone calls.

'Where's the harm, I'm your husband,' Oliver will say, if he sees me frowning at him. But his attitude is entirely different now I'm doing the same to him, albeit if it is by accident. I try to make a joke of it, offer to pay his credit card bill if he likes, but he isn't amused.

Making light of whatever has annoyed him, teasing and joking, attempting to laugh him out of his growing rage before it takes proper hold never seems to work. My good humour only serves to irritate and inflame his temper all the more.

But then nothing I do seems able to prevent the devastating spiral of violence once it starts. Telling him that he's got no right to hit me doesn't work either. Oliver hates me to cry and will hit me, and keep on hitting me, until the tears dry up out of fear. Yet if I remain silent, try to be calm and brave and reason with him, he'll go on and on at me, calling me terrible names, hitting or kicking me till I can stand no more and I'm screaming at him, or cowering on the floor begging for him to stop, or really am sobbing by that time. He's the one who laughs then, saying he has every right to bring me into line. He's *entitled*! He's my husband.

Today, I decide on a different approach. I hit him back.

It proves to be a terrible mistake. I'm not quite five foot three. Oliver is six foot two, and wears a size twelve in shoes. I know that because I've felt the imprint of them on my back and thighs many, many times in the past few months. There's no way I can ever win.

His answer to my show of rebellion on this occasion is to pick me up bodily and throw me over the sofa. I crash to the ground, knocking my head hard on the cedar-wood floorboards, jarring my shoulder. The sofa is set in the middle of the room in full view of the window, and after he's stormed off I lie there for some time in a crumpled heap, sobbing, in total shock. After a short while I hear a knock at the door.

I hastily wipe away my tears with the flat of my hands, comb my fingers through my tousled hair and get shakily to my feet. My head is throbbing from the crack I gave it as I landed, and every bone seems to jangle and ache. By a miracle nothing seems to be broken, no serious damage done, as far as I can tell. Heart quaking, I go to the door. If this is some busybody poking her nose in, I know I mustn't let on what has happened. If Oliver believed for one moment that I was gossiping about him to the neighbours I'd be in for worse punishment.

It's a very kind elderly lady who lives opposite us, just across the road. 'Are you all right, dear?' she asks, her face anxious.

'Oh, yes!' I beam at her with a false brightness. 'I'm fine. Why wouldn't I be?'

'Well, I thought I was seeing things just now, only you looked like you were flying through the air. Then your husband came out slamming the door and I – I just wondered . . .' She looks deeply embarrassed. 'You are all right?'

'Yes, of course. We were playing a silly game, which got a bit out of hand,' I lie. 'Just having fun, a bit of rough and tumble. You know how it is. Unfortunately, it made him late for his golf, so he dashed off in a terrible hurry.' I'm deeply aware that I'm over-explaining and talking absolute rubbish. I can see disbelief writ large and clear in her sympathetic gaze, but I just want her to go away and leave me alone. I try a smile. 'He never can close a door quietly.'

She's still hovering on my doorstep, as if half expecting me to invite her in, perhaps so that she can investigate the scene of the crime more closely. I keep on smiling inanely and finally she takes the hint and starts to back away, but not before suggesting I pop in for a coffee any time I want to talk. I thank her for her kind invitation, but have no intention of accepting. Oliver would really go mad if I risked such a thing. I watch her go with relief then stand behind the closed door breathing hard and shaking with nerves. Keeping up a front is not going to be easy.

There's a small voice at the back of my head telling me that I should leave, that I should get out now, while I still can. But we've been married only a few short months and I feel shamed by my inability to make my new husband happy. How can I admit that my marriage is over, after such a short time? Everyone will think there's something wrong with me. Maybe there *is* something wrong with me, otherwise this wouldn't be happening. I must have done something to deserve this battering. Oliver has said as much a thousand times.

But if *he* is the one with the problem, then surely it's my duty, as his loving wife, to stay and help him put it right. It would certainly feel like failure if I left and gave up so soon. I'm not yet ready to accept defeat.

My parents too would be devastated. I'd never be able to convince them of what he is doing to me. Oliver would deny it and win them round into believing he was innocent, I just know he would. Besides, they're still paying for the wedding.

I'm twenty-five years old and in love, desperate to make my marriage work, to please my new husband. I don't feel I have any choice but to stick it out and try to put things right.

The sofa incident is typical because when he comes home later that day he holds me tenderly in his arms and kisses me, almost goes down on his knees to beg my forgiveness. I try not to analyse what happened and why, I'm just so grateful that he still loves me, still wants me. I have this constant yearning to feel his arms about me, for the man I love to reaffirm his love for me, and I'm so relieved when he takes me in his arms and does just that. Every new marriage has its teething problems, I repeat to myself, and I've come to appreciate how very much I depend upon him. I can't bear him to be angry with me.

I mention the neighbour calling to enquire after me, hoping this will embarrass him into behaving better in future. Instead, he sounds off against interfering busybodies, instructs me to buy blinds to put up at every window. 'We don't want that old faggot watching every damn thing we do!'

I quake at the thought of shutting myself off from the world into a prison of my own making, making me feel more isolated than ever, but of course I do as he says. I order stylish Venetian blinds for every window. Far easier to do as I'm told.

For some reason this morning my head feels remarkably clear, and I know I must do something. It's a week or two later, the blinds have been fitted and our neighbour across the street barely glances at me as I walk by. She's clearly got the message that her concern is not welcome. I feel awful about this, more isolated than ever, as if I'm rejecting her offer of friendship because of something awful and secret that is going on behind these blanked-out windows. Which is true, and it fills me with shame.

I bring Oliver a cup of tea as usual, then beg him to listen to me. I need to explain how I feel in the hope we can shape some sort of solution that will suit us both, try to bring some equality and happiness into our marriage. He dismisses my suggestion with a wave of his hand, not even having the patience to listen.

'What is you want from me now?' he snaps, rather like a petulant child.

I sit quietly on the end of the bed, keeping my voice studiously calm. 'I'd like you to go for counselling, Oliver, to anger-management classes or whatever they call them. I want you to speak to your doctor about this temper of yours. Maybe you're sick.'

His face darkens and he slams his mug down on the bedside table, spilling tea everywhere. 'Are you saying I'm mentally deranged or something?'

'I'm saying you need help.'

'Don't be ridiculous,' he scoffs, and, ignoring the mess, flings himself out of bed and starts to get dressed. 'I haven't time to listen to your nonsense. You'll make me late for work. Haven't you even started cooking my breakfast yet? In any case, we've been over this a thousand times. *You're* the one at fault here, the one ruining our relationship. You've neglected me all summer because of that pathetic job of yours, assuming I'll do your chores when you can't be bothered to cook me decent meals. You make no attempt to look after the house properly. You constantly ignore me by sticking your head in a book for hours on end, and by bringing work home. Yet you complain if I go out with my friends, as if I should be romancing you every bloody night. No wonder I get angry. You drive me to it.'

I listen to his exaggerated claims of my alleged failures and feel like crying with frustration. He does not see any necessity to change his own behaviour or attitudes. Oliver has no ability to share, to give and take, or to see me as anything other than a creature put upon this earth to wait upon him, to kowtow to his every whim and be bullied and controlled if I get it wrong, which I'm bound to do since his demands are so unrealistic.

I try to explain this to him. 'You're too demanding, Oliver. I don't think I can take much more. I know you claim to have been let down by your ex in the past, but there must be more to it than that. You need to admit that you have a problem. If you can only explain to me why you behave in this way, I'm perfectly willing to listen, and to help in any way I can. That's what married people do, they share their concerns and fears.'

'There's nothing to talk about, you stupid woman! Stop trying to manipulate me. Stop bloody nagging!'

He's hovering over me in an intimidating manner and I can see his ears growing red, the familiar white line of tension forming above his upper lip, which is always a bad sign. I push him away and start pulling clothes out of the drawers. 'Then I'm leaving you. I can't go on like this, I really can't.' My heart is in my mouth as I say this, knowing he could easily explode all over again, but I feel I have to use desperate measures to make my point.

He doesn't explode but suddenly sinks down on the bed and puts his head in his hands. 'Christ, Carly, don't do this to me. How could I live without you? I need you.'

'Perhaps you need me too much,' I say. 'You're draining the life out of me, Oliver. You're destroying us both!'

'You don't love me any more, that's it, isn't it?' he asks, his eyes filled with such agony that my heart turns over.

I go and sit beside him, gently take his hand. 'That's not true, I do love you, Oliver, but I can't live like this. I cannot spend my life trying to appease you. I can't cope with these black moods of yours; the way you suddenly blow up over nothing and start hitting me.'

'But I couldn't survive without you, Carly.' Tears are shining in his eyes, his expression morose, the onset of depression in the droop of his shoulders. 'I'd top myself, I would really.'

My heart starts to beat rather fast, and I feel close to tears myself. 'Don't say such things. Please. I don't want to leave you, I just want you to stop hitting me. I need to understand why you treat me so badly.'

'It's because I was abused too,' he suddenly blurts out in soft, hushed tones.

'*What?*'

'It's true. My parents abused me for years.'

This really rocks me back on my heels. I look at him in appalled disbelief, his words sending a chill to my heart. Can this be the reason he's so messed up? I can't quite take it in. Mr and Mrs Sheldon have always struck me as a perfectly nice, friendly couple, a bit straight-laced perhaps, strong on religion, but decent, honest folk. I say as much to him. 'No, surely not. I can't imagine your mother, or your father, doing such a thing.'

He reacts by snatching his hand away, giving me a furious glare. 'Are you suggesting that I'm lying?'

'No, not really, but . . . *how* did they abuse you? What exactly did they do?'

He lets out a shuddering sigh. 'I find it very difficult to talk about.'

'I'm sure you do, but please try.' I lovingly stroke his hand. 'Tell me.'

'They've always been strict and very religious. My mother in particular succeeded in making my young life an absolute misery. She was very impatient, always losing her temper with me. She'd get so angry she'd lock me in a cupboard or beat me with a strap.'

'Oh, my God!' I watch my husband break down in tears and I'm filled with compassion. This must be the reason he abuses me. His parents are the ones to blame for all of this. Not only has he been hurt by a previous relationship, but his own *mother* has abused him for years. No wonder he has a problem relating to women. If Oliver's life has been so difficult, is it any wonder he's an emotional mess? This would surely explain his un-predictable and violent behaviour towards me, wouldn't it? Doesn't society generally assume that a bad childhood can cause a man to become an abuser? He's as much a victim as I am.

I feel a nudge of guilt that I hadn't taken the trouble to learn this important fact about him already.

What I don't see is that he is the master of the hard-luck story. It doesn't occur to me that in describing his childhood as one of abuse, this is the best way to tug at my heartstrings and make *me* feel sorry for *him*. I don't even consider that he might be lying, even though I'm aware he's always keen to get to my parents before I do, to lay the blame for some squabble or other squarely on me, like the time he accused me of flirting with that damn waiter, never owning up to the fact that he'd hit me. I fail to realise that whether or not this story is true, it deflects attention away from the person really at fault: himself. And by focusing on his mother he gets to blame a woman for his mistreatment of women. I don't understand any of this until years later. Right now I simply believe him. Yet another mistake.

'Have you ever told anyone about this?' I ask. 'Have you received counselling for it?'

'No, it's not something I care to talk about,' he confesses, as he pulls me close in his arms. 'I'm sorry if I've taken out my misery on you and treated you badly, but it's all due to this huge sense of insecurity I feel. I promise I'll never hurt you again. I'm sure everything will be fine now that we've confronted my demons. It was so good of you, darling, to suggest I open my soul and explain. What a treasure and a comfort you are to me.' As he kisses me, tender with gratitude, I'm blinded by my love for him, desperate to help my husband overcome his misery.

Nevertheless, as gently as I can, I stick to my argument and try to make my case. 'If you really were abused as a child then you will understand from personal experience how dreadful it feels. If you think about how you suffered, it may help you to stop falling into the trap of abusing others. Me, in fact, since I'm the only one you turn on.'

'But that's because I love you so much, because my feelings for you are so strong. They say you always hurt the one closest to you. I can't seem to help myself.'

'You have to promise that you'll try. Remind yourself how awful it is to live in fear, and yet be told it's all your own fault.'

'Oh, I do see that, darling.' He's kissing me now, anxious to prove his love for me. 'I do understand what you're saying, and you've helped me so much, really you have. Now go and make my breakfast and let's not talk about it any more.'

'That's not another bruise, is it?' I'm again cleaning a bath and as my shirt parts company with my jeans Emma tugs it up still further to frown at the sight of the emerging bruise on my back. 'What happened this time? Not the cupboard door again?'

I hastily tuck the shirt back into place, turning my face away as I'm only too aware that my cheeks are burning. I give a shaky laugh. 'Slipped on the floor when I was mopping it,' I improvise.

'What, not your non-slip tiled floor in your new designer kitchen?'

'The very same,' I jokily reply, in a parody of our earlier conversation.

She says no more on the subject but later, as we drive back to the office, she suddenly says, 'You'd tell me if there was a problem, Carly, wouldn't you?'

I look out at the lake, glimmering silver against the backdrop of woods and mountains beyond, at the glorious palette of colours, of red, saffron and gold. There is nowhere more beautiful than the Lake District in early autumn. 'Why would there be?' But even I'm aware of a slight catch in my voice.

She falls silent again as we wind our way slowly up the hill through Bowness, as usual stuck in a line of traffic. Emma parks in the car park next to the cinema and turns to me, her face serious. 'Marriage isn't always plain sailing. Unexpected problems can crop up, and there's no shame in talking things over with an old friend.'

I've never given her any indication of the difficulties I'm having, but her soft hazel eyes are shrewd and kind as they quietly regard me. 'Everyone has the odd hiccup,' I agree.

'I do realise things haven't always been hunky-dory between the pair of you. Oliver made his feelings on your working evenings pretty plain from the start. He once rang to insist I allow you more time off.'

My eyebrows shoot up in dismay. 'He did what? Why didn't you tell me? He really had no right to do that, I'm so sorry.'

Emma shrugs. 'No sweat, you were just married, still love's young dream at the time, so I didn't mind. Although the way he keeps turning up whenever we're trying to grab a quick drink together or have a private chat about business matters, is seriously weird. As is the suggestion he made that you should give up your car, delivering you each morning and picking you up at the end of each day. How controlling is that?'

I'm appalled that she's observed everything so thoroughly, been harbouring these reservations about my marriage without saying a word, and arrived at some dangerously accurate conclusions. I quickly speak up in his defence. 'My husband has a few problems, admittedly, but he's dealing with them.'

'If you don't mind my saying so,' Emma continues, as if I haven't spoken, 'he seems remarkably possessive. He's far too demanding, seems to like having all his own way and keep you to himself.' She holds up her hands in a placatory fashion as I attempt to interrupt. 'OK, you don't have to say it, I know it's none of my business. But the way he marched into the pub that time and ordered you home was appalling. I'd deck any man who tried that on with me.'

'He didn't *order* me,' I say, feeling rather breathless and annoyed with her, not quite knowing how to deal with this.

'Virtually. I do just wonder where this is all leading.'

I'm smarting with embarrassment by this time, so perhaps my reaction to her concern is impulsive and instinctive rather than wise. Had she not gone into full criticism mode of Oliver I might have confided in her, as it is, I'm totally on the defensive now. I certainly don't pause to think through the effect of my words. 'Actually, you're right. It is none of your business. I've already told you that he has one or two problems, which we're dealing with, but I think that what goes on between myself and my husband is private, don't you?'

There's a long awkward silence while we both sit there, breathing hard, trying to find a way out of this impasse. Emma is the one to break it.

'OK, I'll consider my wrists duly slapped. I'm not one to pry. We'll leave it at that, shall we? Except . . .' She's about to get out of the car but then pauses to rummage in her bag, and hands me a key.

I look at it lying in the palm of my hand. 'What's this?'

'It's a key.'

'I can see that. What's it for?'

'My front door. Should you ever feel the need to use it.'

I look at her. 'Why would I?'

Em shrugs, gives a tight little smile. 'Search me. It's a spare, I don't need it. Call it insurance. Now, what do you say to a coffee before we tackle today's post and hopefully the latest tranche of bookings?'

I swallow a lump that's somehow lodged in my throat. How is it Em is so wise and all-seeing when my family are deaf, dumb and blind? Yet I know I can't tell her. God knows what Oliver would do if I gave so much as a hint as to what went on behind closed doors. Besides, following our recent conversation on the subject, I'm convinced I understand his problem now. Everyone says that child abuse can really screw a person up. And even though he still refuses to see a counsellor, I have every faith that together, Oliver and I can put things right at last. I'm sure I can help him feel better about himself so that he'll stop taking out his bitterness on me. I climb out of the car. But I have no intention of discussing all this private business with my friend. 'I'll go and buy some doughnuts, shall I?'

'Good idea.'

Nothing further is said about the key but I tuck it into my bag anyway, for no reason I can properly explain. Maybe because I've always considered it wise to invest in insurance.

8

It's as if Oliver is two persons. He holds me to this strict regime he's devised, keeping me in line which he feels is his right, slapping me down if he thinks I've slighted or disobeyed him out of lack of consideration or whatever. If I fail in some way, if I overstep the mark and offend him, then I apparently deserve to be punished. He'll call me all manner of abusive names to intimidate me, or refuse to listen properly to what I have to say, wearing me down with pointless arguments.

The strange thing is he'll then storm out of the house in a furious rage after one of these scenes and, minutes later, I'll see him chatting happily with George across the road, or helping Mrs Thomas to trim her hedge. Mr Nice Guy doing his bit for the neighbours.

Why is it, I wonder, that he's so friendly with everyone but me? I wonder what it is about his own wife that brings out the devil in him, that triggers these black moods and changes him into this entirely different person? Other people, neighbours, friends, even my own family, think he's great! He's very liberal and supportive of women in public, but doesn't practise what he preaches in private, certainly not with me at home. He presents himself as Mr Wonderful, so how could I convince anyone of this darker side to his nature?

Em is surely beginning to suspect that our marriage is not quite as wonderful as it might appear. Why didn't I tell her the truth? I wonder. Pride? Shame? Guilt? A hope that things will improve before I need to? All of the above.

The trouble is, since I was the one who told everyone that Oliver was Mr Wonderful in the first place, I'm embarrassed to admit that I was wrong. It's far too shaming to confess that I made a mistake when we've not yet reached our first anniversary, may never do so at this rate.

I badly need some help and advice, but from whom? I'm not aware of any woman's refuge available in this rural area. There must be somewhere I can turn for advice on how best to deal with my problem. I need to learn how I can persuade Oliver to get the help he so badly needs.

I decide against going to see the doctor. Apart from a few bruises, rapidly fading now, I have no physical proof. Oliver has learned from his earlier mistakes and is now extraordinarily skilled at knowing how far he can go without causing too much visible damage. Besides, the doc has known me since I was a small child, knows my entire family very well indeed, and somehow it wouldn't feel comfortable. I realise such information is supposed to be kept confidential but how can I be sure he wouldn't let something slip to my mum.

I go to see the vicar. OK, I'm not the most religious person in the world but I've attended church sporadically all my life, and he married us after all. I've practised what I want to say but sitting before him in the church vestry I find myself stumbling over the words. I clumsily try to explain my dilemma, making it clear that Oliver is not an alcoholic, nor does he use drugs.

'He claims to have been abused himself as a child, and I'm doing my best to help him deal with that, only it's not easy. He is very violent, increasingly so, and I don't know how much longer I can cope,' I burst out, close to tears.

'Oh dear, I'm sorry to hear all of this, Carly. I thought Oliver seemed such a nice young man.'

I dig a bunch of tissues out of my pocket and blow my nose, wipe my eyes, struggling to bring myself back under control. 'Most people do, but he's a Jekyll and Hyde character, believe me. An absolute charmer in public, but not in private, with me.'

The vicar's expression is professionally sympathetic as he asks me how long this has been going on, how it all began.

I relate Oliver's sudden change in attitude over my erratic working hours following our marriage, the story of the failed quiche, and of his objection to the unsocial hours I work.

He smiles and nods as if he understands perfectly. 'A woman's role is not easy, having to balance two disparate areas of her life,' he admits. 'Marriage is a sacred estate not to be lightly undertaken or abandoned, and it is certainly important, in the early years particularly, to be a caring and attentive wife. Have you managed to change your hours?'

I look at him in disbelief. Shouldn't he be asking why Oliver doesn't change his attitude? 'It's a new business,' I explain. 'I can't leave my partner to do all the awkward unsocial hours while I clock off on the dot of five every day. That wouldn't be right. She allowed me what leeway she could in those first months of my marriage, but I have to do my share.'

'Of course, of course.' He coughs, shifts in his seat and looks slightly embarrassed. 'May I ask, Carly, if there might be some other reason behind this problem. Are you, for instance, with-holding sex?'

I walk out, slamming the church door behind me.

Oliver is constantly criticising how I look, saying that I've let myself go, which I don't believe is true at all. I enjoy looking smart and fashionable, as does any woman, but on a number of occasions recently he's insisted that I take a garment back to the shop, accusing me of having no eye for colour. I tend to go for more neutral shades: cream and beige and tan, which set off my fair hair. Oliver says they make me look like a dull mouse. Am I dull? Is that how he sees me? I stand looking at myself in the mirror, a pile of clothes on the bed behind me, already rejected as I try to decide what to wear. I select a bright turquoise blouse, then reject that too. If I wear jewel colours, blues or reds, he accuses me of looking cheap. He likes my lipstick to be quietly restrained in company, barely visible, although he loves me to wear a dazzling sexy pink when we're alone.

We've been asked to go to Sunday lunch at my sister's house, which is the first invitation we've had from her in a long while, but I'm taking great care not to overdress so that I don't inflame her sarcasm. Jo-Jo loves to accuse me of showing off, of making myself appear better than her, and the last thing I want is to cause offence when she's feeling particularly vulnerable over her latest pregnancy. But Oliver's attitude isn't helping. I feel torn between the two of them.

I always try to compliment him when he looks good, which he generally does. I'm fortunate to have such a good-looking guy for a husband. Oliver prides himself on his style and appearance, insisting upon creases in his trousers as sharp as a razor. He likes it when I praise him as it makes him feel good about himself, and he used to be very complimentary about me once upon a time, before we were married. There's been little praise forthcoming recently.

Maybe he goes on about my clothes so much because he no longer fancies me, or perhaps he senses a reserve in me. I freely confess, to myself at least, that I'm less interested in making love than I used to be, although I'm careful not to show it, or risk inflaming his temper by objecting to sex. I'm too worried to relax, too filled with anxiety over how best to deal with this problem we seem to have.

Things are no better between us and I'm desperately trying to think of a way to help him over this child-abuse issue. I wonder if speaking to his parents and getting the full story might help, but I quail at the prospect. They're very correct and proper, and how would I go about it? I can't just ask his mother, straight out, if she ever abused him. It's unthinkable. So I'm still struggling to find a solution.

And whenever I try to raise the subject again with Oliver, he'll roll his eyes and moan. 'Not another heart-to-heart, an in-depth discussion where you complain about the way I allegedly hurt you, or I'm supposed to bare my soul over some perceived problem which is apparently screwing up my mind. I've told you, I can't bear to talk about it.'

'I just want to help.'

'Well you aren't helping, not in the least. So stop going on about it, all right?'

He's developed a knack for blocking the problem out of his head, as well as refusing to accept the evidence of my hurt feelings. He's even showing less compassion towards me these days, simply dismissing my distress by accusing me of making too much fuss.

I can see that this whole situation is making him particularly tetchy, but I feel I must stand by him, and help him come to terms with his troubled past. Even if it weren't my duty, as his wife, I love him and want him to deal with these negative feelings he has, which will hopefully improve the way he treats me as a result. The trouble is, he still doesn't accept that he has a problem.

'Just look at you,' he says to me now. 'I'm not taking you out to lunch in jeans.'

'They're my best, and we're only going to Jo-Jo's. In any case, they go so well with this lovely pale blue top. The very latest style, and quite sexy, don't you think?'

He glowers at me, puts his head on one side and sighs heavily. 'Unexciting, too low in the neck, and the colour doesn't suit you.'

'But . . .'

'I'm surely entitled to care about how my wife looks and what she wears, particularly in public.'

I smile and pop a kiss on his cheek. 'Stop fretting, Oliver. The top, and the jeans, are fine. No one else will be dressed up, not with the children present.'

'You're a damned stubborn, woman, you know that? You do so love to show me up and make me look bad in front of other people. Can't you see that it reflects upon me if you don't look your best? You should be flattered I still fancy you, when you make such little effort to please me.'

I protest vigorously. 'I do try to please you, all the time, Oliver. Of course I do.'

'Well, it doesn't show. There's no easy way to say this, Carly, but you look a mess. Sloppy. You know that I only want what is best for you.' As he has told me a thousand times, over and over, like a stuck record. He looks pointedly at his watch, then orders me to hurry up and change into something more respectable, sounding very like a sergeant-major addressing a recalcitrant private. 'And don't shilly-shally. You know how your sister hates it if we're late.'

I go back into the house to change, as instructed. It's easier that way. Besides, I can no longer judge what I look good in.

He waits for me in the car and when I'm not out in the allotted five minutes, leans the heel of his hand on the horn. Up in our bedroom I dash about like a mad thing, scramble into fresh clothes, touch up my lipstick and hair, and I'm out of the house moments later in such a fluster that I forget to lock the door.

Oliver shouts at me to go back and do it. 'And don't forget to switch on the damn alarm.'

Finally I flop into the car and his eyes roam over me to appraise my choice of outfit this time: a maroon skirt suit, way over the top for a family lunch. He grunts with what might be termed approval. 'I suppose it's a slight improvement, but buy something in a more flattering colour next time, will you, and with not quite such a short skirt. We don't want you looking like a tart.'

It was only when her sister and brother-in-law walked in, looking all formal and smart, that Jo-Jo saw her home through their eyes, with baby stuff and toys everywhere and children running about demented. It must look very much like bedlam. The handsome couple stood awkwardly before her, Carly trying to smile, Oliver wearing his holier-than-thou expression, his mouth tight and grim, making it very evident that he'd rather be anywhere than having lunch with a bunch of rowdy infants.

'My, my, you do look smart,' Jo-Jo caustically remarked to her sister. 'I'm honoured. But for God's sake don't let our Ryan anywhere near that suit or he'll be sick all over it.'

Oliver kissed the air an inch from his sister-in-law's cheek, then escaped out on to the patio with Ed and a glass of beer. Jo-Jo headed for the kitchen to check on the beef, Carly trailing after her. At least the pair of them were talking as they got the meal ready, stilted and awkward though it might be.

The conversation didn't flow too easily as they ate either, but then the entire lunch felt like a living nightmare to Jo-Jo, with one child refusing to eat meat, and another smearing mashed potato all over his high chair. It was a relief when the little terrors were finally sent out to play in the garden. Ed refilled their wine glasses, all except his wife's who wasn't drinking because of her condition, and the adults could at last sit back and relax.

Jo-Jo was acutely aware of Oliver's sideways glances of disapproval in her direction, no doubt aimed at her thickening waistline. It made her feel like a saggy pudding whereas Carly looked all sexy and shapely and smart. But then failing to find a way to stop having babies was a bit stupid. Inevitably, the conversation had moved on to the subject of babies and marriage.

'Would you do it again?' Jo-Jo cheekily asked her sister, as she sipped her boring orange juice. 'I'm not sure I would,' playfully patting her bump and making everyone laugh.

'No, I don't think I would either,' Carly calmly answered, which wiped the smile off everyone's face and stunned them all into silence.

Oliver glared at his wife. 'Why wouldn't you?'

Much to Jo-Jo's amusement he sounded affronted and petulant, deeply offended by the remark, which made everyone laugh all the more. Her own lovely Ed, on the other hand, didn't seem in the least put out by his wife's apparent disloyalty.

Carly gave a little half smile as she sipped her wine. 'I don't know why, maybe because I'm still young and feel I should have enjoyed life a bit more before tying myself down to all this domestic goddess bit. I've decided that I absolutely hate ironing, particularly shirts.'

Jo-Jo roared with laughter. 'Oh, I do agree. I think I'm turning into my mother, or worse into Ed's mother, permanently attached to that ironing board.'

'I wish I'd paid more attention to Mum when she was trying to teach me how to cook,' Carly mourned, letting Ed refill her glass a second time. 'I have to ask the butcher what sort of steak I should buy for a casserole, and I'd no idea kidneys could look so revolting in the raw.'

'I know exactly what you mean,' Jo-Jo agreed, grimacing with distaste. 'Although I do so enjoy a tasty steak and kidney pie, and I love to see Ed in a white shirt, so sexy, so I suppose I'll have to go on ironing them.'

Ed grinned, while Oliver continued to stare at them all in disbelief.

'But couldn't they occasionally do *something* around the house, at least wield the vacuum?' Carly asked, waving her glass about to illustrate her point.

'Come the revolution.'

'Hey, hold on,' Ed protested. 'I often cook the evening meal while you're putting the kids to bed. I'm not entirely hopeless in the kitchen.'

'That's true,' his wife agreed, kissing him. 'And I do appreciate it, really I do. But you don't do cleaning, darling, do you? I don't think Ed knows we even have a broom cupboard under the stairs, let alone what's in it.'

'Oh, Oliver doesn't either. And he seems to think microwaves, cookers, washing machines and irons have one important instruction – "To be operated by females only".' Carly kissed Oliver, his mouth wooden in its fixed smile.

'Quite right too,' Ed joked, and clapped his brother-in-law on the back. 'I don't you how you get away with it, mate. You must give me some tips.'

Jo-Jo was wiping tears of laughter from her eyes. 'Married life not turning out to be quite so blissfully happy as you expected then, Sis?' She couldn't resist teasing her younger sister.

'Oh, I'm sure it'll turn out fine, won't it, darling?' Carly insisted, smiling at her husband who flickered the travesty of a smile in return. 'Or it will be if we survive the first twelve months, or maybe the first twenty-five years which Mum insists are the most difficult. But I still say that marriage comes as more of a shock to women than men. We're the ones who have to keep the home fires burning, do all the washing, ironing, cleaning, bed making, cooking, et cetera, et cetera, while you lads swan off whenever you please.'

Ed said, 'Aw, you can't fool us. Women love all that home-making stuff.'

'And men like to play lord and master. Yet women have rights too,' Carly continued, stubbornly sticking to her argument.

Ed topped up her wine, enjoying the lively debate even as he conceded she might have a point. 'We're all equal, and I, for one, wouldn't dream of depriving you lovely ladies of your due rights, what do you say, Oliver?'

Oliver slipped an arm round his wife's shoulders and gave her a tight little squeeze which caused her smile to slip a fraction, yet he was still smiling, flexing that easy charm of his. 'Of course women have rights, haven't I always said so?'

Unfortunately, the wine had loosened Carly's tongue and stoked up her usually fragile confidence. 'Oliver, really, you certainly don't give the impression to *me* of a man who understands equal rights,' she retaliated, stifling a slight hiccup.

Oliver's laughter by way of response sounded hollow and unconvincing, and as he pretended to kiss her ear, he instructed his wife, very forcibly but quietly, to shut up.

Ed was saying, 'You have to admit though that we're still little boys at heart, so surely deserve some fun once in a while, to escape the kids and the mess, the endless nagging and the do this, do that. To find a bit of peace over a pint.'

'I wouldn't mind a bit of peace,' Jo-Jo yelled, outraged by this remark, and prodding her husband in the chest with a sharp finger.

He played along, laughing at her apparent fury. 'Oh, yeah,

are you planning on taking up pub crawls then? Or have you found yourself that lover at long last?'

'Don't tempt me. How about it, Carly? Why don't we pick up a couple of hunks and make a foursome?' Turning to her husband with a sly smile, she challenged him, 'Maybe we have already, for all you know.'

'I thought you'd turned the milkman down until he won the lottery,' Ed fired right back, his grin wider than ever.

'Ooh, how could you do that?' Carly giggled. 'I think your milkman's gorgeous. I'd have him exactly as he is, stony broke.'

Jo-Jo's eyes were gleaming with laughter as the joke went on and on, getting dangerously out of hand. 'Might be fun to see if we can still pull. What d'you say, girl?'

'Why not?' Carly giggled. 'Maybe it's time we went out and had some adventures of our own.'

'I'm all in favour of that,' her sister agreed. 'Just as soon as I can move again.'

Everyone seemed to find this hugely funny. Carly still sipping her wine, was enjoying herself enormously. Ed was happily peppering his wife's face with kisses, both very aware that neither had the least intention of straying.

Oliver managed only a ghost of a smile, pretending to be amused like everyone else, but clearly not quite able to see the joke. 'You mustn't pay any attention to my wife. She's in a bad mood because she was planning to come here today in her scruffy jeans, and resents the fact I made her change into something smarter.'

'Scruffy jeans?' Jo-Jo said, her mouth dropping open as she regarded her sister, whose cheeks were turning pink right before her eyes, surely evidence of her guilt.

'You should have seen her,' Oliver went on. 'Claimed it really didn't matter what she wore since she was only having lunch with you.'

'It wasn't quite like that,' Carly protested, but nobody heard her.

Jo-Jo scowled at her sister. 'You said we didn't matter?'

'They weren't my scruffy jeans, they were my best ones.'

'*You said it didn't matter how you looked because you were only having lunch with me?*'

'I didn't mean it quite how it sounded,' Carly objected, but Jo-Jo was no longer smiling. The fun and hilarity was suddenly over.

Having stirred up trouble between the sisters, now Oliver did smile, then he grasped his wife's elbow and quietly suggested he take her home, on the grounds that she'd had more than enough to drink.

'I'm not drunk, only slightly merry,' Carly defended herself. 'I was having a good time. Is that not allowed any more? I thought we both were, weren't we, Jo-Jo?'

'I'm not sure what to think, Carly. Oliver's right, you probably have had a glass too many.'

Oliver fetched her jacket and helped her on with it, and having permitted himself only one glass, as usual, he was perfectly capable of driving them home. Jo-Jo noted with some satisfaction that Carly's mood had flattened, was far more muted as they said their goodbyes and drove off. Serve her right. Didn't matter what she wore for lunch with her sister indeed! Who did she think she was?

I say nothing on the journey home, my fuddled brain clearing sufficiently to know that I've overstepped that invisible line good and proper this time. When we get back from Jo-Jo's and we're at last alone, Oliver makes it very clear that he isn't in the least bit amused by my silly jokes.

He's furious I've had the effrontery to reveal any hint of a problem in front of my sister, taking it as a personal insult. I can sense the familiar tension building inside him like a great head of steam so I totter off to the kitchen to put the kettle on, hoping to deflate it with a nice cup of tea. But Oliver isn't in the mood for tea and sympathy. He grabs me by the arms and gives me a hefty shove. It sends me flying and I can't help but cry out as I fall back against the table and slide to the floor. He starts to bludgeon me with verbal abuse about who this alleged lover is and where I met him, shouting and swearing at me, railing and roaring, using foul words and firing questions like bullets from a gun.

'There is no lover!' I sob. 'I swear there's no one, no one at all. It was a *joke!*'

But he really isn't listening. He storms about the kitchen, opening cupboard doors, grabbing a cup or plate and tossing it to the floor, smashing whatever takes his fancy, some of my favourite, most treasured bits of crockery, including some of the tea set Gran and Grandad bought me as a wedding present. I cry out in protest but he ignores me, saying this is nothing to what he'll do to me. He demands to know why I'm so dissatisfied with our marriage, why I was making all that fuss about equal rights. I huddle in a corner hoping to avoid the worst of his rage as he continues to shout and rail.

'How dare you imply that we're having problems?'

Eventually he flings himself into a chair, the ensuing silence overwhelming, marred only by the sound of his rapid breathing. He's finally run out of steam and I get tentatively to my feet, go to rinse my face in cold water and make an attempt to restore some sort of order by picking up shards of broken crockery, cutting my finger in the process. I suck on the flow of blood, try to gather my wits and bring some common sense into the situation.

'For God's sake, Oliver, where's your sense of humour? What I said at Jo-Jo's was just a bit of fun. We'd all had too much to drink. I'm perfectly happy being married to you, honestly. Although you have to admit we do still have a few problems to iron out.'

I reach for the towel and as our gaze locks we both know that there was more than a grain of truth in my complaints.

At that moment we hear a knock on the door, see a flashing light outside. The police! My heart skips a beat as Oliver hisses at me to tidy up, and goes to the door.

9

'Good evening, officer, is there a problem?' Oliver sounds so friendly and affable, so very calm and in control. 'How can I help you?'

I can't quite hear all the conversation but they're apologising for disturbing us at this late hour, claiming to be responding to a complaint from a neighbour. They'd heard noise coming from our house apparently, things being smashed.

Oliver is all sweetness and light, explaining that it was a silly mistake. They ask to come in, say they'd like to speak to me.

'Of course,' he says, throwing wide the door.

'Mrs Sheldon. Is everything all right here?'

I stare at the two officers dumbfounded, unable to think of a thing to say. There's broken pottery all over the floor but not a mark on me. The wine, the sudden change in his mood, and the image of Oliver knocking me down only moments before is somehow fuddling my brain. He's standing before me composed and innocent, smiling with love and compassion, so smartly dressed in his dark Sunday suit and immaculate white shirt, his tie a perfect sheath of silk, that it seems almost laughable he could be the one who created this mayhem. I look at them wild eyed, hair awry, sucking on my cut finger to stop it bleeding everywhere, and wonder desperately what I should say, how I should react.

'I'm afraid my wife has had rather too much to drink,' Oliver explains in quiet, caring tones. 'Family row with her sister. They don't have an easy relationship, I'm afraid. Then she had a bit of a tantrum. I'm sorry if she disturbed the neighbours.'

There are two officers, both men, and they look at me keenly, perhaps wondering if they should breathalyse me. Can you be charged with being drunk in charge of your own kitchen? I wonder, rather hysterically. Then I remind myself that I'm not drunk, not on three small glasses of wine. A bit merry perhaps, a touch tiddly, but not drunk. And I didn't smash a thing, Oliver did.

'Is this correct, madam?' one asks me, and I open and close my mouth in silent anguish. My garrulous chatter and reckless confidence seems to have quite deserted me, leaving me drained and trembling. Dare I tell the truth? Would they believe me if I did? What would they do, arrest Oliver? What then? Even if they did arrest him, wouldn't they almost immediately bail him and he'd come straight back home and . . . I don't care to think what he'd do to me then.

Oliver illustrates what this might be by glowering darkly at me as he stands quietly behind the two officers, rests one finger quietly against his lips, then slides it across his throat. I'm filled with a rush of cold fear and manage only a slight shrug, quite unable to find my voice.

'You have no reason to make a complaint yourself, madam?' the policeman asks, glancing from Oliver to myself and back again. 'You are all right?'

I clear my throat and attempt a smile. 'Yes, yes, I'm fine. I maybe did have one too many. I'm sorry.'

The other officer smirks. 'Lost it a bit, did you?' He turns to Oliver, gives him a sympathetic smile, man to man. 'My wife is just the same. Real temper on her when faced with her sister. Pity about the crockery though. I'd get that cut finger looked at, love, if I were you. It can make a nasty cut.' He kicks at it with his foot then starts to move towards the door.

The first policeman is still walking about the room, eyeing everything up. He comes right over to me and I wonder if he's going to hand me a card, as they do in *The Bill* on TV, maybe suggest I can ring him if I need help any time. 'Kiss and make up, love, that's always best. She's family after all. And maybe try some counselling for that drink problem of yours.' Then he quietly turns and follows his colleague out of the door, which my charming husband holds open, wishing them both a polite goodnight.

After they've gone, we sit at the kitchen table saying nothing for some time. The visit from the police has sobered us both. I'm thinking that at least Oliver won't dare touch me again, not tonight anyway. But I'm wrong. He indulges in yet more verbal abuse, spitting venom at me across the table, but then when I make a move to go to bed, he punches me in the stomach, hard.

'You ever get me in this mess again, you'll live to regret it, if you live at all.'

By the time we finally get to bed I'm wishing the glass or two of wine I'd drunk, at what should have been a jolly Sunday lunch, hadn't loosened my brain as well as my tongue.

'So, no lover then?' he says, as he slips between the sheets.

'No, no lover,' I whisper, sliding to the edge of the bed as far from my husband as I can get.

'No one would have you, anyway,' he snarls, as he snaps off the light, his tone cruelly mocking.

'You wanted me,' I gently remind him.

'Ah, but catching a man is one thing, Carly. Keeping him is quite another.'

'So what did you think of that?' Jo-Jo asked her husband. 'Isn't she *sooo* full of herself? Thinks I'm so unimportant she can't even be bothered dress properly when she's *only* having lunch with us.'

'But she *did* dress properly,' Ed pointed out as he started to stack the dishes in the dishwasher. 'I thought she looked very smart, almost too smart.'

'That's because Oliver insisted she change, otherwise she'd have given me her usual level of consideration. Nil!' Jo-Jo collapsed onto the sofa to ease her aching back. Even though Ed had done most of the cooking she felt drained, ready to crawl into bed and sleep the clock round. Oh, if only she could.

It had been a long, tiring day but there were still the kids to get ready for bed, still the horrors of bath time to face. She'd make the most of five minutes' peace while they were still outside in the garden, playing house under a sheet pinned over the line.

'I only invited her because Mum asked me to, out of a duty to restore family unity. Huh, and you saw how successful that was. Nearly scratching each other's eyes out by the end of the afternoon. I'll hang for that girl, I swear I will. What *is* her problem?'

Ed frowned, pausing in scraping a plate to consider. 'Maybe there is a problem. What was all that stuff about wishing she hadn't married in quite such a rush?'

'Absolute tosh! Spoken for effect, no doubt in an effort to win yet more attention from her adoring husband. Carly thinks the world should be made of rose petals and sunshine. She has a lot to learn.' Jo-Jo eased off her too-tight shoes and lifted her feet up on the sofa with a sigh. 'Ooh, when you've done that, love, will you come and rub my back? I feel like a beached whale having a bad-hair day.'

Ed chuckled but the subject of Carly and Oliver was still playing on his mind. 'You said you saw him in town the other night, but Carly wasn't with him?'

'Hm, that's right.' Jo-Jo had her eyes closed, was drifting nicely to sleep. 'Seeing a client apparently. Never stops working that man. No wonder he's rich.'

'Can't be much fun for Carly if he works so hard and goes out most evenings.'

'I didn't say that he does.'

'Has she? Does she ever complain of being lonely?'

'For heaven's sake, why would she confide in me? I'm only her sister for God's sake! Anyway, who gives a toss what happens at Perfect Villa? She doesn't know she's born, that girl. Gorgeous, adoring, rich husband. Nice house, nice car, no kids. Lucky Carly.'

Ed was beside her now on the sofa, smiling softly as he kissed her neck. 'Not lucky at all. She's missing out on all the fun. And how is my new son behaving?'

'He's going to play for Manchester United. I can tell that because he's already practising his goal kicks.'

'That's good. He'll be able to keep his old mum and dad in the manner to which we'd like to become accustomed. Turn over and I'll rub that back of yours.'

'Ooh, that's lovely. A bit lower . . . yes, there. I wonder if Oliver has your healing hands? Naw! Too stiff necked and proper to be touchy feely.' She turned her head to present her mouth for a kiss. 'Perhaps my sister isn't quite so lucky after all.'

Oliver is still sleeping when I creep out of bed. My heart is beating so loudly in my ears I'm sure he must be able to hear it. I quietly gather up the clothes I've just taken off and sneak out of the bedroom. In the kitchen I pull them hastily on, hopping on one leg as I search for my shoe and fasten zips and buttons at the same time. It would have been much more appropriate to grab a pair of jeans, but I couldn't risk disturbing him by opening a wardrobe or a drawer. I hold my breath as I let myself out of the house, the door closing behind me with a surprisingly loud click. My heart jumps and I waste several precious seconds frozen in fear before scurrying to my car and fumbling for my keys.

I take care to close the car door more carefully, and, heart in mouth, insert the key into the ignition. I glance up at our bedroom window, but it's still in darkness. Then I look across at the front door, terrified that Oliver might burst through it at any moment and come roaring towards me. But I drive away without any problems, without even a neighbour's curtain twitching. Nevertheless, I'm halfway to Windermere before I begin to breathe more easily.

In my bag is another key, the one Emma loaned me, and when I reach her flat, I use it as quietly as I can, not wishing to disturb her at two in the morning.

Even so, my head has barely touched the sofa cushions when

a light comes on in the hall and the next instant she's standing beside me in her nightshirt, blinking and rubbing her eyes.

She looks at me, her best friend and business partner lying on her sofa in the middle of the night, sobbing quietly into her silk cushions, and says, 'I think you need a shot of whisky.'

I never touch the stuff and quickly protest, so she offers to open a bottle of wine instead. 'No, really, I've had enough wine for one evening. I shouldn't even have driven here tonight, I must be way over the limit.' I insist she makes hot chocolate instead, and she does so, giving me a ginger biscuit to dunk. Then she sits beside me, her feet curled under her, saying nothing while I sip it quietly, allowing the hot sweetness of the drink to soothe me.

Her kindness, her blithe acceptance of my presence in her tiny bedsit, her lack of curiosity, all touch me deeply. Then suddenly I'm sobbing and crying, choking over the delicious biscuit and telling her how awful the Sunday lunch was, how Jo-Jo took offence over the blasted jeans Oliver wouldn't allow me to wear, and how he was furious with me for imbibing too much.

She still doesn't speak for several more minutes, and then quietly asks, 'And what happened afterwards, when you got home? What did Oliver do to make you run off like this, even though you're not fit to drive?'

I suddenly realise that I am, in fact, stone cold sober, that I'm hovering on the brink of telling Emma far more than I should. Do I really want her to know that my husband battered me all over the kitchen, smashed half our crockery and made such a row that the police were called; and that they did nothing, believed every lie he told them and left me to an even worse fate? There's a pain in my abdomen where he punched me in the stomach, and my back is aching. I can feel it getting worse as my muscles stiffen up.

I know Em and Oliver don't get on, for whatever reason, but what will she think of him if I tell her all of this? And what will she think of me for putting up with it? But I haven't put up with it, have I? I've been doing my damnedest to help cure him, to survive, and now I've left him. I look at my friend, feeling very close to panic, quite unable to think clearly or make any sensible decision.

'Why are you here, Carly? This can't all be about a pair of jeans or a squabble with your sister. Or even a glass of wine too many. Tell me the whole story.'

I give a little sob. If only I could. How I need a friend right now. Yet the image of Oliver's anger is still painfully fresh in my mind. What if I did tell Emma everything, and he found out? 'We had a row, that's all. He gets so angry, so furious with me.'

'I guessed as much, so what, exactly, does he do to you when he gets angry?' Her tone is gentle, coaxing.

'It was all my fault, I got a bit tiddly. Oliver has a lot of problems, which I'm trying to help him deal with, but oh, I don't know how . . .' At that moment my mobile phone rings, and I almost jump out of my skin.

'It's Oliver,' I say to her, reading the number on the small screen. 'What should I do?' My heart is scudding and I can hardly breathe.

'You don't have to answer,' Emma tells me.

'Yes, I do. I can't not answer my own husband, can I?' He might come round and create a scene, if I don't.

His voice echoes down the line, the signal surprisingly loud and clear. 'Carly, where are you? What the hell are you doing?'

'Tell him you've left him,' Emma whispers by my side.

'Who was that? Who is with you?'

'Nobody.'

'Yes there is, I distinctly heard someone speaking. Are you with him, your lover?'

'Oh, for goodness' sake, Oliver, don't start on that nonsense again. That's why I left the house, left you. I can't stand your obsessive jealousy, or you telling me what to do all the time.'

'Who are you with? Just tell me that.'

I sigh. 'Only Emma.'

There's a short silence, and then Oliver says, 'Do you want to know where *I* am? I'm out in my car, looking for you. I can't live without you, Carly. You are my wife and I love you. You are the reason I get up each day. I couldn't survive if you left me.'

'Don't say that, it's not true.'

'It is true. And if you don't come home to me, now, tonight, then you'll be reading about me in the paper tomorrow.'

'What are you talking about?'

'I've got a length of rubber tube in the boot. I'm getting it out now, even as I speak. I'm fixing it on to the exhaust.'

'What? Oliver, stop that! Stop it!'

'Then tell me you love me. Either come home tonight, this minute, or I'll end it all. *Now*! I can't, won't, live without you.'

'Oliver, don't say such terrible things. You know that I love you, but I can't live *with* you, not the way you've been behaving recently.'

'Come home now, Carly, and we'll talk about it. Otherwise, that's it. I'll do it, I swear. I'm closing all the car windows, I'm running the engine, the tube is here in my hand . . . I can smell the fumes . . .'

'I'm coming, I'm coming. Please don't . . . I'll be home in half an hour.'

I thrust the half-drunk chocolate back in Emma's hands. 'I'm sorry, I have to go.'

She rushes after me to the door, catches hold of me and gives me a little shake. 'Think what you're doing, Carly. Don't go. Stay here tonight at least, till he's had time to cool off.'

I'm shaking my head, frantic to free myself from her grasp. 'No, I can't stay. I'm sorry, but Oliver needs me.'

As I drive home, heart pounding with fear that he may have done something desperate, I feel certain that despite everything that must be true. Oliver does need me. Because he loves me. Otherwise, he would have let me go, wouldn't he?

He's touchingly grateful that I've returned home, as he begged me to do, and I'm so relieved that the black clouds have lifted, that he still loves me, I let him hold me, wincing slightly as he presses against the fresh bruises on my arms.

'I'm sorry, darling. I lost it again, didn't I? Oh, God, I don't know what comes over me,' he says as he examines a nasty purple bruise on my back which I got when he knocked me against the table. 'I'll make it up to you, I swear it. At least we fooled the cops, eh? The last thing we want is for them to start poking their noses into our affairs.'

Oliver makes his feelings on my behaviour very clear. His voice is calm but menacing, and I don't argue. There is to be no further discussion about this oh-so-embarrassing visit from the law. I am never again to cause him to lose his temper to such an extent he starts smashing things. The fault was entirely mine and if I'd kept off the drink . . . blah, blah, blah.

'I'm sorry too,' I tell him, although he hasn't actually apologised.

As always he begs my forgiveness for the beating he gave me, which was, he says, quite against his better judgement. And I, as always, forgive him. His remorse seems genuine, which I feel I must believe, otherwise what future do we have? I'm still nursing an increasingly forlorn hope that he'll change and turn back into the attentive, gorgeous man I first fell in love with. Yet I'm bitterly aware there's a pattern developing and I can't think how to get out of it.

I repeat my apology for my foolish behaviour at the lunch, although I know in my heart that I was reasonably sober when I first voiced my regret at having married in a hurry. The reason I drank too much wine afterwards was because I couldn't bear to examine the reality of my life.

'You won't ever leave me again, Carly, is that clear?' He captures my face between the palm of his hands and smiles gently into my eyes. 'You are all that matters to me, remember that. You're my wife. How would I live without you? You wouldn't wish to have my suicide on your conscience, would you?'

I'm horrified by this, try to say this is blackmail, totally unfair, but can't quite find the courage. What if he means it? What if

Oliver is so badly damaged by an abusive childhood, and by our disastrous marriage, that he does take his own life? How would I live with the knowledge that I'd driven him to it?

This morning I wake to another day and the bleak awareness that things are getting worse, not better. I look at him asleep beside me and feel his rejection like a block of ice in my stomach. I love him still, despite everything, and long for him to relax and enjoy life, for him to be able to enjoy a joke and be happy again.

I'm all too aware I must take care not to say anything which might upset or provoke him, but sometimes the restraint gets to me, as it did after one glass of wine too many. Yet at the same time I'm growing strangely used to these attacks, these furies that suddenly beset him. I've started to take them for granted, half expecting a bad reaction to some innocent remark or other. I'm learning to suffer his slaps and chastisements in silence. That way they're over and done with much quicker.

But why does he care so little for me? That's what hurts the most.

I know that he loved me once. He saw our future together as something wonderful, a world where I was always sexy and beautiful, where I was never tired or overworked, had no independent life of my own and was completely captivated by his charm. In his imagination he pictured a perfect house where we sat on white sofas drinking red wine, entertained friends to dinner with cordon bleu food which I cooked with elegance and charm.

He never saw a house that looked lived in with a wife dashing home late after a long tiring day. Nor did he envision having to play his part in keeping that home running smoothly. Oliver expects to live in an unrealistic world without frustrations or everyday cares and responsibilities, and one devoted entirely to his needs. A fantasy world with a fantasy woman.

A day or two later, as I go over and over the latest incident in my mind, I realise that I must do something. I can't go on like this, allowing him to abuse me, to treat me like a punchbag he can use to take out his frustrations on.

I feel trapped, too fearful of what he might do if I leave, either to me, or to himself, to ever find the courage to risk it again. I'm not even sure which I'm afraid of most. Yet if I don't leave, what kind of life can I hope to have?

If only he would speak to a counsellor. But if he won't, then maybe I should. Surely there must be some way for me to deal with this. I look in the phone book and find a help line number. It takes me several more days to pluck up the courage but finally I punch in the numbers, using the code which disguises the origin of my call before I do so. A woman's voice comes on the line asking if she can help.

'I'm not sure . . .' My voice cracks and I immediately run out of words. I can't think where to begin, how to explain the confusion and despair that I feel, the shame that fills me, the certainty that this is all my fault, even when I know deep down it can't possibly be. Can it?

'I'm here to listen and help if I can,' she says. 'Would you like to tell me your name?'

I hear a car outside and I panic, thinking it might be Oliver coming home unexpectedly, as he sometimes tends to do. I instantly click off the phone. It turns out not to be Oliver after all, but I don't try the number again. Best not to risk it, I think. I'm really not ready to bring strangers into this mess. Not yet. Maybe I'll try talking to Mum first. Just as soon as I can find the courage and an appropriate moment.

In any case, what happened at the lunch on Sunday was as much my fault as Oliver's, I realise that now. I'm appalled that I expressed regret over our marriage, and in front of my sister of all people, ashamed that I let a glass of wine go to my head and that I showed him up in front of everyone. No wonder he was angry with me.

10

I'm speaking to my mother on the phone. I rang her in the hope of arranging an opportunity for us to meet up and talk properly, for me to unburden my heart to her. But she doesn't sound her usual cheerful self, her voice cool and distant, filled with reproach, so I fall at the first fence and don't even dare ask her. She comes straight to the cause of her grievance. 'Have you and Jo-Jo been at it again?'

'Excuse me?'

'She tells me you've had another falling-out, that you put the phone down on her the other day. Cut her off in the middle of a sentence.'

'Oh that, no of course I didn't cut her off. We must have got disconnected, I've no idea how it happened.' I certainly have no intention of going into the details of my married life with my mother.

'And you couldn't ring her back later?'

'I got caught up making Oliver's dinner and I forgot. What's the big deal anyway? We had lunch with them on Sunday and . . .'

'. . . you upset her again. I've heard all about that too; how you were going to wear your scruffy jeans until Oliver persuaded you to change into something more appropriate. Can't you show a little tact and respect for your only sister?'

'I didn't want to overdress because she hates me to look better than she does, particularly when she's fat and pregnant.'

'I hope you didn't say that to her.'

'Of course I didn't, what do you take me for? And they weren't my scruffy jeans, they were a perfectly decent pair, and a lovely new top. What is this, attack-Carly week?'

I hear my mother give one of her loud, disapproving sniffs. 'No doubt you were still in a huff over your last falling-out.'

Somewhere, at the back of my head, an alarm bell is ringing. Has all this stuff come from Jo-Jo? Surely Oliver wouldn't speak to my parents on the subject, let alone try to put me in the wrong yet again, not after all we've been through recently. Since I came home everything has seemed to be fine between us. We didn't talk exactly, as he'd promised we would, but we're reconciled and trying again to make our marriage work. I would just like some help, some advice. I strive to ignore my concerns, try to convince myself this has definitely come from Jo-Jo. My sister loves nothing more than a good moan.

Mum is in full lecture mode. 'I won't have my two girls in a constant state of warfare, particularly when Jo-Jo is carrying. You know how uptight and emotional she gets when she's pregnant. Can't you show a little consideration?'

'I'm sorry,' I say, feeling instantly guilty, realising this is a fair point. 'I really didn't intend to upset her. We were having fun and being silly and it all got a bit out of hand.'

'So I believe. Oliver tells me you were somewhat the worse for wear, and after drinking too much wine you had a temper tantrum and broke some of your best crockery, which was given to you as wedding presents. Really, Carly, what is going on in your head these days? Can't you exercise a little more restraint and control?'

'*When* did Oliver tell you this?' I'm appalled, instantly guessing that the alarm bells were right.

'Does it matter? At least he feels able to pop in the shop and share his concern over your selfish behaviour. Get a grip, girl, for goodness' sake! You don't know how lucky you are to have such a gorgeous, charming man like Oliver.'

How can I begin to explain that this whole, stupid situation was manipulated by my darling husband, whom she thinks is God's gift to mankind? He's the one who objected to my visiting my sister in the first place, who pulled the plug on her call, and refused to join in the fun over lunch. He's the one who checks my petrol gauge, steals money from my purse and accuses me of over-spending, hides my car keys I shouldn't wonder when I think I'm going mad because I can't find them. I work my socks off to make him feel happy and well cared for, try to understand his problems, and all he does is thump me and be obsessively jealous over some imaginary lover he's dreamed up out of nowhere. Mum would never believe the half of it, were I to tell her the whole truth. Nor would I in her shoes. It sounds too contrived, too incredible.

She's still talking, going on and on at me. 'Oliver insists that you're over-stressed, working too hard, and I'm beginning to see he might have a point. Get in a few early nights and stop gallivanting all over the place with that Emma, or whatever it is you two get up to at the end of a day's work. You're a married woman now, not some silly young girl on a night out.'

I don't respond to this, but I can see that Oliver has put a spin on my innocent socialising with Emma too. No doubt also accusing me of being an incipient alcoholic. What is there to say in my own defence that Mum would believe? I wearily change the subject and ask about Gran and Grandad. I offer to pop over and see them later in the week, apologise for my recent neglect. 'And I promise not to upset Jo-Jo again, not while she's pregnant anyway. Honest!'

'Family is important,' she sternly reminds me. 'If you don't keep in touch with people, or treat them properly, you lose them. Even your nearest and dearest.'

'Yes, Mum. Take care. Love you,' and I manage to get off the line without actually cutting her off mid-sentence, but also avoiding a more lengthy lecture, which must be a first. I see that my hand is shaking as I put down the phone. What is happening to me? Why does my life seem to be turning upside down? Why am I always the one in the wrong?

The following weekend Oliver and I enjoy a pleasant evening with his parents. They always make me feel most welcome and I try to imagine how these two lovely, kind people who clearly adore their only son and are supremely proud of his success in the financial world, could ever have abused him. It doesn't seem possible. The very idea of his elegant, gentle mother lifting a strap to her son is beyond belief.

Oliver tells them how happy we are, how he'd do anything for me, and what a wonderful life we have together. It's like listening to the story of someone else's life, not mine.

'Of course she works far too hard,' Oliver gently chides me. 'Don't you think she looks tired, Mother, and a tad overweight? I suspect she grazes on junk food throughout the day.'

I'm privately appalled that he should think me fat, but manage not to show it. I give a sheepish smile and admit there may be some truth in the latter charge at least. 'My excuse is that I need to keep my energy up for all the physical work I do.'

His mother Grace insists I look lovely, as always.

'She's not in the least bit overweight, Oliver, so don't be unkind. In fact, quite the reverse. I'd say you've lost weight since the wedding, my dear. Never still long enough to keep any flesh on you, I should think. Is Oliver being a pain, expecting to be waited on hand, foot and finger? You really mustn't let him, must she, Jeffrey?' She nudges her husband, who grunts something incoherent and keeps on eating his curry.

Oliver smiles. 'I'm only too glad to do my bit. We're a great team, aren't we, darling? And I must say she's getting much better in the kitchen. I can't praise her enough for the effort she's put into learning how to cook. Although she still sometimes dashes off and does something else, forgets to keep an eye on the clock and dries food to a crisp,' Oliver says with a sad shake of his head. 'The beef last Sunday was tough, her Yorkshire puddings didn't rise and her custard curdled. She can't even make a simple quiche.'

Will I never live that down? I manage a stiff smile and swear I'll never make another as long as live. I also privately vow to buy frozen Yorkshire puddings in future. Hopefully he won't notice the difference. Grace, his sweet, gentle mother whom I already like enormously, leans close and whispers in my ear that in the first months of her own marriage, she burned everything, including the toast.

'I hardly had a decent pan left, did I?' she teasingly reminds her husband.

'Practically burned the house down once,' he placidly replies, helping himself to a second slice of delicious home-baked apple pie.

'Give her time, Oliver, dear. You've only been married a few months. She's new to the job, and a busy lady with her own business to run. Cooking takes practice, though I could lend you a splendid, easy-to-follow recipe book, dear, if you like.'

I politely accept even though my cupboard is already stuffed with similar culinary bibles intended to simplify this mysterious art.

Oliver leans over and gives me a kiss. 'Not that I care what she does with my food, or the house. I don't care if she burns everything to a crisp, or if she can't put proper creases in my trousers, I absolutely adore her, and to prove it I'm taking her away for a few days' holiday.'

I look at him in surprise, stunned as much by this unexpected defence of me as this startling news. 'Taking me where? You never said anything to me about this.'

He looks mightily pleased with himself as he laughingly taps me on the nose with one teasing finger. 'I was keeping it as a surprise. Don't you think she deserves a little spoiling, Mum?'

Grace smiles with soft approval. 'I do indeed. A holiday is exactly what you need, Carly, after such a busy season. Where are you taking her Oliver, or is that a surprise too?'

He smiles right into my eyes and my heart flips over, just as it used to.

'Paris, where else?'

'Oh, Oliver,' and I wrap my arms about his neck and kiss him. Maybe our little talk has helped more than I realised.

★　★　★

I still have some worries on my mind and as I help Grace make coffee at the end of the meal, I take the opportunity to ask her what Oliver was like as a child.

She laughs. 'Always needing to be the centre of attention, as he did just now by springing that surprise on you. Of course it's a lovely thing to do, and I'm not denying he's a sweet, generous man, always ready to help others, but he also loves to be appreciated and applauded. He does like everything to revolve around him and his perceived wounds. That's why I was so pleased when he took up with you, Carly. You're so very sensible, with your head screwed on right. You're good for him.'

I'm slightly startled by this, turning her words over in my mind as I set out her best china cups and saucers. But it doesn't resolve the one question that is pounding in my head. I try a more oblique approach.

'It must be quite hard bringing up children. My sister has three, is expecting her fourth as a matter of fact. How she copes I cannot imagine but I've never seen her so much as lift a hand to smack them when they're naughty.'

'Quite right,' Grace Sheldon stoutly agrees. 'Physical punishment shouldn't be necessary if you have a loving rapport with your child.'

'What about tantrums?' I ask her. 'Ryan is coming up to two and can be a bit of a handful in that respect. He just loves to lie on the floor and kick his heels and scream, particularly in the middle of Tesco.'

She laughs. 'Oh, I remember the terrible twos. Oliver was dreadful at that age. Tell your sister to sit him on the naughty step for a while. He'll soon stop screaming and making a fuss when he realises he's missing out on all the fun. But she's quite right, smacking is not the answer. I never lifted a hand to Oliver, nor did his father.'

I frown, trying to absorb the import of this remark as she waits for the coffee to brew, and I see a pink flush creep into her cheeks. 'I don't mind telling you, dear, although it's not something I care to talk about too much, but I lost two babies before I had Oliver, so he was always a very special child.'

'Oh, I didn't realise.'

'It was such a joy to at last hold my own child in my arms, and because there were to be no more babies, I'm afraid we have both rather spoiled him. We tried not to, but every single day I blessed my good fortune. Our entire life was largely geared to that boy's needs. I gladly became a stay-at-home mum and devoted myself to his care, and when his father came home from the office he'd always make time to play with him. We sent Oliver to a good school, had his friends in for tea, gave him a safe routine, and provided him with everything he could wish for. Too much, I suppose, as elderly parents tend to do. Of course we expected him to behave like a proper little man when we took him out for dinner, which we did quite frequently, or in church on Sundays. We were firm but loving parents, I believe,' she tells me with a smile. 'Quite old fashioned in that he had to do his homework on time, and say his please and thank yous. Children like to know where they stand, don't you think, and your sister sounds like she has a similar set of standards. But she's quite right, physical punishment is definitely not the answer. Fetch that dish of chocolates, dear, will you?' she breezily reminds me as she sails away into the dining room, carrying the loaded tray aloft.

I follow, stunned by her little confession, but it's perfectly clear to me that Oliver must have had a very stable and loving upbringing, and a good relationship with his parents. They absolutely adore him, and I do not believe for one moment that they ever abused him. But if that's the case, why did he make out that they did?

'Paris? My, my, lucky you!' Jo-Jo's eyes are green with envy and, for once, I don't blame her. My sister looks tired, worn out by her pregnancy and the demands of three young children. Mum too is having a hard time of it with the elderlies, and I know she's bursting to spill out her latest worries on that score. We're all in her kitchen enjoying a bit of a gossip, eating a slice of her best fruit cake and putting the world to rights. I've told them all about the proposed trip and Mum is once more singing Oliver's praises.

'You are so fortunate in your husband, Carly. I do hope you appreciate him.'

'Yes, Mum . . . I do,' I sigh, but there must have been a slight hesitation in my manner because she gives me a stern look.

'I hope you are treating that man right.'

I stifle a sigh and assure her that I am. 'There are times though when I do wonder why . . .' I begin, and then fall silent. They both wait, somewhat impatiently, for me to finish, but somehow I can't find the words.

It's Jo-Jo in the end who snaps, 'What? Why he doesn't take you to Paris for a week instead of just a few days, or a fortnight perhaps? Why not a cruise on the Med?'

'Stop it, Jo-Jo, that's not what I was about to say at all.' I wonder what exactly I did intend to say. Faced with my family's certainty of my husband's good will I can't think, so I improvise. 'I wonder sometimes why he chose to marry *me*.'

They both look at me in wide-eyed amazement, and then at each other. Mum lets out a heavy sigh. 'Because he loves you, pet. Hasn't he told you so a thousand times? Now stop being so demanding and be thankful for your good fortune. I for one am delighted that both my girls have such lovely husbands. You should both consider yourselves very lucky.'

'If you're complaining that Oliver is no longer romantic,' Jo-Jo says, 'then welcome to the club. You're an old married woman now. Husbands have neither the money nor the motivation to shower you with flowers and gifts once they've caught you. Welcome to the real world.'

'Have you never considered society's attitude towards marriage, women in particular?' I suddenly blurt out, and they both stop chewing cake to look at me askance. 'All that stuff about "love, honour and obey", the vicar saying "who giveth this woman". It's so medieval, don't you think?'

There's a short silence and then Mum bursts out laughing. 'So that's what's going on in your head. You've gone all feminist like that Emma.'

'She's not *that* Emma, she's my friend and partner, and no, I haven't gone feminist at all.'

'Sounds like it. Oliver says that Emma – your friend Emma – is very demanding. That as well as working you too hard, she expects you to sacrifice quite a bit of the time you should be spending with him, to be with her.'

I roll my eyes heavenwards. 'That's simply not true.'

'He says he had to drag you out of the John Peel the other night.'

'It was one drink after work, that's all. We sometimes need to discuss business, and there's little opportunity for that in the office with the phone ringing all the time and clients popping in and out.'

'That's not what Oliver says.'

'Oliver isn't right about everything.'

She frowns with disapproval, as if I've committed a cardinal sin by criticising him. 'What's come over you, Carly? You should be dashing home to be with your lovely husband, not spending the evening drinking in a pub with your girlfriends.'

Jo-Jo interrupts. 'Leave it, Mum, if Carly's working too hard, or drinking too much, she's no one to blame but herself. She's too selfish, too full of ambition and a desire to make money to give her husband a bit of the care and attention he deserves.'

I sigh with frustration, stunned and hurt by this joint attack on me. I try to explain that's not how I am at all, but my sister turns away to stop Ryan from chewing a crayon, and Mum abruptly changes the subject to some tale about Grandpa having started to hoard food. 'He hides slices of apple pie or fruit cake among his socks, would you believe? You have to laugh. Maybe he gets hungry in the night, bless him, and likes to have secret snacks when he's wandering about wondering what time it is.'

'Oh, Mum, that's so sad,' Jo-Jo says. They're talking now as if I wasn't even in the room.

'I certainly don't starve the poor old soul. He eats like a horse, everything I put in front of him. Most of the time he hasn't the first idea what day it is, let alone what time. Dad has caught him twice this week about to leave the house at dawn, still in his pyjamas but with his cap on and bait box in hand, ready to do a day's work. And one evening when he saw your father going off to the football, he asked him if he had enough spending money in his pocket. What year he was in, I've no idea, but clearly not the present. Ken just answered that he was all right for money, thanks very much. Poor old chap. It's easy to smile but I don't know how much longer we can cope. It's nerve-racking not knowing what he might do next.'

Listening to this, and her very real concern, I don't have the heart to make things worse by pouring out my own troubles, even if neither my mother or sister had the patience to listen to me. My problems seem so petty by comparison. Surely I can sort things out for myself. I'm a big girl now.

Haven't we talked things through, Oliver and I? And although I still can't quite get my head around his claim of being abused, which doesn't gel at all with what Grace told me the other day, he does seem much more relaxed. And a trip to Paris could well put everything right between us.

Paris is indeed wonderful, everything I could have hoped for. Just the sights and smells of this beautiful European city seem to bring me alive and revitalise us both. I love sitting at pavement cafés sipping fragrant coffee and watching the world go by. Isn't that what Paris is all about? And Oliver is so attentive, so loving, quite his old romantic self as we devote ourselves exclusively to each other. This holiday is exactly what we need to grow close again.

We have a great time, wandering along the Avenue des Champs Elysées, go up the Eiffel tower to marvel at the view, enjoy a show at the Moulin Rouge, a romantic cruise on the Seine and make love at every possible moment. It's like old times.

We talk more than we've done in an age and I try to explain why I love my job so much, how it makes me feel fulfilled as a person in my own right.

Oliver listens and concedes that he should loosen up a little, give me a bit more elbow room to do my own thing. 'Maybe I'll learn to like the fact you have a business of your own, since you're doing rather well, for now at least. As an accountant I can never say no to a good profit, but you won't always need to work, Carly. Once I'm properly established with a partnership, you can stay at home and be a proper wife.'

I let the comment slide by as we obviously aren't going to agree on that one, and this isn't the moment for any more confrontation. We're having a marvellous time and I've certainly no intention of spoiling it by feminist talk, as Mum calls it. In fact, we don't have a single cross word the entire holiday. It's just wonderful, and I return home refreshed and elated, thrilled that we've grown close again on this fabulous romantic break.

As I tell Jo-Jo all about it, her eyes once more turn green with jealousy. This time I don't care, I'm just so relieved that my marriage seems to be back on track.

And then three weeks later I discover that I'm pregnant.

Oliver is furious. A baby is the last thing he wants right now. I've waited to tell him until I'm absolutely certain, taken the test and everything. Tonight we made love, as we have most nights since we got back from Paris, so it seemed like a good moment to come clean. How wrong I was.

He leaps out of bed and starts prowling about the room in an agitated fashion. 'How could you be so stupid?' he rails at me.

'I don't know. I made a mistake, sorry. I must have missed taking the pill for the odd day. It's easy to forget. Anyway, does it matter, it's happened?'

'Of course it bloody matters! Why do you have to be so incompetent, woman? You've ruined everything. But then you've been determined to ruin our marriage from the start.'

He snatches up our wedding photo and smashes it to the floor, storms about the room getting angrier by the minute and sweeps all the stuff off my dressing table like a man demented. Or perhaps a two year old who can't get his own way. In that moment he reminds me of Ryan having one of his temper tantrums in Tesco. I wouldn't have been surprised if he'd lain down and drummed his heels on the floor. Yet this is not a child but an adult, with the strength of a grown man.

I'm shocked, appalled by his reaction. I was aware that Oliver was in no hurry to have kids, but didn't expect him to react quite so badly to the news. I felt pretty stunned by the news myself at first, and yet secretly thrilled when I realised I was having a baby. I love children and a child of my own would be wonderful. I kneel at the bottom of the bed and try to calm him, to placate him with a teasing, sexy smile.

'Look, don't worry, love. It'll work out fine. Our mothers will be thrilled. Yours certainly will be, she adores babies.' This gives him pause for thought, and I hammer home my small advantage. 'And you should know that an abortion is not an option for me.'

His face is wearing that familiar shuttered look, and I'm beginning to feel slightly sick. 'Damn you, Carly, this is *your* doing. You've done this to me.'

I manage a nervous chuckle. 'I think you had something to do with it too. It's not so surprising, is it? We have been hammering it a bit lately. Blame it on Paris, which was your idea, remember. They say it's a city for lovers, and we've certainly proved that, haven't we? But it'll be great, you'll see. Twenty-six is a good age to start a family, don't you think?'

He puts his clenched fists to his head and almost screams in despair. '*No, I don't*! I'm far too young to have all that baby crap, bottles and nappies, and sleepless nights. I don't want it yet, thanks very much. I need to concentrate on my career and getting a partnership. What the hell were you thinking of to be so careless?'

I'm wondering why everything must turn into such a big issue with him when he hasn't planned it himself. Why he can't simply be happy for us, say it'll be OK and we'll manage. 'What's so terrible about my falling pregnant?' I say to him. 'It's not as if we're short of money, and a baby will be lovely. A product of our love.'

'Don't talk utter crap, you stupid whore!' His hand snakes out and he drags me off the bed to fling me down on the floor. Before I realise what's happening, he starts to kick me. Instinctively I curl into the foetal position, as I've learned to do to protect my head and stomach, but this time he goes on and on kicking me in the back and I scrabble across the floor, desperate to escape, fearing he might never stop. He lunges for me, picks me up and throws me across the room. I'm crying and sobbing, quite hysterical as he starts battering me about the head, apparently forgetting his own rules not to hit me where a mark might show.

This is the worst attack yet and I'm terrified. I know I have to get out before he kills me so I make a run for it. Clad only in my nightie I run down the stairs, out of the kitchen door and down the drive. I can hear him chasing after me but I can't run fast enough. My bare feet skid on the wet tarmac and I fall to my knees, scraping them badly, but I don't even notice the pain. Before I can get up, he grabs me by the hair and starts to drag me along the ground, back up the drive into the house.

'You're going nowhere unless I bloody say so,' he yells.

I catch sight of two middle-aged women standing at the bottom of the drive aghast at what they've just witnessed. I hear one of them ask the other if she should call the police.

Oliver hears them too. He shoves me into the house, slams shut the door and locks it. Running away was the worst possible thing I could have done. I've shamed him in public, in front of perfect strangers, not simply friends or family.

Terrified the police might arrive at any minute and be less accommodating this time, he switches off every light in the house, shuts us both in the bedroom and orders me to stay absolutely silent. I lie curled up tight in bed, shivering in the dark. I'm listening for sounds of a police siren but all I can hear is my own heart pounding. I'm frozen with fear. What should I do if I hear the bell ring? There's no way I can escape, but dare I shout? Would the police break in if they heard me? Will it be the same two policemen? We lie there pretending to be innocently asleep for what seems like hours but no one comes. I realise that the two women must have decided not to interfere in a matrimonial, a 'domestic'. The usual 'let's not get involved' sort of reaction to this type of problem. Oliver realises this too and starts to chuckle. The sound chills me to the bone.

'The cavalry isn't coming,' he sneers. 'No one gives a shit what I do to you.'

For the first time in my life I feel a curdle of real fear, frightened of what he might actually do to me. I'd wanted him to be pleased about the baby, but he's concerned only about the loss of his freedom, the changes a family will make to his own life. A baby will no doubt upset his well-planned routine, and mean I have less time to devote myself to him. Or maybe he's just furious because *he* didn't plan it, didn't give his permission.

Convinced that he isn't about to be carted off to jail, Oliver starts to call me vile names: bitch and slag and other choice words to belittle me. He goes on and on insulting me for my careless stupidity, and for my reckless show of independence by running out of the door. He complains bitterly that I've humiliated him in front of the entire neighbourhood. I cower on the edge of the bed, too afraid to attempt another escape, trying to make myself as small as possible, wishing I was invisible, while he works himself up into a fresh frenzy.

'Are you listening to me?'

When I don't respond he grabs me by the throat and shakes me as if I were a rag doll, squeezing and squeezing till I can see sparks of red before my eyes. My lungs are bursting for air and my head is spinning. Any minute now I know I'll pass out and I'm quite certain that he won't stop till I'm dead. Some instinct kicks in telling me to close my eyes, and I go limp. Maybe if he thinks I have indeed passed out, he'll stop.

It works. Eventually. Just as I'm on the brink of despair. Of course my little play-acting hasn't fooled him at all. He stops choking me when he's good and ready, before he does too much damage.

He releases his grip but only to once again start knocking me all over the bedroom, punching and thumping me, maintaining a furious aggrieved silence so he doesn't disturb the neighbours, which feels even more intimidating than when he shouts and rails at me. He takes hold of my head and bangs it against the wall, slaps my face from side to side with the back of his hand, kicks my shins till they're black and blue.

'Shut up crying. *Shut up, shut up, shut up!*'

But I'm not actually crying now. Dry eyed, I'm gasping and sobbing, I'm trying to catch my breath and I'm begging him to stop. I'm frantically trying to cover my head and stomach and protect myself, terrified he might never stop. I make no effort to retaliate or protest, nor do I any longer attempt to tease him out of his incandescent rage. I am way past such tactics now and my one thought is to survive. The less I resist, the sooner it will be over.

Miraculously, as suddenly as it began, he gives me one last kick and the storm is over.

'You shouldn't provoke me,' he mutters, as he walks away. 'It's your own stupid fault.'

When I am capable of standing again, I stagger to the bathroom to bathe my face in cold water. My throat is burning, it feels red raw and sore, and there are finger marks on my neck. My hand is shaking as I dab antiseptic on a cut lip that is beginning to visibly swell before my eyes. What am I going to do now? How do I get out of this?

I realise that everything has changed.

By staying and trying to save my marriage, despite my best efforts to help him deal with his problems, all of which seem to have failed, I've as good as condoned his treatment of me. I believed him when he claimed that Julie, his first partner, had hurt him badly, and even when he said his own mother had abused him. Until I spoke to Grace herself, that is, and realised the very idea of this gentle woman abusing her only precious child to be utterly impossible. I should have confronted him right away about my discovery, challenged this need of his to appear to be a victim. I should have left Oliver then instead of going with him to Paris.

But it felt as if he were really trying, as if our marriage had been revitalised and we'd found each other again. Now, it's too late. I'm trapped.

Later, as we lie coldly side by side, his venom spent, the tears slide silently down my cheeks. I try not to make a sound but he hears my sniffles all the same. The next instant he puts his knee, or perhaps the flat of his foot, against the small of my back and kicks me out of bed. I knock my head on the bedside table and jar my hip on the floor as I fall.

'For God's sake, stop crying, woman. Shut up! I've had enough of your stupidity for one night. I wouldn't need to touch you at all if it weren't for your bloody hysterics. And if you ever try running off like that again, or leaving me, you'll be sorry. You really don't want to see how angry I could get if I put my mind to it. Just remember that *I* say what you do and where you go, as I've told you before. Got that? Is that quite clear?'

I mumble something incoherent and he leans over the edge of the bed to whisper ominously, mockingly holding a hand to his ear. 'What did you say? I didn't quite catch it.'

Icy fear crawls down my spine. 'I said, yes, Oliver.'

'Good, now shut the fuck up!'

I spend the rest of that night shivering on the floor, too afraid to move or try to escape again. We've been married barely seven months and I feel dehumanised and degraded, as if I have no control over my own life. I'm deeply ashamed that it's come to this, although why I should believe it's all my fault I'm not quite sure. Oliver makes me feel so worthless, so stupid and utterly useless. I do make mistakes, of course I do, I'm only human. I'm young and inexperienced, new to this marriage lark, which has turned out to be not such a lark after all. And getting pregnant was obviously the worst mistake yet.

I'm cold and uncomfortable and deeply frightened lying on the rug. Hot tears slide down my cheeks and neck, but crying isn't going to help. It serves only to irritate him further, so I bite my lip and stay resolutely silent. I feel broken, defeated, knowing I'd do anything to put things right, for this not to be happening, but I'm helpless. There's absolutely nothing I can do.

The only answer seems to be to do exactly as he says, to shut up and let him get on with it. He's the one in control, the one with the power, not me.

★　　★　　★

I'm woken by Oliver lifting me back into bed. He's all over me, weeping with remorse yet again, so very sorry for what he's done and begging once more for my forgiveness. He promises to keep better control of his temper, is adamant that he doesn't want to lose me, that he can't face life without me or he'd fall into a depression. Top himself, in fact. He swears that he'll never hit me again, but I listen to all of this without a trace of emotion. I know in my heart that he won't keep his promises. Something else will irritate and annoy him, and this whole cycle of violence and remorse will start all over again.

He makes love to me but I stare mindlessly up at the ceiling, just waiting for him to be done.

At first I saw these black moods as caused by Oliver's inability to control his temper. I'd suggest he count to ten, go for a walk, or take time out to think what he's doing and where it might lead. But he doesn't seem able to do this. He dismisses these incidents with a shrug, speaks about them as if they're inevitable, something beyond his control and we must simply learn to live with them.

Gradually though, it has dawned on me that he does know exactly what he's doing. He can quite easily choose not to hit me and frequently does, holding his fist over me as a threat but not actually using it. He has the sense to stop choking me just before I pass out. He certainly wishes to avoid any involvement with the authorities, such as the police calling, or my needing hospitalisation. Usually he's careful not to hit me where the bruises show, choosing my body area or my shoulders and arms. He's made a mistake this time by hitting me on the mouth, but he'll learn from it. He always does. He won't do that again but he *will* devise some other way of hurting me. That is the constant fear I have to live with.

When he isn't getting his own way for whatever reason, if I've stepped out of line, or something unexpected that he didn't anticipate has happened, then he'll suddenly turn angry and let fly. It's almost as if he enjoys stoking up his own ire in order to deliver my punishment for the perceived crime I've allegedly committed. He always holds me entirely responsible for the distress he's supposedly suffering.

But I've noticed that even when he's apparently raging out of control, it's as if he's thinking it all through and making studied decisions. When he loses his temper and throws things, it's my stuff that gets broken or damaged, not his. He smashes *my* favourite lamp against the wall, tosses *my* papers on the fire as he did that time, breaks cups and saucers from *my* favourite tea set which Gran bought me. He destroys everything off my dressing table because apparently this baby is all *my* fault.

He's most definitely in charge of his emotions, and of me. He enjoys the power it gives him to subjugate me, to ban me from our bed and force me to spend a miserable sleepless night on the hard floor, to see me begging for mercy. He needs to be in control, which is what this is all about.

I don't go to work that day. I stay in the house worrying endlessly over the problem, desperately trying to decide how best to deal with it. I ring Emma and plead a diplomatic dose of 'flu and take a few days off. I hate to let her down but feel it's necessary for me to stay indoors until the swelling on my lip has subsided. I look as if I've gone ten rounds in a boxing contest and have no wish to humiliate Oliver in public again, or risk inciting curious questions. I dread to think what he might do to me then.

I know I should leave now, today, but I'm filled with fear. I'm certainly not in denial any longer. I realise that I have a serious problem.

Last night when I ran out in my nightdress and bare feet, Oliver was determined not to let me go. He dragged me back and made it very clear that I must never try to leave again, showing not a glimmer of the patience he exhibited the last time when I ran to Emma's. No matter how often I run away, he swears he will always find me and bring me back. In his eyes I belong to him. I'm his possession, and if I ever attempt to break free again, he'll make me very sorry.

I feel like a hostage, and the prospect terrifies me.

Where could I go? How far would I need to run to escape him? I think of the key Em gave me, which I still have secreted in the pocket of my bag. I would never dare to try that again, not after what happened last time. If there were a spare bed at Mum and Dad's I might go there, only Oliver would easily bully me into coming back home. He'd tell lies and win my parents round with his charm as he always does. They'd never believe how bad it was between us, that he'd ever laid a finger on me, let alone that the violence has escalated to this level.

Jo-Jo certainly wouldn't entertain my staying with her, although she'd no doubt find great pleasure in my having to admit that my perfect marriage was a total sham. She's convinced I lead some sort of idyllic existence living love's young dream on caviar and champagne. How wrong she is! Nor, as I've promised Mum, must I risk upsetting her at this stage in her pregnancy.

But it's not just my pride that is hurt. I'm deeply ashamed that I've allowed this happen, confused about how I come to be in this mess, what I've done wrong. I wonder why I didn't recognise this problem in him before we married? Why didn't I leave him after the first time he hit me? Maybe because I couldn't accept what was happening to me, hoped it would all blow over and the problem magically disappear. Or because I was young, newly married and in love, and believed I could put everything right, given time. If only I'd realised then that it would get worse, not better.

I feel so alone, so isolated from my friends and even from my own family.

I long for a normal, happy life, and how can I even think of leaving him, now that I'm pregnant? I can only hope and pray that Oliver will come round eventually to the idea, once he's got over the initial shock. Perhaps this baby will be the very thing he needs to make him more mature and responsible.

*   *   *

I stay home for three whole days, save for one brief outing when I drive over the empty fells to Kentmere where I can walk alone and nurse my wounds with nothing but a lone buzzard for company, and the mewing cry of a curlew. I go over and over everything in my mind. I can't think what to do, how to find the help I need. A stranger would be ideal, some sort of counsellor, but I've no idea how to go about finding one without going through my doctor.

At some point later that afternoon it occurs to me that I might find some answers on the internet. I creep guiltily into Oliver's study and power up his computer.

I could try looking on the computer in the office, except that there's precious little time or opportunity for surfing, since we're normally concerned chiefly with our own website, bookings and emails. Besides, I've no wish to alert Emma's suspicions any more than they are already. And I'm still trying to pluck up the courage to tell her my news.

I type in some key words, find one or two websites, and start reading. There are snippets of advice, stories of how other women cope and the agonies they go through, most of which I can empathise with. The early denial, the self-blame, thinking he might be sick or mentally disturbed in some way. It makes me feel less alone to know that other women have gone through the same mind-numbing questions as I have.

I realise, with a shock, that I'm one of them now. I'm a battered wife. I've acquired a label, one I could well do without.

There's discussion on how society tends to always put the blame on the woman, as if she gets off on violence, as if she says, 'Hey, I love it when you hit me. Why don't you do it some more.' I'm appalled that anyone could believe such propaganda.

Nor is the problem confined to sink estates or the so-called working-class male. There are women from all walks of life suffering, with husbands who are doctors, lawyers, judges.

And accountants.

The words on the screen blur before my eyes as I try to work it out. People always ask why a woman doesn't leave, as if all you have to do is put on your coat and walk out of the door. Of course there are all the emotional ties, the effort you make to try to put things right and save your marriage, as I have done. Issues such as pride and shame and guilt, and battered self-esteem. But actually leaving your husband or partner, isn't as easy as it might sound.

I find plenty of horror stories on the internet of women who've tried to do just that but were forced to return, either because they had no other home to go to, the judiciary insisted their children remain in the marital home, or their husband simply brought them back and made them stay under threat of even greater violence if they ever tried to leave again. Which is what Oliver is saying to me.

Who could protect me? Who would even believe me?

I glance anxiously at my watch. He'll be home in an hour. I must make sure that I log off soon, and leave no trail of which sites I've visited. Isn't there a danger he'll realise I've used his computer? Will he be able to tell which sites I've visited? That mustn't happen. How do I make sure it doesn't? I wonder in a panic. I'm not as computer savvy as Oliver, knowing only as much as I need to do for my job. Isn't there something about clearing the history, or is it the cache? Where do I find that, for goodness' sake!

I'm about to close down when I spot some chilling statistics. They state that almost half of female homicide victims are killed by their partners.

Dear God, I'm beginning to understand just how bad this can get.

I read that some women keep a bag packed ready, in case they need to run. They hide the kitchen knives when their husbands come home drunk. Fortunately my situation isn't quite so bad. I have a comfortable home, food in my larder. Oliver rarely drinks, but apparently alcohol is rarely the cause of woman abuse. Plenty of men drink and they don't all beat their wives. Alcohol may make it worse, but as I have already discovered to my cost, violence is all about attitude, about control and power.

Should I go or stay? What would be the best thing for my child, let alone me? If I left, where could I live with my baby? Could I earn enough to keep us both, and afford child care? What if Oliver decided he wanted the baby after all and tried to gain custody? There are so many factors to consider even if he was willing to let me go, which so far, he isn't. I'm so confused, so concentrated upon getting through each day that I can see only short-term solutions, I can't begin to think long term. I can't get my head around a possible future as a single mum, without him. I'm too concerned with dealing with *now*!

I've already suggested to him that we try counselling, either separately or together, but Oliver point-blank refused to get involved, or to allow me to discuss our private problems in public. Now that I'm pregnant my situation has got a whole lot more complicated. But what if he didn't know? The vicar was useless, and I chickened out of the help line, quite unable to find the courage to speak about it out loud, too terrified of repercussions, but what if I try on-line? That would feel more anonymous. I key in the word counselling, and then suddenly hear his car in the drive.

In a panic I close down all the sites but don't have time to clear the history or the cache as I quickly power off the computer. All I can do is snatch up a duster so that when he marches in and demands to know what the hell I'm doing in his office, I turn to him with a shaky smile and say I'm just giving the computer a wipe down.

'Well, don't. I'll clean my own desk, OK?'

'Would you like a cup of tea?' I ask, ever the good wife, and rush to put the kettle on.

All I can do is bide my time, have my baby in a safe place and hope for the best.

Just as I'm beginning to think that I've got away with it, he comes striding towards me with that familiar light of battle in his eyes. 'You've been messing with my computer.'

I jump and my heart starts to pound. 'No! No, I haven't.'

'Don't lie to me, Carly. I know for a fact that you have.'

'I – I was only checking the weather forecast.' I say the first thing that comes into my head, trying not to show how nervous I feel.

He rests one hand on each arm of my chair, effectively trapping me within it as he spits his venom right in my face. 'No, you bloody weren't. I've checked back through the history and I can see exactly what you've been doing. Reading about other stupid women won't help you one little bit. And don't even consider talking to a bloody counsellor or woman's refuge. I'd make very certain you regretted it. You don't even want to consider what I might do to you.'

An icy shiver crawls down my spine and I'm shaking my head, desperately trying not to cry. Oliver always hates it when I cry. He grips my face with one hand, squeezing hard. 'What happens in a marriage is private. Do you understand? Nobody's business but ours.'

12

It's the run-up to Christmas and everything is a bit crazy at the moment. We have a busy time ahead with lettings at Perfect Cottages, and Mum is frantically preparing the usual feast which we'll all be expected to attend. Oliver is still in a mood, still sulking over my supposed betrayal of our pact not to start a family yet.

I too am feeling quite low, knowing there is nowhere to turn for help. I'm stuck. Trapped. I've made my bed and must lie in it, as they say. I go over and over in my mind how I can save my marriage and make things better between us. Despite all my agonising, how can I leave him now that I'm pregnant? I'm carrying his child for goodness' sake! I surely have a duty to provide my baby with a father, not to run at the first hint of trouble.

I suggest that we don't mention the baby to anyone yet, that we keep the news to ourselves for a while, which will give us both time to adjust to the idea.

Oliver instantly agrees, so I'm surprised when he suddenly springs it on them. We're all enjoying Christmas lunch, about to tuck into Mum's wonderfully tender turkey with all the trimmings when he puts his arm about me and whispers loudly in my ear, 'Shall we tell them our good news, darling?'

I can't help but start and glance nervously into his face, but he's smiling at me, looking so handsome, so delighted and happy that he almost fools me into believing he's as thrilled as I am. 'If you like,' I say.

Then he turns and beams at all the curious faces around the table, a wicked twinkle in his grey-blue eyes, and makes the announcement. 'I'm delighted to inform you that Carly is pregnant. Would you believe it, we're having a baby. Aren't we clever?'

Mum erupts out of her seat, rushes over to give me a suffocating hug and instantly launches into a lecture on what I must and must not do in order to take proper care of myself. Dad grabs Oliver's hand and starts pumping it hard. 'That's great news, lad! Brilliant!'

Jo-Jo goes all weepy. She's still in that post-baby blues period, having recently delivered baby Molly, weighing a healthy seven pounds six ounces. 'Oh, I'm so pleased for you, love, really I am. Now you'll be a proper family, like us.'

'Well done, darling girl!' Gran says, kissing me on both cheeks.

'Well done, Oliver. That's proved your mettle,' Grandad says, lucid enough to take in what is happening for once. He punches Oliver playfully in the shoulder.

There's general mayhem as everyone congratulates us and the information is relayed to the children. They too get all excited at the prospect of a new baby cousin, although Samantha sulkily protests she doesn't like babies because they're boring, and everyone laughs. Dad opens a bottle of champagne to celebrate and Oliver is looking so pleased with himself it's as if he planned the whole thing.

This is so typical of him. Just when you're expecting the worst, perversely he turns all kind and loving and shows himself at his best. Oliver can be really good fun when he puts his mind to it, a wonderfully generous man. I always feel such gratitude for these moments, for the times when he shows me true love and affection, as he did in Paris. I'm thrilled by the way we've rediscovered each other again in the weeks since and feel a great surge of relief and gratitude that everything is going to be all right, after all.

Deep down, despite all our problems, I still love him. Love isn't something you can turn off like a tap, and I still hope and pray that one day he'll grow up a little and change.

It turns out to be a wonderful family day, one in which Oliver treats me as if I'm made of spun gold. He constantly kisses and hugs me, demonstrating his love and affection, finds me a comfy chair when I move from the table, a cushion for my back. He takes an active interest in the inevitable talk of pregnancy and babies that follows, showing not the slightest sign of boredom over topics such as breast feeding and toilet training. When we finally get up to go he fetches my coat, holds the car door open for me. It's a perfect, happy day.

Later that evening when we're alone, I thank him for dealing with it so well. 'You didn't give the slightest hint about your reservations. I'm so proud of you.'

He barely glances at me. 'One of us has to make some attempt to keep up appearances. I can't let your family guess what a consummate idiot their younger daughter is, that she is incapable of remembering to take a simple pill each day.'

I'm stung by this retort, instantly drenched in misery as I realise that the whole performance of his today was simply that, an act put on for the benefit of appearances. A complete lie. He's put on a show to save face, and to make himself look good.

'How can you do that?' I ask him, appalled.

He grunts, eyes half closed as he stretches out in comfort by the fire, uncaring of my disappointment that the joy he exhibited was all a sham. 'Don't start. Everyone was happy, weren't they? What more do you want? You're never satisfied, woman.'

Yet again he's twisting everything round to lay the blame on me. If I went to Mum and Dad and told them all of this, told them the truth, would they believe me? I very much doubt it.

For once my husband goes to bed alone, and I sit mindlessly watching a late-night movie on TV while I contemplate how long it will be before he starts to show any interest in our child.

'Hon, you seem miles away. I think you've forgotten I'm even here.'

Oliver turned to the sexy blonde beside him to give her a long, lingering kiss, tonguing her delectable mouth and sliding his hand up her silky thighs. They were in his car in a lay-by not far from the motorway turnoff, a dark, secluded spot where they'd be unlikely to be disturbed. 'How could I forget when you're so irresistible, and as pretty as your name?'

Poppy giggled softly and slipped a hand round the bulge in his trousers, giving it an encouraging squeeze, then started wrestling with the buckle on his belt. 'You just don't seem quite yourself tonight, sweetie. Anything I can do to help?' She cast him a wide-eyed, coquettish glance out of green, kitten eyes and Oliver groaned.

'You're doing fine, darling, don't stop. But you're right, I am feeling a bit down tonight. Things are getting worse at home, not better.'

The girl nibbled on his lower lip as she eased her hand inside his pants. She wasn't in the least interested in the sorry tale of his marriage, or that nagging wife of his. Oliver Sheldon was a sexy guy, which was all she cared about. She nursed hopes that he'd eventually divorce the stupid cow and marry her. He was going places was Oliver, and Poppy meant to go with him. 'Poor love. You need taking out of yourself. Time for a bit of fun, sweetie.'

She gave him plenty over the next twenty minutes with her usual degree of generosity and verve. She rode him hard despite the confines of the car and the difficulty of negotiating levers and pedals, and he seemed even more aggressive in his love-making than usual, which delighted her.

Poppy admittedly would have appreciated a little more fore-play, perhaps some romantic chit-chat, but Oliver was rarely interested in small talk, and even less so today. Nor was he wiling to indulge in a repeat performance. He took her fast and hard, then putting her from him brusquely informed the girl that he didn't have time as he had an important appointment to attend to. She was annoyed and whimpered her disappoint-ment, as always when he dismissed her so abruptly. Not that

Oliver took any notice. She wasn't in the least important to him; he never gave her a moment's thought once the business was done. And he always cleverly ensured that they came in separate cars to the layby, for the sake of his reputation.

Poppy knew she should give him up and find someone more her own age, but he fascinated her. She was obsessed by the masculine aura of power which emanated from Oliver Sheldon, as all women were. Yet she was all too aware, in her heart of hearts, that to him she was merely an attractive, conveniently willing, pretty little blonde.

She nibbled at his lower lip, teased him with her pink tongue, hoping to persuade him to change his mind and go for a second round. 'I heard old Don will be retiring soon. Won't that mean you'll get offered a partnership soon, sweetie?'

Oliver preened himself a little. 'One can only hope so. I certainly have every reason to believe that will be the case.'

'You deserve it, you're so clever.'

She tried kissing him some more, but his impatience was growing and he suddenly grasped her firmly by the shoulders and thrust her away. 'Now go, be off with you, there's a good girl. I have more important things to do tonight.'

She kept on talking, still seeking an excuse to keep him there. 'Your wife won't be there, will she?'

'Won't be where?'

'At his retirement do? He's sure to have one.'

'Not if I can avoid it. Go on, go.'

'OK, you will call me?'

'As always, darling.' He opened the door and practically shoved her out of the car. 'See you tomorrow.' Then he fired up the engine and gunned the car in the direction of the motorway. If he put his foot down he could be in Windermere in fifteen minutes.

Emma was surprised to find Oliver on her doorstep at nine in the evening, and instantly concerned. 'Is something wrong? Is Carly ill?'

'No. No, not ill exactly, but I would just like a quick word if you've got a minute.'

She invited him in, but he declined. 'This won't take long.' Oliver had no wish to have that partner of hers earwigging in on their conversation, nor to spend a moment longer than necessary in this poky little flat. He was content to remain in the hall.

For some reason Emma couldn't explain she'd never taken to Oliver Sheldon. Far too full of himself. Arrogant and priggish. All that keeping tabs on Carly, the clock-watching whenever she went out for the evening, the suggestion she should give up her car. He was manipulative, like the time he insisted she be excused evening work because they were newly married, bullying Emma into agreeing to his terms. And then there was the mystery of why Carly had found it necessary to use that key in the middle of the night, but had then run back to him. She really couldn't understand what her friend saw in him. Now Emma casually folded her arms and waited for him to explain the reason for his visit.

'The fact is, I'm not sure if she's told you yet, but Carly is pregnant.'

Emma was stunned, yet managed not to show it. 'Well, that's a surprise. I assume congratulations are in order?'

Oliver manufactured a proud smile. 'We're both delighted, naturally. Carly is particularly thrilled as she adores kids. The problem is, she realises it's going to rather screw things up career-wise.'

Emma frowned. 'I don't see why it should. I'm sure we can work round it.'

'Oh, I know it should be quite straightforward in this day and age, nannies and flexible working hours and such. The thing is, Carly doesn't want to go down that road. She was quite happy to have this holiday letting agency to occupy her when she was free and single, but it's become far more demanding than she'd expected. It's been difficult for her, particularly in recent months, to keep up with the work level and the responsibility, not least the long unsocial hours. Now all she really wants is to stay home with the child and be a full-time mother.'

'Goodness, that's the last thing I expected. Look, this has come as a bit of a shock actually. I really do need her. I'm not sure how I could cope on my own.'

Oliver nodded sympathetically. 'I'm sure it won't be easy. I'm in business myself, about to accept a partnership in a large firm actually, so I understand perfectly. That's why I wanted to give you as much warning as possible. Not spring it on you at the last moment that she's leaving.'

'Leaving?'

'As she will most certainly wish to do, once the baby is born.'

Emma let out a heavy sigh. 'I see. Well, that's very thoughtful of you, Oliver. I appreciate your telling me so soon.'

He smiled. 'I wanted to give you as much time as possible to start looking around for a replacement partner. In return, I would appreciate it if you could tactfully inform Carly that you really don't need her any more. You could let her off the hook, as it were, without her even needing to embarrass herself by asking.'

'Embarrass herself?'

'You know how sensitive and shy she is. She hates to be a nuisance or bother to anyone. And she really does want rid of all of this. I'm sorry to say it but Perfect Cottages has put her under enormous pressure lately. I've been really quite worried about her. She hasn't been looking at all well recently, has she?'

'No,' Emma conceded. 'No, she hasn't been quite herself.'

'Too stressed, and now with the baby coming . . .' He held out his hands in a helpless gesture. 'You know how it is. First-time mum and all that. She'd be miserable if she was obliged to hand over child care to some stranger.'

'I certainly don't want Carly to be miserable,' Emma remarked, her voice tight with disappointment. 'Please tell me, why are *you* saying all this to me, and not Carly herself?'

Oliver looked suitably contrite. 'You know how she is, so

sweet and loyal that she finds it difficult to tell you to your face that she wants out. She'd kill me if she ever found out I'd spoken to you. I'm trusting you to keep schtum on the subject. I would just like you to try to make it as easy as possible for her to ease her way out of the business without any sense of guilt. The last thing I want is for her to be upset, which might harm the baby. I hope you understand, and that this conversation can remain strictly private, just between ourselves?'

'Yes, of course.' Emma tried to decide whether she was being manipulated or not.

'I'm so sorry to be the bearer of bad news.' He sounded so genuinely apologetic that she softened a little and smiled.

'It's good news really, a baby for Carly. And of course she must be allowed to enjoy being a full-time mum, if that's what she wants. I'll work something out. Thanks for being so frank and honest with me, Oliver, and for giving me time to sort something out before we get really busy.'

'No problem.'

After he'd gone, Emma closed the door with a thoughtful frown and went to join Glen on the sofa.

'What was all that about?' he asked.

She briefly related what Oliver had told her.

'Heavens, that's a bit of a shaker, isn't it? No wonder you look sad and unhappy.'

'I don't really understand. Carly never gave any indication to me that she would be the sort to turn into a housefrau, the professional stay-at-home mother. But there it is, and I have to accept it. I just wish she'd felt able to tell me herself. It's made me realise that you really don't know people at all, do you?'

Outside, in the car park, Oliver climbed into his car and drove away with a smile on his face. He was feeling really rather pleased with himself, but then he generally found a way to turn a situation to his advantage. Getting rid of Perfect bloody Cottages and having Carly permanently at home, all to himself, was really not a bad idea at all. Quite a pleasing notion, in point of fact.

★　　★　　★

I'm suffering badly from morning sickness, which apparently is supposed to ease after three months, but doesn't appear to be doing so in my case. It's rather like suffering from sea-sickness all the time and food has become a bit of a problem. I ask Jo-Jo about this and she recommends that I eat little and often, never let my stomach get empty or too full.

My sister is naturally supportive over all the issues surrounding pregnancy, birth, and child rearing. I suppose I shouldn't be surprised since she now has four children of her own. I go round to see her quite often and we chat and have a good laugh together. The new baby seems to be growing at a phenomenal rate and I watch with interest, trying to pick up a few tips. Jo-Jo offers me lots of helpful advice and we seem to grow a little closer.

Relations between Oliver and myself have also improved in recent weeks, better than I could hope for. He still goes out a good deal but when he is home he's making much more effort. For once, he really seems to be trying, is constantly fussing over me and making me put my feet up, fetching me cups of tea, even apologising profusely for being so grumpy and bad tempered when he first heard the news.

'I was just scared,' he admits, caressing my still flat stomach. 'But now I'm thrilled and proud. I've a feeling that having a baby could all turn out for the best.'

I'm so relieved to hear him say this that I hug him. 'Thank you, thank you. Everything will be fine, you'll see. I still have to tell Emma yet, but before I do, I need to decide how much time I intend to take off once the baby is born. I can't see it being more than a month or two,' I explain. 'Three at most. It wouldn't be fair to take any more time off than is absolutely necessary. Perfect Cottages gets very busy with bookings in the Spring, and then it's absolutely mad come summer. I'll mess Emma up enough this coming season, just by giving birth. But I don't see why I can't go in fairly soon afterwards, by late summer, if only for a few days a week, taking baby with me if necessary.'

He laughs softly, patient affection in his blue-grey eyes.

'Goodness, you'll be planning to return to your job from the maternity ward next. I know you're always banging on about equality and a woman's right to work as much as she pleases, but isn't that carrying things a bit far?'

'Oliver, I'd be climbing the walls with boredom if I were stuck in the house day after day.'

He laughs. 'I doubt it, not with a young baby to look after. Obviously I'd love to see you have time to relax and enjoy the baby instead of working yourself into the ground, but it's up to you. I've heard you complain enough already about how lonely and isolated you get at times. I wouldn't dream of putting any pressure on you. What do I know, I'm only a mere male? I know nothing about babies.'

He sounds so sweet and understanding, so tolerant of my indecision that I've no wish for this to devolve into another row. And it's so generous of him not to put any pressure on me. I smile and confess that it would indeed be pleasant to have a few months at home with the new baby, were it possible. 'But I can't see how Emma could cope without me. Besides, we need the money. Perfect Cottages is finally making a profit, albeit a small one, and you still haven't got that partnership yet.'

His face darkens and I realise I've put my foot in it, yet again. It's very hard to have a reasonable, adult conversation with Oliver without him taking offence. 'Not that you won't get one soon, I'm sure,' I hasten to add, smiling sweetly.

'I believe a partnership is on the cards. The boss hinted as much only the other day,' he assures me, and continues with surprising patience and diplomacy. 'Maybe when it does come through, you'll give serious consideration to giving up work completely and devote yourself entirely to being a wife and mother. If you wish. If that's what you decide you want, darling. It's entirely up to you.'

He's smiling, looking so happy and sounding so reasonable and agreeable that I don't want to shatter this blissful moment of unity by protesting further that I never saw myself as a stay-at-home mum. Thrilled as I am to be having a baby, I'm keen to get back to normal just as soon as I can fix up reliable child care. 'I shall certainly consider it,' I tactfully agree. 'I may well decide to stay at home for a while. Either way, I'm sure we can make it work, and you know that I love you very much, Oliver.'

'And I love you, darling. So you must concentrate on looking after my son and don't worry about a thing.' He pats my tummy with a gentle hand and I don't object to his assumption that it will be a boy because I'm so thrilled he's referred to the baby with such tenderness. 'Now I have to go out, darling. The boss wants me to go over some figures with him. Do you need anything before I go?'

I shake my head and pick up my book with a smile. This is all going so much better than I'd hoped.

I've been late in to work on a few occasions over recent weeks, needing to take the odd day off occasionally because I felt so unwell. Because it's so unusual for me to be ill, I feel obliged to come clean and finally I confess to Emma about the pregnancy. Her reaction is oddly low key. 'Really? How lovely, a baby. Are you pleased? Are you happy about it? Is Oliver?'

'Yes, yes and yes,' I cheerfully respond. 'Well, he was once he'd got over the initial shock.' Despite her casual response, I suspect that Emma isn't exactly overjoyed by the news.

'We must make proper arrangements for you to take maternity leave,' she says brightly and I instantly reassure her that I intend this baby to make as little difference as possible to our partnership.

'I may have trouble getting around the S-bend once my bump gets too big, so maybe I could take over more of the office duties in the later months. We could perhaps afford to employ a cleaner, part-time at least, by then. After the baby is born I shall of course make every effort to come back to work as soon as possible, if only part-time. I wouldn't dream of leaving you in the lurch.'

We start to talk practicalities and I think I've succeeded in proving to her that I can still cope, baby or not, when she suddenly says, 'Look, you really needn't concern yourself about me. I can easily find someone to replace you, Carly.'

I blink at her, startled by this remark. 'Oh, could you?'

'Of course. In fact I already have someone in mind who'd jump at the chance. Why don't we agree that you take as much time off as you need. Put your feet up, eat chocolate, do whatever pregnant women do, and then enjoy a long sabbatical being a full-time mum. I'll get some temporary relief to stand in for you. Then if, and when, you decide to sell out, I have someone in the wings, ready and waiting.'

I'm shocked and dismayed by this idea. It's almost as if she's eager to take advantage of my pregnancy, keen to be rid of me. I quickly demur. 'I'd rather not sell out, thanks all the same. I want to hold on to my stake in the business, and keep on working for as long as I can. I'm sure I can keep going till I'm at least six months gone, maybe seven.'

'That's up to you, of course, so long as you feel well enough. Then you stay home with Junior for as long as you like, and we'll review the situation say, twelve months after that?'

'Oh!' I'm rather stunned by this suggestion. 'Well, I rather thought I would be coming back rather sooner than that . . .'

Emma smiles at me. 'Why should you? I can manage perfectly well without you. There's really no need for you to worry. As I say, I've already got someone lined up.'

This conversation is not going at all as I'd hoped, and I've got this slightly sick feeling inside, which has nothing at all to do with my pregnancy. 'Well, that all sounds very . . . very organised and efficient.'

'I just want to make things as easy for you as possible, and for myself too of course,' Emma says with a stiff little smile. 'At least I'd know where I was, wouldn't I? I'd have the regular, full-time support I need.'

'Yes, I suppose you would.'

'And of course you can draw maternity pay, if you need it. I'm sure the business can find the money somehow.'

'There's really no need to worry about that,' I foolishly say. 'It's a relatively new business. You can't afford to pay a replacement and maternity pay as well. I'm sure I can cope. Anyway, we can sort the money out later, when we make some long-term decisions, as you suggest. I don't want to put you under any unnecessary strain.'

'Fine, that's settled then.'

Even as I agree that her plans sound sensible, I'm hurt that she seems so eager to be rid of me, and by her cool dismissal of our friendship and business partnership. Yet privately I acknowledge that relations between us have been rather less warm since her caustic remarks about Oliver. And my actually using that key she gave me, hasn't helped. She seems to expect me to reveal all, and I simply can't. There are some secrets too shameful to be shared. I cannot allow anyone to pry too closely into my affairs. That would be far too dangerous and degrading, particularly now with a baby on the way.

As if reading my thoughts Emma looks at me keenly as she quietly enquires, 'You are happy with all of this, Carly, aren't you? Things are OK now between you and Oliver?'

'Why wouldn't they be?' I brightly respond. 'Admittedly, it was all a bit unplanned, but Oliver is being so sweet about it, making every effort to regard the baby as a new beginning for us both.'

'That's good. Excellent! We certainly don't want things to go wrong for you, do we? Although you've still got that key I gave you, don't forget, should you ever need to use it again.'

'I'm sure I won't. You can have it back if you wish.'

'No, it's always useful for a friend to hold a key, not least if I ever lock myself out.' Emma smiles at her own joke, hugs me warmly then the telephone rings and it's business as usual. For now, at least. But I can't help worrying about how I seem to be losing everything: my independence, my friends, and now my job, which is a bitter blow and leaves me feeling more isolated than ever.

13

I see even less of Oliver while I'm pregnant, and never think to question this too closely. To be honest I'm finding the evenings he's out something of a relief, a time when I'm free to relax, to read and do my own thing without being constantly in fear of saying the wrong thing and upsetting him.

Mum's trying to teach me to knit, although I'll never be as good as she is. She can produce a jumper in a week, sitting behind the counter knitting like mad between customers. One Saturday afternoon on a lovely sunny spring day, with Oliver off playing golf, we're sitting together in the back garden as she demonstrates the intricacies of knit and pearl, increase and decrease. She's very patient with me even though she spends most of her time picking up dropped stitches and taking back what I've already knitted. I'm not too concerned as I'm sure she'll keep this baby well supplied with matinee jackets and bootees.

As a keen gardener passionate about her rose trees, Mum is also urging me to do something about my garden, although perhaps garden is too grand a word as this space behind the house is little more than a stretch of lawn which Oliver keeps forgetting to cut. A wilderness, no less.

Perhaps to get her off the subject of my horticultural failings, as well as resolve the issue which daily torments me, I pretend I've read something in the *Daily Mail* and make a few carefully worded, and very general remarks on the question of violence in marriage.

I can't quite find the courage to come right out into the open and tell her the truth. For one thing she'd never believe me as she absolutely adores Oliver, and sees no wrong in him. I'd have my work cut out to convince her. Nevertheless, a part of me feels I should try.

We get on well enough, I suppose, despite her grumbles and lectures. I've always been more of a daddy's girl, although that brings its own problems. Dad is so proud of me I can't bear to let him down. I'm convinced Mum won't understand, that she'll blame me. She would be sure to ask a whole lot of difficult questions such as why I didn't ever mention this before? Why didn't I leave right away? How can I possibly claim to still love him? She would never be able to comprehend the fear I have that I couldn't cope without him, that my strength and belief in myself has gradually seeped away, leaving me drained and exhausted. I now doubt my own ability to deal with anything properly, feeling sometimes as if I've lost my identity.

I'm also afraid of upsetting her, of course. Most of all, I dread having to admit that my dream of a happy marriage is dead. The whole sorry mess would then be on public view and Oliver would be furious, so angry I dread to think what he might do.

So I carefully circumvent the personal by remaining in the general. I idly comment that living with a violent man must make a woman feel trapped, as well as destroying her self-esteem. 'What would be the right way for her to deal with such a situation?' I ask, as casually as I am able.

With absolutely no experience of such things, and not picking up on the hidden meaning beneath my words, nor even noticing my tension, she comes out with the usual comment that she really cannot understand why a woman would put up with such treatment. I listen horrified to my own mother making such outrageous remarks as, 'It takes two, you know. Some women must ask for it or provoke him in some way,' and 'the silly woman must have known what she was letting herself in for when she married him'. I shudder.

How easy it is to pass judgement when you're not emotionally involved.

I concentrate on my stitches, trying not to let her see that my hands are trembling. Push in the needle, wrap the wool round, slip it over and off. Nope, lost that one too. She reaches over and patiently puts it right. Picking up dropped stitches is easy by comparison with mending a marriage.

'And what if she didn't?' I ask, as I watch her sort out the muddle. 'What if his behaviour came as a complete shock to her, and she still wants to save her marriage, still loves him?'

Knitting furiously, my mother snorts her derision but doesn't trouble to answer my question. 'I put it all down to sex. It turns them on, women like that. I wouldn't put up with it. I'd walk out.'

I feel slightly sick hearing my own mother take this clichéd attitude. It's so easy to make such pronouncements when you're not the one facing the possibility of physical abuse. I try again. 'But what if she can't walk out? What if she tried that once and her brutal husband brought her back, threatened to hurt her badly if she ever tried again?'

My pint-sized mother laughs as if I've made a joke. 'I'd give him what for, that's what I'd do. A taste of his own medicine. What happened to the woman in the article you read? Did she divorce him?'

'I'm not sure,' I say, floundering, yet determined to plough on now that I've got this far. 'Do you think violent behaviour is some kind of mental sickness? Could a doctor help?'

She considers me with a frown. 'How would I know? Anyway, why get yourself worked up over some woman in the paper? You mustn't dwell on morbid subjects, not while you're pregnant, love. Thank your lucky stars Oliver is such a lovely man. He'd never lay a finger on you, or that child.'

I go back to discussing the possibility of creating a rose bed.

The sickness has finally passed and I'm having a fairly easy pregnancy. I feel marvellous now, absolutely bursting with energy. Blooming, as they say. Oliver's parents pop over to see me occasionally, laying down fussy little rules about what I should and shouldn't do, how I mustn't stand too long, stretch up too high, or lift anything heavy. I listen to all their advice, smile and settle for following my own common sense. They are not happy that I'm still going in to work every day, neither is Oliver, who grumbles and groans the whole time about it.

'Why shouldn't I work? I feel fine,' I tell him. 'Stop fussing. It's only for a few more weeks then I'll be house-bound, stuck indoors like a beached whale.' I smile at my own silly joke but the prospect alarms me. I've tried on several occasions to resurrect the subject with Emma but she absolutely refuses to discuss the matter.

'We can talk it all through later, once Junior has arrived and made his presence felt. In the meantime we mustn't upset you, or the baby. You're not to worry about a thing, Carly. We're coping fine.'

There's a middle-aged woman called Wanda already coming in three days a week to learn the ropes, and I'm beginning to feel side lined in my own agency.

My condition has ceased to be a novelty to Oliver. He's thoroughly bored with attempting to take an interest in our constant chatter about babies. When Jo-Jo pops round with Molly he swiftly retreats to his office. Not that I mind. I'm happy to sit and indulge in baby-talk with my sister, and watch in adoration as her latest offspring lies on the rug and kicks her bare legs with great exuberance and much happy gurgling. It's good that we have something in common at last.

'Is he attending the fathers' ante-natal classes?' she asks, and I laugh and shake my head.

'Never mind, I'm sure he'll fall in love with baby the minute she's born.'

'It's a boy, apparently,' I say.

'Did they tell you that? You never mentioned it.'

'No, I didn't want them to tell me what sex it is, but Oliver is quite certain.'

'Ah, well, let's hope he's not disappointed.'

I sincerely hope so too as his good humour and patience is

rapidly evaporating. I'm not unduly surprised, far too used to his volatile nature by now to do anything other than philosophically accept this change of mood, with as much good grace as I can muster. Even when I was being sick in a morning he still expected me to cook his breakfast, which I did without complaint, and then went and threw up in the bathroom sink afterwards.

At least that dreadful nausea is over with now but he still expects his routine to continue unchanged, despite my increasing bulk and the difficulties I find in keeping on top of everything. He seems to be getting increasingly fussy, back to running his finger over window ledges and lecturing me about making savings by always cooking from fresh. I listen and agree with him, then pop something in the microwave as I have neither the time nor the energy to slave away over a hot stove these days. I make very sure though that I wrap the packaging in newspaper and dispose of it carefully where he won't find it.

He constantly asks how much things cost and I lie about that too. Far easier than face another row or listen to him pontificating about how kitchen towels might be cheaper at a different supermarket, if I took the trouble to look. I don't argue, or tell him that I've no time for such things, or he'll make me give up work right away, and I'm anxious to keep going for as long as I can.

He has long periods when he sulks and moans endlessly about the responsibility that a family imposes, and the cost of it all as we check out the price of prams and cots and baby buggies. He frequently goes on about how a baby will tie us down and spoil our freedom. Since he's the only one who seems to have any freedom, the point seems largely academic. I don't argue with him on that subject either. It's far wiser to say nothing.

The reality is, he's quite his old self again, back to criticising and bullying and making me feel small and stupid. Worse, the boundaries of how far he's prepared to go to keep me in line by using physical violence are changing. Perhaps it has dawned on him that he can't punch and kick me quite as he used to, because of the baby. Instead, he moves on to a more calculated pain.

It all begins one afternoon when Emma sends me home early because I'm feeling pretty sick again. Strange how I still get these episodes of nausea from time to time. The doctor tells me it's anxiety and I should learn to relax. I'm bored so I wander into Oliver's office, power up his computer and do a bit of surfing, carefully keeping off the women's refuge sites I visited previously. I do some idle browsing, look up sites listing baby names and try them out to see which I might like. Belinda Sheldon. Rosie. David. I read blogs about babies and pregnancy, visit sites offering help and advice on parenting, and feel a huge ache inside that some of the joy which should be present at this momentous time in my life is missing.

I finish off with a game of Solitaire and then shut down, and think no more about it as I go to make our evening meal.

Oliver comes to me as I'm sitting that evening with my feet up, still struggling with my piece of knitting. I'm thinking that I might manage to actually finish this matinee jacket by the time my child is starting school.

He leans over my chair, smiles at me as he presses one finger to my lips, making it plain that I mustn't make a sound. Then he takes the wool and needles out of my hands, grasps my arm, and twists the skin in opposite directions, a Chinese burn he calls it.

A scream starts somewhere in the back of my throat but again he presses one finger against my mouth, effectively silencing me. 'Ssh,' he says. 'Not a sound. We don't want the neighbours to hear, do we?'

I stare at him wild eyed, almost pass out with the pain, and I'm biting so hard on my lower lip I can taste blood.

'You've been in my office again, haven't you? I obviously didn't make it clear enough the last time. You don't touch anything of mine, right? Understand? You don't ever go into my office.' He stops what he is doing so that I can answer.

'I – I understand, Oliver. I'm sorry!' My voice cracks in a throat raw with pain.

'Just do as you're fucking told.' Then he walks away, quietly closing the door after him.

This is a trick he repeats frequently over the coming weeks whenever he's in one of his black moods, or wishing to reinforce his control over me for some reason. Keeping me in line, he calls it.

'Why are you doing this?' I'll cry, begging him to stop. 'Why are you so cold and so calm?'

'But you say you don't like me to get angry,' he taunts me.

He'll yank my arm up my back till I collapse and fall to my knees, or he'll pull back each finger as far as it will go, till I'm begging him to stop, terrified it might break at any moment. Of course, he makes sure that it doesn't break. The visit from the police, busybody neighbours, particularly the two old ladies in our drive, has had some effect upon him. And Oliver has no wish to answer awkward questions in Casualty or at the doctor's surgery.

Throughout this carefully calculated torture I'm not allowed to cry out or make a sound. Nor does he shout or rail at me. He carries out these peevish, sadistic acts in complete silence, sometimes with a smirk of pure pleasure on his face.

He seems to have learned new tricks, and it's absolutely terrifying.

I'm eight months gone and I've finally given up work. Summer is almost upon us and the super-efficient Wanda now sits at my desk, dealing with my mail and regularly updating the website. She's the one who dashes out to clean and prepare the cottages and apartments for our guests, answers their telephone queries and checks on them to make sure all is well. The timing of this baby is just about as bad as it could be, but there's nothing I can do about it. I'm still hoping that by late summer or early autumn, long before the bookings start coming in for next season, I'll be ready and able to return to work, albeit with a baby in tow.

Oliver has at last been given the partnership as one of the other partners is taking early retirement. The firm is planning to hold a dinner dance before they all go away for their summer break, a sort of leaving party for old Don, to which all wives and girlfriends are invited. Except me, apparently. I found the invitation quite by chance among Oliver's cufflinks in his chest of drawers, but he doesn't think I should attend. Today's argument is about why he refuses to take me.

'For God's sake, you're pregnant! You've nothing decent to wear for a start, and it certainly isn't worth buying anything new, now you're so far gone.'

'That's not a problem. I can easily make myself something.'

'Don't be ridiculous,' he says. 'You'd need a bell tent,' and he storms out, back to the office, his football match or his quiz league, or whatever he has planned for this evening. I sit and morosely flick through my latest library book, feeling fat and really quite tearful with disappointment, then I pick up the phone to speak to my sister.

Say what you like about Jo-Jo, she's generally there for me in a crisis.

Once I stop crying long enough to properly explain my problem, she's all decisive and positive. 'Just let me get this lot to bed and I'll be round.'

She brings with her an out-moded blue chiffon dress with a long full skirt. She cuts off the bodice and lets out the gathers which she binds with a dark blue velvet sash that finishes in a trailing bow at the back.

The alterations are soon done and I try it on.

She teams the skirt with a lovely stretchy, sparkly, off-the-shoulder black top, and I have to say it looks fantastic. I've never been a skinny-minnie but my breasts are even fuller than normal, and draw the eye nicely away from the bump beneath.

Even Oliver, when he sees it later, admits I look good, but still isn't keen on my going, insisting it'll be too much for me.

'You certainly couldn't dance,' he tells me.

'Why couldn't I? I could waddle around the dance floor to the slow numbers at least, and I can still enjoy the dinner.'

'What if you went into labour?'

I can't help but laugh. 'We'd call the ambulance. Anyway, I'm weeks off yet. And if I were to go into premature labour, it would be even more frightening if I were on my own at home.' I don't remind him that I so often am these days.

'I still don't think it's a good idea.'

'Why?'

'I just don't. Pregnant women shouldn't go to dinner dances. I don't want you making an exhibition of yourself.'

I look at him keenly. 'You aren't embarrassed, are you, because I'm eight months gone?' His ears turn bright red and I laugh and call him a Victorian fuddy-duddy, trying to tease him out of his ill humour. I'm absolutely determined to go. I've been stuck in this house for weeks now, and feel the need for some fun.

The dinner dance is indeed great fun and I'm made a great fuss of by Oliver's colleagues. One of them tells me he informed them I wasn't well enough to attend. I laugh at this, assuring them all that I'm having a marvellous pregnancy, absolutely bursting with hormones and energy. Afterwards, I gently tease Oliver for being so old fashioned in his attitude.

I never think to question that there might be another reason altogether why he didn't want me to be there.

The dinner is delicious and the guys all dance attendance on me, fetching me lemonade and nibbles, telling me I look gorgeous. And I'm never without a partner as they take it in turns to perambulate me gently round the floor.

Tony and Jane are there too, of course, and there's an awkward moment as we engage in rather stilted conversation, striving to be polite at least. I haven't seen Jane since the time I called at her house and she told me Tony and Oliver weren't as friendly as they used to be, seeming to think this was because we'd moved into a new house in a posh neighbourhood.

'You never did call in for that coffee,' I remind her.

'No, I didn't, did I?' And taking Tony's hand, she drags him on to the dance floor.

'Goodness,' I say to Oliver. 'What did we ever do to offend those two?'

'God knows!'

It's rather a smart hotel and I go to the Ladies powder room for a rest and to freshen up. I'm sitting in a comfy chair taking a breather when Jane breezes in.

I smile, politely admire her dress while she pointedly assesses my condition.

'Not long to go then?'

'No, could arrive at any moment, in fact,' I cheerfully inform her.

'And Oliver is pleased, is he?'

I smile tightly and assure her that he is. She turns towards the door as a pretty young girl enters. 'Ah, Carly, meet Poppy. She works in the same office as Tony and Oliver. Poppy, this is Carly, Oliver's wife.'

'Pleased to meet you.' I politely hold out my hand but she ignores it, a slightly dazed expression on her face. Not the brightest star in the universe, obviously, I think. I laughingly ask if my husband is a tyrant to work for, but she still looks lost for words. Shy perhaps, so I try again.

'Does he insist you keep everything very tidy?'

'Oh, yes,' she blurts out, and then starts talking very fast. 'Every paper-clip and pen must be in its proper place, the filing done right away, phone calls recorded. He's incredibly picky. You've got to get everything just right or he's on to you.' Her smile instantly fades as she suddenly remembers that she's speaking to her boss's wife. 'But that's only fair, I suppose. It's a very busy office with some quite important clients.'

Jane seems to have vanished but the girl watches me for a moment as I push off my shoes and wiggle my aching toes.

'You look all in,' she says, then adds, rather cautiously, 'he

never mentioned you were pregnant. At least, we only heard
about it a few days ago,' she acknowledged. 'When he said that
you were coming tonight after all.'

I laugh as I stroke my swollen bump. 'It was a last-minute
decision. Oh dear, and there was me hoping to disguise my
pregnancy in this lovely outfit my sister made for me.'

She looks at me with a puzzled frown. 'Is that what you've
been trying to do?'

'I'm joking.'

'Oh, I see.' She gives an embarrassed little laugh.

Silly girl, I think. Definitely one sandwich short of a picnic.
She must drive Oliver to distraction. He hates stupid females.

'I like your outfit,' she says, studying me more closely. 'You
look very . . . very elegant. Oliver never said how lovely you
were. Your hair is gorgeous, so thick and beautifully cut. I like
the colour too. I wish I was a natural blonde.'

I smile in astonishment. 'How very kind of you to say so.
I'm flattered. Oliver obviously works with some lovely people.
This evening has been a real morale booster for me. Generally
nobody looks twice at a pregnant woman. I feel a complete
frump most of the time. I can't tell you what a relief it will be
to be free of this bump.'

'I've got to go,' she says, and suddenly dashes off in her
clumpy wedges and too-short skirt. I chuckle softly to myself.
Nice girl, I think, if a bit dim, and clearly overwhelmed by
meeting her boss's wife. And it would seem that Oliver is every
bit as fussy in the office as he is at home. An absolute tyrant
to work for, every paper-clip must be accounted for. Why am
I not surprised? I can't help but laugh. As I head back to the
dance floor I wonder vaguely what happened to Jane, but
mentally shrug the problem away. She obviously wasn't for
hanging around for a girly chat.

I enjoy the dance enormously, have a wonderful evening
despite my sorrow over the loss of this old friendship, and revel
in this small taste of freedom. It's been wonderful to get out
of the house and enjoy the music and laughter, to listen to

office gossip even if most of it does go right over my head. I'm disappointed when Oliver decides we should leave early. He collects my coat and firmly insists it's long past time I should be in bed.

'Don't be a stranger,' the guys from the office call out as we leave.

'Wasn't that fun?' I say.

'You certainly seemed to enjoy yourself,' he replies.

It all starts to go wrong the minute we arrive home.

We've been in the house barely five minutes when he starts accusing me of flirting with his colleagues.

I can't help but laugh. 'Don't be silly, how can a pregnant woman flirt? Your friends would have more success with a beach ball.'

'You certainly seemed to be enjoying their attention.'

'Maybe that's because I don't get much of that from you these days. You're rarely ever home.'

'Oh, so it's my fault now, is it?'

'For goodness' sake, Oliver, they were just being friendly.'

'You made a complete fool of me.'

'How?' I blink up at him, surprised, as I thankfully slip off my shoes. 'I don't understand.'

'You told everyone you've been perfectly well all through your pregnancy when I'd already said you'd been sick. You made me out to be a liar.'

'No, I didn't, don't be silly. I just explained that I was mainly sick at the beginning, during the first few months, and only occasionally now. I felt fine tonight. Absolutely marvellous. Look, we've had a lovely evening, let's not spoil it with a row. It's late and I'm tired and I really can't take your getting angry with me tonight.' Shoes in hand, I pad off upstairs to bed.

I realise at once that I've made a bad mistake. Oliver hates it when I walk away from him, or ask him not to get angry. He's always the one who must decide when an argument is over, so he follows me, still ranting on about how I've no consideration for his feelings.

'It's *you* who makes me angry,' he shouts. 'You try my patience to the limit, you do really. I think you enjoy making me look bad.'

'Don't, Oliver, please.' I slip out of the long skirt and sparkly black top, thinking I'll be able to tell Jo-Jo tomorrow that the outfit was a huge success, very much admired. She'll be pleased about that, never having been a wallflower herself, pregnant or not.

Oliver snatches up the skirt and flings it across the room. 'And you looked utterly stupid waddling round the dance floor in that home-made frock.'

I can feel the traitorous tears starting to form at the back of my eyes. 'Why do you always have to spoil things by picking on me? We've had a lovely evening, everyone admired the outfit and nobody was in the least embarrassed by my bump. Nobody except you, that is.'

'And I don't count, I suppose.'

'Oh, for goodness' sake, Oliver, I'm not listening to any more of this. I'm exhausted. Even that silly little girl, what was she called, Poppy, thought my outfit looked elegant. And she seemed to think you should have mentioned what a lovely wife you had,' I teasingly remark as I slip into my dressing gown and head for the bathroom.

Oliver stands glowering for a second then strides after me. I automatically flinch away from him, realising he's completely flipped, yet again.

'Why won't you ever listen to me?' he spits at me, his face inches from mine, at his most intimidating. 'Why are you so bloody stubborn? I told you not to flaming well come to the bloody dinner dance.'

An icy shiver crawls down my spine but I turn away, determined to say nothing more. What is the point?

I've reached the top of the stairs on my way across the landing when he suddenly lunges at me and gives me a hefty shove.

To my horror I lose my balance and start to fall backwards. I cry out, try to grab hold of the banister rail but miss it completely. 'Oliver,' I shout. Then I'm rolling and bumping to the bottom of the stairs, my hands clutched about my swollen belly.

14

I've landed with a heavy thud, all the wind knocked out of my body. Oliver is still standing at the stop of the stairs, making no move to come and help. I'm so terrified I might have hurt my baby that I lie there for a long time before I find the courage to roll over on to all fours and slowly get to my feet. By then there's no sign of him. I assume he's gone to bed.

I stagger into the kitchen, shaking with shock, and make myself a mug of hot chocolate. The next few hours are an absolute agony as I wait to feel my baby move again. Even when it does, I remain fearful for its safety.

Next morning I suggest I go to the hospital for a check-up but Oliver won't hear of it. I can see why he's against the idea. It would mean difficult questions and explanations over how this 'accident' occurred.

'We don't want anyone poking their noses in our affairs. Anyway, you're making a big fuss over nothing. The baby will be fine,' he insists. 'Don't they swim about in liquid, or something? It was all your own fault. You would never have fallen if you hadn't started an argument at the top of the stairs.'

I stifle a gasp and try to work out how I could possibly have avoided falling when he shoved me so hard, but confine myself to gently pointing out that I didn't start the argument, he did.

He lifts his hands in a gesture of despair. 'For goodness' sake, it was only a little shove, meant to calm you down.'

'I was perfectly calm. Quite tired, if you remember, and I did ask you not to get angry.'

'I wouldn't ever need to get angry, would I, if you weren't so bloody obstinate? You're always so ready to make me look a complete idiot in front of my colleagues. I surely deserve some respect in public. You ask for it, you do really.'

When he finally goes off to the office, I crawl back into bed and curl up in misery, worrying about my baby.

I must have fallen asleep because I'm woken by a voice downstairs in the kitchen. 'Hello, is anyone in? Carly?'

I realise it's Dad. It's not often he calls but I'm always glad to see him when he does. I quickly struggle out of bed, not wanting any awkward questions or have him start fussing over me, but I can hear his light quick tread on the stairs.

'Are you up there, love?'

'I'm coming,' I call. 'Put the kettle on, I'll be down in a minute.'

'Right.'

I hear him go off into the kitchen while I quickly dress, run a brush through my hair then join him in time to accept the steaming mug of tea he puts into my hand.

'What's wrong, love? Aren't you feeling well?'

I laugh and try to make light of it. 'We went to that dinner dance last night, and I'm afraid I overslept.'

'Good for you. I should think Oliver encouraged you to sleep in, didn't he? Did you overdo it a bit, love? Not drunk, I hope.'

'Didn't touch a drop. Come into the lounge.'

'Not on them white sofas, no,' he demurs. 'I'm happier here, thanks.'

We sit at the kitchen table, chatting contentedly as we sip our tea.

'I had a great time last night,' I tell him, nervously wondering what Dad's reaction would be if I revealed what took place after the dance. I have this slight ache in my back and I'm aware that both knees are badly bruised as a result of my fall. I keep them tucked under the table out of sight so he doesn't notice as I surreptitiously rub them from time to time. Though maybe I should tell him. Maybe this is the moment to reveal all. 'It was good to meet Oliver's work colleagues at last, even though I had a job persuading him to take me.' I'm tentatively trying to lead up to it slowly, but without much success as again he interrupts.

'Too over-protective, I suppose. I was a bit that way with your mum when she was carrying Jo-Jo, though I wasn't quite so strung up the second time.'

'Oliver can be over-protective at times,' I agree, 'but not always. He hates it if I say the wrong thing in front of his colleagues. He's not protective then, he just feels insulted.'

Dad looks at me with a considering frown, then laughs. 'He's a man, full of pride and with a man's fragile ego. We all have this grand image of ourselves as the big provider, the fount of all wisdom, particularly at work in front of our mates. You mam says I'm just the same.'

I smile and sip my tea. My mind is whirling and I can't think how best to deal with this. Dad is so happy for me, so proud. I'm still his little girl and the last thing I want to do is upset him. Or have him upset Oliver.

'Apart from the effects of a late night, how you are feeling in yourself, Princess? You do look at bit tired. Don't overdo it now.'

'I won't. Don't worry. Anyway, you can't call me that silly name now I'm an old married woman.'

He looks affronted. 'I can and I will. You'll always be my princess.'

'Didn't you tell me that one day I'd find my knight in shining armour, my Prince Charming?'

'And so you did, love, I'm pleased to say.' Dad glances about him at my beautiful designer kitchen with its white-painted cupboards and stainless-steel equipment. The very best of everything. 'You've done very nicely for yourself.'

'I'm not talking about material things,' I say. 'All parents seem to promise their daughters a fairy-tale marriage, and I do wonder sometimes why they do that. It's not a very sensible thing to promise, is it? I mean, how many princes do you meet in the real world? It must be extremely rare, that happy-ever-after walk into the sunset.'

'It is indeed, which is why you are so very fortunate, girl. Our Jo-Jo is lucky too, though she doesn't always appreciate that fact. But making sure a marriage keeps on working is largely up to the two people concerned. It takes constant love and care, as your mum and I have told you both countless times. Plenty of give and take. I only have to look at my own parents, your Gran and Grandad. Fifty years they've been wed, and they're still in love, even if Gramps is becoming progressively more senile and difficult to control.'

I start to speak, to say that love isn't enough, but he's still talking, telling some tale about Grandad which is apparently driving Mum scatty.

'The old man has started to save plastic bags from the supermarket, would you believe? He's got a drawer full of them, and those labels off fruit cans. I can't think why. Got very shirty with me when I asked. And you know how your Mum is passionate about her garden, and Grandpa loves to potter about and help. Unfortunately the poor old chap can no longer remember which are weeds and which are flowers. She has to watch him like a hawk or all her new plants end up on the compost heap. You have to laugh, or you'd cry,' Dad admits with a sigh. 'You can have me put down, love, if I ever reach that stage.'

I try to interrupt. 'Dad, I've got a bit of an ache.' But he's still talking and doesn't hear me.

'Mum found weed killer in among the sauce bottles the other day. We know it must have been him putting it back in the wrong cupboard, but where's the point in telling him? He'd never remember. We need eyes in the back of our heads, we do really. As for the length of time he takes in the bathroom, I'd never get off to work if . . .'

'Dad . . . I . . . I fell this morning.' The truth is stuck in my throat, lodged there like an unpalatable lump of stodgy porridge. 'Do you think I should go to the hospital?'

He finally focuses on what I'm saying. 'Fell? Fell where? Why didn't you say? Good grief, don't say your contractions have started?' He leaps up, appalled, spilling tea on the pale blue kitchen kelim and I pause to worry over what Oliver will say when he spots the stain.

'No, no, nothing like that. I feel fine, just the odd bruise here and there, but the baby's been very quiet today. What if it was hurt when I fell?'

Dad is suddenly all action. 'Get your coat on, I'll drive you round to the doctor right now, just to be sure. No, I'll fetch your mum first, that'd be best.' He panics a bit, running on the spot almost like a cartoon, before finally hustling me out of the door and helping me carefully into the car.

'Don't move. Don't even breathe. No, cancel that, keep breathing. Just sit there and gently breathe for the baby.'

'Right, Dad. Could you get in the car and drive please.'

Mum and I sit facing the doctor and he naturally wants to know how and where I fell. I spin some yarn about falling off the back door step when I took out some washing early in the day, wearing only my bedroom slippers. I pretend I fell down one step, not thirteen. Unlucky for some, I think.

He gently lectures me about proper footwear, listens to my tummy through his stethoscope and when he sees the anxious expression on my face, lets me listen to the tiny precious sounds of life, like a ticking clock in my tummy. 'Can you hear it? Baby is absolutely fine. No need to worry at all. But take better care with those steps in future, no more wearing of bedroom slippers, and absolute rest for a day or two.'

Mum takes me back home, fussing over me and issuing similar stern lectures. She offers to ring Oliver but I quickly put her off. 'No! Don't do that. I'm fine. The doctor says there's no real cause for concern, so let's not mention it to Oliver. He'll only worry.'

'Course he will, bless him. Never stops fretting over you, that man. Pops in the shop constantly to say how concerned he is that you aren't getting enough rest. He's a treasure is your Oliver. All right, we'll keep this to ourselves.'

I feel like a complete coward. I chickened out of telling Dad, now I can't bring myself to tell Mum either. I can't summon up the courage to say those dreadful words, that my husband, the knight in shining armour who came and carried me away on his white charger, the much-longed-for Prince Charming, actually pushed me down the stairs. And he did this knowing full well that I was carrying his child. 'Oliver is very busy at the office now that he's been made a partner,' I say, rather weakly.

Mum smiles proudly as she settles me in a chair in a sunny corner of the garden for the afternoon, brings me a sandwich and another cup of tea and tells me how lucky I am to have such a clever husband.

'Yes,' I agree. 'He is clever. Very clever indeed.'

The last month of my pregnancy is something of a trial. I've a pain right down my leg. Something to do with the baby resting against a nerve and the doctor insists I stay in bed a good deal with the foot of it propped up on a stack of encyclopaedias to raise it several inches from the ground. This is supposed to relieve the pressure. I worry that this pain may actually be a result of my alleged 'fall' but try not to dwell on that too much. I also suffer a good deal of heartburn, all of which bores Oliver to distraction. It's impossible for him to sleep in the same bed at such an angle, so he moves into the spare room.

I'm secretly delighted and find being alone in the big double bed a wonderfully liberating experience, free of the fear of being kicked out of it, which has remained a favourite punishment of his, although not recently, thank goodness. Having finally mastered knitting sufficiently to knit a woolly teddy bear for the baby, much more fun than a matinee jacket, I spend most nights with my legs propped up, sipping milk for the heartburn while I knit happily away. I feel remarkably calm, the nearest I've come to contentment in a long time.

The birth is surprisingly easy, although my labour is long drawn out as is often the case with a first baby but with no real problems, not even a single stitch. I haven't put on a great deal of weight, being only just over nine stone, but then I probably lost weight during the first months of my marriage, without my realising it.

My beautiful daughter is born on a bright day in June and I fall instantly in love with her, knowing I can cope with anything now as she will make my life worthwhile. She seems so tiny and precious with perfect fingernails like miniature shells, inquisitive blue eyes and a downy fluff of fair hair, and so fragile at just five pounds twelve ounces, but I will take good care of her and I shall enjoy watching her grow and develop. At least something good has come out of this debacle of a marriage.

I can see that Oliver is disappointed I didn't provide him with a son. He looks at me with that expression on his face which loudly states, you couldn't even get this right, could you? But I don't care what he thinks and feels any more. I have my lovely baby, my beloved child. I call her Katherine, Katie for short. She is my star.

Despite the fact we now have a baby in the house, Oliver's routine remains unchanged. His bacon and egg must still be on the table by seven o'clock precisely each morning. Fortunately, Katie wakes me up early anyway, but I could do without the hassle of having a breakfast to cook as well as dealing with her. I try suggesting that Oliver cook breakfast for me for a change, since I'm the one awake half the night. He looks at me as if I've suggested he fly to the moon.

'It was just a thought.'

My smile is weary, my eyes red with exhaustion, my hair like a bird's nest as I can't remember the last time I shampooed it, but he doesn't even notice. He's already grumbling about the lack of attention I'm giving him since the baby arrived, and seems to think I should still have time to sit and enjoy breakfast with him in a leisurely fashion, as I used to. I explain that this isn't always possible, that feeding a baby isn't a five-minute chore, but I suppose he's right in a way. I am obsessed with the baby. I adore her and pour into this small scrap of humanity all the love I have kept bottled up inside of me.

Katie is so small that she can only take a small amount of milk before she nods off to sleep, so a feed can take ages. I confess I frequently nearly nod off myself, so do usually go back to bed for an hour or two after the early-morning feed. I'm dropping on my feet and need to catch up on whatever sleep I can, as all new mums do.

Unfortunately, one morning, Oliver comes back to the house for something or other he has forgotten, and finds me still in bed.

He stares at me appalled. 'For God's sake, what are you doing there, you lazy slag? It's nearly ten o'clock.'

I leap out of bed in a fright, terrified he might be about to give me a beating but he's in a hurry to get back to the office so I get away with it. When he's gone I find my heart is still pounding, which shows how very jumpy and nervy I am when he's around.

I make very sure on that particular evening that his dinner is ready on time, and, as always, every item of baby stuff is cleared away before he arrives home. Katie too has been tidied away into her cot, out of sight and out of mind. He hates to see any sort of mess, any evidence, in fact, that we have a child. The house must revolve around *him*, not a mere baby.

I jokingly ask my sister how she copes with this problem, and Jo-Jo just laughs, saying Ed has to put up with the mess, and a great deal more besides.

'He helped create these children, so they're just as much his responsibility as mine,' she cheerfully remarks. 'You tell Oliver that.'

Naturally, I wouldn't dream of doing any such thing.

I'm not permitted to sit on our new white sofa with the baby on my knee, in case of 'accidents', not even allowed to feed her in the warmth and comfort of the lounge. I must go upstairs to the nursery which he has had specially decorated and fitted out with all the latest equipment, baby alarms and gizmos.

At first I'm secretly outraged at being shuffled off into a corner, but then come to see this room as a private haven for Katie and me, a place where we can feel safe and secure.

I buy myself a rocking chair and love sitting cuddling her in the quiet of the night, listening to her soft baby noises as she suckles, the sound of her breathing.

It irritates Oliver enormously if his sleep is disturbed, or when she goes through a spell of not sleeping because of evening colic. Nor does he take kindly to her crying, which interferes with his demands for peace and quiet of an evening. He complains he's tired from too many disturbed nights so again moves into the spare room, as he did during the last weeks of my pregnancy.

Again I feel nothing but relief.

Mum and Dad are regular visitors, as they love to pop in to see their latest grandchild. I frequently hear Oliver declaring to them how proud he is of his new family, but then he'll make it very clear to me, once they've gone, that the demands the baby makes are entirely my responsibility, and not his. The only time I ever see him hold her is when Mum puts her into his arms so that she can take a photograph. I can see quite clearly how very uncomfortable he feels, but I doubt anyone else notices.

Oliver takes very little interest in his daughter, leaving me to do all the nappy changing and getting up at night with her, but if something seems to be wrong, if she sicks up her feed as babies tend to do, or if she screams the place down, then he instantly turns into some kind of expert. He tells me I must have left her too long between feeds, I'm neglecting her, or I'm giving her the wrong food and should change it. He thinks she shouldn't ever cry, and if she does it must be because of my inadequacies as a mother.

I'm concerned that my milk seems to be drying up. Perhaps Mum's right and it's because I've lost a bit too much weight too quickly. There never seems to be time to eat properly, and I don't seem to have much appetite. I start Katie on a bottle and one evening I suggest Oliver feed her.

He looks at me horrified, but I smile encouragement and show him how to hold her, how to hold the bottle to make sure there is no air in the teat. He doesn't get it quite right and Katie starts to cry. He at once tries to hand her back.

'No, try again, darling. Don't worry, just let her take the teat right into her mouth.'

'It might choke her.'

'Don't be silly. She loves her bottle. Go on, try again.'

'You should be breast feeding her, not giving her this rubbish.'

I have to laugh. 'It's not long since you were complaining that I'd ruin my figure by breast feeding. Oliver, please just offer her the bottle. She's hungry.'

But he loses patience, dumps her on my knee and tells me it's not his job, and he won't be responsible for feeding bottled poison to a child. Then he marches off downstairs to the quiet privacy of his office.

'Never mind, my precious,' I murmur to Katie. 'I'm sure your dad loves you really. You just have to grow a bit first before he feels brave enough to cope.'

As the family get caught up in their own lives again, and call in to see us less often, I begin to feel quite lonely and isolated, sadly lacking in adult conversation. I'm delighted, therefore, when Emma calls one afternoon. She's brought a present for Katie, a pretty pink frock, and some flowers for me. She kisses me on each cheek, apologises for not having come sooner but explains that Oliver had insisted visitors were limited to family members only.

I'm surprised by this but say nothing. Relations between us are still a little cool so I wonder if she's making this up, or exaggerating what he actually said as an excuse to have a dig at him.

I take her to see Katie, who is fast asleep, which is such a relief I daren't disturb her.

'Maybe you'd like to hold her when she wakes for her feed?' I suggest.

'Oh, I can't stay long,' Emma says, glancing at her watch. 'Another time maybe. Don't wake the little mite for me.'

I make coffee and ask Emma to fill me in on what's happening at Perfect Cottages. I feel desperate for some news, for a bit of girly gossip and chit-chat. I'm also eager to hear how Wanda, my replacement, is getting along. I'm already making plans in my head for my return to work but Emma's answer is not encouraging.

'She's coping fine, an absolute gem. Wanda has taken complete charge of the website, keeps it regularly updated, and has found several other suitable tourist websites to link it with, which has bumped up our bookings enormously.'

I smile and say how pleased I am, but feel slightly hurt that she's doing so well and no one seems to be missing me. We all imagine ourselves to be indispensable and it's never pleasant to realise that we aren't.

'I've every intention of getting back to work just as soon as I can, of course,' I say, but Em seems unconvinced, almost uninterested.

She shrugs. 'Don't worry about it. There's really no rush. I dare say Wanda would be happy to continue indefinitely.'

It's not what I wish to hear and I suggest that maybe I could do some paperwork at home.

'Such as? Accounts aren't your thing, are they? I deal with those, and Wanda and I both handle the bookings. We've employed a couple of cleaners now, but you're not up to coping with that side of things yet, are you? Besides, you know Oliver wouldn't like it if you started work too soon.'

I stifle a sigh and quietly concede this is true.

'How is the new father coping?' she asks, a certain tartness in her tone which I studiously ignore.

'He's getting the hang of things, slowly,' I lie, not wishing to divulge my husband's complete lack of interest in our child.

'Good. Excellent.' She glances about her as if at a loss for words, then mentions one or two regular clients who have booked holidays this season and have asked about me.

I'm pleased and flattered by this but then minutes later she's gulping down her coffee, reaching for her bag and edging out of the door. I appreciate how busy she must be but I'm sorry to see her go so quickly.

'Call in any time you're passing,' I say.

'Of course, and do take care of that precious baby.'

Then she's gone and the emptiness of the house folds in around me.

A day or two later I drive down to the supermarket as I often do on a Thursday morning, Katie strapped in her baby seat in the back. It's a pleasant break from the house and I deliberately make a detour so that I can call in on Emma at the agency. She seems surprised to see me again so soon, and I make an excuse about visiting Booth's Supermarket at Windermere, but we both know I've come an extra couple of miles out of my way.

'I felt like a drive by the lake,' I say, by way of an excuse. 'I thought you might like to see her awake.' I place Katie in Emma's arms and she is entranced.

'Oh, Carly, she's beautiful. Absolutely gorgeous!'

Wanda too comes over and we all coo over the baby for some minutes.

'I've also come to invite you to the christening. I forgot to mention when you called the other day. In fact, I'd like you to be godmother, well, one of them. Jo-Jo will be the other, naturally.'

Em looks at me in astonishment, her cheeks faintly pink. 'Oh, that would be wonderful. Have you asked Oliver? Does he mind?'

I frown. 'Why would Oliver mind? You're *my* friend. Will you do it?'

'I would be proud,' and we smile at each with real warmth for the first time in months. Wanda is beaming too.

'I'll trot out and buy cream cakes,' she says. 'This surely warrants a celebration.'

15

The christening takes place on a beautiful summer's day with Oliver proudly showing off our beautiful new daughter. He fusses over me endlessly, telling everyone how clever I am, how beautiful, what a lucky man he is. It always feels like a minor miracle to me that he can be so charming and affable in public. Emma and Jo-Jo both act as godmothers, with an old friend of Oliver's as godfather. Katie cries at the appropriate moment and afterwards everyone comes back to the house where Mum and I had earlier prepared sandwiches and snacks.

There is only one awkward moment when Oliver's mother Grace slips the baby into his arms and notices at once that he isn't used to holding her. But instead of challenging her son on the matter, she turns on me with a surprising sharpness to her tone.

'Really, Carly, you must stop being so possessive over this child and allow Oliver to feed and hold her sometimes. Look at the poor man, he hardly knows which way up to hold her, or where to put his hands.'

I must have look stunned because she goes on, 'It's no good looking guilty, dear. Oliver has told us how you keep her all to yourself and don't let him have a look in. Which isn't very sensible, is it? I have to say you look quite worn out, so do learn to share her a little more, get some rest, and try not to be quite so obsessed with the baby. You're making Oliver feel left out and unhappy.'

I look at him in surprise; at the sad, woebegone expression on his handsome face and am yet again astounded at this ability he has to put on such a convincing act for the benefit of our parents. But I accept her criticism without protest. I certainly have no wish to challenge him on the issue.

'Would you like to feed her, Mrs Sheldon?' I ask, which pleases my mother-in-law enormously and the moment passes. I'm becoming increasingly accustomed to this remarkable facility Oliver has for saying one thing to me, and quite the opposite to everyone else. I simply can't win.

'Do you think there's something wrong between those two?'

Jo-Jo looked at her husband and blinked. 'Wrong? What could be wrong?'

'I'm not sure, only I can sense an atmosphere, a certain sang-froid between them, don't you think?'

Jo-Jo, struggling to feed a child who was currently determined to scream the place down, was not at her most patient. She looked at her husband, wild eyed. 'Don't talk rubbish. Carly adores Oliver, won't hear a word said against him. He's her knight in shining armour, her Mr Wonderful. Hasn't she been telling us so from the moment she first clapped eyes on the man? My darling sister has it all. Her husband has his partnership and no doubt doubled his salary. They live in this fantastic house, and now she has a family as well as a terrific career. Lucky Carly! And look at me, a complete frump.' She pinched a roll of fat on her stomach, still not completely having lost the weight she gained since Molly's birth. Each succeeding birth made it harder for her to do so.

Ed laughed. 'You look gorgeous, as always.'

'No need to pretend, Ed Dickson, I certainly do not look gorgeous, and I saw you chatting up Emma earlier. I thought she looked unusually sexy today, but then we don't often see her in a dress, do we? And that hair! Why pink streaks, I wonder? Doesn't seem quite the right colour for such a strident feminist, does it? They should be purple for the suffragette look. You spent enough time talking to her, what do you think? Are you and she having an affair?'

'What?' Now it was Ed's turn to blink, the poor man completely taken aback by this accusation.

'Is that where you go every evening, to see the lovely Emma?'

'For goodness' sake, what's got into you? You know damn well where I go of an evening, working overtime at the garage, trying to make enough money to feed my family. And it's not quite every evening so don't exaggerate, Jo-Jo.'

His wife lifted the baby from her breast and leaned her against her shoulder, rubbing her back. Molly was instantly sick all down Jo-Jo's new blouse. 'Oh, no, this is the first time I've worn·this.' Ed grabbed a cloth and tried to help clean her up but she slapped his hand away. 'I wouldn't blame you if you were having an affair,' she sniffed, the glare she gave him rather giving the lie to this statement. 'Is it any wonder with a wife that looks like the back end of an elephant.'

'I'm not having an affair.' Ed put his hands on his wife's shoulders and kissed the top of her tousled hair. 'You're just in a state because you're tired, and Molly is fretful. There is no one in this town, in the entire world can hold a candle to you. Why would I need to look elsewhere?'

Tears filled her eyes. 'You know why. I just never feel like it any more. Never! I'm exhausted, worn out, fat, an old woman before my time. And you're still young and handsome, why wouldn't you look elsewhere when you now find yourself married to an old crone who isn't even interested in sex any more.' Then she shoved the screaming baby into her husband's arms and fled to the bathroom in floods of tears.

Emma's comment about my not being good with accounts reminds me that I've neglected filling in my housekeeping book recently. I spend an hour or so one morning trying to bring it up to date. My mind isn't properly on the task as I keep going over the things she said, or implied.

Could it be true that Oliver tried to stop her from calling, or was she making that up because for some reason she doesn't approve of him? Was she trying to tell me that she didn't want me to return to work, ever? Does she prefer Wanda to me? If so, why? I remember too her earlier remarks during my pregnancy when she suggested I might want to sell out, and I chew on the end of my pen. Stepping down from the business isn't something I've ever seriously considered, and it troubles me deeply. I can't imagine not working. I love my job and have no wish to give it up or hand over my share of the holiday letting agency to the super-efficient Wanda, or anyone else for that matter.

I glance in panic at the housekeeping book which is more fiction than fact, then hear Katie start to tune up so I stuff it under a cushion to deal with later. She is my priority now. Pleasant as it is to visit the office and enjoy coffee and cakes with the girls, it's obviously too soon to be thinking about going back to work just yet. I tell myself that my friend and partner is only showing due consideration, which is kind of her. And I also hope that my mother-in-law is wrong and I'm not becoming obsessed with the baby. But I do feel as if I am the only one truly responsible for her care.

I forget all about the housekeeping book until Oliver digs it out from under the cushion later that evening. We're about to sit down to eat our evening meal, salmon in a watercress sauce which I bought from Marks and Spencer, the only fish Oliver will tolerate. He's pushing it about his plate with a fork while he examines the housekeeping book with careful scrutiny, then subjects me to a fierce grilling on this entry or that, querying prices and quantities. I field as many questions as I can, then hold up my hands in surrender, the smallest tremor of fear running through me.

'OK, I'm sorry. I admit I haven't been keeping it properly up to date recently and may have got one or two details wrong. I've been too busy with the baby.'

'Don't make excuses, Carly. You're always too ready to pass the blame on to someone else, even your own child.'

'That's not what I'm doing at all,' I hotly protest. 'I'm saying it's entirely my fault if there are mistakes in the accounts, but I've been busy.'

He gives me a withering look and there's a slight curl of disdain to his upper lip. 'You're obsessed. Minding one small baby shouldn't take up every hour of your day. It's not like you have anything else to do now, is it? You should pay more attention to me, your neglected husband since you no longer have to dash all over the place for that stupid agency of yours. Did you make this sauce, it's disgusting.'

I ignore his opinion on the sauce, which is delicious, and concentrate on making my point. 'Minding one small baby takes up far more time than you might imagine, and as I'm new to the job I confess it is fairly nerve-racking. I'm absolutely shattered, not least from lack of sleep.' I try a beguiling smile. 'It might help, Oliver, if you didn't expect the house to be so clean and perfect when you arrive home each evening. I do my best but babies seem to take up so much *space!*'

'Rubbish! I see no reason to allow standards to slip.'

Before I can find any suitable reply to this I hear the first hiccupping sounds of Katie's cry. I start to go to her but he grabs my arm.

'Leave her. Finish serving the dessert first, then you can go.'

'But she's clearly in distress.'

'Are you deaf? What was it I just told you to do?' He fastens his hand around my hair and pulls me to within an inch of his face, speaking to me slowly and quietly, as if addressing a rather stupid child. 'I assume there will be a dessert, or can't you be bothered to do that properly either?'

'There's a fruit pie.' That familiar surge of panic courses through me as I see the contempt in his face, and I'm aching to go to my distressed child.

'Good, then serve it, please. Don't I at least deserve to come before a wailing baby?'

What would his mother say if she could see her precious son now?

'Of course, Oliver,' I bleakly respond, and serve him the sweet. Upstairs, Katie's crying reaches fever-pitch and it's a wonder I don't smash the pie in his face. Oliver insists on a full three-course meal each evening, although I cheat a bit by not telling him that I buy ready-made food from M&S or the supermarket, and pass it off as my own. Mainly he doesn't notice, but as I place the slice of cherry tart before him, ready to make a dash the second he is served, he grabs me by the wrist.

'Cherries? Where did you buy these?'

'The greengrocers on Highgate. Er – they are in season – aren't they?' I stammer, not sure if they are or not. 'Don't you like them?'

'We'll soon see, won't we? And for God's sake shut that child up.'

I make my escape at last on a stifled sigh of relief.

Following my next visit to the supermarket I go into the nursery to put my loose change in Katie's piggy bank, and I'm shocked to discover it's empty. Many of our friends and family have given Katie money either when she was born or at the christening, and as I don't need anything more in the way of equipment for her, I've kept it in her piggy bank, intending to open a proper account for her at the building society once I could find the time to organise such things. It must have contained forty or fifty pounds, plus I've added odd sixpences and shillings whenever I have some spare change. Now it's empty.

I can't think how this can have happened. When I challenge Oliver on the matter, he freely confesses that he's borrowed it.

'*Borrowed?* But it's Katie's money. I was about to invest it for her future.'

He snorts his disdain. 'That's years away yet. I need it more than she does. She's only a baby, for God's sake! Do you know how much it costs to run this house?'

This is an oft-repeated complaint, difficult to refute, except to say that he chose it, but I don't dare say this right now. I go away and weep quietly in the nursery, wishing I'd invested the money for Katie right away. I feel I've let her down. Is this the kind of father Oliver is going to be? Utterly selfish and greedy?

But there's a greater shock to come when a day or two later I open a letter from the bank manager complaining about the size of our overdraft. Overdraft? We don't even have an overdraft, not so far as I know. Apparently I'm wrong.

When I tackle Oliver on the subject of the overdraft, he says it came about by mistake. And this from a professional accountant! Commensurate with his new status as a partner, he's changing the Ford Mondeo for a BMW, and apparently the firm isn't prepared to pay the difference. 'It's only temporary until the money comes through from the guy who bought the Mondeo, and I get my next pay check. Nip in and tell the old buffer that, will you?'

'Me?' I'm appalled.

'You can surely manage that, can't you? I don't have time. Tell him it'll be cleared next week and I don't expect to have any charges.'

'But . . .'

'Carly, just do as I ask.'

So I'm the one who has to go to see the bank manager and explain all of this, the one to suffer the lecture on why it would have been better to ask permission first. I could hardly say that my husband never asks anyone's permission to do anything, is in fact manically determined to live life on his own terms.

I'm beginning to despair of ever achieving a peaceful life, aware that I can't go on like this for much longer. I can't understand why Oliver would spend money we don't have, without even telling me. Why he would need to steal from Katie's piggy bank. He earns a good salary.

Oliver senses that I'm upset and annoyed about the piggy bank and the loss of Katie's investment, and avoids the issue by becoming cold and distant and barely speaking to me for days. It's a trick he uses often.

I find his silence difficult to cope with, perhaps because I'm feeling increasingly vulnerable right now. Apart from being over-tired from looking after the baby largely on my own, I feel an increasing despair over my future. Since giving up work I seem to have lost what little independence I had. I feel I'm becoming far too dependent on him, not only emotionally, but financially. I've no idea what money we have, and I have none of my own save for the housekeeping allowance which Oliver gives me. I desperately regret having refused the maternity benefit which Emma offered, but I daren't go to her now and admit that I need it after all. Oliver controls our finances completely. He handles, or rather mishandles, our money, although what he spends it on I'm not sure. What can he be doing with it all?

Oliver parked his splendid new BMW in his designated spot, marked with his name now that he was a partner, and sauntered across the car park to the office. Tony was already at his desk, talking to Poppy. The pair of them looked up as he entered, then the girl put her nose in the air and turned away.

Oliver stood in the centre of the floor, hands in his trouser pockets, watching with a smirk on his face as she flounced off in high dudgeon.

'Trouble in paradise?' Tony sarcastically enquired.

'Dearest Poppy has been in a huff for months, ever since the office dinner dance, the silly mare. Claims she felt cheated and badly let down because I forgot to mention my wife was pregnant. As if that had anything to do with her? Surely the silly girl didn't imagine I was ever going to leave Carly? Certainly not for a sulky child, anyway. It wasn't as if I promised her happy-ever-after or any of that nonsense, and I must have spent a small fortune on keeping the stupid girl wined and dined. Still, easy come, easy go. Women are like buses, lose one and another will be along any moment. Anyway, what's it to you?'

Tony shrugged. 'No skin off my nose who you lay, although your wife might have an issue with it.'

Oliver laughed. 'What the eye doesn't see . . .'

'. . . the heart doesn't grieve over, yeah, I've heard the theory. Not sure if it holds true, certainly where women are concerned, and Carly deserves better.'

'You're an expert on my wife now, are you?'

'I've certainly known her longer than you have, and would treat her a good deal better if she were *my* wife.'

'Which, fortunately, she isn't, so keep your nose out of my personal affairs.'

'Affairs being the operative word,' Tony swiftly reposted. He was sick of Oliver's arrogance. The guy had his own office now that he was a partner, but could never resist stopping off to plague him every morning with his caustic, clever remarks. And his casual, couldn't-give-a-damn attitude towards Carly infuriated Tony. She did indeed deserve better, and her husband messing about with other women had entirely ruined a perfectly good friendship between them. Tony couldn't bear to look her in the eye these days.

'And you've never had the guts to stray, I suppose?' Oliver caustically asked as he sifted through the mail.

'Nope, wouldn't dream of it.'

'Has your own darling wife never cuckolded you either?'

Tony bridled. 'You leave my wife out of this.'

'Maybe I should check her out a bit more thoroughly, see if she'd be worth having.'

Tony went red in the face, his jaw tightening to a hard jutting ridge of fury. 'If you so much as lay a finger on my wife I'll slit your fucking throat.'

'Language, language,' Oliver laughed. 'It's true that I've grown somewhat bored with sweet Poppy who has a brain the size of a pea, although I shall miss her other attributes.'

'How is Carly?' Tony growled, striving to keep his anger in check and remain calm as he booted up his computer.

Oliver frowned, blue-grey eyes narrowing with displeasure. 'Like all women who have just given birth, I suppose, completely obsessed with babies and becoming strangely detached from the world around her.' It wasn't simply that she never troubled to disagree with him any more, or beg his forgiveness as she used to do whenever she made a mistake, she no longer even seemed to care. He gave a harsh laugh. 'She's angry with me for borrowing a few quid from the baby's piggy bank. What the hell does it matter? The child is barely three months old, so what does she need the money for?

'And you have your women to pay for,' Tony sarcastically acknowledged, quietly entering his password as the Welcome screen appeared.

'I do indeed. Women! We can't live with them, and have no wish to live without them.'

Tony began to punch numbers into his computer, his mouth set tight and grim. 'It helps if you're content to live with only one.'

Oliver laughed. 'Oh, very droll. Monogamy is not my style, old sport. Although I'm certainly coming to the conclusion that sulky girls are more trouble than they are worth. Maybe a more mature woman would be less demanding, and not quite so histrionic. It's useful too if they're married. No strings. I shall keep my eye out for a likely candidate. For some reason I never seem to have any difficulty in finding one, the old charm offensive still seems to do the trick, wouldn't you say? But then I do appreciate a woman with a mind of her own, such as your own lovely Jane, for instance. Far more of a challenge, don't you think?

One Saturday afternoon I'm ironing in the kitchen when my elderly neighbour from across the street comes running in to tell me that smoke is pouring out of the upstairs window. I grab the nappy pail which I'm using to soak the towelling nappies I put on Katie at night, and run up the stairs while my neighbour pauses only long enough to fill another bucket. Flames are leaping out of the linen cupboard and we fling the contents of the two buckets onto the fire to quench it. Water, Napisan, wet nappies and all. We both then dash to the bathroom to refill them and keep going until the fire is finally out and we are both coughing and choking, and the linen cupboard is black with smoke.

I've dragged some items out of the cupboard, hoping to save them. Among them is my grandmother's quilt which she made for me when I was a small girl. She would tuck it round me as I sat on her lap drinking hot chocolate, listening to a bedtime story. It's starting to smoulder and blacken, here and there a ripple of flame and I grab it and run out on to the drive where I beat it against the tarmac, afraid of this treasured memory going up in flames too, along with everything else.

I stamp on it hard, pounding the soft fabric with my feet, stamping and stamping, quite unable to control my emotions as tears roll down my cheeks. The quilt can be repaired but so much else has been lost. It's a disaster! I should feel deeply fortunate that my neighbour spotted the smoke and was so quick off the mark, otherwise the entire house might have burned down. Even so, I'm devastated.

I feel rage inside, as hot as the flames which consumed my precious belongings. I'm filled with anger, not simply at this terrible loss, but because I know Oliver will blame me for this fire, even though I didn't cause it.

Every scrap of linen I possessed, every sheet and pillow case, every towel and item of bedding for the baby has been destroyed. It has either been burned or blackened beyond any hope of salvation. A good many of Katie's clothes which were airing in neat piles, have also gone up in flames. I'm absolutely heartbroken.

My neighbour is very kind and makes me sit down to calm my nerves and dry my tears, while she makes us both a cup of tea.

'What will your husband say?' is her first question as she hands the cup to me, and I look up at her in startled silence, quite unable to answer.

This is the lady who saw Oliver throw me over the sofa, and I don't have the strength left to keep on pretending it was all some silly game, not right now. I shake my head and say nothing. Katie is still blissfully asleep in her pram in the hall, completely unaware of the panic going on around her.

We sip our tea in silence for a long while then very quietly my neighbour says, 'Don't worry, dear, I'm sure everything will be all right. It wasn't your fault, after all. It was just an accident.'

I clear my throat but nothing comes out beyond a croak, and even that hurts my throat which feels raw with smoke. A trivial problem by comparison to the fury I still have to face from Oliver, and my heart skips a beat. My fault or not, he will undoubtedly blame me, as he does for everything that goes wrong in our lives.

She puts out a consoling hand and gently squeezes mine. 'I have no wish to interfere, and won't say a word to anyone about what goes on here. You can rely on my discretion, if that's what you want, dear. But in my experience, violent men generally go worse, not better.' Then she sets down her empty cup, kisses the top of my head, and leaves.

I put my face in my hands and sob.

Strangely, and to my huge relief, when I tell Oliver about the fire, for once he does not blame me. He doesn't fall into a tantrum or one of his black moods. He calmly calls the insurance company and they come to inspect. They can find no obvious cause and decide it was probably an electrical fault on the immersion heater. They pay up without argument. Nothing in that cupboard was more than eighteen months old, being all wedding gifts and baby items, save for my grandmother's quilt which had fortunately only been charred around the edges and can be repaired.

But I don't see a penny of that money. Oliver cashes the cheque and that's the last I hear of it. I tentatively mention that the fire has made us rather short on sheets and towels, and that Katie has scarcely an item of clothing or bedding left to her name. He dismisses the former problem by saying we can ask relatives to buy us more for Christmas, and the baby's losses as immaterial.

'She's growing at such a rate they'd be useless anyway in a month or two,' is his comment.

Mum, bless her, picks up her knitting needles and sets about helping to replace the perished baby clothes, and perhaps for the first time begins to question the state of my marriage.

We're browsing through the market in Kendal and she's holding up a pretty lemon cotton dress that's for sale on one of the stalls. 'Surely Oliver didn't really say it wasn't important that Katie didn't have any clothes to wear?'

I concede that he may have a point when he says she's growing at such a tremendous rate many of the items we've lost would soon be too small for her anyway.

Mum considers this argument and then nods. 'Ah, well, that's generally the way with babies. Still, that's easily remedied. You simply replace the items with a larger size. This is lovely, don't you think? Shall I buy it for her?'

'There's really no need.'

'Of course there's a need. The poor child has barely a stitch to wear following that fire. Thank God she was downstairs and out of harm's way. Anyway, I'm her grandmother and it's my privilege to buy baby clothes for my adorable grandchild.'

The stallholder dutifully gushes over the sleeping Katie while she wraps the gift and Mum digs out her purse. Then as we walk away, she returns to the subject of the insurance claim. 'You'll need to replace her bedding too, I suppose. Might I ask how much you've got to play with?'

The one good thing about Mum is that she's easily distracted, so I mumble something about having forgotten to buy cheese while we were on the market, and rush back to get some. I also buy wool so that she can crochet Katie a new cot cover, which makes Mum very happy. The question about money is thankfully dropped.

The following week Oliver gives me fifty pounds and I'm so thrilled I impulsively kiss him. And then I discover where he got the money from. He's sold my car.

16

I'm confined to the house even more now that I have no car. There is a small convenience store on the edge of the estate where we live, although not as good as my parents' shop. They act as a small post office too, which is useful for stamps and such-like, but if I wish to visit my sister, or my parents, or go to Kendal, I have to catch the bus at the end of the road. It's infrequent and slow, and I have all the hassle of negotiating a baby, baby buggy and the usual proliferation of shopping bags. An absolute nightmare!

Not having a car will also mean that I won't easily get to call in at the agency office to keep in touch with Emma. Catching the bus to Bowness and back could take the entire afternoon. I realise that I'll be worn out by the time I do arrive back home, but I'm determined to go. I desperately need to get out of the house for a break.

'You should've given me a ring,' she scolds me, as I struggle into the office looking all hot and bothered, bitterly complaining about buses which take forever wandering around every back lane and stopping at most hamlets and villages en route. 'I can't believe you came all this way by bus. You should've said if the car was out of commission. I could've popped over to pick you up.'

'I don't need you to pick me up. I can manage fine, thanks very much,' I tartly respond, aware I'm being unnecessarily short with her, but I hate to appear needy. I do little enough in the way of work for the agency as it is, without demanding Emma act as chauffeur for me as well.

'OK,' she says, backing off. 'I'll put the kettle on in a minute, when I've just dealt with this client.'

Katie is crying, the wheels of the buggy have got caught up with the door mat and a young man steps forward to help extricate the tangle. I'm filled with shame, embarrassed by my sharpness in front of a client, and a rather good looking one at that.

He's tall and dark, in his late twenties or early thirties, I guess, with clear green eyes and designer stubble on his chin. 'I'm so s-sorry,' I stammer, as I wheel the buggy over his foot.

He grins. 'Didn't feel a thing. These boots are made for walking, and pretty tough.'

I look more closely at him, at his fleece and waterproof trousers, notice a huge rucksack leaning drunkenly against the door. 'You're on a walking holiday?'

'Right.' He's gazing at me so intently I find my cheeks growing warm and I turn quickly away, thankful when Emma comes to my rescue.

'This is Mr Hathaway, one of our regulars for our more rural lets.'

He thrusts out a hand, large, and capable and lightly tanned. 'Tim. Pleased to meet you.'

His grip is firm and solid, like its owner, I assume, and he holds onto my hand rather longer than necessary. His smile is wide and friendly and I find myself smiling back at him. 'Carly Sheldon.'

'Carly is my partner, and part owner of the agency,' Emma informs him.

'Ah, excellent!' He looks strangely pleased. 'We're bound to meet again then, so feel free to run over my foot any time.' This comment reminds him that I have a child in tow, and he quickly adds, 'And this is . . . ?' He glances down at the squalling, red-faced infant who is my pride and joy.

'This is Katie, but she's not at her best right now.'

Emma butts in, all efficiency, perhaps thinking I might descend into baby talk if she doesn't interrupt. 'Right, Tim, here are the keys. Thanks for calling in to pick them up. I hope you enjoy your stay. Any problems, you know where we are.'

He gives me one last smile before hoisting up his rucksack

and easing himself with difficulty through the door and down the stairs.

'Wow!' I say, unable to stop myself.

Emma laughs. 'Yeah, what a hunk. Makes you wish you were single again, doesn't it?' She heads back to her desk, gathering up papers and files as she does so, half glancing at them as she continues, 'So, what happened to the car?'

She looks very efficient and in charge as she sits in her office chair and slides it up to the computer, very content with life and her place in it. Wanda, she informs me, is out supervising a new cleaner who is preparing a property for new clients arriving later that day. I feel out of touch, old suddenly, a frumpish hausfrau, and experience a spurt of envy for Emma's obvious confidence at managing this business without me. But then I know I couldn't hope to achieve what she has in such a short time. I don't seem able to cope with anything.

I concentrate on lifting Katie out of her buggy, and, finding she's dirtied her nappy, start rummaging in the changing bag for a clean one. 'The car has been sold,' I finally confess.

'Goodness, that's a bit drastic, isn't it?'

'I – I decided I didn't need one at the moment,' I lie, not wishing to go into detail.

'I see. Well, you might have warned me,' she says tightly. 'I assume that means you'll now be stepping down from the agency altogether?'

'What?' I look at her, stunned. 'Are you asking me to resign? To sell out my share? Just because I've sold my car?'

'It's an option you should perhaps seriously consider.'

'Why?'

Emma gives a little grimace of distaste as I peel off Katie's dirty nappy, then gets up to switch on the kettle and starts to spoon coffee into two mugs. 'Actually, not simply because of the car, although I'm surprised you've decided to get rid of it. But because of the baby. How old is Katie now, nearly five months? You've hardly been near the office in all that time so you've obviously decided you prefer to stay at home. The sale of your car confirms the issue, otherwise how would you manage to come back to work without transport? But then, it's your prerogative to choose.'

I open my mouth to say that it wasn't actually my choice at all. But I can't really do that without admitting it was Oliver who sold my car, and that he did it without my permission. That it is Oliver who makes all the decisions in our house.

'Let me think about it,' I say, feeling harassed as I struggle with baby lotion and nappies, and a screaming infant on my lap. 'I need a little more time.'

'OK.' Emma watches all of this performance with a sympathetic smile, and when I'm done and Katie is clean again, picks her up for a cuddle. 'But I should point out that I don't actually have much, time, that is. It's almost Christmas, bookings are pouring in, and we're up to our eyes in work. As you know, this is nothing to what it will be like when next season really gets going. Like it or not, it will soon be make-your-mind-up time, Carly. Either you're coming back to take a full part in this business, or you sell up. I do need to know pretty soon.'

'Do you think we could have lunch?' I suddenly blurt out. 'I need to talk to someone and . . .'

'. . . and I'm it?' She smiles, and I remember what good friends we've always been, that we did start this business together, that she is my daughter's godmother. Could I find the courage to tell her everything? Dare I risk it? And if I did, what could she do to help? What do I want her to do? Offer sanctuary and protection? Is that even realistic?

I'm still chewing over these questions in my mind as we stroll down to the John Peel, our favourite pub, and order a ploughman's lunch each. Emma is chattering on about the healthy state of the agency's profit and loss account, of the rush of bookings they've already had for next season, and describing the new properties they've taken on. I'm feeling more and more left out of the excitement of it all, my fragile confidence rapidly evaporating. My life seems to be in free fall and I have no control over it whatsoever.

'That's enough of me rabbiting on about the agency. So what was it you wanted to talk about?'

Our lunch arrives and I postpone the evil moment as we dig in to the delicious food. We talk about Katie of course, and the christening. I tell her about the fire, although I don't add that by refusing to replace all the lost linen and clothing, and by selling my car, Oliver is punishing me for my apparent carelessness for allowing it to happen. I don't say that he blames me for everything, that our failing marriage and his brutal treatment of me is apparently all my fault too. I'm trying to find a way to admit my marriage isn't working without actually going into too many details, but the words stick in my throat. How could I possibly tell her the truth?

Well, actually, my husband kicks me about the bedroom like a battered old ball. How would Emma react to that? Or if I told her of the other things he does to me, the way he puts me down all the time, makes me look stupid in front of my parents, intimidates and bullies me, and uses more sadistic tricks? If I told her that I was afraid of him. What would her opinion of me be then?

I sigh, knowing only too well. That I'm a fool for putting up with it, which of course I am. So why don't I just walk out of the door? It's easy, isn't it? As simple as a mouse running away from a cat. How can I explain that not so very long ago it was too soon for me to leave him, and now it's too late.

Maybe she reads something in my silence as she suddenly says, 'You didn't choose to sell the car, did you? Oliver did.'

I stare into my empty coffee cup, unable, or unwilling, to meet her probing gaze.

'Silence isn't the answer, Carly. I've suspected for a while that there's a problem. Look, if there is, I don't believe for a minute that it's your fault, so tell me. Speak! This *is* what you wanted to say, isn't it? Why did he do that? Why did he sell your car?' When I still say nothing, she sighs. 'OK, let me guess, he sold it in order to keep you at home. What else does he do to control you? Come on, you can tell me. I want to help. How can I help?'

I shake my head, indicating there's absolutely nothing she can do, too choked with emotion to speak, my mind paralysed by indecision and fear.

She gives my arm a gentle squeeze. 'Tell me, Carly. Spill the beans. Get it off your chest for God's sake.'

I look at her in anguish, open my mouth to speak and close it again, the unspoken words blocking my throat. Wouldn't it be a betrayal of our marriage if I revealed these problems? Wouldn't it prove that I'd failed? My mind is a turmoil of emotion, Oliver's face looming large amongst my jumbled thoughts. He would never forgive me.

'Why aren't you open and honest with me like you used to be when we used to giggle behind the girl's lavatories at school?' She sounds irritated but then looks into my eyes, a quick indrawn breath and in a quiet, shocked voice, says, 'My God, you're scared of him, aren't you?'

I'm on my feet in an instant, glancing at my watch, mumbling something about having to hurry to catch the bus. A moment later I'm rapidly walking away, pushing the baby buggy out on to the pavement and heading back up the hill. Emma hurries along beside me, strangely silent.

I suddenly say, 'The key . . . the key you lent me . . . the one I foolishly used that time.'

'Yes?' I sense her casting me an anxious, enquiring glance.

'I wondered if maybe you'd like it back.' Now why on earth did I say that? Isn't it my only lifeline?

'Do you want to give it back?' she asks, sounding shocked.

'I – I'm not sure. I . . .'

'Carly?'

I look up and see Oliver climbing out of the BMW which he's double-parked outside the office. My mouth goes dry and I'm swamped with relief that I've said no more, that I've held on to my chilling secret. What was I thinking of to even imagine I could reveal the smallest part of it?

'What brings you to our neck of the woods?' There's a note of cool animosity in Emma's tone, and I know she's thinking that he must have followed me here, checking up on me as he has done so often in the past. I'm thinking this too and it's really rather disturbing. Oliver's grey-blue eyes narrow in his unsmiling face as he swiftly assesses the situation, no doubt trying to guess what we've been talking about. He's bound to assume we were talking about him. I forget sometimes, how very paranoid he can be. I simply want to get in the car and escape before Emma irritates him further. I start to unbuckle Katie and lift her out of the buggy.

As I turn to put her into her car seat, Emma hugs and kisses us both. 'Keep it,' she whispers in my ear, and I know she's referring to the key.

'I'll call you . . . about my decision,' I reply.

As we drive on through Bowness and up the hill to Windermere, Oliver's silence is chilling and I too say nothing, keeping my gaze fixed on the small shops and Lakeland stone cottages as we pass by. At the T-junction by the station he pauses before turning right, and acidly remarks, 'You never told me you were coming here today.'

'Should I have done?'

'I would have preferred it if you had.'

I don't question this remark. I don't have the nerve. I sink down in my seat and wish I could vanish in a puff of smoke, wish I were invisible or a million miles away from here. Oliver says nothing more but I'm left in no doubt what to expect when we're finally back home with the door locked behind us.

He is generous enough to allow me to put Katie down in her cot before he starts to interrogate me, punctuated with the usual slaps and punches. Fortunately I am able to say, in all honesty, that Emma and I talked exclusively about business.

'If you were planning to go back to work, forget it. We don't need your pathetic earnings now that I've been made a partner, and I certainly don't want that woman poking her nose into our affairs.'

'I haven't decided what I'm going to do yet,' I recklessly reply, desperately striving to hang on to the last shreds of my independence. 'Who knows, I may need a job one day.'

Oliver glares at me, his tone sardonic and mocking. 'When you finally summon up the courage to divorce me, you mean? I don't think that's likely to happen any time soon, is it, Carly dear? You need me. You couldn't possibly cope on your own. Remember that if you were to ever consider leaving me, you'd find yourself alone and penniless. This house is in my name, don't forget.'

I'm not sure whether I'm being brave or foolhardy, but I face up to him. 'I don't believe that matters these days. I'm your wife so I would get my share. You're obliged to provide for me.'

'And what about your precious child? Would you run away from her too? Because I'd make damn sure you weren't granted custody.'

I instinctively gasp, shocked by this. 'You wouldn't be so cruel! In any case, you'd never win custody. I could get a solicitor to make sure that you didn't.'

But he laughs in my face. 'I'm an accountant, I'm not stupid. Believe me, I know all the tricks. I have a good income and a fine home, whereas you have no transport, no job, no income of any kind. You'd have nowhere to live for a start. Do you really want to bring up your child on a sink council estate, which is all you'd get from social services? Do you imagine they would allow you to when I can offer our child so much more?' My blood runs cold as he warms to his theme. 'I would simply make sure that I got the lion's share, and you the absolute minimum. I could accuse you of having a lover, of turning into an alcoholic, and of not being a fit mother.'

'But that's a complete lie! I don't have a lover. I've never had a lover, despite all your jealous accusations. And I *am* a fit mother!'

'That's why you carelessly started a fire when your baby was asleep in the house, is it?'

A chill creeps down my spine as a terrible thought strikes me. Could Oliver have somehow set that fire? Did he deliberately tamper with the wiring in order to accuse me of being an unfit mother? Christ, surely even he wouldn't risk our baby's life just to discredit me? 'That was an accident!' I yell, banishing the thought.

'It was complete carelessness on your part. Hadn't you been smoking and gossiping with a friend, that old woman from across the road? It's so difficult to prove your innocence, isn't it?'

'How can you make up such bare-faced lies? You know perfectly well that I don't smoke. And having one glass of wine too many at Sunday lunch doesn't make me an alcoholic.'

'Oh, right, and you're being so drunk the neighbours felt obliged to call the police was an accident too, was it?'

I'm enraged, longing to get really angry with him but doing my utmost to curb my temper, knowing no good would come of losing it. 'That's not how it was,' I quietly respond, 'and you know it. You created that row, smashed all those cups and plates, not me.'

He puts back his head and roars with laughter. 'Says who? Prove it. Go on, prove it, if you can. It would be so easy for me to conjure up evidence of *your* guilt, irrespective of whether or not it's true, exactly as I did when those police officers came asking a lot of damn fool questions. And what about that young man you were talking to at the agency's office today, for instance. Who is he?'

'What young man?' A cold chill runs down my spine. If Oliver saw me talking to Tim Hathaway that must mean he'd been hanging around for much longer than I'd imagined. Was he at the pub too? Watching us? Listening in to our conversation? I feel suddenly faint as I recall how near I came to confiding in Emma. What on earth would have happened if I'd done so with Oliver close by, listening to every word I said? 'If you mean Mr Hathaway, the walker, he's a client. That was the first time I'd met him today. Tell me, Oliver, did you follow the bus? Or did you come home early, as you so love to do to check up on me, and then realise where I'd gone? Why didn't you come in and say hello to Emma when you first arrived? Why wait till after we'd had lunch? Why hide?'

His smile is wintry and doesn't reach his eyes. 'Much more fun to watch you both gossiping and making your little plans, scheming your little schemes.'

I've heard enough and I turn away from him in disgust. 'You're sick, do you know that? An absolute creep to follow me about in that shameful way. Am I to be allowed no freedom at all then? No transport, no job, no independence, just because I'm your *wife*?'

'You have what I give you, what I allow you to have, and don't you ever forget that,' he yells at me as I march away up the stairs. 'Don't ever consider bailing out, Carly. You'd find it far too expensive, and dangerously risky.'

Upstairs I throw myself on the bed too angry to cry, but I know that he's won. Again.

It's all about survival. Despite my moment of recklessness, I do indeed take his threats seriously, however flawed and fraudulent they might be. Very seriously indeed. I'm worn out by a constant feeling of dread, by this suppressed anger burning deep inside me, the pent-up emotion, the fear and desperation. But I daren't even begin to express it. Far too risky. I feel drained, constantly tired, overwhelmed by a strange lethargy that robs me of energy. There are no more bus trips to Bowness. Sometimes I can't even bring myself to step outside the door. I can't remember the simplest thing, can't think straight. My rashness in disagreeing with him that night cost me several more bruises, but I'm not a masochist. Generally I make very sure that I say nothing to inflame his temper. I am learning to protect myself.

I concentrate entirely on getting through each day, on surviving each display of temper. I can't focus on anything beyond that, cannot view my marriage as an entity over which I have any control, or visualise any future for us. I'm far too concerned with coping with the day-to-day, with telling silly fibs and practising little deceits, with being resourceful and courageous, being really quite cunning at times. Far removed from the pathetic, passive creature everyone imagines when they think of battered wives. But then survival requires me to scheme and cheat, and be underhand.

I may need to appear submissive at times, be excessively wary and cautious of my husband's volatile moods, go along with his wishes against my better judgement at times, but I need to make sure that he doesn't hit me *now*. I make every effort to appease him. I tell myself that by tomorrow, or the next day, or the day after that, I might have thought of a way out of this mire. Maybe then I'll be able to work out a long-term strategy and escape plan.

The memory of the two occasions I attempted to run away are still painfully fresh in my mind: how he cajoled and tricked and even dragged me back. I'm aware that even when I'm not attempting to leave, such as my trip to Bowness to see Emma, Oliver works on the assumption that I might be, and keeps a very close watch on my every movement. It's chilling, and deeply disturbing. I'm far too afraid of him to try again, even though I castigate myself for being weak and soft.

But then I can't afford to take too many risks. I have Katie to think about now. And Oliver does have all the aces. Where could I live? Even if I go back to the agency, how could I care for her and work at the same time? Could I earn enough to keep us? No doubt social services or the council would find me accommodation, in some grim, run-down housing estate where I'd be at risk of being attacked by strangers every time I set foot out of the door. I certainly have no wish to bring up my child in such a place. Or they might take her away from me altogether, put her into foster care if they weren't satisfied with what I could offer.

And all of this supposes that Oliver would actually let her go? Despite his lack of interest in our child, I believe him when he says he would fight me for custody. He would do that simply to bring me to heel, to score points and win. The thought of losing my baby is too terrible to contemplate. Surely staying is by far the least of these evils.

I'm learning to be resilient, perhaps brave sometimes to the point of being foolhardy. I'm in a living hell and it takes all my strength to keep my life on an even keel. I never feel relaxed as I have to be forever on my guard against upsetting him, and when it goes wrong I crawl inside my invisible shell and wait for the storm to pass. I seem to lurch from one crisis to another and I can't think beyond that, cannot distance myself from the present day sufficiently to visualise any alternative future.

I feel like a hostage who has to barter with her captor for leniency. Yet it's worse in a way because it's my own husband who has captured me, and I have this instinctive need to reach out to him for help.

I wonder sometimes if Oliver too feels trapped, enmeshed by his own desire for power and control. We're caught up together in this destructive situation, an ever-recurring pattern of abuse. I no longer ask myself whether I love or hate him, whether it's right for me to stay or leave. I've given up questioning such things. I'm defeated. He's won. Consciously or unconsciously I'm way beyond such reasoning. My one object now is to survive.

He becomes increasingly distant in the days and weeks following, cold and distant towards me, often not speaking to me for days on end. I try to tell him about my conversation with Emma, to explain how lonely and isolated I feel and that I really would love to get back to work, if only part-time. I beg him to reinstate my car, to at least talk to me. Finally I'm forced to admit that I can't stand the way he's ignoring me. His whole demeanour is unnerving, frightening.

Then one Sunday morning I recklessly say I'd prefer anything to this cold, endless silence. 'At least if you had another woman I'd have something definite to deal with.'

'It's interesting you should say that,' he blithely responds. 'Because there is someone as a matter of fact.'

17

I am utterly devastated. It feels like the ultimate betrayal. Has Oliver ever told me anything close to the truth? My entire marriage seems to have been built on lies. In the awful recriminations, explanations, and row that follows, Oliver makes it clear that it's all my fault. I'm the one who has driven him into another woman's arms because of my 'constant complaints', my 'nagging' and my 'need for independence'. He complains about my 'hysteria', and I freely confess that at times I have got a bit hysterical when he's beaten me, particularly in the early days. Who wouldn't?

Apparently the first affair was with Poppy, the rather pretty girl I met at the dinner dance, but now he's taken up with my old school friend, Jane. I can hardly believe it. *Jane*, of all people, and she was so critical of Oliver, telling me she thought him far too full of himself. She was jealous because she imagined we'd moved up in the world to a detached house on a posh estate. She's clearly not so condemning of him now. No wonder she's never made any effort to return my call, and was so cool and distant at the dance. She must have deliberately orchestrated that meeting between myself and Poppy, and then decided she rather fancied him herself.

I'm in complete despair, haunted by the images of the man I love, the man I believed loved me, making love to another woman, to the person I once thought of as my *best friend*.

I can take no more and go to my sister.

'Can I stay here tonight?' It's the following day and I've walked most of the two miles to her house, although a kind neighbour spotted me struggling with Katie, baby buggy, and a heavy overnight bag, and gave me a lift for the last half mile. Now I'm sitting in my sister's lounge telling her all about Oliver's betrayal, explaining that I'd like some time on my own. 'I just need some space, a little peace in which to think and decide what I should do about it.'

Jo-Jo sighs. 'You won't find any peace here. This house is pure bedlam.'

I look at her and frown. She looks tired with dark rings under her eyes, her cheeks pale and puffy. It's half past ten in the morning and she's still in her tatty old dressing gown. I find myself starting to worry about her. Is she sick? Is one of the children sick? I know she's exhausted, and who wouldn't be with four young children to care for, but my sister seems oddly detached, as if she isn't in the least interested in my troubles, isn't even listening. 'Did you hear what I said? Oliver is having an affair.'

'Join the club,' she bitterly remarks, and pours us both a glass of wine. 'I think we need something a bit stronger than tea and sympathy today, don't you?'

'Have you even had breakfast?' I ask, taking the glass she offers me. 'And what do you mean by join the club?'

She shrugs as if she really couldn't care less, then takes a long slug of wine, pushes back her tousled hair which clearly hasn't seen sight of a brush for some time. 'I'm quite convinced Ed is having it off with someone too. Possibly your Emma.'

'What?' I look at her in horror. 'You have to be joking! Ed absolutely adores you, and Emma and Glen are very much a couple, even though they aren't married. In any case, Ed would never do anything to risk losing his children.'

Jo-Jo starts to pout. 'Are you saying that's the only reason he stays with me, because he loves the kids?'

'No, I'm saying that he absolutely adores you.'

'He's been working a lot of overtime lately, or so he says. For all I know he could be over in Bowness with the gorgeous Emma, that so-called business partner of yours.'

'Oh, for goodness' sake, Jo-Jo, he is not in Bowness with

Emma. You're having delusions. Of course he's working a lot of overtime! You have four children to keep for God's sake, and *you* don't bring any money in.'

She almost bites my head off. 'Don't go all sniffy on me because I had to give up my job. I do my best but how can I possibly work with four kids to look after? It's all right for you and Oliver. You've loads of dosh. For us, money is tight.'

I sigh with exasperation, wondering how it is that every time I go to my sister with *my* problems, we end up talking about *hers*. Patiently, I try again. 'Ed is not having an affair, not with Emma or anyone. You're imagining it. You're seeing problems where they don't exist, just because you're tired and depressed. Stop it. Stop feeling sorry for yourself.'

'I'm not imagining things. It's not good between us right now. We never have sex. Never! I never want it, never feel like it, so why would he stay faithful?'

'Because he loves you. I'm sure it will pass, this feeling. I dare say your lack of interest is only because you had a more difficult birth this time, and you're over-tired. But you've nothing to worry about where Ed is concerned, really you haven't. He's a one-woman guy, absolutely faithful, no doubt about that. Ed is a good husband and an excellent, caring father. Oliver, unfortunately, is neither.'

'Oh, for goodness' sake, now who's exaggerating? I saw him fawning all over you at the christening, and his precious baby. He was clearly a man content with his lot. Has he been neglecting you lately? Has he forgotten your birthday or something?'

'It's not my birthday, as you very well know.'

'So having a baby means it's no longer just the two of you in wedded bliss, and endless romantic evenings out. Get real. That's life! Buy yourself a new sexy nightdress,' she says irritably. 'That'll soon bring him running.'

I put down the glass of wine untouched. 'Well, if I was wanting tea and sympathy, I've obviously come to the wrong place.'

She gives my overnight bag a long, hard stare. 'And if you

were thinking of staying, forget it. I couldn't even lend you a clothes line to sleep on. House full. No vacancies. Didn't you see the sign when you came in?'

I pick up my bag, tuck Katie back in the baby buggy, and leave. What is the point in talking to her, of trying to expect her to understand? Why would she even care about me? She's only my sister, for heaven's sake. And if she won't listen to what I have to say about Oliver's infidelity, she certainly wouldn't be interested in hearing the rest of my sordid tale.

I walk out of the door without a backward glance. I certainly don't give her the satisfaction of seeing my tears.

I go instead to see Dad. I call in the shop at lunchtime while Mum is at home making dinner for the old folks, and tell him that Oliver has been unfaithful and I don't think that I can go on. Despite all the stuff that has gone badly wrong in my marriage, I'm heartbroken. I feel bitter and angry, as if all my efforts, all my striving to help Oliver overcome his problems have been for nothing. Dad is clearly angry too, and upset that I should be hurt in this way. He hugs me close, offering what comfort he can, but then to my utter horror urges me to be brave and not do anything rash.

'You must think of Katie, think of what's best for her. If Oliver truly regrets what he's done, there's no reason why your marriage shouldn't recover. You may be able to find it in your heart to forgive him.'

I can hardly take in what he's saying to me, hardly see him for my tears. Of course, I've said nothing about the other problems in my marriage, not a word about how Oliver treats me, by now buried so deep that the doors against it are shut tight. I'm quite incapable of opening them and speaking about this to anyone. I'm too conditioned to keeping it a secret, too well trained, almost brain-washed into silence.

'But I need your help,' I beg him. 'I need you to talk to Oliver. Maybe you can make him see sense, make him understand that he's destroying everything we ever had together.'

I suppose I'm clinging to the fragile hope that my dad, who's always been my hero, can somehow resolve all my problems with a bit of straight talking. I seem to expect him to do this without even knowing the whole sordid story. Madness, I know, but I'm not thinking clearly.

A part of me still longs to save my marriage, to make it happy and joyous as I'd once dreamed it would be, as my parents' marriage is. Another part of me is no longer in denial, sees only the reality and wants to run as far away as humanly possible from this mess, if only I could find a safe place to run to.

Dad is reluctant to interfere but promises that he'll help in any way he can. He agrees that he and Mum will call this evening, and we'll talk through what is best to be done.

If I'd hoped that a family discussion would put everything right and my loving parents would provide me with the support I need, then I'm soon to be bitterly disappointed.

I don't mention to Oliver that they're coming until the last possible moment, afraid of what his reaction might be. Needless to say I'm right to be concerned. He's furious to learn that I've discussed his affair with my parents and has great difficulty in restraining his anger.

'How dare you ask them over without even checking with me first?'

I look at him, my eyes blank. 'Did you ask me if you could have an affair?'

Oliver takes control of the meeting from the start. While I put on the kettle and make tea he gets in first with his defence. I can hear him saying how sorry he is, how filled with remorse, that he never meant this to happen. He's explaining how we were having a few problems and everything got on top of him. He sounds so genuine even I begin to wonder if this can be true. Did I neglect him, was that why he looked elsewhere? Oliver has a way of making me doubt even my own name.

I carry the tea through and Mum casts me one of her 'What

have you been doing now?' sort of looks. I ignore her, pour the tea and pass round the cups. I've steeled myself to face this meeting and I'm quite certain I was right to ask for their help. I have every faith that Dad can put things right for me, as if by magic. I need someone on my side, and who better than my own parents?

But I have to admit it's not looking good. Everyone seems edgy and uncomfortable as we all sit politely sipping tea, except for Oliver who is striding about the room in an agitated fashion, constantly running a hand through his hair. He looks very much like a man at the end of his tether.

'I've tried so hard to make our marriage work,' he's saying. 'But everything I do is wrong. I seem to have no importance in her life. All Carly cares about is her job, not me, not the house, not spending time together as a proper loving couple should, just her precious job. I don't mind confessing that the drinking was the worst, the lowest point so far. Never in a million years had I imagined that my lovely Carly would turn into a wino, practically an alcoholic, smashing crockery, having hysterics, arguing with the police . . .'

'The police?' Dad is shocked. 'I knew nothing about any police.'

My mouth has fallen open but Oliver is all conciliatory. 'It's all right, Ken, I took the blame. I fobbed them off, let them think I was the one who'd had too much to drink, not her.'

'For goodness' sake,' I say, unable to hear any more. 'This is all absolute nonsense, I . . .'

Oliver interrupts with something very like a sob. 'You see how she denies all responsibility. Carly seems to imagine she can behave exactly as she pleases and it really doesn't matter how much she hurts me.' He gives me one of his anguished, loving glances. 'You know how I absolutely adore her, how I'd do anything for her. She is my *life!*'

I begin to feel a dreadful predictability about this entire discussion. Mum is hanging on to his every word, Dad still hesitating to get involved, perhaps sensing something isn't quite right, but not sure what. He's clearly embarrassed and I can see he's wishing he were anywhere but in my lounge discussing the intimate details of my marriage. He looks at me as if for some sort of clue, but I'm not sure how to react. Doesn't he see that it's all lies, that this whole performance is a sham?

Oliver goes to sit next to Mum on the sofa and she gently pats his shoulder. 'I know I've made terrible mistakes, Viv, but I couldn't bear the way Carly ignored me. She's been completely obsessed with the baby. She rarely even acknowledges my presence much of the time.'

Mum gently points out that all new mums are like this. 'It's fairly normal behaviour but it passes in time, I do assure you, when the child starts to get stroppy.' Another of her fierce glares comes my way, and I see that this is all going terribly wrong, that I'm the one on the rack here, not Oliver.

'I do see that now,' he says, as if making a confession. 'And I realise that having an affair was a childish, stupid reaction. It was very wrong of me, but is it any wonder I was tempted with the way she's been behaving? I can see that I've made things worse between us, not better, but she still imagines she should have the same freedom she enjoyed when she was single. Carly is so stubborn, so obstinate.'

Dad snorts and admits I always was a little madam in that respect, then quietly adds, 'Some might see obstinacy as a strength. She might be a bit quiet and shy, but she never gives up if things get tough, does our Carly.'

Thank you, Dad, I think, and manage a small smile but then, perhaps rashly, I decide this may well be the moment to reveal how Oliver has attempted to knock this stubbornness out of me.

'Maybe that's the reason he hits me.'

Silence greets this remark, but I'm unrepentant. There, I think, the words are out at last. I've said it. I've told them the truth. I look at my parents, from one to the other of them and I'm surprised to see no reaction of any kind. They aren't shocked, aren't even surprised, and Oliver simply rolls his eyes heaven-ward, then shakes his head in mock despair.

'Didn't I say she'd bring up that old chestnut again. You see how she never lets it drop. Once – once only did I hit her, a little slap, that's all, and she tripped over a rug and fell and hurt her head. You remember how sorry I was at the time. I called in the shop specifically the following morning to confess and apologise, if you remember. That was when I was upset over her flirting with the waiter,' he elaborates, just in case they've forgotten the exact details. He sounds so reasonable, so genuinely concerned and upset, and I'm amazed to see there are actually tears in his eyes. What a brilliant actor this man is.

'But will she forgive me? She never stops banging on about that one stupid mistake. Now I've made another, and I doubt she'll forgive me for that either. You see how difficult she is to deal with. No matter how hard I try to please her she's never satisfied. And you surely must know – Viv, Ken – that all I want is to make your lovely daughter happy?'

There's much more nauseating stuff along these same lines but I've stopped listening. I can see that my parents are drinking it all in, carried along by his evident sincerity. And it's true, he is very convincing, utterly charming and plausible. Had I not known better, I would have believed him myself. I am swamped with despair and a sensation of complete helplessness.

'You made a bad error of judgement,' Dad tells him. 'It's one thing to look at other women, enjoy the view as it were, but quite another to get involved with one.' He turns to me then and asks if I'm prepared to forgive Oliver and try again. 'Do you want this marriage to survive, Carly?

There's a long awkward silence while I seriously consider the question. The whole room seems to be holding it's breath. At last I quietly remark that I'm not sure I do. 'I don't see how I can go on.'

I see at once how shocked and disappointed my father is. He immediately responds with a lot of spiel about marriage being for life. Dad means well but he's very old-fashioned.

He still believes divorce is a shocking thing, viewing it very much as a last resort, a state he doesn't believe we should have reached so early in our marriage. He's lecturing me now about pulling together, about give and take. Doesn't he realise that my husband only takes, and I'm the one who gives, gives, gives? I start to say this but my mother interrupts, sharply reminding me of my marriage vows.

'You don't run away when the going gets tough,' she scolds me. 'Marriage is for better and for worse.'

'All I seem to have had so far is the worse,' I say, unable to keep the bitterness out of my voice. 'I can't go on like this.'

'Don't be ridiculous! You've had a wonderful start to married life, but if things go wrong you have to set to and make them come right, not wallow in self pity. You have to pull together.'

'I *can't*,' I repeat, like a stuck record. There's a constriction in my throat, trapping any other words, any further explanation, blocked by the sight of Oliver's cold grey-blue eyes warning me to tread carefully, that if I say too much, I'll regret it.

The moment Mum glances up at him, his expression changes to one all innocence and concern. 'You see how stubborn she is? This is what I have to put up with the entire time.' He holds out his hands as if in desperate appeal. 'I don't believe Carly gives a toss about me. She doesn't love me any more.' Then he puts his head in his hands and begins to quietly weep.

'Oh, Carly,' Mum says, sounding cross, and puts her arms about Oliver, not me.

I stare at them all, dumbfounded. It wasn't supposed to be like this. They were supposed to take *my* side, help *me* deal with my husband's betrayal, not lecture me about forgiveness and allow *him* to accuse *me* of all manner of stuff. I feel as if the world has gone mad, or I have.

'He's lying,' I gasp. 'Everything he says is a lie.'

'Stop it, Carly!' Dad snaps. 'This isn't getting us anywhere. You have to look at the reality of life, not some rosy, idealised dream. Stop squabbling, the pair of you, and start talking like adults for a change.'

Oliver smirks, evidently still bent on exercising his considerable charm with my trusting parents, maintaining that this silly little affair has been blown out of all proportion, and they are drinking it all in. 'It meant nothing, a stupid mistake because we've not been getting on too well lately. I'm perfectly willing to try again. I swear Carly is the only woman I have ever loved.'

'But why haven't you been getting along?' Mum asks, genuinely puzzled. 'What on earth is the problem?' She fires this question at me, in a tone of voice which doesn't encourage confidences, let alone the revelation of dark secrets, and I'm seeing now that this entire meeting was a bad idea. I feel as if I'm trapped in a corner, damned if I speak and damned if I don't. It's all going wrong and I make one last desperate effort. I mention the unofficial overdraft and my having to go to the bank manager and apologise. I tell them that Oliver stole the money from Katie's piggy bank.

Dad is appalled. He issues a stern lecture to us both on our immaturity and foolishness, on how selfish we're being by fighting over money when Oliver has such a good job and must be earning well.

Oliver interrupts. 'I didn't steal Katie's money. Carly is absolutely paranoid. I took it because I fully intend to invest it in a special account in her name.'

'I'm sure you do,' Mum says, patting his hand.

Only I can tell that he's lying.

'He sold my car,' I cry, but even here Oliver draws their sympathy, launching into a long explanation on how finishing off the house has turned out to be far more expensive than he'd accounted for.

'I'm sure we'll recover, but I didn't think a car for Carly was an important issue right now, not while she's at home with the baby.'

'Of course it isn't,' Mum snaps. 'I certainly never had a car of my own when I was at home with my babies, and you can always ring an order through to the shop, Carly, if you want me to bring anything over, or need a lift into town.'

Now I'm being made to seem greedy, like a spoiled child, when all I want is a little independence and consideration. My parents both come from working-class backgrounds, have known hard times, including a recession in the early nineties when their business very nearly went under, so my complaints seem trivial by comparison.

The men are talking among themselves but I've stopped listening. Mum is still ranting on at me, telling me how I should appreciate my good fortune, be grateful for having such a beautiful baby and really shouldn't have any problems at all.

I know that I've lost. They want me to sweep my problems under the carpet, forgive Oliver for the affair, accept my lot, and get on with life. They believe I have a romanticised view of the world, should grow up and stop expecting everything to be perfect. Maybe they're right. Maybe I do expect too much. Maybe this is how life is for everyone.

'Life is messy,' Dad sternly informs me. 'Accept that fact.'

'What you both need is a break,' Mum informs us. 'You haven't been away anywhere together since that weekend in Paris when you got pregnant. Why don't you go for a lovely holiday by the sea, with little Katie. It's time you learned to be a family.'

Oliver actually kisses my mother on the cheek, which must be a first. 'Viv, you're a treasure. That's a wonderful idea. Why don't we do that, Carly?'

Dad is beaming, as if he has single-handedly saved the world, or our small part of it at least.

What more can I say? It's hopeless. They think Oliver is genuine in his remorse, that he is desperately sorry and still loves me, that the sun shines out of his arse.

To be fair, they remain blithely unaware that there has been far more violence than that single slap he so conveniently confessed to, and which supposedly caused me to trip and fall over the rug. Even that incident was far worse than the tale he told them, let alone how badly his violence has escalated since. But they don't believe a word I say, so why waste my breath?

They've been won over completely by his charm, as per usual, and any shreds of courage I managed to dredge up to face this meeting have long since evaporated. I'm rapidly withdrawing into myself again, falling back into my depression, quite incapable of opening that particular Pandora's Box. I want only to run away and hide.

Unfortunately, hiding isn't an option. Oliver shows them politely out of the door, shaking Dad firmly by the hand and giving Mum a warm hug. Once they've gone, he switches off all the lights and with a silent jerk of his head, orders me upstairs. I know what is coming, yet am equally certain that there is no escape. Where could I run? Nowhere. There's no support from anyone. I'm on my own.

I'm completely trapped in this living nightmare, so I meekly do exactly as my husband says.

18

Where am I going? What am I doing? Why have I agreed to forgive Oliver and try again? I can no longer trust a word my husband says. He lies to me, lies to my parents, is a cheat, a bully and a total control freak. Yet I'm trapped. Right now I can't think of any feasible alternative. I'm beyond hope, so sunk in misery and depression I can't think at all, although the future terrifies me. I'm haunted by his betrayal, blame myself entirely. If I'd been a good wife to him instead of being so hopeless at everything, so useless and unattractive, perhaps he wouldn't have felt the need to look elsewhere.

'I would never have looked at another woman had you and I been getting along as we should.'

He's so drummed this into my head, I've come to believe it. Nor am I convinced that the affair is over, no matter how much he might claim it to be.

I know that I should give up on our marriage and leave, despite what my parents say, and I tell him so. But he swears that he still loves me, that we can still make it work. He weeps and begs me to give him another chance, tells me how sorry he is that he's screwed up, how much he needs and depends upon me, how we can still be happy.

As always I end up consoling him, and, despite the small warning voice in my head, find myself promising to stay. I know he's past master at getting *me* to feel sorry for *him* but I'm secretly relieved that I don't have to step out into the unknown right now. I feel so alone, so vulnerable. Who could I turn to?

Certainly not my unsympathetic family. Oliver has effectively cut me off from them. I've really no idea what other lies he may have told them about our problems, what tales he has spun to win their support, but they undoubtedly believe his version of events and not mine. I don't feel able to argue any more, all the fight has drained out of me. I certainly don't feel capable of coping on my own, or of making decisions of any sort. It's all too frightening.

Even if I went to Emma's, what could she possibly do to help? She would be no match against Oliver's fierce determination to hang on to me.

I feel so tired, exhausted much of the time, nervous and jumpy, depressed, and really rather ill. I'm deeply ashamed of my own inadequacy but quite incapable of doing anything about it. If I left, I'd be constantly looking over my shoulder, expecting him to appear at any moment and force me to return. He might even take Katie away from me. I know he's capable of anything.

As if sensing my panic in the days and weeks following that family discussion, I often sense him smiling at me with sad compassion in his greyblue eyes, those same eyes which I once fell in love with. 'The problem is that you've let yourself go, Carly, which is a pity, because you used to be so sexy.'

He's right, I think. I am a mess. I've lost weight, and I'm appalled by the dark rings under my eyes, by the gauntness of my face. I slob about the house all day in old jeans and a T-shirt, rarely bothering to even put on lipstick. No wonder he's having affairs.

'We'll be OK,' he promises. 'We just have to try a bit harder.'

By *we* I realise he means me, but the fact he's willing to try is such a relief that I hang on to the belief that a solution to our troubles might be found.

There are days, though not so many now, when my brain clears slightly and I begin to work out a solution. I look for a place to hide, for some means of escaping. But I always come up against the same obstacles. I have no job, no home other than this one, no money of my own, and absolutely no confidence in myself that I could cope. My head starts to buzz with half-formed plans, then it all gets far too complicated and I give up. My brain feels paralysed, my emotions frozen.

My only consolation is that since the punishment he meted out to me following that disastrous family meeting, he hasn't lost his temper once, or laid a hand on me. He's his old charming self again, attentive and caring. Nothing is too much trouble. Seeing how tired I am he tells me to put my feet up and rest. He brings me breakfast in bed, the first time ever.

I should be feeling the smallest degree of optimism for a new beginning, but somehow I've lost heart. I feel numb, utterly devoid of emotion. All hope gone.

Katie's first Christmas passes in a blur, not special at all, despite my eagerness to make it so. The piggy bank is still empty and there is no evidence of any savings account being opened in her name, and I'm only too aware that the overdraft at the bank has still not been paid off.

I'm going through the motions of normality, when really nothing about my life is the least little bit normal.

In January, we do go on holiday, exactly as Mum suggested. We fly out to Tenerife and stay at a small family hotel by the sea in Los Cristianos. The sun shines and the days are pleasant enough. I take lots of happy photos of Katie enjoying dipping her toes in the sea for the first time and patting at the sand castles I have built for her.

Oliver is surprisingly tolerant and attentive, apparently making every effort to save our marriage, but there is an awkwardness between us, a distance we can't quite bridge. I look at this man I married and see a stranger. We're not coping well, superficially pretending to get along, perhaps for Katie's sake, or because we've grown accustomed to keeping up appearances.

The nights are pure torture. Were I able to contemplate a return to normal sexual relations between us, it would be impossible. Katie absolutely refuses to settle. She spits out her comforter and screams the place down hour upon hour.

I try every desperate measure I can think of to quieten her, pacing the floor of the bedroom as I sing to her in my arms, bathing her in case she's too hot, rubbing her back and tummy, feeding her, changing her. Nothing works. Oliver's patience is evaporating rapidly and I'm close to exhaustion. I decide that she's missing her own cot and the familiarity of her daily routine, or maybe she's picked up on the heavy atmosphere between the two of us. Whatever the reason, her behaviour is profoundly embarrassing.

Not unreasonably there's a complaint from the hotel management. Oliver loses his temper and orders me to pack our bags. We're leaving. So much for happy families.

Back home, Katie instantly returns to her old sweet self. She is my pride and joy, my sanity. I devote my entire day to her, making her delicious, home-made puréed food rather than buying ready prepared. I take her for walks, and endlessly play with her. Late each afternoon I try to remember to clear away all her baby things in good time before Oliver comes home. He hates to see the lounge littered with her stuff: the bouncy baby chair where I rock her, her squeaky duck and the cuddly teddy that I knitted for her, her plastic bricks and little postbox into which she posts each one, with my help of course.

One day he comes home slightly early, as he likes to do sometimes, just to keep me on my toes, and he finds the knitted teddy lying in his own chair. He picks it up, about to toss it into the stove when I rush in and stop him.

'You can't do that, it's Katie's favourite toy. I knitted it for her myself.'

'Good lord, don't tell me you've learned to knit. Then why aren't I saving myself a fortune by having you knit my sweaters in future?' He's hanging on to the teddy and there's an undignified tug of war going on between us.

'Don't be silly, Oliver, you know I'm not capable of knitting a sweater.'

'You're not capable of doing anything right,' he scoffs, 'and for God's sake shut that child up. Does she never stop crying?' Thankfully he releases his grip on the teddy, and I take Katie upstairs.

I'm desperately tired, never quite getting enough sleep, partly because of listening out for Katie, but partly because the moment I wake, I start worrying about the future.

Every evening I bathe and feed her, then I sit in the rocking chair in the little nursery and cuddle her before putting her down to sleep. Sometimes she goes all night now without waking, but I never mind if she does wake up because it gives me the opportunity to cuddle her again. Babies, I've discovered, are exhausting creatures, and Oliver still shows little interest in her, but I no longer care. I love her to bits. Nothing else matters so long as I have my child.

Life continues in this way for some time, outwardly peaceful, but it's a shaky peace. In theory Oliver has turned over a new leaf, ditched the lovely Jane, and is a devoted and attentive husband. In practice nothing very much has changed at all. Oliver continues to go out several evenings a week and I'm quite convinced the affair with my erstwhile friend is very much on-going. Inevitably his good intentions falter and the sulks and the black moods return, together with his long-drawn-out gloomy silences. And his desire to control is as strong as ever. I never complain, never say a word. I suppose I've reached a kind of acceptance of my lot, a dangerous one perhaps, but a state of complete resignation.

Another spring is upon us with the sweet scent of bluebells and May flowers on the air. Katie is almost ten months old now, sitting up and taking an interest, but the minute she sees Oliver she just waves her little hand, as if assuming Daddy is on his way out somewhere. She doesn't see him as a part of her life. I'm beginning to feel very much the same. Could I at last be growing less dependent upon him, and is this a good thing, I wonder?

I've begun to think that violence turns him on. After he's gone through the usual ritual of apologising and nursing me better, begging for my forgiveness, sometimes in tears, then follows the love making. I find that sickening. It certainly doesn't turn *me* on, and our sex life, so far as I'm concerned, is of little interest to me now.

I go through the motions, trying not to expect too much and not to imagine how he must have enjoyed making love to Jane, my one-time best friend. Perhaps still does. But it's hard, and there are obviously times when I am less than enthusiastic. Refusal to have sex, however, is not an option, not unless I want the whole spiral of his anger to start up all over again. I never object, even though I rarely feel in the mood these days. But then Oliver isn't a man who takes no for an answer.

He no longer troubles himself with foreplay, irritated that I'm not as sexy as I used to be, as he frequently and caustically informs me.

'You're useless in bed. You don't even try.'

'Wanting to make love doesn't start in the bedroom,' I tell him, but he doesn't understand. I loathe this ability Oliver has to dismiss his treatment of me as of little consequence, and to use my vulnerability to his advantage.

One night I wake to find him on top of me.

'What the hell are you doing?' I'm only half awake but he's pulled up my nightdress and he's pushing himself inside me, obviously willing to take me even while I'm asleep.

I try to push him off but he grabs both my wrists with one hand and holds me down while he thrusts himself into me, hard. He's strong and powerful and there's no way I can escape. I'm dry and closed, not even remotely aroused, and I cry out as he hurts me badly. He takes not the slightest notice, ramming into me with everything he's got.

When finally it's over, he slumps to one side, ignoring me. I'm shaking now, and crying. 'You *raped* me!'

'Don't talk rubbish! How can it be rape? You're my *wife*!'

The sex was brutal, awful, disgusting! He didn't care that

I might not have felt like it, that I might still be upset over the beating he'd given me only hours before, that I was asleep. He wanted sex so he took it. He seems to imagine he has that right, simply because we're married. When I go to the bathroom and wash myself I find I'm bruised and sore. I feel unclean, dirty, used, as if he really doesn't care who I am or what I want. As if the only reason I exist is to please him.

Carly's father was becoming concerned about his daughter. He didn't think she was looking at all well, and the holiday, by all accounts, had not been a riotous success. He was beginning to wonder if he'd tackled that family discussion quite as well as he should. Was there something more he could have done, some aspect of their relationship that perhaps they were unaware of? He never had taken to Oliver quite as much as his wife had, but Viv had laughed at that, saying what man could ever be good enough for a precious daughter, in a father's estimation. Just as she was laughing at him now for suggesting they might be missing something.

'All our Carly has missed out on is more discipline when she was young. You spoiled that girl something shocking.'

'Rubbish! You don't spoil a child by loving them. She's not happy, Viv, I can see it in her eyes.'

'If she isn't, then it's for her husband to put that right, not you. Though she must be partly to blame. He's a lovely man is Oliver, and she's neglected him something shocking, been too full of what *she* wants, instead of being a good wife to him and giving him the kind of attention he deserves. I always said her starting that business was a bad idea. It takes up far too much of her time, and that Emma is so demanding, and very left-wing.'

Ken let out a heavy sigh. 'Please don't bring politics into this. We've enough to worry about already. Emma is a nice girl. A shrewd businesswoman, friendly and outgoing. I rather like her.'

'She wears dungarees and has pink streaks in her hair.'

Ken laughed. 'She's young, so why not? Anyway, the pink sets off those auburn curls of hers nicely. She's really rather sexy.'

Viv looked at her husband and made a little scoffing sound in her throat. 'Don't you start getting ideas.'

He grinned at her. 'As if.'

'Our Carly wants things too much her own way. A woman shouldn't give up and run away just because her marriage hits a problem,' Viv repeated, like a mantra. 'We've not brought her up to be a coward.' So saying, she marched off, head held high, not prepared to listen to any possibility that the gorgeous Oliver could possibly be to blame.

At lunchtime when Viv popped home to make the old folks' dinner, she found the precious daughter in question standing on her doorstep with tears in her eyes, baby buggy, bags and baggage clustered about her feet. Viv took one look and said, 'If you're going to tell me you've left him, I don't want to know.'

'That's exactly what I've done.'

'Well, don't think you can stay here. As your father and I have already made clear, we've no wish to interfere in your marriage. We've done what we can to help, now it's up to you two to sort out the mess. I certainly don't think it's a good idea for you to leave Oliver on his own right now. What about that other woman, whoever she is? She might move in and take your place.'

'She's welcome to him,' Carly replied, an unusual asperity in her tone.

Viv was not amused, nor showed the slightest sympathy. She folded her arms across her chest and regarded her younger daughter with a steely eye. 'So what happened to the fresh start?'

'Can I at least come in? I've no wish to discuss my personal problems in full view of all the neighbours.'

Seated in the kitchen with a mug of tea in her hand, Carly tentatively pointed out that there were further problems, besides the affair, which she was convinced was still going on. 'What if I told you he forced himself on me?'

'Oh, for goodness' sake!' Her mother put her hands to her ears and refused to listen. 'I don't want to know. What happens in a marriage is personal and private. There's nothing I, nor your father, nor anyone else for that matter, can do to help. Whatever it is, another women, money, sex, the problem is yours, not ours. The pair of you have to sort it out for yourselves.'

Carly said, 'On the grounds I've made my bed so must lie in it? Thanks a bunch for your support.'

Viv sighed. 'In any case, Carly, I'm beginning to think that you're very prone to exaggeration.'

'You've made it very clear that you always believe him, and not me. But what if I'm right and your belief in him is wrong, what then? What if he does more than force sex upon me?'

There was the smallest hesitation as Viv considered her daughter. What was she trying to say? What was she hinting at? For a fraction of a second Viv experienced the slightest shiver of a doubt, one she swiftly dismissed, her faith in her son-in-law unshaken. If her daughter wasn't looking quite her normal self right now, she put that down entirely to her having to cope with a young baby. Every young mum had dark rings under their eyes from lack of sleep. 'You always were stubborn, Carly, but refusing to forgive your husband when he's humbly apologised for that stupid affair, is taking obstinacy too far, and refusing to have sex won't help either. Give the man a chance.'

Carly stared at her mother, her eyes becoming oddly blank, totally without expression. 'What about Katie, doesn't she deserve a little consideration?'

Viv glanced down at her granddaughter, whom she adored, before issuing a further lecture on the responsibilities of motherhood.

Carly gave a bitter little laugh. 'That's rich, coming from you.'

Viv bridled. 'I've always been a good mother to you.'

Tears shimmered in her daughter's eyes. 'That's true, actually, in a rough and ready sort of way you have been a good mother to me, despite your hectoring and criticising. So be one now.'

In the end, Viv reluctantly agreed that Carly could stay for one night only. It was her husband who insisted on this when she rang to tell Ken she'd be a bit late getting back to the shop because Carly had come home and wanted to stay. She'd been forced into a corner, the pair of them ganging up on her, but she'd no intention of making things easy for the girl.

'You can't have your old room back. The elderlies have that now, and your father uses Jo-Jo's old room as a home office. Not that you'd be wanting to stay long, I shouldn't think, once you've made whatever point it is you're trying to make to your lovely husband.'

Carly sighed. 'I'm not sure what I want. That's the whole point. I need time to think, but the sofa will do for now.'

'You might as well make yourself useful then. There are a couple of chicken breasts in the fridge I was going to cook for the old folks' dinner. Then you could do the ironing for me, peel some potatoes ready for when we come home, and . . .' The list went on, Viv quite oblivious to Carly's stifled sigh.

When she returned that evening, Viv remained adamant in her decision. 'One night only, remember. Then you'll have to make other arrangements, or sort out this latest problem, whatever it is, between you.'

'She can stay as long as she likes,' Ken corrected his wife.

Carly cast her father a grateful smile and hastened to explain that she desperately wanted a little more time. 'I just need some space to get my head together then I might be able to work out what I should do. The way I'm feeling right now I'm quite unable to make a decision of any sort. If Oliver calls I don't want to see him. Don't even tell him that I'm here.'

Ken assured his daughter that they would do as she asked. 'And so will your mother.' He gave his wife a stern glance.

Viv snorted her disdain and absolutely refused to discuss the matter further, particularly not in front of the old people.

She marched over and switched on the television set, thereby effectively closing the discussion.

Carly spent the evening huddled in a corner of the sofa, not saying a word and trying to ignore the curious glances from her grandparents, although as always both of them were very kind and loving towards her. She offered no explanation as to why she was there, quite unable to tell her sorry tale, and they didn't ask.

She slept that night, or rather didn't sleep, on the sofa. Viv could hear the girl tossing and turning, sometimes prowling about the kitchen, perhaps getting a cup of tea in the early hours. Carly fell asleep from sheer exhaustion just before dawn. Moments later, or so it seemed, she was shaken rudely awake.

'It's Oliver,' her mother said. 'I've put him in the kitchen, but he's anxious to see you.'

'You've *what*? I told you I didn't want to see him, that I needed some space, and time to think.'

'The poor man is in pieces.' Viv handed her a mug of tea. 'He sounds quite suicidal. He really does regret that silly affair, which he very reasonably points out was over months ago, and he's desperate not to lose you. At least come and talk to him. Better still, pack your bags, stop being so holier than thou, and go back home and mend your marriage.'

The spell of good weather is over and spring has turned cold and bleak, exactly as I feel. I'm sick of my own company, sick of my unhappy marriage, weary of life in general. I feel totally alone, without any support from anyone, not even my own family.

Most of the time I feel unwell and just get through each day as best I can. I'm suffering from constant headaches, sickness and depression. My periods are erratic, I can't sleep, can't eat. I'm having problems with my stomach and sometimes throw up whatever I've eaten, and I constantly experience panic attacks, some days feeling quite incapable of even stepping out of the door.

I'm lying in the bath now, my face wet with tears as I gently soap my latest collection of bruises. I feel utter despair. I seem to spend my entire life apologising to my husband for my failings, yet I'm quite sure that even if I suddenly turned into Little Miss Perfect, Oliver still wouldn't be satisfied. There would be something he'd find fault with. Even my apologies irritate him. Nothing I do can ever be right.

He treated my 'running home to Mum' as a personal insult; furious I had again showed him up in front of my parents. And, as always, I was duly punished.

'You're my *wife*!' he shouted at me. 'You belong to *me*. I hope you didn't shoot your mouth off. What we do in our own home is private, *and nothing to do with anyone else*! You keep schtum, right? You stay here, where you belong, and behave yourself, or you'll live to regret it. You really wouldn't like to know what I could do to you if you really pissed me off.'

He has me by the throat while he's saying all of this, shaking me till my teeth chatter in my head.

I don't have the strength to argue with him, to point out that I'm not a possession, like his car, his mobile phone, or his laptop. In fact they probably come first, before me. But I no longer care. I no longer have the energy to stand against him. I'm certainly not capable of properly explaining to anyone what is happening to me. My life is a mess. *I* am a mess. I'm broken. Destroyed. I truly believe that I am a useless wife and a hopeless mother. I'm no good in bed. I have let myself go. I'm boring and dull, and ugly, quite unworthy of anyone's love. Not even my own mother cares about me, and my sister is too wrapped up in imagined problems of her own.

They all like Oliver because he appears so charming, so friendly and affable. This morning, being a Sunday, he's gone to help Dad to clip the hedges. After that Mum will no doubt cook him a snack, despite his already having enjoyed the breakfast I cooked for him earlier, and he'll butter her up some more with his charm.

But underneath all that glossy good will is a darker, far more cruel and complex personality. He's nothing but a sham, a complete lie. Oliver likes to be liked. He loves to look good in front of others. I too was once fooled into thinking him a wonderful, caring, attentive and loving man. Even his possessiveness didn't trouble me, not at first.

I begin to wonder if I love someone who doesn't exist, who never did exist. I thought I could cure his problems with love and understanding. I can see now that was a false hope.

There is no way I can change him. Oliver's bad attitude towards me, perhaps towards women in general, is entrenched in him. He sees no reason to change, would deny there was even a problem. He absolutely refuses to accept responsibility for his own behaviour, believing I am the one at fault, that he has the right to treat me as he does, that he is entitled to be so demanding.

He once seemed to like the fact that I was strong and independent, a woman with a mind of my own, with ambitions for my new business. Now he sees me as some sort of threat. He is adamant that he must remain in charge, and in order to achieve that he intimidates me and puts me down all the time. I fantasise sometimes about killing him, or of him being involved in a tragic car accident. I'm always ashamed of such thoughts afterwards, filled with fresh guilt. But I manufacture these evil thoughts because I'm aware of what he is doing to me. I know that he bullies me psychologically, mentally and physically, that I'm powerless to stop him, powerless to escape. Too conditioned to his abuse, too afraid of what else he might do to me.

Sometimes, in my dreams, I feel as if I'm searching for something, trying to find myself: that happy, bubbly, affectionate girl I once was, but she's gone. She seems to be dead. I can see no way out of this nightmare.

The steam is clearing a little and I notice Oliver's razor lying on the sink. I reach for it and slip out the blade, hold it in the palm of my hand. It would take very little to end all of this agony, to be free of the beatings, the fear, this feeling of utter worthlessness. A few strokes on each wrist, that's all. I doubt it would hurt much, no worse than the pain Oliver constantly inflicts upon me. I take the blade between my finger and thumb, press it lightly against the warm damp skin of my wrist.

The telephone starts to ring. I guess that it is Oliver ringing from Mum and Dad's, checking up on me, making sure that I am where I'm supposed to be, here at home waiting for him. For once I do not rush to answer it. I let it ring. The sound seems to grow louder, echoing in the empty house, filling all the deserted rooms, except that it suddenly occurs to me that the house isn't deserted. Katie is in her cot, and if I do this she'll be quite alone, not only in the empty house, but forever.

I drop the razor blade in the soapy bath water, instantly swamped with guilt. What am I thinking of? I have a child now, a beautiful baby. I'm a *mother*! Who else would love and care for her? Not Oliver. Katie needs *me*. Katie loves me.

I climb out of the bath shaking with emotion, filled with shame. Whatever the answer is, this isn't it.

19

A week or two later I pick up the phone and call Emma. 'I need to see you. I've thought things through and I've decided that I don't want to sell out my share of the agency. I'm thinking of returning to work.'

She comes right over, within the hour, bringing cream cakes as a peace offering, and we hug, and brew coffee, and don't stop talking for hours as we iron out the details. I have no money, no car, and absolutely no confidence in myself, but I explain about Oliver's affair, using that as an excuse for me to reassert myself.

'Is it still going on?' she asks.

'I suspect so, although he claims it's over.'

'Why don't you have him followed? Hire a private detective or something.'

I give a bitter little laugh. 'And pay them with what? That's half my problem, Em, I have no money of my own. I only have the housekeeping, doled out piecemeal, that Oliver gives me. I couldn't afford to run a car even if I still had one. I have to do something or I'll go mad stuck behind these dreadful Venetian blinds. I thought I'd start by working mornings only, if that's all right with you. Then I can get the bus and be home in good time to pick up Katie and make the evening meal.'

'I take it your sister is having the baby?'

'I haven't asked Jo-Jo yet, but I'm hoping to persuade her.'

'And Oliver, is he agreeable?'

I try not to meet my friend's shrewd gaze. 'I haven't told him yet either, but I will. This time I'm really determined that I'm coming back to the agency, no matter what he says.'

'Excellent,' she agrees, giving a wide smile. 'About time you stood up to that man. He isn't God, and you shouldn't do every damn thing he tells you.'

'He's my husband.'

'Oh, for goodness' sake! Look, tell me to mind my own business if you like, but are you sure this is the right solution? You staying with him, I mean.'

'It seems the best solution for now,' I coolly reply, making it very clear that I've no wish to discuss the private details of my marriage.

Emma frowns. 'But there are problems, aren't there? Don't lie, this is me. I've seen the bruises, Carly. I'm not stupid. I think you should talk about this to someone. If not to me, then to a lawyer, or the vicar perhaps?' She sees me wince, and goes on, 'Or a marriage counsellor.'

I try to imagine explaining Oliver's behaviour to a lawyer, doctor or marriage counsellor. The prospect is daunting and quite beyond me right now. 'I admit we have had some problems but Oliver refuses to consider counselling. He's already made his views on the subject very plain.'

'But . . .'

'When I feel ready to talk, I'll let you know,' I tell her, rather curtly.

She sighs. 'I'll consider my wrists slapped over that suggestion. I'm your friend, Carly, I'm just concerned about you, that's all. I want to help.'

I soften a little, and smile. 'You do help, just by being my friend, and I can't begin to tell you how grateful I am for that. I'm so glad we got over whatever it was that created a wedge between us.' There's silence for a moment as we both privately acknowledge it was Oliver who did that, somehow managing to drive us apart for a while. I decide this isn't the moment to go into this facility he has for controlling me, or for being two faced and telling lies. I clear my throat and stoutly go on. 'But it would be better – safer – for me, if you didn't get involved. Making a scene with my husband tends to have rather a – a negative effect.'

'I see.' She's looking very sombre. 'I'm sticking my neck out here, but you know you can always come and stay with me. You still have that spare key.'

I inwardly cringe as I remember the occasion when I attempted to use it. What good did that do me? None at all. Oliver always manages to get the upper hand. 'I really don't think that's the answer. Right now I've forgiven him for the affair and we're giving our marriage another try.' I fish the key out of my bag while I say this and put it on the table where we both stare at it. 'Take it.'

'Are you sure?'

'I'm certain.'

Reluctantly she slips the key into her bag, and a bleakness swells inside me as I watch one possible escape route vanish.

But I'm way past talking about my problems now, can't allow myself to indulge in self-pity. Perhaps because I've come to accept Oliver's behaviour as normal, a part and parcel of life that I've learned to deal with. Even the police would term the problem as *only a domestic*. I remember how the two police constables were easily put off by his excuses when they were called to the house in answer to a neighbour's complaint. They automatically believed him and not me.

Emma is the only one on my side, and I can see by her face that she doesn't believe I'm doing the right thing. I shrug, indicating that I need to give it one last shot. 'I have Katie to think of. I can't risk losing her. I'd prefer not to talk about this right now, if you don't mind. Let's concentrate on business, shall we?' I tuck my legs under me and curl up in a corner of the sofa, turning in on myself again, as if trying to escape from reality.

'Talking might help,' she persists, looking seriously concerned. When I say nothing more, she sighs and gives in. 'OK, when you're ready, let me know. In the meantime, if there's anything I can do, anything at all . . .'

'I need to rebuild: myself, my life . . . I need you to help me do that. I just want you to agree to my returning to work.'

'Absolutely! That's fine. I'd be delighted to have you back, Carly, you know I would. When can I expect you and what are you going to use for transport?'

'I shall start as soon as I can fix it up with Jo-Jo. As for transport, I'm not sure. Initially I'll have to make do with the bus. One problem at a time, but I'll manage somehow.'

'Good for you, girl. I'll look forward to hearing from you.'

The minute Emma leaves I get right on the phone to my sister. It takes some doing but I eventually persuade her to help. Once I make it clear I'll pay her to mind Katie, she's all for it. One more baby is neither here nor there, she says, and she could do with the extra cash.

I don't even ask Oliver his opinion on the matter but simply inform him of my decision. I prepare myself for a row, for the usual battering, but he says nothing. Not that we do talk much these days. There doesn't seem to be much left to say.

My mother is scathing and deeply critical of my decision, issuing yet another long lecture on the responsibility of motherhood. And this from a woman who has worked in the family shop all her married life, paying any number of child minders to care for Jo-Jo and me. Is this her guilt finally coming to the surface, I wonder.

Only my father seems in favour of my decision. 'I'm glad to hear you're going back to work. Maybe getting out and about a bit more will bring the colour back into your cheeks, love.'

'I do hope I can cope.'

'Of course you'll cope. Having a baby doesn't rob you of your motivation to make something of your life.'

Having a controlling husband does, I think.

'I've every faith in you,' he says, giving me a hug.

'I know Mum isn't too happy about my going back to work. She thinks I should stay at home with Katie.'

'She'll come round. I'll work on her. Never forget, you're still my princess.'

'Oh Dad, thanks for your support.' I kiss him and feel quite choked, my throat blocked with tears, and with all the unspoken secrets.

I realise it will be hard parting from my baby even for a few hours each day. Jo-Jo accuses me of fussing too much when I insist she keep careful record in a little book of what she gives Katie to eat. 'I have some experience in feeding babies and toddlers,' she caustically remarks.

'I want to make sure we don't duplicate anything, that between us Katie gets a properly balanced diet.'

It feels strange to be giving instructions to my sister, professional earth-mother that she is, but I want to do the best I can for my child. I'm suffering enough guilt over leaving her, although I really don't have a choice. It's essential that I start to rebuild my life, that I begin to think ahead.

The day arrives and I put on mascara and lipstick, a touch of blusher to each pale cheek. Perhaps Oliver will find me more attractive if I look more like the woman he fell in love with. I worry that I may no longer be able to squeeze into my office suit since having the baby, but it hangs loose on me. I've lost more weight than I realised, which worries me a bit.

But then there's a lot to worry about: whether I can crank up my rusty brain sufficiently to cope with the many tasks demanded of me at the agency, whether I'll have the confidence to deal with people's problems with quite the casual ease I used to. I worry whether Katie will be all right without me, and if I can bear to be parted from her.

I almost don't have the courage to leave the house. I stand in the kitchen with Katie in my arms, her bag of toys and nappies at my feet. I'm breathing hard and my heart is hammering in my chest. I must do this. If I back out now, if I fall at the first hurdle, I may never find the strength to go through it all again.

I strap Katie into the buggy, and deliver her to Jo-Jo with yet more instructions till my sister is sighing heavily and shoving me out of the door. 'For goodness' sake, Carly, go. Get to work! Katie will be fine.'

My first day turns out to be far less difficult than I feared. Somehow, the moment I sit at my old desk, pick up the phone and start to answer a query from a client, I become a different person. I catch a glimpse of the old Carly, the one with skills at her fingertips, and little by little as the day progresses my confidence slowly builds. This is the way for me to escape, I realise: step by step. I cannot change Oliver, but I can change myself. I have to rebuild my own identity, and not let him know I'm doing it. I'm determined to succeed, alone and without help, if necessary.

There was a time when I was in complete denial over our problems, then I went through a stage of looking for a reason to explain his behaviour, which I didn't find. I came to believe that it was all my fault, largely because Oliver drummed this into me over and over again. His constant complaints and criticisms still pound away at my fragile esteem and make me feel more and more worthless.

But failing to achieve Happy-Ever-After is as much his fault as mine. More so, since he's the one in charge. I need to regain control of my own life. I must fight this constant downward spiral of guilt. I seem to have lost everything: confidence in myself as an independent woman, belief in my own judgement, even the rights over my own body. I have to lift myself up, out of the perpetual pattern of abuse and depression, and the way to do that is surely to find myself again and put my own needs first.

Then when I have the strength, and everything in place, I can take that last irrevocable step and finally break free.

'How did it go?' Jo-Jo asks, as I pick up Katie in the early afternoon.

'A bit nerve-wracking at first, but it's going to be OK. I'm glad I've made the decision to go back.'

'You're fortunate to have the choice,' Jo-Jo acidly remarks, unable to resist a barb.

Katie, she assures me, settled very quickly and she never noticed I was gone. She apparently played happily with her cousin Molly, ate her lunch without difficulty and enjoyed a short nap. I experience a pang of fresh guilt but I swallow it whole.

'See you tomorrow,' I call, as I walk away, optimism warming my heart for the first time in months. It feels good. Hope is reborn.

'So, madam has decided to return to work, apparently in need of more money, more stimulation, whatever, and is now filled with guilt. Serve the silly mare right,' Jo-Jo caustically remarked.

'That's putting it a bit harsh. Why shouldn't she return to work? You did when we only had the one child,' Ed said. He was washing up while Jo-Jo warmed milk for Molly's bedtime feed, the only bottle left in her day which she was still clinging to and Jo-Jo had no wish to stop.

'That was different, we needed the money, she doesn't. Oliver is rolling in it.'

Ed idly poured more washing-up liquid into the hot water, then as the bubbles swelled and pilled up, realised he'd rather overdone it and tried to pop them. 'But your sister isn't rolling in it. She's even had to sell her car, which is a bit mean of him, don't you think?'

'Why would she need a car?' Jo-Jo sulked, who drove a beat-up old Ford Fiesta, still going strong after twelve years.

'Living out in the sticks as they do, I should think it's essential. Don't be prejudiced, love. She's entitled to earn some money of her own, and to enjoy a bit of independence. Don't you think that beneath all that charm and affable blokeishness, Oliver is something of a control freak?'

His wife considered this as she screwed the teat on the bottle. 'I always thought the guy was a bit too full of himself, never did understand what Carly saw in him. To her he's Mr Wonderful, Mr-can-do-no-wrong.'

Ed took a moment before answering. 'I'm not so sure. I think she's been looking a bit below par recently.'

'She looks a total mess,' Jo-Jo agreed, with the kind of brutality only a sister can display. 'Let herself go completely since she had the baby.'

'Then maybe it'll be a good thing for her to get out and about a bit more. Maybe she needs some stimulation, some of her old independence back.'

Jo-Jo scowled. 'She can only do that, so long as I'm willing to have her child.'

'But at least your minding Katie earns you a bit of pocket money for yourself, eh?'

Jo-Jo was outraged. 'That's what you think it is, do you, pocket money? I spent all of it, every last penny if you want to know, in the supermarket. I didn't exactly use it for a girls' night out.'

Ed gave a wry smile, then pulled his wife into her arms, unperturbed by her fury. 'Maybe next time we should spend the money on a grown-ups night out, just you and me.'

'In your dreams.' She slapped him away, tried to wriggle free. 'Stop that, your hands are all wet and soapy.'

He stuck a soapy bubble on the tip of her nose, then kissed her mouth so that they were both covered in the stuff. Jo-Jo squealed, gathered up a handful and rubbed the bubbles all over his face, like a clown might with a custard pie. Ed of course retaliated and by this time they were giggling, which excited the children who all gathered round, wanting to join in the game. Stacey grabbed a handful of suds out of the sink and slapped it on to Samantha's head. Samantha screamed and slapped some back on her, which turned into a battle royal. Then Ed piled a coil of soap on each of his daughters' heads, and Ryan, too small to reach the sink, started chasing bubbles and soap suds all around the kitchen, shouting with laughter. The dog caught their excitement and joined in the fun, barking and careering around like a mad thing.

The silly game finally stopped only when the entire family was soaked through and they all collapsed on the sofa in a soapy heap.

'We must be mad,' Jo-Jo gasped.

'Or happy,' Ed agreed, cuddling his family close. 'One of the two.'

They both grinned at each other then cheerily set about the mammoth task of calming down four children sufficiently to get them dried and into bed. Later, as they sat with a cup of tea watching TV, Ed said, 'I've made an appointment to see the quack.'

Jo-Jo jerked as if struck, turned to look at her husband with horror-filled eyes. 'You aren't sick, are you?'

'Nope, but I thought that before we have this night out, or better still a weekend away, assuming your mother will have the kids, of course, I should get a small matter attended to first. Four children is fine, five could be considered overdoing it a stretch.'

His wife was regarding him in all seriousness, a small frown puckering her brow. 'What are you saying, Ed? Are you suggesting that you . . .'

'Have the snip? It was your suggestion, and it seems sensible, then perhaps you'd feel more relaxed and normal service could be resumed.'

Jo-Jo began to cry. 'Oh, Ed, I do love you.'

'Will that convince you that it's *you* I love, and nobody else?'

'Nobody else would have you,' Jo-Jo sobbed.

'I should hope not.'

Coping with the pressures of the agency and a small baby isn't easy. I don't expect help from my husband, and I don't get any. Oliver is of that breed of male who believes that the roles of men and women are entirely different, which nicely excuses him from such boring chores as doing the dishes or wielding a vacuum cleaner. Instead he amuses himself by issuing a stream of caustic remarks, instructing me on how best to do these tasks.

His mood is sour. He's seriously annoyed that I've defied him by going back to the agency. Sometimes he'll sulk in silence for days, which he knows unnerves me badly and makes me feel very jumpy. At other times he'll lose patience and grumble, either accusing me of being obsessive over the baby or, perversely, of neglecting her and being too engrossed in my job. He naturally objects to the fact that I'm not giving him the attention he deserves, that I'm neglecting my wifely duties.

'Being married means that you should spend time together,' he sanctimoniously informs me, as if he's devoted every moment of our marriage to nurturing our relationship.

It's like the early days all over again, with him commenting and criticising on any sign of a lessening in the high standards he expects in his home. He's back to running his finger along the window sills, tut-tutting if he sees Katie's plastic stacking bricks left lying on the rug, and is as unforgiving as ever if dinner is not ready on time.

But I'm an expert now at deception. Pans and food can instantly appear almost out of nowhere, and if I hear the car turn into the drive and I haven't tidied up, I have a remedy for that too. I throw everything into the nearest drawer, or under a cushion in the time it takes for him to lock the car and walk to the front door. When he enters I'm standing waiting for him, a smile of welcome on my face as I kick a plastic brick out of sight under the dresser. Perfect house, perfect wife, exactly as he likes it.

There's also a packed bag tucked away at the back of the linen cupboard. Just in case.

I'm aware that none of these strategies is a long-term solution, but they help to get me through each day while I attempt to rebuild my confidence. If I make a mistake, or get something wrong, he takes his retribution with a smile on his face, reminding me how he said all along that I wouldn't be able to cope. Any sign of failure on my part seems almost to give him pleasure.

Oliver's opinion of my career is low. In his view I sit about talking on a telephone taking bookings for a few hours, which must be easy, not like his own sweat and toil. He does everything he can to put me down. 'It can't last, this fad of yours to go back to work. You can't cope with one job properly, with bringing up a child, let alone two. Trying to be in two places at once will prove too much for you and you'll start making mistakes, which will alienate clients and damage the business.'

'I'm sure you're right,' I agree, determined not to enter into an argument, or let his caustic comments get to me.

'I suppose this is all to do with that chap I saw you talking to?'

'What *chap*?'

'I wouldn't know his name, would I? The one you claimed to be a client.'

'You mean Tim Hathaway? Mr Hathaway is a client. He lives in Manchester and comes to the Lakes regularly to walk.'

'*Mr Hathaway*. I bet you don't call him that when you're cosying up with him in the pub.'

'Stop this, Oliver. I don't cosy up with him anywhere.'

He leans close, almost spitting in my face. 'You're a slag, you know that? A whore. A lousy cook and a bad mother.'

Again I remain silent, but in my head I tell myself very firmly that I am none of these things. I am absolutely determined to hang on to the fragile threads of my new-found confidence. I refuse to allow him to destroy me while I make these first tentative steps to freedom.

I open a building society account which I keep secret from Oliver. When – and I say *when* to myself now, not *if* – I finally summon up the courage to leave him for good, then Katie and I will need all the money I can lay my hands on. I hide the Building Society book in my undies drawer, sending up a silent prayer that Oliver never thinks to rummage in there.

In the meantime, work is my salvation. Knowing that Katie is to be well looked after is vitally important to me, but being back in the office means there's now a part of each day when I can start to find myself again. I can try to discover the happy girl I once was, the girl I seem to have lost.

20

Despite my insisting that it isn't necessary, there are days when Oliver comes to pick me up. How he manages to take the time off work I don't dare to ask, but it's happening more and more and it irritates me enormously. I'm quite happy catching the bus home, and although it's a long walk from the bus stop and then the couple of miles home from my sister's house, I quite enjoy it, as does Katie. Sometimes we stop off at the play area and I'll push her on the swing for a little while. She loves that.

But I'll see the BMW roll up just across the road from the office, or Emma will warn me that he's arrived, and my heart will sink. The moment I see him park the car I know that I must instantly stop whatever I'm doing, quickly grab my things and leave. Oliver does not care to be kept waiting.

On this particular day as I dash down the stairs and out on to the pavement I bump right into Tim Hathaway.

'Hey, we really must stop meeting like this,' he jokes, grasping my arms to steady me as I almost lose my balance.

Some instinct causes me to look up into his eyes and there's that same shock, almost of recognition, and a warm glow kindles inside me at the sight of his smiling face.

But I'm acutely aware of Oliver watching me from across the road, so my response is perhaps rather cooler towards him than it would normally be. 'Sorry,' I say, rather primly. 'I'm in rather a hurry.' He's frowning at me, clearly puzzled by my abruptness. I feel awful, realising he must think me very rude. Then he shrugs and smiles in that good-natured way of his, showing perfect white teeth, and that he hasn't taken offence.

'I was hoping to ask you to join me for a coffee, or maybe a swift half at the John Peel?'

'I'm married!' I blurt out this remark without thinking, and instantly realise it's a foolish, presumptuous thing to say. Why didn't I simply point out that my husband was across the road, waiting in his car?

'Um, it wasn't an offer of holy matrimony I was making actually, just a chat over coffee or a beer, to talk about cottages, walking, and stuff. Course, I wouldn't be averse to discussing other things, although I freely confess marriage isn't on my mind right at this minute. That's not to say it mightn't have been, or something very like it, were circumstances different.'

I'm thoroughly embarrassed now, at a loss to know how to extricate myself from this muddle of my own making. And then it becomes a whole lot worse as Oliver suddenly appears at my side. I'm instantly drenched in fear, terrified he might have overheard our conversation.

Taking a firm hold of my elbow he glares at Tim. 'I'd be obliged if you'd keep away from my wife.'

Tim's jaw drops open. 'Excuse me?'

'You heard.'

Then Oliver marches me across the road and bundles me into the car. As we drive away, I'm all too aware of Tim standing watching me from the pavement. I'm shaking with suppressed rage, not sure how best to react.

Oliver instantly launches into attack. 'That was him, wasn't it? Go on, admit it. That was your *friend*, wasn't it? Had you planned to have lunch together?'

I grit my teeth, desperately trying to remain calm. 'I've already told you that Mr Hathaway is simply a client. I'm not getting into this argument, Oliver, as I've told you many times. And there's really no need for you to take time off work to pick me up. I'm quite happy catching the bus.'

He grabs my wrist and twists it. 'It would suit you wouldn't it, if I never came near? Well, I don't want my wife acting like a slag with every Tom, Dick and Harry.'

'Oliver, please stop this nonsense and concentrate on your driving.'

'It's your fault if I get angry. You drive me mad. I can see now why you were so keen to get back to work. It's not your independence you're missing, it's lover boy.'

He continues to harangue me all the way home, but I stop listening. I shut my mind to his filthy language and tell myself that I'm not any of these things he is calling me. I concentrate on the work I've done that day, each small achievement I've made. I've learned to be circumspect, and very careful. Agreeing with him, and smiling at my own supposed folly, is undoubtedly the best policy. Oliver still makes the rules.

Tim calls again the next day and makes a point of apologising for whatever offence he might have caused, asking if there's a problem.

'No, of course not. There's really no need for you to apologise. Why would there be? I'm the one who should be apologising. Oliver can get a bit – a bit possessive at times. I'm sorry.' I smile dismissively, making it clear that I've no wish to discuss my husband's paranoia. Far too embarrassing.

'I can see why he thinks he's a lucky guy.'

There's a small silence, one which I don't attempt to fill as my cheeks are burning. I fuss over papers on my desk, trying to look busy.

Tim says, 'I thought you seemed a tad brusque even before he came over. I wondered if I'd offended you in some way, or stepped on your toes again with my big clumsy boots.'

I laugh. 'Don't be silly.'

'Good. Can I buy you that drink now then? A swift half down at the John Peel. Or a coffee perhaps?'

I look up at him and freely confess, to myself at least, that I'm sorely tempted. 'I don't think my husband would approve of that either.'

He looks at me quite calmly. 'No, I don't suppose he would, but the offer is still open.'

'Maybe some other time,' I say, and quickly walk away.

Just before two o'clock, a little later than I usually leave as I was held up on the phone by a client, I'm rushing down the hill to catch the bus. I'm battling with an umbrella that's turned inside out in the wind and the rain as the bus comes sailing past me. It doesn't stop, its wheels splashing through puddles and drenching me in water.

'Damn, damn, damn!' Now I'll have to wait for the next, which will make me late picking up Katie, earn me a telling-off from Jo-Jo and cut it very fine for getting all my chores done before Oliver arrives home. I again regret the loss of having transport of my own, when I suddenly become aware of a car drawing up behind me. For once I'd be happy to face my glowering husband, except that it isn't a BMW but a battered old Jeep that has seen better days, and Tim Hathaway is at the wheel.

'Looks like you could do with a lift,' he offers, throwing open the door. 'Considering the weather.'

I jump in. 'Bless you! I'm supposed to be collecting my daughter, and waiting for the next bus would make me terribly late.'

'No problem.'

We negotiate the traffic in silence for a while, apart from my giving a few basic directions. Then Tim starts to chat, telling me about himself in a friendly, open manner. He's thirty-two and a geography teacher at a school in Manchester, and he's single, although he was involved in a long-term relationship for a time. Now his only companion is a tabby cat called Spiky (because of his fierce claws) and his hobby is walking. His aim is to climb as many of the Lake District peaks as he possibly can before he gets too old and decrepit.

I laugh. 'That will be a long time in coming. I should think you could climb them all at least twice before then.'

'I'm doing a fairly short walk next weekend. Castle Crag. Maybe you and your husband would like to join me?'

'My husband isn't into hiking.'

'That's a shame! What a pity to live in the Lakes and not be interested in exploring this marvellous scenery.'

'He's a very busy man.'

A slight pause, and then, 'And a lucky one too.'

'Why?' I ask, in all innocence.

'Because he has you.'

I'm ashamed to find my cheeks grow warm and I turn to stare out through the rain-splattered windows, saying nothing as I sink into my customary shyness. I'm relieved when we reach the end of Jo-Jo's road and I tell Tim he can drop me here. The last thing I need is my nosy sister catching sight of this gorgeous young man.

Tim stops the car, pulls on the brake and turns to me with a wry smile. 'Now you'll have to return the favour by agreeing to have that drink with me after all.'

'That's bribery.'

'Not at all. Quite a clever ruse, I thought. Surely one small glass of beer won't hurt, although I realise I shouldn't ask, since your husband seems to be the jealous type.'

I say nothing to this but politely thank him for the lift and get out of the car.

'It's half term so I'm here all week. I'm doing Striding Edge tomorrow, so maybe Thursday? I'll pop in the agency office around lunchtime. OK?'

'I'll see,' I say, struggling to close the door of the vehicle which doesn't seem to fit properly. By the time he drives off with a cheery wave, I find that my heart is pounding and I'm feeling decidedly flustered.

'Your sister informs me that you got a lift home as you missed the bus. That was rather careless of you.' Oliver has been in the house barely five minutes and already he's finding fault and interrogating me.

I privately resolve to be as pleasant as possible, give a small shrug as I reply with a smile. 'The bus times are infrequent and irregular, and unfortunately I got held up on the telephone with a client and missed the one I usually catch.' My subterfuge did nothing to put my sister off the scent either, since it was clear I hadn't come by bus. I'd arrived at her house at quite the wrong time.

Oliver is equally unconvinced. 'What client was this?'

'Just a client. I can't remember her name. When did you see Jo-Jo?'

'I called on my way home through the village, in case you were still there, gossiping. Who gave you the lift?'

Jo-Jo had asked that too. I give Oliver the same answer I gave my sister. 'A client.' It sounds a feeble excuse even to my own ears, so I concentrate on shaking the washed lettuce in a colander. My heart is thumping and I know that Oliver must have called on Jo-Jo deliberately, just to check up on me. He always needs to know what time I leave, which bus I catch, what time I arrive home.

'Anyone I know?'

'What? Of course not. How would you know any of our clients?' He's still waiting for further details, so I supply them. 'A rather nice elderly couple actually, from . . . from Liverpool, I believe. They were going this way, saw me battling with my umbrella in the rain, and offered me a lift. It was very kind of them, don't you think?' I'm amazed how easily the lies slip from my tongue. They make me feel rather breathless, and I turn away to hide my burning cheeks. I toss the salad, and go to check on the salmon poaching gently in the oven.

'You should have given me a ring. I would have come and collected you.'

'No need. I was fine. I wouldn't need a lift if I still had my own car. Ah, good, the salmon is perfect. I think we're ready to eat now.'

The very next day I talk to Dad about the problem I'm having with transport and he solves the car issue for me by shaming my penny-pinching husband into buying me a cheap, second-hand Fiat. Ed checks it over for me and pronounces it healthy and safe.

I'm thrilled and delighted. I can just about afford to run a car now that I'm earning again, and Oliver will have no reason now to come and pick me up. It feels like a minor miracle, a triumph. One up for me at last.

★ ★ ★

My small burst of optimism doesn't last long. One morning Mum rings to say that my grandfather has had a stroke and is seriously ill. She's nursing the old man at home because he's too ill to be moved. Mum seems to have spent half her life caring for people, first her father who was crippled with multiple sclerosis, then her own mother when she became old and sick, and now my father's parents. No wonder it all gets a bit much for her at times. She had a difficult childhood and money was tight, so if at times she seems tough and inflexible, it's because she's had to be. Yet at five foot nothing she has more energy than an entire rugby team. She makes me feel totally inadequate. I just wish she could learn to be a bit less hard on herself, and on me. But she's my mum and I love her to bits.

As if that's not bad enough, Gran goes down with the 'flu. There seems to be an epidemic in progress this spring and people are falling sick in droves. Jo-Jo is sick too, and her children are going down with it one by one. Oliver's mother also has the 'flu so I have to take Katie into the office with me and look after her myself. I think Emma would have preferred me to stay at home, particularly when I hear her curse as she trips over the baby buggy in the tiny, overcrowded office, or Katie starts to cry. But I'm determined to keep going and maintain the progress I've already made. And then I go down with it too.

I can't remember ever being so ill. I feel dreadful. Oliver remains robustly healthy and refuses to take any time off work to help, leaving me to suffer alone even though I have a small baby to look after. He still doesn't consider he should take any responsibility for Katie. I spend a miserable week in bed, trying to keep warm, hoping Katie doesn't become ill with it too. So far she seems quite lively, with nothing more serious than a runny nose.

I'm just beginning to feel marginally human again when Emma rings to say that she has the 'flu now, as has Wanda, and could I possibly get in to work tomorrow as there's no one to man the phones.

I drag myself out of bed the following morning, still feeling decidedly ropy although the worst of the aches and pains have gone. I fasten Katie into her car seat and drive to the office. Thank goodness I at least have a car now.

Fortunately we have no changeovers today, but I'm kept busy replying to emails and answering telephone queries. By the end of the day, I'm exhausted. Instead of going straight home I pop up to Mum's to see how Grandad is, and find that she too is in bed with the dreaded influenza. His condition remains unchanged. The poor old man is drifting in and out of sleep, with Gran sitting by his bed feeding him occasional sips of water or trying to persuade him to take a little beef soup. The old lady is seventy-eight and not in the best of health herself, so every now and then poor Mum has to crawl out of her sick-bed and go to help her to turn him, or let him use the bottle, then crawl back to bed again.

Dad has to carry on as best he can opening the shop each day, with precious little in the way of assistance because of the 'flu epidemic. He works long days so I promise to do what I can to make things easier for them all.

The next ten days or so are an absolute nightmare. Coping alone at the agency isn't easy. The phone never stops ringing, as if everybody has suddenly decided to plan their holidays in order to make themselves feel better. I've also a couple of changeovers later in the week for which I could really do with Wanda's help. Every night when I arrive home after another exhausting day I cook a large casserole, big enough for the entire family, for Gran and Dad and Mum, as well as for Oliver and myself. I take the food up to Mum's and do whatever I can to help while I'm there: making cups of tea, doing some of the washing that has piled up, generally tidying and seeing to Gran and Grandad.

Oliver complains bitterly, objecting to my 'neglect'. I can't believe how selfish he is. Why didn't I notice that before I married him? I certainly won't be accused of neglecting my family.

'My grandfather is ill,' I tell him. 'He's *dying*! Why don't you help instead of criticising?'

He looks at me in astonishment, as if I'm mad to suggest such a thing, then slams out of the house saying he'll go and eat at the pub.

'Yes, you do that,' I shout after him, and throw the meal I prepared for him into the pedal bin. It's a small triumph but short lived. He returns in an even more foul mood and, despite being as stone-cold sober as ever, insists upon sex, which I'm not in the mood for at all. Not that this troubles Oliver. He never bothers with romancing me now. Making love is all about pleasing himself, not me.

This time I don't let him bully me. I carry on going over to Mum's, doing what I can. Jo-Jo does her share, once her own family are on the road to recovery. She seems bursting with energy, filled with unexpected exuberance, and finally confesses that Ed has undergone a vasectomy.

'So there'll be no more little accidents, no more bambinos. Four is enough, even for Ed.' She leans close and whispers in my ear. 'And it's also reawakened my libido, knowing I'm safe from falling pregnant again. Joy of joys, now we can bang away without a care in the world.'

'I'm glad for you,' I say, truly meaning it, but for the first time in my life, I feel a burst of envy for my sister.

My lovely grandad still needs to be watched like a hawk even though the stroke has hampered him. Sometimes the old man forgets where he is, struggles out of bed and goes wandering off. We have to keep the front door locked at all times, just in case. Mum's rest is constantly disturbed as she has to coax him back into bed, then calm Gran's fears.

The two women spend a good deal of time drinking tea together, and worrying. The doctor calls regularly but there's nothing he can do. Just a matter of time, he says. Keep the old man comfortable, give him a little water to drink. Then one morning Grandad suddenly sits up in bed and starts asking for toast and his favourite marmalade. It must have been his final burst of energy because a few short hours later, he dies.

The funeral is hard for us all. My grandfather was a sweet and gentle little man, barely five feet two inches tall with white wavy hair, glossy black when he was young, a real dandy in his hey-day. I remember, as a child, how he filled my head with exciting stories of Robin Hood and King Arthur. I remember family holidays where he would take me to visit ancient castles and historic mansions, Roman forts, and Scottish glens where the clans clashed in battle, filling my young head with a passion for history and for books in general. I love him dearly and grieve for his loss.

I'm also grieving for my marriage, which seems to be going nowhere. A week or so later it dawns on me that I haven't had a period for some time. I came off the pill for a while when I was weighed down with sickness and depression, and only started taking it again once I'd recovered from the 'flu. Now I realise that I must be pregnant.

My heart skips a beat and I'm filled with trepidation. I love children and normally would have welcomed a brother or sister for Katie, even if I have no wish to match my sister's quartet. But another child is the last thing I need right now. I know it would spell disaster for my marriage. I'm proved to be absolutely correct. I don't expect Oliver to be pleased by my news, but even I am shocked by his blunt reaction.

'Get rid of it!'

I vigorously protest. Abortion is not an option so far as I am concerned. The pregnancy may be unexpected, even unwanted in the circumstances, but surely not a total disaster? I try to explain all of this to him, but he's too busy reminding me how incompetent I am.

'I haven't done a test yet,' I admit, my voice going all shaky. 'But wouldn't a new baby be lovely? It might be just the thing to cheer us up.' I don't quite believe this myself but I'm doing my best to be positive.

Oliver is adamant. 'You're not having another child, and there's an end to the matter. I won't allow it. See the doctor and fix up an abortion.'

21

By the end of the week I still haven't made an appointment to see the doctor, nor have I done the pregnancy test. Inside my head something is telling me that whatever the result, it isn't going to help. I'm beginning to question if my marriage is even worth saving. Before I can actually do the test and face the truth, whatever it might be, I feel a desperate need to be alone, to think, and to work out exactly what I feel about this latest development. I leave Katie with Jo-Jo, now fully recovered, and drive out to the nearby dale of Kentmere.

I must have walked for miles. I gaze at the wild amphitheatre of mountains that circle the head of the valley, which look as bleak on this cold spring day as I feel. Yet I need to be out in this empty landscape, breathing in the freedom of the open fells. There are precious few farmhouses in the scattered hamlet and I welcome the loneliness of the place. I'm desperate for some privacy right now. The lofty mountains seem to represent escape to another world, far beyond Windermere which lies a few miles to the north-west, to a world I've hardly had the chance to explore yet. I'm still only in my twenties, but feel like an old woman. I pass Kentmere Hall with its ruined pele tower and wonder how many women throughout history have faced the prospect of an unwanted child. How many have lived with a brutal, controlling husband, and walked, crying, over these fells, as I am doing? How many of my friends and neighbours, I wonder, are also keeping quiet about what goes on behind closed doors? What dark secrets do other people keep from their neighbours?

What is it in a man that makes him turn violent, that causes him to beat and humiliate the woman he once claimed to love? I wish I could ask my sympathetic neighbour from across the road. But despite her having witnessed two of my disasters, the sofa incident and the fire, she painstakingly avoids intimacy, doing little more than passing the time of day with me. She will send me the odd reassuring smile from across the street, as if to remind me of our shared secrets, and of her continued discretion. Very occasionally she will stop to drool over Katie, but if she sees me out with Oliver, she doesn't even glance my way.

I wipe away my tears and watch the sheep crop the lush grass in the rolling pastures. I come to a small copse and I'm captivated by the display of fresh green leaves and wild lilac. The sweet fragrance is calming, a balm to my troubled soul. I lie beneath the trees, breathing it in as I go over the details of my marriage in my head, thinking everything through with a rare clarity.

I wonder why I never saw through his charm from the start. Perhaps because he didn't allow me to. He clearly uses it as a mask to disguise the flawed man beneath, and to manipulate me, his victim, in order to keep me under control. Oliver seems to believe that he's entitled to order his own private universe according to his personal needs, and he wishes me to see him as the centre of it.

A skylark soars high in the sky, singing joyously, reminding me of the carefree days of my youth, of the dreams I once had. All I'd wanted was to love him, to have a family and carry on working in my little business. Was that too much to ask?

I stare at this innocent piece of plastic in my hand, which apparently holds the answer to my future. If I am pregnant, and agree to an abortion, what then? Do we carry on as if nothing had happened? Can I continue to love a man who treats me with such contempt? A man who beats and controls me, and wants to kill his own child? I don't think so.

And if I'm not pregnant, will that make everything all right again? It would be a relief in the circumstances, yes, but would it make me happy? Would it solve the problems in my marriage? I very much doubt it. Wouldn't I be living in constant fear of this happening again? Wouldn't I feel compelled to give up all hope of another child, a brother or sister for Katie?

I feel a lump of raw emotion in my throat. Pain and regret for what might have been. Isn't it time to stop fooling myself and start making some tough decisions?

I take the test and it comes up negative. As I sink back on the soft turf with a sigh of relief, my eyes fill with tears, and my heart twists with fresh pain as if a knife has been plunged into it. What do I do now?

When my crying finally abates, a strange calmness comes over me and I begin to walk again, my vision and my thoughts becoming clear and unwavering. It's as if I'm reaching down inside myself to the young girl I once was, to the core of me that remains Carly Holt, a person who is no one's wife, or mother, or daughter, but simply herself. I feel that I've at last found the part that is the real *me*. I may have lost that youthful innocence which was once full of joy and hope, the girl who had boundless faith in the future and in herself. In her place is this beaten, broken shell. I'm now the kind of person I loathe: someone who lives in fear and jumps at her own shadow. Yet surely the core of her is still present, still burning somewhere deep inside?

I begin to talk to myself, which could mean either that I'm going mad or I'm getting it together at last. Whatever, it seems like a good way to drum up my courage. I'm speaking quite firmly, ordering myself not to be a wimp.

'You have to stand up for yourself and not allow him to bully you any more. OK, brave words easier said than done, but you've done well these last few weeks,' I say, mentally patting myself on the back. 'Getting back to work was a real milestone. There might not be as much money as I would have liked in my secret account, but I've surely gained in other ways.

'I'm stronger, feel slightly detached from Oliver for some

reason, less needy and dependent upon him.' I think this must be a good thing. Evidence, surely, that I'm making progress.

Oliver will be relieved, naturally, when I tell him it was all a false alarm, that there is to be no pregnancy. He will no doubt use the false alarm to berate me even more about my alleged incompetence. But what then?

Mum and Dad have suffered enough recently and the last thing I want is to inflict the break-up of my marriage upon them at this juncture. Yet I have to consider my own future, and Katie's. I have to be brave and explain to Oliver that I'm leaving him, and this time I mean it.

I move my things out of our bedroom. I do it quickly, before he comes home. It feels like a huge step and I'm nervous of his reaction, but I have no intention of continuing to sleep with him while I make the necessary alternative arrangements for my departure.

As expected, Oliver takes the news of the mistaken pregnancy as further proof of my own stupidity, and coldly instructs me to take more care in future.

I'm in the nursery changing Katie's nappy, and Oliver is leaning against the doorjamb, a look of pure disdain on his face. He makes no move to pick her up and kiss her. I do so, giving my daughter a loving cuddle.

'The reason I'm having irregular periods is because I've lost so much weight, and feel so unwell. Had you even noticed?' I ask.

He gives a heavy sigh of exasperation. 'You should stop going on those fad diets and eat properly, Carly. It's all your own fault if you're too skinny.'

Is he deliberately missing the point? Does he prefer to turn a blind eye to the fact that he is the one who is making me ill? I could take issue with him on the subject, tell him that my weight loss, my constant headaches and sickness are a result of being forced to live with his brutality. But it would only degenerate into another row. Instead I take a deep breath, desperately striving to ignore the slow, heavy thud of my heart as I summon up every ounce of courage I possess. My hands continue with the task of cleaning and changing Katie while I tell him, in quiet, measured tones, that I've moved into the spare room. 'It's only temporary. I would like us to be civilised about this, but I truly believe that our marriage is over. By the end of the week I fully intend to have found alternative accommodation for Katie and myself, and we'll be moving out. Permanently.'

The silence following this carefully rehearsed statement is long and frightening, and, apart from a slight narrowing of the eyes, his face is totally devoid of expression. He seems to be waiting for something, perhaps for me to offer some sort of explanation, as if such a thing were necessary.

I lift Katie in my arms, trying not to meet his gaze as I cuddle her, feel the warm weight of her against my breast. She is so very precious.

'I've no wish for another row, we've surely had enough to those, but I've come to a decision. I can't go on like this any longer, Oliver. As soon as I find suitable accommodation, hopefully within the week, two at most, I intend to leave. In the meantime I'll continue to cook for you, and look after the house, but I will no longer be paying my wages into our joint account. I shall keep it for myself, and for Katie, although I'm obviously prepared to pay my share of housekeeping expenses, food and so on, until I leave.' I pause, but still he says nothing.

'I'm sorry it's come to this, but I've really tried, Oliver. I've done everything I can think of to make our marriage work. Unfortunately, I seem to be the only one who is trying, and this latest scare, this – false alarm – made me realise that there is no hope for us at all. I appreciate that there are occasions when an abortion may well be an appropriate response and the right thing to do, but this isn't one of them. We're married. We're in good health and can easily afford another child. We even once loved each other, or at least I thought we did. Had I been pregnant, I could never have agreed to getting rid of it, as you so callously ordered. Even though I'm not a Roman Catholic or anything, I believe life to be sacred. I believe in responsibility, something you choose to ignore. I just couldn't bring myself to kill my own child, even if it was little more than a tiny scrap inside me, for no other reason than selfishness. I'm appalled to realise that you could.'

His face seems to harden, the mouth tightening in that familiar way, yet still he doesn't answer my charges. He stands immobile, hands in his pockets, glaring at the floor.

I wait for his response. When it doesn't come I begin to breathe more easily. Maybe Oliver too can see we've finally come to the end of the road. 'OK, so that's all I wanted to say. What about you?' I mean, does he accept my decision. Does he accept it?

He glances at his watch, as if I'm keeping him from some pressing engagement, and then asks, 'I suppose dinner is ready, is it?'

'Oh, yes, of course. And we can discuss the details later – if you wish. Yes, I'm sure it is ready. We'd best eat.' I take a tentative step towards him and he backs away from the door to let me pass. At the top of the stairs, Katie still in my arms, I turn and see that he still hasn't moved. He remains standing with his hands in his pockets, his expression impassive. I manage a small smile. 'You'll be down in a minute then?' I turn and walk slowly down the stairs, keenly aware of his eyes following my every step.

Katie is teething and rather fractious. She's sitting up in a high chair now and Oliver always insists that she join us at the table where she is expected to behave impeccably. We sit at the table together, to all outward appearances an ordinary happy family, yet the silence is heavy, intense. Oliver has still made no comment on my announcement, and I'm beginning to breathe more easily, thinking it's a done deal, that even he can see it's the only course for us now.

I take the spoon off Katie. Usually she can feed herself,

when she's in the mood, but today I'm having to encourage her. Her cheeks are red and she keeps rubbing her small fist over her sore mouth, grizzling miserably. I'm playing games with her, pretending the spoon is an aeroplane, dive-bombing her mouth. It usually works, but this evening she turns away and cries. I wipe the food off her face and patiently try again.

Oliver, however, has no such patience. 'You're a hopeless mother,' he snaps. 'Look at the child, won't even take the food you offer. What is it you're trying to make her eat?'

'Stewed apple.'

'Well she obviously doesn't like stewed apple.'

'She loves it. Her gums are hurting.'

'Then leave her alone.'

'She has to eat something, Oliver.'

'Give the spoon to me.'

He snatches the spoon out of my hand and attempts to shove it into Katie's mouth. She stubbornly resists, keeping her mouth shut tight, then pushes the spoon away with her hand. Furious, he wags a finger in the baby's startled face. 'You'll eat your dinner and like it, if you know what's good for you, child!'

'Oliver . . .' I'm half way out of my seat in an instant, urging him to be calm. She might only be young but what kind of atmosphere is this in which to bring up a child? Miraculously, Katie opens her mouth and allows him to shovel in the stewed apple.

'There you are,' he says with quiet satisfaction. 'You just have to be firm.' At which point, she spits it right out again, all down his clean shirt, squares her mouth wide and starts to scream.

'She has my stubborn streak, I'm afraid.' I'm trying not to smile, even as I see Oliver's own face turn red with rage. Katie is rubbing the remains of the stewed apple all over her face with a small tired fist. It's in her hair, down her clothes, up her nose. 'She's far too upset now to eat,' I tell him, 'and tired out, I'm afraid. It's been another exhausting day for her. I'll put her down.' I get up to take her but he orders me to sit still.

'Sit down. I'll decide when this meal is over, not you, and

certainly not some dratted infant. I'm not being ruled by a mere child. She can't be allowed to *win*!'

'She's a baby, Oliver. She's teething. Her gums are sore. She's not trying to fight you.'

Oliver spoons up more stewed apple and again attempts to shovel it into the open wailing mouth and once more Katie spits it out, this time right in his face. Quick as a flash, Oliver slaps her, leaving the imprint of his fingermarks on the pale skin of her leg.

I'm horrified. 'Please don't do that,' I say, trying to still the tremor in my voice, but my words have no effect whatsoever.

His gaze bores into mine, the fury in them almost palpable. 'You might think you can just walk out on me, and I might let you, you useless tart. You can have affairs, refuse to be a proper wife to me by showing no interest in sex. You can argue with me and question every decision I make, go back to your bloody job and ignore and reject everything I've ever done for you, *but this is still my child and she'll do as I bloody say.*'

Before I realise what he's about to do, he snatches Katie up out of her high chair and marches upstairs to her bedroom. I race after him, desperately trying to make him give her back to me. He has her under one arm, and, ignoring me completely, suddenly twists her into the crook of his arm, as if she were a ball, and throws her the length of the nursery into her cot. I cry out in protest as I see my child fly through the air, limbs flailing. By a miracle she lands in the cot, flat on her face, shocked into silence. He could so easily have missed, and she would then have smashed against the wall. We could have a dead, battered baby lying in the cot right at this minute. Without pausing to check she isn't harmed, Oliver turns on his heels and storms out of the house.

I rush to the cot to comfort my near-hysterical child. For me, it's the final, defining moment. This proves that my decision to leave was absolutely correct. This is the end.

I cuddle her in my arms, her red face wet with tears as she gasps and screams in terror. I'm kissing and soothing her, checking her arms, her legs, her small hands, her spine; pacing the room, quite unable to keep still. I'm filled with rage. I have never known such anger. Suppressed for so long because Oliver doesn't believe I should show any emotion, it has festered and bubbled inside me. Now it erupts. Had he still been in the room with us, I think I might very well have tried to kill him.

I've put up with so many beatings, his peevish little tricks and malicious punishments for almost two years. I'm ill as a result of it all. Possibly, I realise, on the verge of a complete breakdown. He has so diminished me as a person that I've come to accept the situation as normal and unavoidable, something I must tolerate without complaint, which has to be wrong. No woman should be expected to put up with such treatment. No man, not even a husband or partner, should be allowed to treat his wife or partner as Oliver has treated me.

If only I hadn't felt so desperate to make our marriage work, so ashamed, so vulnerable, so filled with self-doubt and indecisiveness. But he made me that way. He deliberately set out to undermine me, continually insisting that I was the one to blame. It's a most effective method of control.

But I am not to blame. I am not the one at fault.

Where once he saw an attractive, independent woman whom he loved, now he sees only my alleged failings. Early in our marriage I loved him so much I was determined to do everything I possibly could to make it work. By the time I realised this was fruitless, it was too late. He'd destroyed me, robbed me of my self-esteem and turned me into a cowed, miserable creature, terrified of resisting him. I wish now that I'd been brave enough to ignore his threats, to risk any possible reprisals, and left him long since. I should have sought help from someone, made my parents listen, talked to Emma, my nosy neighbour, an internet helpline or the police, *anyone*. If only I'd had the courage. If only I hadn't felt so utterly down-trodden and beaten, quite unable to even think straight.

I'm damned if I'll let him destroy my child in the same way.

Over these last few weeks while I've been privately congratulating myself at winning back some control over my life, rejoicing at my small faltering steps, of the slow but steady progress I'm making towards independence, Oliver has obviously been simmering with silent resentment. The erroneous pregnancy finally brought everything to a head, forced me to think clearly at last, and allowed me to summon up the courage to face him with my decision.

Tonight, I believed he had accepted that our marriage was finally over. I should have known better. He never had any intention of letting me go, took his revenge for my rebellion not on me, but by turning on my child.

Cold fear washes over me. How can I possibly protect her through the years ahead? She's now an abused child, a victim, as I am. But we don't have to remain so. Whatever the cost, I must put a stop to this once and for all. I cannot allow this terrible thing that has happened to me to ruin her life too.

I waste not a moment. I snatch up a few essentials for Katie, collect the packed bag I've hidden in the linen cupboard, get in my car and drive away. I'm not sure where I'm going, no idea how I'll survive, or if this small burst of courage will last but I know this is the right thing to do. Whatever risk I take by leaving him, there are greater ones if I stay.

22

Seeing me appear once more on her doorstep with bags and baggage, my mother instantly embarks on the usual lecture. It's a chilly night, just starting to rain, and I might well have been forced to spend it in the garden shed had not Dad gently moved her away and ushered me inside.

I tell my parents bluntly that my marriage is over, for good this time, and could Dad please help me find a flat to rent somewhere. I'm traumatised by what has happened. Despite all my best efforts, my love was not enough for Oliver.

I offer them no explanation, feel too numbed by recent events to talk. I'm frozen, paralysed, perhaps by the shock of what I've just witnessed him do to my child. I can feel myself start to shake but it's Gran, not my own mother, who gathers me into her arms and takes me over to the sofa. Mum is too busy trying to press me into explaining what exactly has brought me running home this time.

Dad shushes her and finally succeeds in holding her in check, but I can tell them nothing, am quite incapable of speech. I sit huddled in a corner of the sofa with Katie in my arms, refusing to allow anyone to take her from me and put her to bed. In the end, seeing how distressed I am, Mum makes me some hot chocolate, Gran brings blankets and a pillow and they all creep away and leave me to grieve alone for the death of my dreams and hopes.

I spend a sleepless night on the sofa, even worse than before, and, finding me still awake when he comes downstairs at six, my father makes me a morning cup of tea. He doesn't ask any questions or issue any lectures, simply promises he'll start looking into the question of a flat to rent that very day.

I hug and thank him, desperately struggling to swallow my tears.

He does gently point out that the task of finding accommodation in the Lake District at a price I can afford will not be an easy one. 'You might have to consider bunking down with Emma, or Jo-Jo, for a while,' he warns.

My heart sinks. I was aware of this fact and yet to have him say this in so many words is not what I want to hear right now. As he's about to go out of the door I call after him, panic in my voice. 'If Oliver comes into the shop, don't tell him where I am.'

'I wouldn't do that, pet, although he's sure to guess.'

'Then please tell him to stay away and leave me alone. It's very important that you make him understand I won't allow him to bully me into returning this time.'

There's a long pause while Dad absorbs this remark, and then he quietly nods. 'I'll make sure he understands. You stay here with your Gran today. I'll call Emma and tell her you're ill. And don't answer the door to anyone.'

I take his advice, but realise that I can't stay hidden forever. Nor can I keep my dark secrets quiet for much longer. Eventually, it's going to all have to come out. When Mum comes down later, she doesn't probe, clearly schooled by Dad to say nothing. She behaves as if it's perfectly normal to find her daughter and granddaughter camping out in her lounge, and, to be honest, that helps enormously.

I give her a hug as she prepares to leave for the shop. 'We'll talk later, right?'

'Whenever you're ready,' she agrees.

Emma rings me on my mobile later in the morning and I take her call, realising she's probably seen through Dad's excuse: that the sickness was more diplomatic than real.

'I can't talk right now, Emma,' I say, 'but I may be needing to crash on your floor for a while, or maybe I could bunk down at the office for a bit.'

'No problem,' she agrees. 'Whichever you prefer. If there's a crisis, take all the time off you need.' She doesn't ask why I might need time, or why I'm pretending to be ill.

'I shall want to be busy actually, after today,' I tell her. 'Very busy.'

'That's good, because we are. *Very* busy.'

'Good. I'll see you tomorrow . . . or the day after . . . as soon as I feel up to it.'

'I'll be here.'

When Dad gets home that night he informs me Oliver did indeed come into the shop, no doubt anxious to put his own spin on the events which led up to my leaving. I don't ask what those are. I don't want to know. Whatever Dad said to him must have had an effect because in the days following, my husband makes no attempt to contact me, not even to phone. He seems to be staying well clear, which is good, but that doesn't mean that when I eventually do emerge and try to pick up the threads of my life again, I won't be constantly looking over my shoulder.

I don't in fact go in to work the next day, or the day after that. I seem to be quite incapable of doing anything. Free at last from Oliver's domination and control, I expect to feel relief. I had imagined that all the pent-up emotions would spill out of me and I'd feel released and renewed. It isn't like that at all. Maybe I'm in denial again, or suffering from some sort of post-traumatic stress but talking about my marriage seems quite beyond me. Instead I experience only a sad disillusionment and a deep sense of failure. It all seems so unreal, as if this were happening to someone else.

Nor can I talk to my parents. I sit chewing my nails, fussing over Katie, worrying and weeping. I can't bear the thought of revealing to the world how he has treated me, how much abuse I've been forced to endure in the forlorn hope he'd eventually see the light and change.

I realise it is essential that I do start to talk before I go entirely mad and this whole thing destroys me. But my feelings of depression show no signs of abating, and I'm still struggling to eat. I need to get up off the sofa and get back to work. I need to do something positive. Why am I the one hiding away suffering shame? I ask myself. Why is all this tearing me apart when I am the victim, not the perpetrator? Yet somehow that's how it feels, as if I'm the one responsible for Oliver's despicable behaviour.

But then, hasn't he told me so a thousand times?

Mum marches me to the bathroom scales where we discover that I've lost over two stone in weight. I'm barely six and a half stone. My system seems to be shutting down altogether, and she insists I see a doctor, at once.

I dread going to see him but in fact Doctor Mac, as we call him, proves to be surprisingly supportive and sympathetic. He instantly recognises the problem and asks me straight out if Oliver has been violent towards me. I nod, carefully avoiding his eyes.

'Then you've done the right thing by leaving him, both for your own sake, and for Katie's. Many women don't manage to do that either for financial or emotional reasons, out of fear, or a false hope that things will improve. In my experience, men who abuse women in this way don't ever change. If anything, they get worse.'

I recall my nosy neighbour saying very much the same thing. Why didn't I listen to her?

Nice as he is, I'm too afraid to tell him about the incident in the nursery, of how Oliver threw Katie, like a ball, across the room. That only good luck, or Oliver's bowling skills, saved her. The last thing I want is a social worker poking her nose in, maybe blaming me for not protecting my child sufficiently. It's one thing to tell me I'm not responsible, quite another for me to absorb that fact. All I can be sure of right now is that I'm working hard to rid myself of this deep sense of guilt and shame, but it's going to take time for me to fully recover. I do ask Doctor Mac to check her over, which he does, very thoroughly, assuring me she is very healthy and making good progress.

He prescribes anti-depressants for me, encourages me to eat little and often, not to over-face myself with too much food at first, and to start making plans. 'Have you told your parents?'

I shake my head and he urges me to do just that. 'Don't bottle it up, Carly. Tell them. They can help. And if he comes looking for you, don't let him talk you into trying again or you'll be right back where you started. Don't look back, Carly, look ahead. You need to put this child, and yourself, first in future. Is that clear?'

'Crystal.'

Once I've plucked up sufficient courage to start, my parents listen in horror, shocked into silence, in particular my mother who adores Oliver and has refused to hear a word said against him. I reveal only a fraction of what has happened, and there are things I really can't tell them, not yet, perhaps not ever, but it is enough.

Dad becomes very angry and Mum starts to quietly weep. I've never seen her so upset and vulnerable.

'I never realised . . . I never thought you were suffering like that . . . Oh, God, I know you hinted at it once, love, but I thought you were making it up, because you couldn't forgive him over that stupid affair. I didn't believe Oliver could be so cruel. He's so kind, so gentle and charming.'

'Not all the time,' I say. And then it all comes rushing out of me, all my pent-up resentment and pain. 'He uses his charm offensive as a means of control. It's not genuine, merely a part of his armoury. He likes everyone to think him a great chap because he likes to be liked, to feel good about himself. It's all *me, me, me,* with Oliver. He has to be the best, the only one getting attention. The winner. He has to be dominant, always in charge, and nothing brings him greater satisfaction than to have a brow-beaten, intelligent woman at his command. I was supposed to supply his every need, whether emotional or physical, like some sort of slave obeying his orders without question or complaint. And like a fool, because I loved him,

I did just that. I denied there was a problem at first, then desperately tried to help him deal with it, thinking there must be a good reason. But there wasn't, other than his huge ego, and his certainty that he's entitled to control the universe, or at least his section of it. And an unshakeable belief that men are important and women are rubbish. My efforts to placate him, to endlessly prove that I loved him, were entirely useless. He never loved *me*, he just loved the idea of *my* loving *him*.'

Mum looks at me askance. 'Oh, Carly, you're far too young to sound so bitter, and so cynical.'

'I'm not young at all, Mum. I'm old, certainly in experience. Oliver has made me so. His behaviour is so manipulative. He has a terrible temper but he doesn't just lose it; he's perfectly aware of what he's doing, and could stop any time he chooses. I know that's hard to understand. *I* don't fully understand. He loves to put me down in order to get what he wants. If I don't do as he asks, or carry out his instructions to the letter, then it's because *I'm* stupid, not because he expects the impossible. He's pathologically fixated on having a perfect life, perfect home, perfect wife. He even writes rude names in the dust on the window. Oh, I could go on and on, but I won't, I can't.' I start to cry again and Mum holds me close at last. The soft warmth of her feels so good.

'I doubt I could ever trust a man again,' I sob.

'Yes, you will. One day,' she says, stroking damp strands of hair from my face. 'Just because one apple is bad doesn't mean the whole barrel is,' and she smiles.

'At least I'm no longer in thrall to him,' I say, trying to sound positive even though I feel anything but. 'And while I freely admit I'm still very afraid of him, I've finally found the courage to break free. Nothing he does to threaten me now – *nothing* – will persuade me to return to him and try to repair my marriage. I'm done.'

Dad speaks through gritted teeth. 'He'll not touch you again, love. Not without going through me first.'

Mum is so upset that she bursts into tears again and cries

for a long time. I find I'm the one having to comfort her now. I think she's shocked by her own inadequacies as a mother at failing to recognise the truth. She too is suffering from shame, blaming herself for not protecting me, for being too absorbed in her own problems. Gran quietly comforts us both, wisely reminding us that if we persist in taking the blame, that is exactly what Oliver wants, and the last thing we should be doing.

She puts on the kettle and we embark on yet more tea and sympathy.

Jo-Jo comes round the following morning, avid with curiosity and bustling with self-importance. She has Molly with her who she puts down on the rug to play with Katie. The little girl at once gets up and starts dashing about, showing off her new walking skills. I concentrate on making coffee while Jo-Jo calms the toddler down but, once she's happily playing with Katie's bricks, my sister turns on me, eager to dish the dirt. We're alone in the house, thank goodness, as Mum and Dad are at the shop and Gran is next door chatting to her friend.

'So what's all this I hear about you and Oliver splitting up? He called to tell us that you've left him because you're having an affair. I must say I was shocked. Aren't you the sly one?'

'Oh, for goodness' sake Jo-Jo, he's lying. I am not having an affair.'

She raises her brows in mocking disbelief. 'And who is it you're not having this affair with?'

Through gritted teeth I tell her there's no one, no one at all.

My sister adopts an air of casual surprise. 'Oh, I thought his name was Tim something, a client, I believe. So that's how you met him, is it, through the agency?' Her face suddenly clears. 'He's the one who gave you a lift home, isn't he? My, my, you are a dark horse.'

I give an exasperated sigh as I hand her a coffee. 'Tim Hathaway is indeed a client. He's a geography teacher who likes to come to the Lakes to walk, but – watch my lips – listen carefully. *I am not having an affair.*'

'Then why would Oliver say that you were?'

'Because he's a slime-ball who loves to pass the blame for his own bad behaviour on to me. He's the one who's had the affair, and much more besides.'

'So what has Mr Perfect done this time? Screwed some other little chick in his office?'

If she weren't my sister who, despite everything, I love dearly, and if I weren't so anti-violence, I'd thump her one, I would really. I sink on to the sofa and put my head in my hands, then I tell her in a dull monotone why I left my husband. She doesn't interrupt, despite having to intervene in a squabble over bricks between the babies, but listens in complete silence. I don't look at her, aware that she's feeling obliged to unscramble all the clichéd assumptions and petty resentments she's nursed in her head about me, and view the reality with a clearer vision. It won't be a comfortable image for her. She puts the squirming Molly back down on the rug, and sits on the sofa beside me. After a long silence she finally speaks.

'He beat you?'

'He did.'

'Why didn't you tell me?'

'Would you have believed me?'

Another long silence, and then, 'I might have, eventually, if you'd tried hard enough. Why did you stay with him? If Ed ever laid a finger on me I'd walk out of the door and never look back.'

'No, you wouldn't.'

'I would.'

'No, you'd want to know *why* he hit you. You'd fight for your marriage, as I did, because you love him. Then you'd get in so deep you wouldn't be able to get out. If Ed were anything like Oliver, which thank God he isn't, he wouldn't let you leave. It's far more complicated than you might imagine, far too difficult to explain, Jo-Jo. You'll just have to take my word for it.'

She opens her mouth to protest further but, seeing my

expression, closes it again, the words unspoken. Jo-Jo has always been jealous of me, the baby sister, the one with the good job, with a comfortable lifestyle she envies, never quite able to recognise her own good fortune. I've always considered jealousy a completely pointless emotion, but now I envy her. I wish I'd married a lovely caring guy like Ed. I long for my life to be normal, for me to have a happy marriage like everyone else, yet my marriage is over and I must face reality and start to rebuild my life. There is no going back.

Then she says a surprising thing. She tells me that she never did like Oliver. 'In fact, I was the one who sent you that anonymous letter. I saw him kissing Sandra Fuller just weeks before your wedding.'

I stare at her in shock. 'So if you'd spoken to me outright, as a loving sister should, instead of sending that stupid letter to Mum and Dad, you might have spared me all of this?'

There are tears in her eyes now, and she has the grace to look embarrassed. 'I thought Mum and Dad would tell you, but they threw the damn letter straight in the fire. I didn't think you'd ever believe *me*. Oliver was very much Mr Wonderful in your eyes.'

Even as I gaze in fury at my sister I know what she says is true. We would have quarrelled bitterly, I expect, but would I have believed her? I very much doubt it. I suspect my stubbornness would have kicked in, and, recalling how very much in love I was at that time, I would have clung to the belief that he was innocent. I hug Jo-Jo and tell her it's not her fault. 'You're right. Even if I'd believed you he would have soothed my fears with his charm, as he has done countless times since. Well, I've done the right thing now.'

She can see how distressed I am and puts her arms around me and hugs me back. 'You have, love. If that's the game he's been playing, then you most certainly have done the right thing in leaving him. You've obviously seen sense at last. And not before time. I'm surprised you stuck it as long as you did.'

That little caustic remark at the end of her sentence makes

me see that it's going to be a long hard road ahead; that some people, even friends and family, may never fully understand.

It is two weeks now since I left Oliver and shame still gnaws at me. When I walk down the street I'm so self-conscious that it's easy to assume everyone is looking at me and gossiping behind their hands. I can see it in the way they glance covertly at me, as if trying to spot the bruises. I can hear them whispering, 'Did you know that she left her husband? I've heard that he used to beat her.' Followed by the usual, 'She must have asked for it.' Or, 'She obviously enjoyed it or she would have left sooner.'

I want to scream at them: *The only thing that stopped me leaving him was Oliver himself.*

But I say nothing. I'm still badly bruised, both inside and out. Will the taint of shame that I loved such a man ever leave me? I wonder.

Those who know my husband refuse to believe the story at all, insisting that the very idea of this charming man being violent is all a figment of my vivid imagination. Grace, his mother, is furious with me when she hears. I confess I don't have the courage to face her with the truth myself, so she learns of it via the gossip grapevine, or maybe Mum rang her, I'm not sure. She comes to the agency in Windermere, marches up the stairs, her husband trundling along behind, and accosts me in my own office.

'I'd like to know exactly what you've been saying about my son? How dare you accuse him of *knocking you about*?' There's a curl to her lip, a mocking edge to her tone as she trips out this old-fashioned phrase, quite at odds with the sweet-natured lady I've come to like and admire.

'I dare because it's true.'

'So tell me *when* he hit you, and *how*! What had you done to provoke him?' As if we were children scrapping in the school playground.

Oliver's father looks deeply uncomfortable, almost hanging

his head in shame, but he doesn't interrupt as his wife rants and rails at me for a full ten minutes or more, vehemently defending her beloved only son. She accuses me of driving him to it by being both frigid and a harlot who has enjoyed affairs with all and sundry. I listen in silence, privately appalled by her reaction, but deeply aware what a shock it must be for her to learn all of this. How does a mother come to terms with the fact her precious son is a wife-beater? Finally, I can take no more and hold up my hands to implore her to stop, apologising for the fact I really can't talk about it right now, and I walk away.

Emma briskly shows them both the door.

Other people's attitude towards me becomes almost a form of amusement. Some friends cross the street rather than face me, perhaps too embarrassed to know what to say, or as if what has happened to me might be catching and put their own marriages at risk. Others drag their husbands away if they see them speaking to me, as if I might want to steal them. Some are patronising and offer to loan me their cast-off carpets and bits of old furniture since I'm now homeless. One or two tell me that they knew all along about Oliver's affairs but didn't like to say. It's hurtful to see how much people love to gossip, and I have to steel myself to deal with it. It certainly teaches me who my real friends are.

To my amazement an old friend, whom I haven't seen in a long time, turns up one day quite out of the blue. Tony arrives at the office asking to speak to me. Emma show him in and leaves us to it. He's clearly embarrassed and I don't wonder at it. Yet in a way we're both in the same boat since Jane, his wife, and also once my best friend, is still heavily involved in an affair with my husband, or so I assume.

'I heard what happened,' he says, by way of explanation for his sudden appearance. 'I wondered how you were coping.'

'I'm fine, thanks. And you?'

He shuffles his feet, not quite looking at me. 'Jane and I, we . . .

we're still together. She's not with Oliver any more. I believe he's moved on and got himself a new woman, so I'm standing by her.'

I'm surprised by this but try not to show it. 'I see. Well, I hope it works out for you.' I tell myself that it makes no difference to me if my husband has yet another new mistress. Maybe it will help me come to terms with just how fickle and unreliable he is. 'Do you know where Oliver is living, by any chance? He doesn't seem to be at the house, and there are matters to be settled, decisions to be made.'

He looks surprised that I don't know. 'He's living with this married woman, in Heversham, I believe. She left her husband the same day Oliver left you.'

I want to say that Oliver didn't leave me, that I left him, but it seems trivial so I don't bother. What does it matter what Tony knows, or thinks?

'I suppose you'll be getting a divorce?' he says. 'I hope you won't cite Jane as co-respondent, she's really had a bellyful of him.'

I don't answer this comment either, although I understand now why he called. It was to protect his wife, and his own marriage, not out of concern for me. In my heart I know divorce is inevitable. I just haven't started to think ahead that far yet. I'm still suffering from a lack of confidence, and even censure in some quarters. 'Tony, why did you and Jane stop speaking to us, long before – before she and Oliver got together?'

Dark brows lift in surprise. 'I thought you'd have realised by now. Because I knew he was having it off with Poppy, then I saw him in his car with a girl from the mailing room. I knew he was cheating on you, so how could we carry on being friends, just as if nothing was going on? I couldn't do it. Oliver hated my self-righteous, pious attitude, as he called it, which is why he took his revenge by screwing my wife.'

I'm shocked by this, and yet it is so typical of my husband. 'Oh, Tony. You lost your wife because you were trying to protect me?'

'I haven't lost my wife. At least I hope I haven't.'

'I hope so too.'

He grins at me suddenly, and it warms my heart to see it. I've missed Tony and Jane, my dear old school friends. I felt so alone without them for so long.

Tony seems to be reading my thoughts. 'Maybe we can all three of us get together again one day,' he says optimistically. 'Talk about old times.'

I take his hands and give them a gentle squeeze. 'I don't think so, do you? But thanks for coming. I appreciate it.'

'What are friends for?' he says, quite unable to see the contradiction in his words.

23

I'm still at my parents' house and Oliver has rung many times, wishing to speak to me, but I refuse to take his calls. Finally he sends me a note requesting a desire to see Katie. I'm utterly flabbergasted by this. From the moment of her birth he has shown not the slightest interest in our child. Most evenings he would be off out almost the moment he'd finished eating, and even when he was home he never offered to put her to bed, or even to hold her. Most of the time he ignored Katie's very existence.

Now, because I've left him, he claims that he wants to spend more time with her. He's clearly wanting to put himself in a good light when it comes to the divorce proceedings. The note says he'll ring to make arrangements for a visit later in the week. I've no choice but to agree, but I'm nervous and furious all at the same time. It's so typically manipulative of him.

I slip round to see his parents, wanting to soothe relations between us a little and thinking they might like to see their granddaughter. I'm wondering if they would agree for Oliver to take her to their house on the days he has access, so that I would at least know Katie was in good hands.

They make a great fuss of her, although conversation with me is stilted. I try to tell them that I did everything I could think of to save our marriage but Grace walks away, head high, ostensibly to put the kettle on, but I know that deep down she blames me. Jeffrey, Oliver's father, leans over and whispers an explanation.

'Grace and Oliver have always been very close. He is the child she never thought she'd have.'

'I understand, and I'm genuinely sorry things have turned out this way. I just want her to know that I loved him very

much, still do in a way, but I simply can't live with him. He . . .'
I look into his father's sympathetic gaze and my words falter.
Jeffrey finishes them for me.

'He didn't treat you well.'

'No, I'm afraid he didn't.'

'Other women?'

'That too, as well as the other stuff.'

'If he was a little rough at times, I'm sure it was unintentional.'

'I'm afraid I cannot agree with you there.'

He struggles for a moment, seeming to have trouble dealing
with this, which I don't wonder at. 'Then I can only apologise
on my son's behalf.'

'Isn't that something he should do for himself?' I suggest.

Jeffrey makes a gesture with his hands, conceding my point.
'Grace finds this hard to accept because Oliver has been brought
up in a morally upright home. We always insisted on him attending
church every Sunday, and I made it clear to him when he was
growing up that women are delicate creatures and should be
treated accordingly. If they care for us and nurture us; love, honour
and obey us, then we should treat them with all due appreciation.
While a husband may deserve all due deference and duty from
his wife, in return he should show her loyalty and love.'

There's something slightly troubling about this statement, bland
and well meaning as it might sound, and I try to work out what
it is. I instinctively want to protest that I'm not in the least bit
delicate, that normally I can stand up for myself very well. I'm a
modern, intelligent woman but I don't expect to be constantly
belittled and humiliated, or beaten black and blue by my husband.
Then I realise that Jeffrey's view of a wife's role is very like that
of his son's: believing her chief role in life is to nurture and care
for her man. I never actually thought of myself as a feminist,
leaving that particular battle to Emma, but neither do I see men
and women's roles in this clichéd, traditional way. I believe there
should be equal caring, and respect, from both parties.

Fortunately I'm saved from going into all of this, and possibly
becoming embroiled in an uncomfortable argument, by Grace

returning with a tray of tea and biscuits. We all sit and politely drink it while she plays with Katie on the rug.

She still hasn't addressed me directly, and I attempt to talk to her about Katie, giving details of her weight and progress at her latest check-up. Even then she responds by talking only to the child, saying, 'Who's a clever girl then? Aren't you getting to be a big girl?' and suchlike nonsense. I glance at Jeffrey who smiles sympathetically. He is clearly concerned and means well, but I wonder how much his old-fashioned views on marriage, and Grace's obvious spoiling, have influenced their son and helped to turn him into the selfish, demanding creature he is.

We're just finishing our second cup when the doorbell rings. Grace is still engrossed with Katie, so it is Jeffrey who gets up to answer it, but he hesitates as he reaches the hall.

'Oh dear, it's Oliver, I'm afraid. What would you like to do, Carly? Perhaps it would be better if you left by the kitchen door. We don't want a scene.'

I hastily agree and begin to gather our belongings together, Katie's coat and feeding cup, my own jacket and bag, feeling flustered and nervous at the prospect of a confrontation with Oliver.

Jeffrey calls out to his son. 'Hold on, lad, we won't be a moment.'

It's one of those doors with a narrow panel of stained glass down the centre, and I suddenly see Oliver's face peering through it. I realise instantly that he will have seen the stroller in the hall. I'm filled with trepidation as I make a dash for it, dragging it backwards into the kitchen. My fears are confirmed as a roar of rage explodes through the letterbox.

'Is that you, Carly? Open this door, Father. I wish to speak to my wife.'

'Not right now, son. Hold on a minute.'

Grace is outraged. 'I will not shut my son out of his own house.'

'This isn't his house any longer, Mother,' Jeffrey reminds her, in the kind of stentorian tones which issue a chilling reminder of Oliver's own.

I'm trying to stuff Katie into the buggy but she's screaming and resisting every effort by stiffening her legs and arching her back. Grace is also hindering me by accusing me of being cruel to my child and deliberately keeping her from her father. I'm beginning to panic, tempers are growing short when suddenly Oliver loses his entirely and smashes the door in. He simply slams his fist straight through the glass.

I don't linger to check if he's hurt, or to see how Grace and Jeffrey deal with this disaster, I snatch up my bag, grab the buggy and run out of the kitchen door, down the back garden and out on to the street behind the house where thankfully I parked my car. I'm all fingers and thumbs, gasping and sobbing with fear as I struggle to fasten a distressed child into her car seat. I can hear voices raised in argument, roars of fury emanating from my husband, Jeffrey clearly in the throes of issuing a stern, moralising lecture, and hysterical sobs from his mother.

Nausea clogs my throat. If he can smash in a door and behave like this with his own parents, what will he do to me? Oliver bursts on to the street just as I finally manage to stuff the key into the ignition and fire the engine into life. I drive away leaving him shouting after me, much to the entertainment of the neighbours.

I'm so distressed by the time I get to Windermere, Emma urges me to see a solicitor. 'You can't allow him to hound you like this. Do you think Oliver followed you to his parents' house?'

I'm appalled by the very idea. 'Surely not?'

'Then how did he know you were there?'

'I'm not saying he did. I assumed it was simply chance that Oliver happened to call to see them while I was there. A coincidence.'

Emma raises her brows in disbelief. 'When has Oliver ever relied upon chance or coincidence? Whatever the reason for his dreadful behaviour, you must get someone on your side. You need to see a solicitor.'

Recognising this as sound advice, I do so before the week is out. He's a large, flabby man with a bald head, spectacles, and a crumpled dark blue suit. He half glances up as his secretary shows me into his office, before continuing with whatever he was scribbling on a file, completely ignoring me. I take a seat and wait, glancing about me at shelves lined with dusty legal tomes, black and white etchings of Helvellyn, and Ullswater. Finally, he puts down his pen and looks at me over the top of his spectacles. His eyes are pale grey, too small for his round face, and would probably have shown more interest had I been a grubby mark on the beige carpet.

'Mrs Sheldon, I understand you are wishing to sue your husband for divorce.' I half expect him to yawn, feeling very much as if I'm nothing more than an item on a conveyor belt.

'I am, yes.'

'On grounds of adultery, I assume. I'm sure you've no wish to wait two years for desertion, or embark upon a long-drawn-out battle over who has behaved the most unreasonably by refusing to help with the washing-up or eating fish and chips in bed.' His face twists into a grimace and I realise he's attempting to make a joke and raise a smile. It's not particularly effective.

I clear my throat and take a breath, preparing myself for a lengthy explanation. I've carefully practised what I wish to say because I'm afraid of saying the wrong thing and making a fool of myself. But before I get a word out he reaches for a bunch of forms and starts firing questions at me in a bored tone of voice which clearly states he's done this more times than he cares to count. Mainly he's asking for basic details: names, ages, address, date of marriage, employment.

I tell him about Perfect Cottages.

'Hmm, in that case I doubt you'll be granted much in the way of legal aid.' He informs me of the likely cost and I blanch, thinking I might be obliged to ask Dad for a loan.

Pushing financial considerations to the back of my mind for now, I confess that I've no idea who my husband's latest mistress is. 'I'm aware of the names of two other women with whom he has had affairs,' I hasten to add. 'But with this latest one I know only that she's also married, has left her husband and she and

Oliver are living together, in Heversham I believe. She's older than him by ten years, or so I've been told.'

He snaps up his head, quite sharply, and clicks his tongue. 'Ten years! I doubt it will last. Are you certain you wish to proceed? Perhaps marriage counselling . . . ?'

I'm surprised by this remark and show it. 'I'm absolutely certain. There were other problems in my marriage.'

'I'm sure, I'm sure.' He sighs, looking mildly irritated, shuffles papers about on his desk, glances at his watch, as if to make clear that his time is precious, and certainly expensive, and he really has no wish to sit listening to the moans of an abandoned wife. He makes a great show of clearing his throat. 'Supplying names won't be necessary, and could only serve to put you in a bad light were you to offer such details, unless the divorce were to be contested. He isn't planning on defending the case, is he?'

I swallow, not sure how to answer this. Oliver has given ample evidence in recent months that he has no wish to let me go or end our marriage, yet the news that he's co-habiting with another woman, so soon after our break-up, has shaken me somewhat. It's left me feeling confused and unsure of him, but then there's nothing Oliver enjoys more than confusing me. I stiffen my resolve with a quick indrawn breath. 'I hope not.'

The solicitor shrugs. 'There would be little point in any case, if one party is determined the marriage is over, it generally is.'

'I most certainly am determined.'

He nods. Pulls out another form. 'Is there a child of the marriage?'

I tell him about Katie, then try a question of my own. 'What will happen about custody? Can he contest it?'

He gives me a hard stare. 'Is there any reason why he would? Are you having an affair yourself?'

'No, of course not, only Oliver has threatened to fight me on custody.'

'He has every right to do so, of course. Young children are generally left in the care of their mothers although the judge may decide it can be shared equally between you. It's increasingly common these days.'

My heart sinks and I feel slightly sick. Shared custody isn't something that I've considered and it comes as something of a shock. I try again. 'I'm worried because he isn't in a particularly stable frame of mind at the moment. He was involved in a terrible row with his parents the other day, and his behaviour . . .'

He interrupts before I have time to finish. 'These things happen. Divorce is a traumatic experience for all parties concerned.'

He isn't looking at me, apparently too engrossed in pulling out yet more forms, pencilling in the odd detail here and there. I'm growing increasingly bemused by his lack of interest, and by the pile of paper stacking up on the desk before him. I'm still trying to find a way to lead in to a discussion about Oliver's true nature, to describe how controlling he is, but the solicitor isn't making it easy for me. I take a breath but once again he interrupts me.

'How long did you say you were married?'

'Just over two years, but problems emerged fairly early on. He was violent.' There, I think, in quiet triumph. I've said it.

He puts down his pencil and I wait for him to ask for a full explanation, for me to describe some of these events. Instead, he asks, 'Any broken bones, photos of bruises, visits to A & E?'

I shake my head. 'He was very careful where he hit me.'

'The adultery should be sufficient to prove irretrievable break-down of the marriage. Why hang out all your dirty washing?' and he hands me a bulky fistful of forms.

I'm apparently expected to furnish him with all necessary financial details: income and expenditure, rent or mortgage payments, community charge, water rates, premiums on endowment policies, insurance, bank accounts, pension. Copy of my most recent P60. Even the age of my car, its make and model and probable value. He reels off a list that sets my head spinning, then gets to his feet and I realise the interview is over.

'My first task is to file a petition which gives notice of your intentions to the respondent, your husband. I'll call you when I receive his acknowledgement of service. Hopefully it should all be perfectly straightforward. In the meantime, I would advise you to work out some sort of visitation rights. You'll find it less expensive in legal costs if matters regarding children and finance, always stumbling blocks, can be worked out amicably between the pair of you from the start.'

I feel a beat of fear. Do I trust Oliver with Katie? Although the solicitor has made it plain that I'm legally obliged to allow him access, the prospect terrifies me.

Moments later I'm out on the pavement, feeling bemused and bewildered. I know in my heart that Oliver will do his utmost to make this divorce anything but straightforward. I'm alarmed that the solicitor didn't seem interested in hearing details of Oliver's treatment of me, of how he beat and humiliated me. Was he doubting my word simply because my leg wasn't in plaster or I hadn't taken gory photos of my injuries? His one concern was to achieve a fast and cheap divorce. But then isn't that what I want too? So why should that bother me? Do I want my personal and private affairs plastered all over the local press, as might well happen if I insist on revealing what went on behind closed doors? My dirty washing hung out on the line, as he aptly described. Of course I don't. A fast and simple divorce sounds good.

The following Sunday, Oliver calls at my parents' house to collect Katie. Dad and I are alone, Mum and Gran having been packed off to the neighbour's house next door, well out of the way. I'm shaking with nerves, sick to my stomach at the prospect of seeing him again, let alone handing Katie over. What if he hurts her again? Or if he refuses to hand her back? I keep thinking how vulnerable she is, and what little interest he's shown in her until now.

He's taking her out for the afternoon, for a gentle stroll and a picnic by the lake, something he's never done in his life before. His solicitor rang to arrange it yesterday, a woman with a crisp, no-nonsense sort of voice. Dad took the call and, after relaying the details to me and gaining my agreement, made the necessary arrangements. I'm so glad he's here with me now.

When I hear the knock on the door I feel suddenly faint and light-headed, close to collapse. Dad opens the door and addresses my husband in brisk tones.

'Good morning, Oliver. We have Katie all ready for you. Carly has packed her bag with nappies, food, everything she might need. Please have her back by four o'clock sharp, in good time for her to have her tea and bath before bed.'

I wonder if he'll accuse me of creating an incident at Grace and Jeffrey's house, but he doesn't even mention it. 'Of course,' Oliver says, smiling. 'I wouldn't dream of interfering with her normal bedtime routine. Hello, sweetie,' he says to Katie, who turns and buries her head in my neck.

Dad lifts her from my arms and my heart clenches. I feel as if she's being torn from me, but I make no protest as he straps her into the buggy. I crouch down to kiss her. 'Have a lovely afternoon with Daddy. I'll be here waiting for you when you get back.'

There's a small puckering frown on her smooth brow as she looks first at me, and then at Oliver, as if none of this seems quite right to her but she can't work out exactly what is wrong.

'Wave bye-bye to Mummy,' Oliver says, then picks up the bag, hooks it on to the buggy, and with a curt nod in my direction, wheels Katie away.

How I stopped myself from running after him and snatching her back, I really can't say. Dad's gentle hand on my arm perhaps.

Katie flaps her small hand, her small face beaming at me.

The BMW is parked some distance from the house, presumably in a pathetic attempt to avoid being seen by the neighbours. Dad and I stand at the door watching as Oliver straps Katie into the car seat, stows the buggy in the boot, and with a cheery wave, drives off. Only then does Dad close the door with a heavy sigh, and I collapse on to the sofa, arms wrapped about myself, and begin to rock back and forth in great distress.

The afternoon seems the longest in my entire life. I'm

comforted by both Mum and Dad, and Gran is a tower of strength with her calm, wise way of looking at the world.

'Don't let it worry you, he's only making a point,' she tells me.

'I'm sure he isn't doing any such thing,' Mum argues. 'Whatever Oliver and Carly may feel about each other, they both love Katie.'

Gran thinks differently. 'I'm not so sure. When have you ever seen that young man take any interest, Viv? I've never seen him so much as walk his child down the road, or take her to the playground. Did he ever offer to do so, Carly?' I shake my head. 'Or to feed her, or change her, or put her to bed?'

'No, never.'

'There you are then,' Gran says with satisfaction. 'He's making a point, and once he's made it, he'll soon grow bored and leave Katie alone.'

I'm not so sure. I think that Oliver may well do all he can to win Katie, like a prize, just to prove that he can.

It's the following week and I'm back at the agency, working nine till two, making an effort to move forward and be normal. Katie is back with Jo-Jo and I've given my sister strict instructions not to let her out of her sight, and never to allow Oliver to take her without ringing me first to check if it's OK.

When Katie returned from her Sunday afternoon outing, she was strangely quiet and subdued, clinging to me like a limpet for the rest of the evening. I learn later, from our garrulous neighbour who seems to have spies in all the right places, that there was also a woman in the car, his fancy piece, as she describes her to Gran. I worry what Katie made of that, of seeing her daddy with another woman, and how the pair of them behaved in front of her. I wonder whether this woman, this stranger, held my child, fed her and changed her nappies. Somehow I find the idea revolting.

'Please instruct your good friend not to give me any more details about my husband,' I tell Gran. 'I really don't want to know.'

She looks at me with sad, faded eyes. 'Ignorance is not the

best policy right now, Carly. You need to know as much as possible about what he's up to.'

I know that she's right, but why is it so unbearably difficult?

It's on Friday afternoon that Tim Hathaway clatters up our stairs in his great big boots, and strides, grinning, into my office. My heart does a little flip at sight of him, and I'm quite certain that my cheeks redden for no reason whatsoever.

'I've come to claim that coffee you promised me,' he says, sounding decidedly firm. 'And don't even consider saying no, as a refusal can often offend.' He picks up my jacket and holds it out for me.

He looks so smilingly pleased to see me, so vibrant and energetic, so full of life, that I find myself laughing for the first time in weeks. Just seeing him standing there, legs astride, with that wry grin on his handsome face, reminds me that I'm still young, only twenty-six, not at all the withered old crone I feel inside.

'No strings,' he adds more quietly. 'Just coffee.'

I can feel myself weakening. 'Well, maybe a quick one then, just five minutes. OK?'

'OK.' I allow him to lead me away.

We go to a coffee bar across the road where Tim orders an espresso for himself and a latte for me, plus a couple of chocolate chip muffins. I demur, saying I'm not hungry but he insists I need the calories. He's probably right. We sit at a marble-topped table and I start to crumble my muffin, nibbling the odd chunk while Tim eats his with gusto and genuine enjoyment. I suspect this is the way he tackles everything in life, with true joy and exuberance. I've forgotten how that feels.

He explains that he's here for the weekend, this time to tackle Helm Crag, known locally as the lion and the lamb because of the configuration of the rocks. 'Why don't you come with me?'

'I don't think that would be appropriate.'

He nods. 'I heard that you and your husband had broken up. I'm sorry, although I have to say that what little I've seen of him didn't impress me much.'

I smile at this. 'He can be very impressive, when he puts his mind to it. Otherwise, no, you're right. He can be . . .'

'A real shit?'

I giggle. 'Difficult.'

'So you aren't going to be shedding too many tears over him then?'

'Not any more.'

'Excellent! Forward march. Fresh fields and pastures new.'

I laugh out loud at this. 'If you mean am I looking for another fella, no I am not. Another relationship is the last thing on my agenda right now.'

He slides one hand over mine and gently squeezes it. 'Of course it is, I realise that, Carly. I wasn't trying to push you into anything. But we could be friends, maybe? I could offer a shoulder to cry on, if needed. A friendly chat. Well-meaning, if not necessarily impeccable advice, and plenty of fresh air and exercise, should you desire it.'

'If only life could be that simple.'

'How is your little daughter?' he asks, more seriously, and I'm suddenly crying again, despite having just vowed never to do so again. I find myself describing the misery of Sunday, and Katie's strange silence and clinginess afterwards. He listens patiently without offering any solutions, then goes and buys us more coffee.

'Feeling better now you've got that off your chest?' he gently asks, and I nod.

'Good. I wish I could be more help, but I can at least lend a sympathetic ear. My sister went through a divorce and it was most unpleasant for her, but you have to hang in there and get through it as best you can. There is a light at the end of the tunnel.'

'Yes,' I say, responding to his warm smile with a shy one of my own. 'I can see that now.'

'I'm here most weekends, Carly, if you need a friend. Remember that.'

'I will.'

'Why would she need a friend when she has a husband?' The deep voice from behind nearly has me jumping out of my skin. I whirl about to face him. 'Oliver! What on earth are you doing here?'

'Good job I am. This all looks very cosy. Didn't take you long to latch on to lover-boy again.'

'*Oliver*, for God's sake, stop that!'

Tim is frowning and I'm feeling hugely embarrassed, but Oliver is clearly enjoying himself. He leans over and gripping me firmly by the elbow, hisses in my ear, 'I'd like a word, if you don't mind.'

I wrench my arm free. 'Actually, I do mind. I don't think we have anything to say to each other.'

'Oh, yes, we do.'

'Then you can say it to my solicitor.'

He snorts with laughter. 'And double the legal bill, I don't think so.' He turns to Tim. 'I think you should go. I need to discuss some important issues with my wife.'

'Not now, Oliver.'

'Yes, now. Or are you saying that such issues as the welfare of our child are less important than spending time with your lover?' He asks me this loaded question with contempt in his tone.

'You need to know,' Tim quietly remarks, 'that I am not her lover. Unfortunately.'

'Beat it!'

I'm shivering inside, shaking with silent fury and a familiar sensation of helplessness. Tim gets slowly to his feet, his gaze fixed firmly on mine. 'I'll be just outside.' His eyes are telling me that he's there for me, should I need him. I simply nod and wearily accept the inevitable. Oliver always manages to get what he wants. Whether I've left him or not, he's still very much in control.

24

I feel like a displaced person, dividing my time between my parents' sofa and Emma's floor. I even spent a few nights in the office, me cuddled in a sleeping bag behind my desk, Katie ensconced in a drawer doubling as a make-shift cot. I had use of a microwave and a kettle, and it certainly saved on petrol getting to and from Windermere, but it was far from ideal as it meant I had Katie with me all day, which was hard work. I did try asking my sister if I could squeeze in with her children, or have them double up while I rented a room off her, but she wouldn't even consider it.

'There are quite enough people in this house already, thanks very much. I'm sure your rich husband can afford to pay for you to rent a place somewhere.'

'That's just it, I want to be independent of Oliver, Jo-Jo.'

'Oh, for goodness' sake, get real, Carly. Screw him for every penny you can, but don't expect me to bail you out.'

I gave up on the argument and went back to sleeping under my desk. I've been asking everyone I can think of for weeks if they know of a place available long-term on a reasonable rent, and then just as I'd almost given up hope, Caroline, a friend of Emma's, comes up trumps.

She rattles a set of keys. 'It's somewhere in the country between Staveley and Burneside, near the River Gowan so you can enjoy riverside walks. Come on, let's go and find it.'

The cottage is more isolated than I would have liked, some distance from the road, surrounded on all sides by fields and backing on to a wood. It's one of a row of four but the others are holiday cottages, so are rarely occupied until the height of summer. It's also very small, with no front garden. Nevertheless I'm excited at the prospect of a home of my own, however humble it might be. I'm hoping that once the divorce comes through there will be some settlement from Oliver when he'll either put the house up for sale, or pay me a fair share for my portion of it. Knowing my husband as I do, I'm not expecting this operation to be either simple or quick.

I push open the door, which sticks a little from the damp, and I'm hit by a none-too-clean smell which is not encouraging. The cottage is dark and overwhelmingly green: carpet, paintwork, a three-piece suite which looks as if it has been branded with any amount of gravy, egg and tea stains over the last fifty years, and a hideous, green-tiled, 1950s fireplace. The walls are a symphony of green and beige swirls in polished anaglypta. I smile, determined to be positive, and throw back the dusty curtains, also green, to let in more light. 'This is lovely, at least it will be once I've given it a lick of paint here and there. It is all right for me to brighten it up a bit, isn't it?'

'I'll check, but I shouldn't imagine there'll be a problem. The cottage belonged to Caro's mother, who's recently died. I think she'd be happy to sell it, if you were interested. You might get it for a good price since it needs considerable work doing to it and isn't in the Central Lakes.'

I perk up even more and look at the cottage now from a more professional point of view, as I'm accustomed to doing when offered a possible property to put on our books. The sitting room is small, with a tiny kitchen behind. Beyond that lies a tiny, unkempt garden which could be made pretty with time and effort. It even boasts a small paved area currently occupied by a rotting bench that has seen better days.

Upstairs are two bedrooms of roughly equal size, and a bathroom in a depressing shade of avocado that was probably installed as the latest thing in the early sixties. 'It's rather tired, but certainly has possibilities. With a wood-burning stove in place of that 1950s fireplace, new kitchen, new bathroom, complete redecoration, floorboards stripped and waxed, and completely refurnished in bleached pine with a nice squashy sofa, it could make a cosy, charming home.'

Emma laughs. 'That's more like it. Time to start fighting back. I was beginning to worry about you. I'll leave you to settle in, and if you decide you like it, you can always put in an offer. Here's Caro's number, together with details of what she requires as monthly rent. It might be worth checking if she'd reduce that a little, in view of its condition.'

I glance at the piece of paper and wince. 'I would definitely welcome the possibility of a rent reduction, since I'm a bit hard pressed for cash right now. I'll give her a ring and see if we can come to terms.' I'm filled with a sudden surge of optimism. Creating a home for Katie and myself would be fun, and represent a new beginning for us.

But when Emma's gone, leaving me to mooch about on my own for a while, the professional mask slips and my confidence rapidly dissolves. I'd have to get a mortgage, maybe a bridging loan as well. I don't have any money of my own until after the divorce goes through, maybe not even then until Oliver decides what he's doing about the house.

I stare out over the empty fields and woods and feel desperately, achingly alone. I think of all the work I would need to do to the place, without any assistance, and am filled with self-doubt and indecisiveness. What am I doing here? How could I possibly cope on my own in the middle of nowhere with a small child, let alone attempt any of the renovations? I must be mad to even consider it. Panic clutches at my chest and I pull out my mobile, desperate to ring Oliver. I need to ask him what I should do, what's the best way forward, can I really afford to pay this rent? Could I afford to take on a mortgage? Am I being sensible to even consider buying this cottage?

I've punched in the first three numbers before it dawns on me that turning to my husband every time I hit a problem is the last thing I should be doing. What am I thinking of? I switch it off, and, finding my legs are shaking, sink into the smelly green armchair, my head in my hands. Oliver is right. I am stupid and inadequate. Quite incapable of coping on my own. I must be mad to be even considering this.

'Cooee! Hello, oh there you are. I thought I heard someone. I'm Sue, from the end house. Are you the new tenant?' I'm confronted by a woman as round as a dumpling, with frizzed hair clipped back from her smiling face. 'I wondered if you fancied a cup of tea. I've got the kettle on.'

'Oh, that's very kind of you.' I jump out of the chair, a bit nonplussed to be confronted by a smiling stranger when I'm in the throes of grieving for a lost marriage. 'I thought none of these cottages was occupied, that they were all holiday cottages.'

'They are, except for mine, which is more of a second home. I work in Manchester, at the archives, but come up here as often as I can get away.' She glances about her at the dingy green decor. 'Bit grim, isn't it? I thought it might cheer you up to see mine, show you what can be done with these cottages.'

And indeed it does. By the time I've admired Sue's array of shining copper kettles, her smart little kitchen, and become acquainted with her excellent shortbread, I'm feeling much more optimistic. Ready for anything. I thank her for her kindness and head back Windermere, bursting to ring Emma's friend and get the whole thing fixed up.

The divorce proceedings have shuddered to a halt. Oliver still hasn't returned the acknowledgement of service. This is a document sent by the court at the same time as the divorce petition, which Oliver is expected to fill out and return. My solicitor informs me that it is a perfectly straightforward document and should cause no problems. Apart from an obvious check that he has received the divorce papers, it asks Oliver if he intends to defend the case, and does he admit adultery.

Unfortunately, Oliver is proving to be elusive. He appears to have moved out of the matrimonial home, and so far my solicitor has been unable to trace him in order to serve the papers on him. Why am I not surprised? Oliver never admitted to anything in his life, so why should he do so now? He'll be keeping his head down somewhere, determined to make things as difficult as possible for me. But if he hopes that I might weary of the battle, give up and go back to him, he couldn't be more wrong.

When I ring Grace to ask if she has any news, her tone is decidedly frosty. She claims not to know where he's living, tells me he's off work because he's so upset. Which means we can't even contact him at his office.

I try not to worry and turn my attention to making plans on how best to do up the cottage. I've come to an agreement with the owner that I'll rent it for twelve months with an option to buy at the end of that time, should I find it suitable. It sounds like a good deal, and gives me time to sort myself out financially.

But any improvements will have to be made on a shoestring. I can only afford a few cans of paint at this stage, but I set to with a will, determined to at least banish the green walls. The task seems daunting but Emma offers to help, as does Glen, her partner. It's a quiet Saturday so she closes the office and rings to say she's on her way. To my complete surprise, Tim is with them. I feel that familiar uplift of spirit which always happens when I see him, instantly followed by a rush of guilt and fear. I find myself glancing up and down the deserted lane, as if to make sure we're not being watched.

Emma breezes in bearing brushes, mops and buckets, and a bright innocent smile. I instantly remonstrate with her, 'Why did you bring Tim? I'm not sure that was a good idea.'

She gives me an arch look, then glances at the grim, dark walls and equally depressing carpet and furnishings. 'He volunteered. Anyway, I doubt you can afford to be too picky. You look like you need all the help you can muster.'

I have to confess this is true, so welcome him with a philosophical smile, hoping against hope my in-laws, Grace and Jeffrey, don't decide to drop by out of curiosity.

I've persuaded Jo-Jo to have Katie for the weekend while

I blitz the place, and in no time the four of us have dragged out the stained green velvet settee, the chairs and sagging bed, and other Victorian monstrosities. We rip up the carpet, along with several layers of smelly linoleum which lie beneath. I've hired a skip and it soon fills up with the contents of the cottage. The kitchen and bathroom will have to make do with a good scrub until I can afford to have them replaced, but scouring off the thick layer of grease that coats every surface should improve matters considerably. The two men make short work of knocking out the old fifties fireplace, and Tim assures me he can easily fit the second-hand multi-fuel stove I've bought.

Glen has hired an amazing piece of equipment which steams the anaglypta off the walls, and in no time the two men are working their way through the entire house. Emma and I follow on behind, cleaning off the bits they miss, filling cracks, sanding the paintwork, and using a great deal of elbow grease as we scrub and mop, and generally dispose of the mess.

The work is exhausting, leaving little energy for chatter. With Radio One blasting away, people humming and laughing, the day has a warmth and companionable quality to it; yet I still feel slightly detached, all hollow and empty inside, as if I'm clinging to the edge of a cliff and about to fall off. When we stop for a break in the middle of the day, I stroll down to the river for a breath of fresh air. Tim comes to join me.

'It looks an impossible task at the moment, doesn't it, but it'll soon pull together.'

'I'm sure it will,' I agree. But can I pull myself together, I wonder? Why do I keep experiencing these panic attacks, this terrible need to call Oliver and ask his advice? Am I quite incapable of thinking for myself, of making decisions about my own life?

As if sensing my mood, Tim says, 'It can't have been easy for you, walking out on a bad marriage. I admire your courage.'

I glance up at him in surprise. 'Do you? It all seems so very difficult I can't seem to think straight. I don't know who I am any more, or whether I can even cope on my own, let alone look after Katie properly.'

'I'm sure that's a natural reaction, and you're making a great job of looking after Katie already. Look, I've no wish to pry, and I may be jumping to completely the wrong conclusion, but I've heard it said that the most dangerous time for . . . for an abused woman, is the moment when she finally breaks free. The divorce, in fact. So do take care, Carly.'

I look at him in astonishment. I've told him nothing about the reason for the break-up of my marriage, and I know in my heart that Emma would never betray a confidence. He must have put two and two together himself, perhaps making judgements about Oliver's behaviour, or perhaps my own gives away more than I realise, to a keen observer. 'You're quite astute.'

He gives a self-deprecating smile. 'It has been said. I accept this is none of my business, but I want you to know that you aren't on your own, not at all.' He puts a hand on my shoulder and gives it a comforting squeeze. 'If there's anything you want doing, just let me know.'

He's so close I can sense the warmth from his body. I feel a great urge to smooth my hands over his arms, bare to the elbow beneath the rolled-up sleeves of his check shirt, lean into those strong masculine shoulders. I hear a rustle in the undergrowth and glance back over my shoulder, nervous suddenly, as if I sense we're not alone. I step back, away from his mesmerising closeness, and manage a stiff little smile. 'You've helped already, just by coming here today.'

'I meant in other ways. If you need support of any kind . . . protection . . . or just a friend. I'm here for you.'

I'm touched by his offer, and deeply embarrassed, but instead of thanking him gracefully, I mumble something incoherent about having to get back to the decorating, and scurry away.

By the end of a long tiring day, the cottage is stripped and ready for painting, and we relax, chatting happily together as we sit eating fish and chips and drinking beer. Tim and Glen are talking through the mechanics of installing the stove, and the long black pipe that acts as a chimney. It sounds very complicated but the pair of them seem quite optimistic they can manage it OK. Emma and I are discussing colours of paint for the various rooms, how to eradicate the green.

I'm exhausted from all the hard work, but it's a happy sort of weariness, with hope and optimism in it, something I haven't felt in a long time. I still have to work out how I can afford to furnish the cottage, let alone find the money to finish the renovations and actually buy the place. Oliver invested most money into the matrimonial home, nevertheless I did put all my savings into it too, and for the two years of our marriage paid a share of its upkeep. It may not be much, but surely I'll get something out of the break-up?

Except that we need to find him first, issue the necessary papers, work out an agreement on property and custody. It all seems too much and I wouldn't even have got this far without the help of these marvellous friends. I'm suddenly overwhelmed with emotion. Tears well up in my eyes and Emma is at once all concern.

'What is it? What's wrong? Have I said something?' She has streaks of dust and cement on her pretty face, her pink-tinged hair looks wilder than ever and her usually pristine nails are a total mess.

I shake my head, try to smile and start to cry instead. 'I'm sorry but I'm trying to find the words to tell you all how very grateful I am,' I sob, sounding very like a child in infant school. 'You've all been so kind. I don't know how I could have coped without you.'

They watch appalled as I start to blub, my cheeks growing pinker by the second, rush in with comforting words, saying how it was no trouble, how much they've enjoyed it. Thankfully, Tim deflects their attention away from my embarrassment by starting to tell some tale about being chased by geese on his last walk over Scafell. He makes it sound so funny that in seconds we're all hooting with laughter.

Then my phone bleeps. It's a text from Oliver, warning me that he wishes to pick up Katie at noon tomorrow. My good humour and fragile happiness evaporate instantly, and a familiar dark cloud descends.

'Oh goodness, that means I'll have to slip round to Jo-Jo's, she won't want the responsibility of handing her over.'

'Don't worry,' Emma says, slipping an arm about my shoulder. 'We'll hold the fort here while you do the necessary. And don't let him bully you. That man has put the cause of women back fifty years. Don't let him get away with any more. Remember you're free now.'

I respond with a vague smile, not wishing to discuss my personal affairs in front of Tim, but I see by the way his brow creases into a small frown that he's concerned by Emma's words. He senses me looking at him and our eyes meet. For once he doesn't break the moment with his usual casual grin or one of his bad jokes, instead he holds my gaze without smiling. He seems to be attempting to remind me of his earlier offer, to instil some sort of strength into me, and for the life of me I can't tear my own eyes away.

There's no doubt in my mind that I like him, but it's far too soon to be even considering another relationship. Apart from tying up the loose ends of my failed marriage and starting the long slow climb to rebuild my life, I know there is still a great deal of healing to be done. I'm still raw and sore inside from all I've been through. More than anything I need time to find myself again, to restore my confidence and self-esteem, and to learn to trust again. Besides all of that, it would be foolish and dangerous for me to take any sort of risk where Katie is concerned. My child is everything to me, and I will do nothing which might damage my hopes for full custody. I finally manage a feeble smile in an effort to convey these thoughts to him. His eyes kindle with warmth and I see that he understands.

'Here's to a brighter future,' he says, raising a bottle of beer by way of salute.

'To a brighter future,' everyone echoes, and I see at last that I'm not alone at all. I have friends.

It's difficult coping with a young child and a stressful job. Katie seems unsettled by the move, cries a good deal, and I don't get much sleep from having to keep getting up to comfort her. I'm still working on the cottage, putting the finishing touches to the paintwork, and constantly making improvements. The walls are now covered with a smooth lining paper and painted a tasteful cream, except for Katie's room which is a pale shell pink. Emma has revealed an amazing talent for painting cartoon characters, which she is creating in bright colours all over the walls. So far she has done Squirrel Nutkin and Mrs Tiggy Winkle. Katie is entranced. Tim has installed the multi-fuel stove, with Glen's help, and it works beautifully, so we're cosy and warm, our home clean and bright.

Friends and family generously lend me some basic pieces of furniture: a small sofa with squashy cushions, bed, kitchen table and chairs, a pretty rug, enough to get by for the moment. Mum has provided curtains for the living room and Gran has given me a set of crockery which she insists she never uses. Even Jo-Jo comes up trumps by lending me a few pots and pans for the kitchen.

I'm grateful for everyone's help. Money is tight and I'm very much on the breadline, with still no progress made on the divorce. I realise I'll have to go through all the rigmarole of getting maintenance set up, either coming to some agreement privately with Oliver, or, more likely since he's already proving hard to pin down, through the Child Support Agency, or whatever it's called now. But I can't quite bring myself to do that, not yet. Hard up as I am, it's such a good feeling to be completely free and independent of Oliver, that I'm putting off the evil moment.

I'm told that the divorce could take anything from four to six months to come through, once we get it underway. I've put everyone on the alert to keep a look-out for him, even the nosy neighbours are keeping an eye out, and of course he hasn't even been in his office for the past few weeks. Stalemate.

'He can't hide forever,' Dad keeps muttering.

'And at least while he's in hiding he isn't pestering to take Katie out,' Gran adds with a wicked wink.

I smile to disguise my impatience. I'm so anxious to get on with things, now that I've finally summoned up the courage to leave him, and I can hardly wait for the decree absolute, when I really will be free at last. I'm troubled by Tim's warning: how the moment of a permanent break is the most dangerous but I firmly shake the fear away. I just long to be normal, to have my life back.

Dad takes me over to the house to collect my clothes and books, and personal belongings. I insist he leaves me to go through things quietly, on my own.

'Put everything you want to take in the kitchen. I'll be back in an hour to load up. Sure you'll be all right?'

'I'll be fine, thanks.'

I'm very far from fine as I watch my father drive away. It feels strange to be in the place I once called home, which was supposed to represent a happy future with the man of my dreams. A dream that never materialised. I wonder where he is right at this moment, if he'll ever come back to live here in his beloved house which he took such care in designing. But he needs to come out of hiding and face reality first, something Oliver isn't too good at.

I try to imagine another woman living in our house. *Her* toiletries in the bathroom, *her* clothes in my wardrobe, *her* dressing gown behind the door where mine used to hang. A stab of pain takes my breath away at the thought. Is that because I still love him, or regret the loss of what we might have had together if things had been different?

Does Oliver love her, I wonder? Or is it simply convenient for him to have found another woman willing to look after him? Does he humiliate and criticise her? Has he hit her yet? Or is he waiting until he's more sure of her, as he did with me? Once I'd said those fatal words, *I do*, signed the register which seemed to also sign away my freedom, his attitude towards me began to change. I became his possession and not a real person with a mind of my own any longer. If only I'd realised how bad it would get and broken away sooner.

I turn away from these thoughts, unable to bear them. I did break free in the end, and now it's time to move on, to look forward, not back.

I wonder what he's told his boss about our separation. I've no doubt he will be putting the blame for our break-up entirely upon me, concerned that his personal life doesn't interfere with his standing in the office, or his opportunities for promotion.

I take only what is necessary, some essential bed linen, my own clothes and Katie's. I dismantle her cot and stack it in the kitchen together with her high chair and other bits and bobs. Oliver may well need to buy replacement items for the times she visits him, but he can afford to. I'm not interested in any of the furniture, which was all Oliver's choice, not mine, and certainly wouldn't fit into my tiny cottage.

My heart twists as I discover our wedding album in a drawer, and I find myself quietly weeping over the photographs which he insisted must be absolutely perfect. Everything had to be perfect that day, I remember. He would constantly be making requests for changes, apologising for any inconvenience even as he changed things to suit himself. I recall the excessive care he took over making the arrangements, which at the time I believed was out of a need to help, a way of showing consideration to my parents. I should have recognised then his obsessive need to control.

I can see now that there was evidence of his true nature even before we married, while we were still going out, in the way we always did what *he* wanted, mainly saw *his* friends. I was so besotted I allowed him to make all the decisions, whether it was which film we went to see or where we went for our honeymoon.

He always was jealous and possessive, contriving to distance me from my friends right from the start. Instead of being concerned by this attitude, I was flattered. But then he was always so charming, so adoring, putting me up on a pedestal and worshipping me like some sort of goddess. Any reservations I might have had were overshadowed by what I saw as evidence of his love.

I'm sobbing by this time, overwhelmed by sad memories, and I jump with fear as a hand touches my shoulder.

'Come on, love,' Dad says. 'No point in dwelling on the past or on what might have been.'

'I'm sorry, it all gets a bit much at times.'

'Course it does. I only wish you'd felt able to tell me what was going on.'

'That wasn't your fault,' I insist, pressing my face into his broad chest as he strokes my hair. 'I was too screwed up, too brain-washed to keep quiet. Too full of shame and guilt, and obsessed by the desperate, futile hope that I could put things right. In the end I came to be too much under his control to find the courage to break free.'

'Well, you have now, so don't worry about Oliver Sheldon any more. Your mum's got a bit of dinner waiting for us back home. You take one last look around, while I start loading the car.'

At the cottage later, I take great pleasure in setting out my books on shelves Dad has knocked up for me, hanging my favourite pictures on the nice clean walls, dressing my bed with my own duvet and bed linen. It's starting to look like home at last. Katie beams at me as she bangs on her pegs with a wooden hammer.

'We're going to be fine,' I tell her, popping a kiss on top of her head. 'We're going to be absolutely fine.'

And then my phone starts to ring.

25

I see Oliver's name flash up on the screen of my mobile phone, but even though I'm keen to find him, I'm reluctant to take the call. This is my first night sleeping under my own roof, now that the smell of paint is less overpowering, and I don't want my peace disturbed right at this moment. But Oliver is still the father of my child, arrangements need to be made concerning Katie, the divorce, and more pressing financial matters, so finally I ring him back to see what it is he wants.

My ear is instantly assaulted by the volume of his anger. He's furious that I dared to take stuff out of the house without asking him first, demanding to know how he can possibly cope with Katie now that I've taken all the baby equipment away.

I patiently answer his question. 'You could buy new equipment.'

'Why should I?'

'Because we can no longer share, now that we are living apart.'

'We shouldn't *be* living apart. You should be here, with me.'

I ignore this remark. 'In any case, Oliver, Katie will be living with me, not you, so you won't need quite so much. And while we're on the subject, where exactly *are* you living? My solicitor could do with an address, so that we can get this divorce underway. I assume you're with your lady friend?'

'No, I am not!' he roars, rushing to assure me that he's split up with Jane. 'And *I* never wanted this bloody divorce in the first place.'

'I'm not talking about Jane. I mean your latest mistress, who I believe you are living with in Heversham?'

I seem to have caught him off guard as there's a short startled silence. He seems stunned that I know this. 'That's not true,' he growls, his voice low and filled with a raw anger that makes me shiver, even down the phone. 'As a matter of fact I'm back in my own house. She was nothing more than a friend who helped me when I was low, almost suicidal. Not that you would care.'

I know that he's lying, on all counts, but the next instant he's weeping, telling me it was all a bad mistake, that she wasn't right for him. It's me he really wants, not some old married woman. He'll never stray again, blah, blah, blah. He's begging me to come home, telling me how much he misses and needs me, how he cannot bear to live without me.

My heart lurches and I steel myself against weakening.

'I'm so miserable without you, Carly, I'm not sure I can go on,' he groans, that oh-so-familiar note of self-pity creeping into his voice. 'Why are you putting me through all of this? You're being so silly, sweetie. I know that you love me really. We need each other. We belong together. You can't possibly cope without me.'

'I'm doing fine, actually.'

He hears an unexpected confidence in my voice and his tone hardens. 'What the hell's going on? Is there someone there with you, telling you what to say, what to do?'

'No.'

'There must be. Is it your father? Tell him to mind his own bloody business. You can't possibly deal with the complexities of a divorce, or of life on your own with a small child. You *need* me!'

'I don't need anyone, Oliver.'

His voice roars down the phone. '*You bloody do!*'

'Don't swear at me, Oliver, or I'll ring off.' I'm not feeling half as brave as I sound, but I grit my teeth and plough on. 'Perhaps you'd care to tell me what you've decided about the house.'

'I think you mean *my* house.'

I decide to leave this part of the argument to my lawyer. 'Do you intend to sell it, or to pay me out? I would at least like the money back that I invested in it. We ought to be working out these sort of details. I need to know where I stand.'

I hear him take an exasperated breath. 'You're the one who left *me*. You deserve nothing.'

'I think I do, for putting up with you for so long, if nothing else.'

'You're getting damned stroppy all of a sudden. And *I* want a list of the items you *stole from me*!'

'I didn't steal anything. I merely took what I needed, mainly personal possessions, plus a few essentials to which I'm surely entitled.'

'You're entitled to *nothing*! You should be at home with me now, being a proper wife, not sneaking about stealing sheets and towels, or living in some God-forsaken cottage in the back of beyond.'

A chill creeps down my spine. How does Oliver know where I'm living? How can he know unless . . . 'Who told you . . . ? I mean . . . what makes you think I'm living . . .' I blurt out, before I have time to stop myself.

He interrupts me with a laugh that drenches me in ice-cold fear, and I have to sit down as my legs will no longer support me. 'I know all about your pretty little country cottage, about your friends and your lover helping you to do it up. In fact I know where you go and what you do every minute of every day. I even saw lover-boy canoodling you by the river.'

'*What*? We weren't canoodling, we were talking. Were you watching, you bastard? *Where were you?*'

I instantly regret letting him get to me but his chuckle chills me to the bone. 'Wouldn't you like to know? Close enough to recognise the identity of lover-boy. But then I'm never far away from you, my darling. I need to watch over you and look after you, don't I? You're my *wife* for God's sake! There's no one for me but you, and vice versa. You surely know that's true, Carly?' His voice purrs seductively in my ear.

My teeth are chattering and I can hardly hold the phone I'm shaking so much. I cut him off and slam the phone down on the table. My reaction must have infuriated him because seconds later it rings again, the phone almost bouncing with fury across the table. I take the call and his anger booms out at me, filling my peaceful haven with his ominous presence.

'You *bitch*! Don't you dare hang up on me. You get back home this minute or you'll be bloody sorry! And you can forget about any pay-out from the house. It's mine, as are you. You belong to *me*, Carly, remember that. Don't imagine for one minute that you can just walk away and . . .'

This time after I've clicked off, I switch off the phone completely. Then I panic, worried in case Emma or Mum need to reach me. I make a mental note to get a landline installed, ex-directory, as quickly as possible.

Right at this moment the cottage no longer feels likes a safe haven, or the symbol of a new beginning. I feel suddenly very alone and extremely vulnerable. I'm terrified Oliver might still be around somewhere, watching me even now. I'm scrabbling in my bag for my car keys when the door bell rings and I drop the whole lot on the floor, giving a little cry of fear.

A face appears at the window, ghostly and pale. 'Carly? Are you in there?'

I run to the door with relief. It's Tim, and oblivious of everything I pull open the door and fall into his arms. He feels so strong and safe, holding me in a warm embrace, his chin pressed against my hair. I breathe in the scent of him with heartfelt relief, clean fresh soap and the tangy scent of spring grass.

'He rang again, right?'

I nod, quite unable to speak. Tim quietly collects up my bag, address book and all the detritus that fell out of it. He finds my keys, jiggles them in his hand.

'I just called to check you were OK. Since it's your first night at the cottage I thought you might welcome a friendly face. Are you sure you want to stay here tonight, or would you like me to take you to your mum's?'

I shake my head. 'No, I'm fine, thanks. A moment of panic, that's all, I'm determined not to allow Oliver to chase me out of my new home.' I take a breath. 'Coffee?'

He grins at me. 'Sounds good.'

Dusk is falling and I go over to the window to see Tim's old Jeep standing right outside the cottage. As I pull the curtains closed, I try not to imagine my husband watching us from some shadowed corner.

A day or two later I'm at Mum's house, helping her sort through some old curtains, looking for something suitable to cut down to fit the small window in Katie's room. We're trying not to talk about the divorce but it's on both our minds. The whole thing has affected her so badly, she can hardly bear to mention Oliver's name.

'He's made a fool of us all,' is her constant complaint, taking his betrayal almost as a personal insult. 'If only I'd known what was going on.'

I don't answer this, don't even attempt to remind her of the times I tried to talk to her, my every effort blocked. What good would it do? Guilt is already consuming her. She feels she's let me down, failed to protect her own child.

'It's so unfair that you're grubbing around through other people's cast-offs while he's swanning off with his fancy woman and we don't even know where he is to serve him with the damn papers. It's so wrong!'

'He'll crawl out of the woodwork eventually,' I say, with more confidence than I feel. I'm desperately trying not to reveal to Mum that I too am anxious. Surely the longer he manages to evade me, the harder it will be. I'm frightened my solicitor might suddenly decide that the whole thing is hopeless, or that I've run out of time. Is there a time limit, I wonder? That's something else I must check. A divorce will surely cost more the longer and more complicated it is, and money is something I don't have much of. My head aches with everything I'm trying to remember and cope with.

'Oliver isn't good at responsibility, or accepting blame, so he isn't going to make this easy for me.' I've no sooner spoken these words than the door bell rings. I go to answer it, feeling decidedly weary and increasingly defeated. Could Oliver win this battle simply by disappearing off the face of the earth?

'Mrs Sheldon?'

'Yes.'

It's a young man with a clip board. 'Sorry for the delay but I went to the wrong address. I used the one on your husband's credit card, instead of the delivery address, and then your neighbour across the street directed me here. I've come to deliver your new bed.'

'My new bed?' I frown at him, not understanding.

He nods, looking almost pleased with himself for having so diligently tracked me down. 'That's right. The one you chose on Monday at our Kendal store? If you'd just sign here, I'll bring it in, Mrs Sheldon.'

'My God,' Mum softly remarks, as she comes to stand beside me. We look at each other, as we both realise what has happened. Oliver, or his new woman, has ordered a bed and it's arrived here, by mistake, thanks to my nosy neighbour friend who lives across the road and has witnessed more of my travails than I care to recall.

'Young man,' Mum says, all polite smiles and easy charm. 'Do you have a record of the correct delivery address?'

'Oh, yes,' he says, frowning at his clip-board. 'But I was assured by Mrs Sheldon's neighbour that I would find her here, so this is where I must bring it.'

We've found him at last! I make a mental note to thank the dear lady the very next time I see her.

Mum says, 'Why don't you come in for a cuppa? Leave the bed in the van for the moment. I think there's a little favour you can do for my lovely daughter here.'

As the young man happily tucks into ginger nuts and coffee, Mum carefully explains the circumstances. As she talks, his cheeks seem to puff out and go all red, rather like a hamster who has swallowed too many nuts. He is so embarrassed by his faux pas at attempting to deliver a bed ordered by the mistress of a straying husband to the house of the abandoned wife, that he is more than willing to hand over his new address. Oliver turns out not to be living in Heversham at all, but in Silverdale, much further away. No wonder the young man was anxious to avoid the long drive.

'I'm afraid you will still have to deliver the bed. We certainly don't want it here,' my mother tells him.

'No, no, course you don't.' He hastily thanks us for being so understanding over his 'confusion' and takes off as fast as he can get out of the door.

Mum and I hug each other, then I pick up the phone to give the good news to my solicitor. He sounds rather less bored when I tell him Oliver's address. 'Progress, at last.'

'Onward and upward, love,' Mum says, giving me another hug. 'We'll show the bastard he can't beat us.'

My phone rings constantly over the next few weeks, twenty or more times a day, but whenever I see Oliver's number come up, I don't answer, determined not to give in to his bullying. He starts ringing me from different phone numbers: from his office, from call boxes, or from friends' houses, which throws me completely. I'm never sure if it's him or perhaps a client wanting to rent a house, until I answer.

When I get wise to that too, he calls in at my parents' shop and accuses them of deliberately keeping him from his child. They listen in shocked silence, my mother in particular is very distressed by this show of temper and for the first time begins to see what I have had to put up with.

I don't attempt to stop him from seeing Katie. That wouldn't be wise, although I always arrange to meet him at Mum's. I have no wish to encourage Oliver to come anywhere near the cottage. It breaks my heart every time he calls for her, knowing he isn't in the least interested in his child, only in hurting me.

'I'll try to have her back on time,' he'll say, a smirk twisting his handsome face, meaning nothing of the sort.

'Please make sure that you do. Last time you were very late and she got quite fractious. This has all been very confusing and upsetting for her, so I would appreciate it if you didn't take out your venom on our daughter. Routine is very important to a child. Where are you taking her, to your mother's?'

With Katie clasped tight in his arms, he sticks his face up close to mine and hisses, 'What business is it of yours? None, unless you start to be a proper wife. I'll take her where I damned well please.'

I swallow the protest that comes instinctively to my lips, smile at my baby and kiss her, then clasp my hands tightly together so that Oliver can't see they're shaking as he strolls nonchalantly away. Once again I'm left with the bitter taste of defeat in my mouth.

I've at least received the necessary acknowledgement forms from his own solicitor now, and various others have been filed and signed. I was afraid for a while that Oliver might contest the divorce and refuse to admit unreasonable behaviour, or a break-down in our relationship.

'He'll admit to anything,' Emma scoffed, 'except that he's laid a finger on you. He won't want the fact that he's been violent towards you becoming public knowledge, or his bosses might not like it.'

I look at her and frown, but I think that she's probably right. Oliver is a proud man, with high ambitions, anxious for people to see him in a good light. And exactly as Emma predicted, all the papers are duly signed and returned and the divorce is at last back on track, proceeding smoothly, save for the fact that we still haven't discussed financial details, or Katie.

I'm filled with relief and a strange, surreal sort of happiness as I suddenly see a light at the end of a very dark tunnel. The divorce is going to go through, and within a few short months, I'll be free.

My celebrations are somewhat premature as we instantly hit another blockage. Oliver is outraged at having to provide details of his mistress's income, in addition to his own. No doubt she is too, whoever she may be. It's not something I care to know about either, but apparently it's the law. I ask my solicitor about this and while he agrees that the courts have no jurisdiction to compel the cohabitee to pay anything to the wife, or children, nevertheless her income is usually taken into account.

'She will be contributing to the living expenses of the house they share and a court will very likely take the view that her income is therefore relevant. She might not think it fair, but . . .'

'It wasn't exactly fair of her to steal my husband,' I finish for him with a wry smile.

He continues as if I hadn't interrupted. '. . . the Family Proceedings Rules empower a judge either to order her attendance, should he deem it necessary, or for her to disclose documents such as pay slips or bank statements. This often causes bad feeling but the information can be insisted upon.'

In due course the information is indeed forthcoming but Oliver makes me pay for having won the first round so easily by harassing me with a further stream of abusive phone calls.

Everywhere I go I'm constantly glancing over my shoulder, fearful that he may emerge at any moment to confront me, that I'll see him lurking somewhere, watching me. I often see his car parked at the end of the lane, or crawling in the traffic a few cars behind me as I drive to Windermere. I start to change my routine, leave home at different times, become quite neurotic about varying my route, but no matter what I do, his car will suddenly appear in my mirror, silently pursuing me.

I can feel him, a dark presence, a shadow stealthily moving just out of my sightline. He's stalking me, harassing me, making it very clear that no matter what I do, or where I go, I can never escape him entirely. It's as if he wishes to make it very clear that he is still very much in control of my life.

I'm sinking into depression again, fearful of going out. I may have won the odd skirmish, but I feel as if I'm losing the battle before I've hardly started. How can I hope to win the war? Wouldn't it be easier to just accept defeat and go back to him?

When such traitorous thoughts creep into my head, I look at my darling daughter and remember what he did to her. I warn myself that he would hurt her again, and worse, if I went back. I've no intention of allowing my child to suffer the kind of abuse that I came to take so much for granted. At whatever cost, I must protect her.

One evening as I'm making my hot chocolate before going up to bed, I hear a scuffling noise at the door. My heart jumps and I rush to turn the key as I realise I've stupidly left it unlocked. The door swings open before I can reach it and Oliver is in my living room, hands in pockets, his mouth twisted into a grimace of distaste as he stands glaring at me.

'Get out! You've no right to walk into my cottage uninvited.'

'I have every right. I'm your husband.'

'Not for much longer. I'm warning you, Oliver, either you go now or I'll call the police.'

He laughs. 'Go on, call them. We'll see who they believe this time.'

I glance frantically about the small room, desperate to recall where I set down my mobile phone, but before I can move a muscle he grabs me by the throat and forces me to my knees.

'That's where you belong, on your knees, doing as I tell you. Don't think you can win, or steal a penny from me to which you're not entitled, you *whore*.' Then he walks out, slamming the door behind him, leaving me breathless and weeping. I run to lock the door and shoot the bolt. Never will I make that mistake again.

My sister is now surprisingly sympathetic, her change of attitude very much tinged with guilt. Even so, her sisterly advice is still coming thick and fast, if with a little more consideration for my plight.

'So what are you going to do about child care? I've been

glad to help out but I'll admit it's been a bit of a strain. I'm not Superwoman, and with four children of my own . . .'

'I know, don't worry. I do realise I shall need to make alternative arrangements,' I assure her, giving her a hug. 'I'm truly grateful for your help, Jo-Jo, but I'm looking for a nursery that's not too expensive, and a bit closer to Windermere.'

There's so much to organise I feel quite exhausted at the daunting prospect of finding something within my budget. Katie too is obviously tired, her pupils big and dark. Is she teething again, I wonder, or disturbed by all the changes in her little life? She stiffens and starts to cry, rubbing her face and resisting my attempts to slip on her coat.

Jo-Jo scribbles something on a slip of paper and hands it to me. 'Try these people. They don't charge the earth and have an excellent reputation. She's jotted down the name and telephone number of a small private nursery quite close to the office, and I quickly secure a place for Katie. The cost of it is rather alarming, but I'll find the money somehow.

My sister's solution to being short of money, of course, is perfectly straightforward. 'Screw hubby for more maintenance then.'

'It isn't quite as simple as that.'

Maintenance payments are proving erratic. My solicitor has arranged for Oliver to pay a sum into my account each month but it's very hit and miss. Sometimes it's there on time, more often than not it's late or not paid at all. But I say nothing, make no complaints, unwilling to create yet more hassle, as it only rebounds on me rather than Oliver. If not paying me the proper amount each month means he'll stay away, then so be it, I can live with that. I want him out of my life.

Early one morning just as I'm getting ready to leave for work, I take a call on my mobile. It's Oliver, of course, and he's even more irate than usual. 'I understand from my solicitor that you are considering court action over non-payment of maintenance.'

I've considered no such thing but I don't say that. This threat has obviously come from my solicitor, or perhaps the Child

Support Agency is on to him, I'm not sure, but I realise it wouldn't be wise for me to get involved. I feel the usual shakiness inside as I mumble some non-committal response.

'Are you listening to me, Carly? You need to understand that if you pursue me for money, I'll make your life absolute hell.'

'You're doing that already, Oliver. I'm aware of your car following me everywhere I go. Have you nothing better to do with your time? Can't you let go and get on with your own life?'

'You still aren't listening, you stupid cow. You are my wife! You will remain my wife for as long as I say, until I'm ready to let you go. And you will be content with whatever money I can afford to pay. You will not sue me for non-payment, or anything that I've done to you in the past will feel like a walk in the park compared to what I *will* do if you defy me in this.'

I find my voice at last. 'I won't sue you, Oliver, but if you persist in following me, or harassing Katie, I'll slap a writ on you so fast your head won't stop spinning till you land in jail. I'll hit you where your heart is, right in your pocket.'

I put down the phone. Minutes later I have my head down the loo, vomiting up my breakfast.

26

Life falls into some sort of routine over the coming months. Katie is happy in the new nursery, and Emma and I are busy keeping the tourists suitably accommodated as summer progresses. Tim makes a point of calling to see me most weekends, either by coming to the office or to the cottage. I try to dissuade him from doing this, afraid Oliver might spot him, but he's so friendly, so very kind, and makes no unwelcome approaches, that it's difficult to object too much. Besides, I like him, and enjoy his company. He's turning into a good friend, but I'm careful to make it clear that it can be no more than that.

We'll walk by the river or through the woods, sometimes going for a picnic in Kentmere or by the Lake, and once up Coniston Old Man with me carrying Katie in a sling on my back, and Glen and Emma chugging along too. None of these outings are in any respect a date. Tim doesn't seem to mind. He's sensible enough to realise that this isn't the time for me to be taking on a new relationship, and seems quite content to wait for all this muddle of a divorce to be dealt with.

I haven't seen much of Oliver for weeks now. He's not even demanded to take Katie out. Just when I've convinced myself that, as her father, he has a perfect right to see her as much as he likes, he seems to have tired of that particular game, proving to me that he isn't really interested in his daughter at all. But I've begun to relax a little, to see an end in sight to my torment. I begin to think of a future when all of this will be settled and I'll finally be free, when I'll be in a position to consider the future and think about my own happiness. I can't wait.

Perhaps it's because I feel as if I'm almost there that when Tim asks me out for a meal, I accept, albeit with some degree of caution. Or because Emma has barged into the conversation and offered to mind Katie for me.

I give her a look but she laughs. 'OK, I don't know much about kids, but Katie is an expert. We'll cope, she and I and why shouldn't you have a little fun for a change?'

I'm instantly assailed by doubt, not sure if this is such a good idea, after all, and say as much.

'I'll deliver you home early, not a minute past ten o'clock,' Tim hastens to assure me, eager to take advantage of Emma's generous offer. 'If that's what you want.'

So I agree. Now, trying to decide what to wear, as fluttery as a young girl on a first date, I'm wondering what on earth I've let myself in for. 'This is all wrong,' I say to Emma, who is sprawled on my bed watching with some amusement as the discarded outfits pile up. 'I'm still a married woman.'

'Only for two more weeks, and hell, it's just dinner. He's not offered to ravish you, not yet, though I dare say he wouldn't mind. Anyway, it's up to you to keep the brakes on this relationship, for now, eh? Once you get that magic piece of paper, that decree absolute, you can please yourself.'

'I'm not ready for any sort of relationship,' I argue. 'I just want to be free.' I pick up my phone, insisting I'm going to ring and cancel, but Emma talks me out of it, saying Tim has some important news to tell me, and maybe that's what this 'date' is all about.

Something squeezes inside me. Is he going to tell me that he's going away? I try to imagine a life without Tim hanging around, without his solid friendship, his cheerful good humour, and it seems a very dull prospect indeed.

He picks me up early, at seven, his old Jeep rattling along my lane and the familiar deep-throated roar of its engine warning me in advance so that I'm out on the step waiting for him when he pulls up. It's a warm summer's evening and I've opted for a simple, strappy T-shirt and black jeans as I've no wish to appear as if I've tried too hard. I glance only once over my shoulder as I climb aboard, but I can see no sign of Oliver's car.

'Hi,' he says, smiling warmly at me. 'You look great. Lovely, in fact.'

'You look pretty good yourself.' He's dressed in a blue checked shirt, a navy sweater with the sleeves pushed up his arms, revealing the shirt sleeves beneath, and baggy jeans that have seen better days. He looks relaxed and very attractive in a rough and ready sort of way, comfortable in his own skin. I rather like that.

He shifts the gear stick with a loud grating sound which makes us both laugh, and the vehicle bounces off along the rutted lane. I don't even look back once to see if we're being followed, but there's a strange little wobble deep in my stomach.

We have a pleasant, jolly evening, chatting away the whole time like the good friends we've become. He's describing his various adventures at university and during his gap year in Thailand and Australia, then tells loads of funny stories of his early trials in teaching. I find myself relaxing, enjoying the meal and his company immensely, happily describing my hopes for developing the agency. We don't talk about Oliver, or the divorce.

'I do have a bit of news you might find interesting,' he says as we set down our spoons after demolishing a delicious portion of raspberry Pavlova. He's suddenly avoiding direct eye contact and my heart sinks. This is it. This is the moment when he tells me that he's leaving. All this stuff about previous trips is simply a prelude to announcing that he's going off on another. OK, so we're good friends, I think, but nothing more. He's never kissed me, never said that he even fancies me, although there have been times when he's certainly given that impression. And how do I feel about him? I ask myself. I daren't even consider what my answer might be to that one.

'I've got a new post.'

'Oh, how interesting. Where?' I try to smile and look pleased for him, waiting for the blow to fall, waiting for him to tell me that it's in India or Thailand.

'I start in September at the Lakes School.'

There's a buzzing in my head as I try to take this in. Some new emotion is forming inside me and I can't quite grasp what it is. 'The L-Lakes School? The one just down the road?'

He grins at me. 'That's the one.'

'You're moving *here*, to the Lakes?'

He laughs softly and quietly takes my hand in his. 'I am. I wonder what the attraction can be?' He's smoothing my fingers one by one and something like an electric current is running up my arm. Very carefully he sets my hand aside, as if he's noticed the effect his touch is having, or has perhaps experienced something similar himself, and his eyes are dark as they gaze into mine. 'I've no intention of rushing you, Carly. I can wait, and hope that when you've fully recovered from – from this current crisis, and from your trauma, that you and I can perhaps become more than friends. I hope so, anyway.'

I can't think of a thing to say by way of response, can't even find my voice. There's something mesmerising about those eyes, that lazy smile, and I can feel myself being drawn irrevocably closer. Dangerously close. Fortunately, the waiter arrives with our bill and we both smile and ease back in our seats on a sigh. There's plenty of time, after all, and this isn't the moment for declarations or decisions. I must remain cautious, at least until a week on Friday.

It's the day before the divorce hearing and there's a sick feeling in the pit of my stomach that refuses to go away. I've hardly slept for days and I feel bone weary and jumpy with nerves. It's a benign September day, warm with autumn sunshine, the kind of day which should make me feel glad to be alive, but I'm far too anxious to appreciate it. I wish I could simply fast-forward the next twenty-four hours and be out free and clear on the other side of that court room. I've taken the afternoon off work to see my solicitor one last time. I want to have it straight in my head exactly what will be expected of me. He explains the procedure, very fully, and assures me that the whole thing will be over in a matter of minutes, that neither party is actually required to attend unless we wish to do so.

'I think I should be there. You don't know my husband,' I tell him. 'What if he should suddenly spring something on us at the last minute, one of his nasty surprises, or decide to defend the divorce after all?'

The man actually smiles. 'That's extremely unlikely. Everything has been agreed and sorted. We've even thrashed out the final details of custody and access for Katie, so there's really nothing more he can do. Like it or not, we'll bring him kicking and screaming into court and you can be rid of him once and for all. Now go home, relax, enjoy a glass of wine. Get an early night. Tomorrow you'll be a free woman.' It's the most consideration he's shown for my welfare since the whole dreadful process began. I feel shattered, wrung out, and a strange sort of numbness is forming in my head. Maybe he's right. An early night sounds like a good idea.

I arrive at the cottage late afternoon and leave Katie still strapped in her car seat as I go to unlock the door. As usual I'm loaded up with shopping, mainly nappies, plus baby buggy, my brief-case, and a pizza I intend to warm up for my supper. I start carrying the stuff into the kitchen, placing the pizza carefully on the tiny table. I drop my briefcase, park the buggy, then head back out to the car for Katie.

She isn't there. The car is empty. For one endless moment I stand transfixed, unable to believe my own eyes. Then I'm rushing around in a panic, screaming her name, crying and sobbing. Oliver seems to come out of nowhere and steps in front of me.

'Lost your daughter? How very careless. As incompetent as ever, I see.'

'Where is she? What the hell have you done with her?'

He wags a chastising finger. 'You can't go on blaming me

for everything that goes wrong in your life. She's only a child. You should take proper care of her.'

'I did take care. She was strapped in her car seat. *Where is she?*' There's a tight pain in my chest and I can hardly catch my breath. 'What the hell . . . ?' I stop myself from asking what he's doing here. I think I can guess.

He shifts his cool gaze to my face. 'Dear me, darling, you look dreadfully pale, almost ill. Would you like to sit down?'

He looks as if he's about to take my arm and I back away, lift up both hands to ward him off even as I'm desperately glancing about me, trying to see where he has hidden her. Why isn't she crying? Is she still asleep? Has he hurt her? Fear is curdling my stomach but I'm doing my utmost to remain calm. It never pays to spook him. 'Stop playing games, Oliver. You shouldn't even be here. Please give me Katie and go home. You can have your say in court.'

'Ah, but this doesn't even need to go to court. I'm here to put a stop to this whole stupid fiasco.'

I let out a bitter little laugh. 'It's far too late for that. Tomorrow I'll be a free woman, and it can't happen soon enough for me.'

'No, you won't, not unless I allow you to be, which I don't. I never wanted this divorce in the first place. So, OK, you've had your little strop, you've made your point, now call it off and start behaving as a proper wife should. I need you and Katie to come home with me.'

'I'd rather die!'

'That could be arranged, if necessary.' He grabs my wrist in an iron grip and, twisting me round, pulls my arm as high up my back as he can. I hear clicks and cracks and my shoulder screams with pain, but I bite hard on my bottom lip, making not a sound. I've learned all too well what pleasure he derives from making me cry and squeal. I absolutely refuse to give him the satisfaction now. He shoves me through the door into the living room and throws me down on my own sofa, then pushes his face so close to mine I can see each bead of sweat forming on his brow.

'Do you realise you've made a laughing stock of me in the office?'

'I think you've done that to yourself, Oliver. I've done nothing. I'm the victim in all of this. You and I could have been very happy together, had you been more of a loving husband and less of a bully.'

He grabs a lock of my hair and uses it to pull me up from the sofa, laughing softly as he sees tears form in my eyes. 'You think *I'm* the one responsible for our failed marriage, do you?'

'I do.' I'm struggling to remain calm, to think clearly when suddenly my mobile starts to ring. It surprises us both but before I can react he plunges his hand into my jacket pocket and whips it out.

'It's your interfering friend, dear Emma.' He snaps off the phone, drops it to the ground and grinds it to pieces with the heel of his shoe. I suck in a breath, trying desperately not to show my fear. Outside, somewhere in the lane, I hear Katie start to cry. My heart leaps with relief.

'I must go to her. Let me go to her.'

'You'll stay here until I'm done with you. Just for once, you'll do as I bloody say.' He adopts a tone of exasperated patience. 'Oh, Carly, if only you'd learned that simple rule from the start then we wouldn't have needed to go through all of this, would we, you silly girl? You know that I love you. And *I* know, deep down, that you still love me. We need each other.'

'You love no one but yourself. You never have.'

'Stop arguing, Carly. You've done everything you can think of to make life as difficult as possible for me. You're still doing it. You've shown not one scrap of gratitude for the care I've taken of you, or how I've tolerated your determination to flirt with every man you see.'

'That's a complete lie. You're the one who's indulged in affairs, probably from the start. Not that I care who you sleep with now, Oliver, since it certainly won't be me, ever again.'

'You still aren't listening, darling. Didn't I just take great pains to remind you that you belong to me. You're my *wife*!'

He's edging me backwards, towards the stairs. My heart begins to pound but at last I come to life and start to resist, although, as he still has hold of a handful of my hair, this isn't easy.

'No, Oliver, I am not your wife. Technically perhaps, in theory, but not in practice. Now let go. Go home and stop behaving like a bloody idiot.'

He starts to drag me up the stairs by my hair. Resistance is futile but I try to take a hold of it myself, closer to my scalp, to ease the pressure. The ploy isn't working and I'm gasping with pain.

Once in the bedroom he hits me across the face with the back of his hand, sending me flying backwards and I fall, hitting my head on the edge of the dressing table. I must have briefly passed out because I come round to find him mopping blood from the back of my head with a bunch of wet toilet paper.

'Still playing the drama queen,' he scolds, sarcasm harsh in his tone. 'I knew you were only pretending, and not really unconscious.'

I'm sprawled on the floor and I start to struggle to get to my feet but he pushes me back down, pressing me to the carpet as he launches himself upon me. I slap at his face and hands as he tries to capture both my wrists with one iron grip. We're engaged in a fierce tussle and I'm quite certain he intends to rape me. Instinctively, I bring my knee up hard into his crotch and he howls in agony. It's something I should have done years ago.

I scrabble away backwards like a crab, but with one hand still holding his private parts, he makes a grab for the front of my jacket with the other, pulling me back towards him. He starts swearing at me, all his favourite and now so-familiar abusive words, spitting them in my face, but he's still in agony and has lost some of his power. He's the one now impeded by pain and I manage to break free and scramble to my feet. I'm gasping for breath, I've no phone, and Katie's cries have notched up several decibels. I turn and run down the stairs but he's right there behind me, grabs my ankle and I fall headlong across the rug. I kick out at him, catching him right on the nose, making him yelp. I'm terrified he might get to Katie before I do, might try to hurt her as he did before.

I summon every scrap of my flagging energy and I'm screaming at him now, something incoherent, then I'm on my feet again, facing him. He has the poker in his hand, and he's breathing hard as I step back away from him.

Some part of my brain becomes aware that Katie has stopped crying, and this troubles me, until suddenly I see Emma framed in the door behind him. She's holding Katie safe in her arms, watching Oliver very carefully. I start to breathe again, gather my wits, and stand my ground.

'I'd put that down if I were you, Oliver. It's not going to do you any good tomorrow if I go into court covered in bruises. It might almost do me a favour. It's over, this farce of a marriage, and nothing you can do can put it back together, not now.'

'There's a great deal I can do. I've seen lover-boy coming to the cottage, picking you up, taking you out for long romantic walks, and meals for just the two of you. I dare say he stays the night, eh? Does he get a kick out of stealing what is rightly mine?'

The familiar chill settles around my heart but I brush it away. I can smell freedom and I've no intention of giving in to his bullying ever again. 'You can't twist this thing around and lay all the blame on me, Oliver. I won't allow you to do that. I belong to no one but myself. I don't have a lover. I've never slept with any man but you, more's the pity. I'm not your chattel to use and hurt in any way you wish. I'm a free woman with a mind of my own. Accept the inevitable with good grace. It's over. I'm not coming back to you, not now, not ever. And if you want to avoid becoming a laughing stock, or a focus of gossip in your office, then stop this right now. I'm seeking a divorce in as civilised a fashion as possible, but it could get worse. I could tell all. I could take the gloves off and really dish the dirt, as they say. I doubt your boss would be too impressed by the story I have to tell of how you've used and abused me throughout our marriage. My telling the truth could easily put paid to your hopes for further promotion, don't you think?'

'You wouldn't dare.'

I manage to smile at him, quite calmly. 'Try me.'

'I'd believe her if I were you,' Emma says from the door.

He jerks round, taking in her presence, and Katie's, with a low growl. She walks calmly into the room and comes over to me and hands me my daughter. Katie's little face is still wet with tears, her lovely blue eyes wide with fright but as she puts out her arms for me, her smile is beatific.

I look over her head at my soon-to-be ex-husband. 'You're such a fool, Oliver. Such an arrogant prick. You're the one who's lost out here, not me. So what's it to be? A civilised divorce, over and done with in a few minutes, or a no-holds barred contest which I'm certain to win?'

Those grey-blue eyes which once used to look at me with such adoration, and then with a perverted pleasure at the pain he inflicted upon me, narrow keenly as his mind clicks over the likely repercussions that would surely follow. The publicity would badly damage his image, could even lose him his job. I can see him at last begin to face the reality of his options, his brash arrogance begin to disintegrate before my eyes. Then to my utter relief, and without another word, he turns on his heel and strides out of the door, out of my life.

'You're shaking,' Emma says, as she puts her arms about me.

'But this time *I've* won. In less than twenty-four hours I'll have my decree nisi which will become absolute in just six weeks. I'm free at last.'